LEIGH BLACKMORE, born in Sydney in 1959, is a writer, researcher and editor who has been variously called 'Australia's leading horror expert' (Hodder press release), 'the dark doyen of Australian horror (author Terry Dowling), 'the ghoulish guru of Australian horror' (Julia Lester, 3RRR Adelaide) and 'Mr Horror' ('The Times', ATN Television). Blackmore published and edited (with B. J. Stevens and Christopher G. C. Sequeira) *Terror Australis: The Australian Horror and Fantasy Magazine* (1988-92). His anthology *Terror Australis: The Best of Australian Horror* (Hodder & Stoughton, 1993), Australia's first mass-market horror anthology, was praised by Robert Bloch (author of *Psycho*) as "a landmark venture…a monument to the advancement of the genre." Leigh is a regular essayist and reviewer on the horror genre for such journals as *Dead Reckonings* and *Spectral Realms*. His work has thrice been nominated for the Aurealis Award (for both fiction and criticism). He recently completed his debut novel, *The Eighth Trigram*. His hobbies include films, music (listening and playing) and eternally rearranging the books in his library of 10,000-plus volumes. He lives with his family and black cat, Katie, in the Illawarra, NSW.

# Praise For Leigh Blackmore's Writing

"'Uncharted' by Leigh Blackmore is an extraordinary story— second person, present tense, with two alternative endings If it didn't work, if it didn't engage me, I would have called it pretentious and overambitious; but it does work, so I'll call it clever and ambitious instead." – *Andromeda Spaceways Inflight Magazine*

('Uncharted') – "…impressive work…" – Terry Dowling, *The Australian*

"'Uncharted' is a tale of spare textual elegance, an interstitial fantasy which resists easy closure." – *Robert Todd Carroll*

"'Dr Nadurnian's Golem'…What else would you expect from Leigh Blackmore, other than a tale about peoples' long-held fascination with dark magic?

"'Dr Nadurnian's Golem' provides an insight into what might happen when a man delves too deeply into the black arts." – *Orb Speculative Fiction*

"'The Hourglass'…starts slowly but builds nicely with a mixture of twisted sexuality and occult ritual." – Bill Congreve, *Mean Streets*

"Leigh Blackmore's 'The Hourglass' is a masterpiece." – Ellen Whinnett, *Launceston Examiner*

"'The Hourglass' is…a powerful story about mystical sex and murder." – *Avid Reader* magazine

"'The Infestation' is a metaphysical approach to storytelling, a haunting, Lovecraftian tale of dark mystery.

"'The Hourglass' is stylish—evocative sexuality and a clever idea." – *The Mentor*

# NIGHTMARE LOGIC

## TALES OF THE MACABRE, FANTASTIC AND CTHULHUESQUE

### BY
### LEIGH BLACKMORE

IFWG Publishing International
Gold Coast

www.ifwgpublishing.com

For Margi Curtis

Wise Woman, Walker between the Worlds


For Danny Lovecraft and Margaret Barnes

(who encouraged me)


For S. T. Joshi

Indefatigable scholar and editor of the weird


For Ramsey Campbell

For 50 years of delicious chills


For Lindsay Walker

Who introduced me to the Eldritch Gentleman from Providence

# TABLE OF CONTENTS

"They cannot scare me with their empty spaces
Between stars—on stars where no human race is.
I have it in me so much nearer home
To scare myself with my own desert places."
– Robert Frost

"Believe me: the secret for reaping the greatest fruit-
fulness from existence, and the greatest pleasure, is to
live dangerously! To found your cities on the slopes
of Vesuvius! To send your ships sailing out into
uncharted seas!"
– Nietzsche

"The waking have one world in common,
Sleepers meanwhile turn aside, each into a darkness
of his own."
– Heraclitus

## Auctorial Note

Oh nothing, really. Just always wanted to use the word 'auctorial', that's
all. You can go ahead and read the stories now…

# AUTHOR'S ACKNOWLEDGEMENTS

## To Friends and Colleagues

I would like to thank the editors who first published some of these stories: Jeff R. Campbell, Steve 'SCAR' Carter, Henrik Harksen, Rob Hood, Robin Pen, Charles M. Prepolec, Robert M. Price, Cat Sparks, Keith Stevenson, The Tertangala Editors Collective, The Tide Editors Collective.

Thanks also to the following reviewers who praised various tales herein (in print or online): Martin Andersson, Mike Barrett, Ron L. Clarke, Bill Congreve, Margi Curtis, Terry Dowling, Sarah Endacott, Russell B. Farr, Mario Guslandi, Rich Horton, William Patrick Maynard, Anthony Oakman, Gavin L. O'Keefe, Scott A. Shaeffer, Bryce Stevens, Peter Tennant, Mark Valentine, Peter Watts, Ellen Whinnett.

For "Cemetery Rose," thanks to Danny Lovecraft for raving to me about rose breeds, Kent Blackmore for information on the Davenport Brothers burials at Rookwood Cemetery, Rick Kennett for the word 'Necrotourist' and Bryce Stevens for the creature made of sticks. Thanks to Andrea Gawthorne, Margi Curtis, and Bryce Stevens for feedback. Thanks to Paula M. Berenstein (USA) for the Australian Horror Writers' Association's Hallowe'en 2006 podcast dramatisation of the tale on *www.writingshow.com*.

For "The Infestation," thanks to Steven Paulsen for reading the tale live-to-air on Rick Kennett's 3CR and 3MDR Community radio show "Pilots of the Unknown," and to Rick for including it.

For "Uncharted," thanks to my test readers Angela Groutsis, Margaret Barnes, Kate Bookallil, Cherie Curchod, and Bronwen Williams.

Uber-special thanks to Margi Curtis for many suggestions which have improved these stories.

For conversations on writerly process, gracious hospitality and most importantly, friendship, thanks to Terry Dowling, who has inspired me continually to raise the bar of both standard and ambition.

Thanks to Tal Chalak for weekend breakfasts, I Ching and use of 'The Bunker' where parts of this book were typed up in the Earlwood days.

To Rick Kennett; BJ Stevens; Cat Sparks and Rob Hood; Bill Congreve; for keeping the flame of horror burning in this country. You guys rock.

To the *good* members of the Australasian Horror Writers Association in 2011; they know who they are.

For encouragement and friendship, thanks to Rohan Curtis-Wykes and Lily O'Sullivan; Cecilia Drewer Hopkins; Victoria Felix aka PAE, Andrea Gawthorne, Danny Lovecraft, Rod Marsden, Gavin L. O'Keefe; Adrielle Spence, Benjamin J. Szumskyj; Richard Trowsdale and Meredith Jones; Iain and Llyn Triffitt; Pete Wilson & Stella Leonides; Ian and Cheree Walker, Kyla Ward and David Carroll (also for vulture imitations and Nights of the Evil Coconut); Leon Wild.

To the Parade of Cats: Bhuric, Beltane (the Snuffler from the Stars), Persephone, Hades, Isis (RIP all), and Katie (Puss-Niggurath)– creature of fur and claw, most companionable of the *felidae*.

Most of all, heartfelt thanks to Gerry Huntman, who believed.

# Introducing Leigh Blackmore

## by Darrell Schweitzer

I will admit I don't know Leigh Blackmore. I have seen his name around for years, and he has occasionally bought books from me, but that is all. We have never met. One reason for this is that he lives on the other side of the planet, in Australia, while I live in the eastern United States, and the one time he seems to have come to my side of the planet, to attend the Lovecraft Centennial Conference in Providence Rhode Island, I just happened to be out of North America for the first time in my life that weekend, in Rome, Italy, poking among the ruins of storied Antiquity before heading off to a World Science Fiction Convention in The Hague, Netherlands. So we missed one another by about 4000 miles.

But I see from his biography how much we have in common. A very early interest in weird and fantastic fiction. Lovecraft. Amateur and small-press publishing. Some scholarship. The both of us have collaborated with the esteemed S.T. Joshi on bibliographies, Lord Dunsany in my case, his a supplement to *H.P. Lovecraft and Lovecraft Criticism, an Annotated Bibliography, 1980-1984*. In his youth he discovered Michael Moorcock, sword and sorcery, H.P. Lovecraft and the *Weird Tales* school, the anthologies of August Derleth and Peter Haining, the works of Ramsey Campbell, etc. etc. It all sounds very familiar. We don't have everything in common, of course. His first publications were Lovecraftian sonnets in R. Alain Everts' *The Arkham Sampler* (new series), a form I have yet to master. But what I realize very strongly is that he and I are members of the same tribe. I am sure we would get on famously if we did meet, as we would seem like long-lost cousins to one another. Lovecraft remarked that in his day weird fiction enthusiasts were a very scattered community indeed. In Providence, he knew only C.M. Eddy. Everyone else came through correspondence, at least in the early years. Clark Ashton Smith and Robert E. Howard met no other members of the *Weird Tales* circle until the widely-roaming E. Hoffmann Price came to call. Today of course we have conventions, and the internet has to some degree superseded postal correspondence, but there is still this sense of great distance and of tribal affinity when two of us do encounter one another.

Blackmore writes a mean sonnet, by the way. Another place we intersected was in the 2013 edition of his poetry collection, *Spores from Sharnoth and Other Madnesses*. This is the second edition, with an introduction by Joshi and a back-cover blurb by yours truly, which says, among other things, that "Leigh Blackmore's verse will appeal strongly to fans of H.P. Lovecraft and Clark Ashton Smith, and of the older, traditional *Weird Tales* school of writers." I go on about elegant lines, spooky sonnets, cosmic vistas, and the like.

That's all true, but it applies to his fiction just as well. He has range. He can write everything from an extension of Lin Carter's version of the Cthulhu Mythos ("The Return of Zoth-Ommog") to a Dunsany fable, to existential weirdness in the manner of Thomas Ligotti to straight, visceral horror ("By Their Fruits") in which a hatchet-murderer does in his mistress and suffers a fate nastier than anything in E.C. Comics. His "Waiting for Cthulhu," a short, sharp parody of Samuel Beckett's *Waiting for Godot*, is *very* funny.

You might momentarily get the false impression that all this is a bunch of fan fiction, a mere regurgitation of things Blackmore has read, but, trust me, it is not. There is nothing wrong with being part of a tradition. We all stand on the shoulders of giants. We sidestep the blunders of pygmies. (The difference between these two is an essential literary survival skill.) Leigh Blackmore is a much more interesting guy than that. I am sure that if we met I would also be interested in hearing about the broad swaths of his life and career that have nothing in common with my own, his extensive musical career and his involvement in the occult. He also worked as a bookseller for many years, hosting literary events featuring such major figures as Harlan Ellison, Storm Constantine, Terry Pratchett, Douglas Adams, etc. He's gotten around. He's met and befriended lots of the movers and shakers of fantastic fiction. His activities have ranged from Lovecraft fandom (he contributes to the Esoteric Order of Dagon amateur press association) to co-editing the magazine *Terror Australis* between 1987 and 1992. *Terror Australis: the Best Australian Horror* (1993, edited by Blackmore alone) was a pioneering effort, the first mass-market anthology of Australian horror. He has been a guiding light, something like the August Derleth or Farnsworth Wright of Australia. He also lectures at universities and is a frequent panelist at conventions. He runs a manuscript appraisal business, called Proof Editorial Services.

He is a member of the Society of Editors, served as president of the Australian Horror Writers Association (2010-2011). He has produced a considerable body of criticism, conducts workshops in magick, reviews horror fiction for *Dead Reckonings*, has written screenplays and radio plays, and lectured alongside the renowned S.T. Joshi on Lovecraft as part of Joshi's speaking tour in 2019. Somehow Blackmore also finds time to eat, sleep, breathe, and, incidentally, write such fiction as you find gathered in the present volume.

Enjoy.

– Darrell Schweitzer
Philadelphia, Pennsylvania, USA,
July 18, 2023.

# TALES OF THE MACABRE AND FANTASTIC

# THE SACRIFICE

*That's right, stumble,* I thought, *fall to your knees from sheer exhaustion. There is no-one to help you now. You are unable to rest until it suits me.*

They danced before me, their eyes glazed, their peasants' garb tattered and fluttering in the moonlight. At their head danced the piper, his instrument glittering in his hands as he fluted the weird melody that I had taught him, his legs moving under the same spell as that which had been cast over the ghastly-faced decadents he led.

The ground raced underfoot and the scenery changed with alarming rapidity; on and on they would dance under my direction, struggling against physical pain but unable to stop, across the countryside's ever-changing face until gasping, trembling from exertion, barely able to continue, they arrived at their destination.

"Astaroth will be appeased tonight, but the demand is heavy. I must find a way before the night is out." With my cloak wrapped around me, keeping pace with the jerking, melody-enthralled offerings of human flesh ahead of me, I pictured again the isolated hut in the valley which I had visited but an hour before.

It was one of a number of makeshift dwellings which dotted the landscape, inhabited, as they all were, by ignorant and superstitious shepherd folk. None was more than a hovel, as befitted the abysmal poverty of the people, who barely managed to exist in the harsh climate. The dilapidated structure, which I had visited this night, had been one of the only huts left inhabited after the sacrifices which had been made thus far.

The piper by my side, I approached the door of the hut, smiling as I heard the foolish muttered prayers of the family within, and carefully inscribed the rough wooden door with a crescent moon, the symbol of my beloved Lady Astaroth. Then stepping back, I waited—and they came.

There was terror in her eyes then, but I knew that it would be replaced by weariness as the peasants began to stumble after the piper as he strode away across the glen into the darkness. Yes, stumbling they came, and stumbling they still were, following blindly the piercing sound of the silvery flute.

But now, the line in front of me slowed somewhat as it plunged into the black forest. It was a matter of small concern—we were nearly arrived in any case. Through the trees I followed the straggling line, until it burst out into the moonlit clearing with its improvised rock altar. There I allowed the peasants in their shabby skins and furs to drop like puppets cut loose from their strings.

The piper lowered the flute from his lips and helped me raise one of the inert bodies and lay it on the altar.

Raising my eyes to the moon, whose pale beams illuminated the clearing, I recited the ritual invocation and then withdrew a long, curving knife from the folds of my robe. With great care and with a steady hand, I neatly cut the peasant's throat from ear to ear. As the warm blood flowed out onto the stone surface, I noted with ironic anticipation the shape of the gash—a perfect crescent.

The minutes passed quickly as I disposed of the others in a like manner. They went silent and uncomprehending to their deaths.

Now, however, the problem still faced me. The ramshackle dwellings of the shepherd folk were now entirely without occupants; all had fallen to the knife in the name of my quest. But I needed another sacrifice, just one, if my Lady Astaroth was to take me to my reward. My love for her was strong, and my thoughts were filled with uneasiness for a few moments.

And then I found a way. It was so simple, and I needed that sacrifice.

I turned around. "Come here," I said to the piper, dreaming of eternal love beyond the stars.

# IMAGO

Elizabeth stepped out onto the unfamiliar street, seeing the world as if for the first time. This was not the town where she was born and raised. Life was going to be different. Today she felt liberated, free to be herself and secretly elated, as though she had gotten away with something. She had dipped her hand in the biscuit jar and not been found out.

It was the hottest summer on record, so the television news said. The street where she lived now was lined with glorious liquid ambers; box-brush trees surrounded the yard. A huge, black butterfly, its wingspan a full hand-width from tip to tip, fluttered up above her neighbour's letterbox and over the trees. How beautiful it was!

She saw herself as wading enthusiastically into life's waters for the first time. Still, she was little more active than before. That summer it became her habit to watch the cats sunning themselves on the iron rooftop next door. She loved the way they seemed to collapse into soft boneless curves of furriness. In the evenings she would sit out on the balcony overlooking the back yard, letting the cool dark seep soothingly into her. At night she was sometimes awakened by possums scrabbling on the tin roof—the noise they made!—or squatting on the dustbin lid, foraging for food scraps.

Winter crept in too early. By late June the ground in the parks was sodden with rain. Black trees scraped up against her window at night. The sound of rain dripping off the roofs was obscurely comforting. Dreaming, she would find herself sitting in a dark room. In these dreams, which were saturated with a light sluggish as golden syrup, she sat self-contained, arms crossed protectively over her chest, her mouth a tight line. At times she would wake sweating in the cold dark, but then, falling uneasily back to sleep, she would forget the gloom.

She would wake in the morning greedy for new experience, even something as uneventful as walking down to the shops. On these walks she would watch people, mainly younger than herself, going about their daily lives.

Along Crown Street shoppers spilled from store doorways, chattering and laughing, mingling with the methadone patients who hung out in the Mall. Elizabeth studied the faces. She felt happy watching the girls with their skimpy midriff tops and uniformly vacant expressions, the boys with their mobile phones and scruffy haircuts.

Elizabeth had a secret. Life had dealt her some knockout blows. Now she had put everything behind her, as though she had taken the sum total of her previous life, folded it up and packed it, like so many faded skirts, into a suitcase, which she had carefully stowed in a battered locker on a train station somewhere and had promptly forgotten. She walked away from the suitcase—her school teaching, her fifty years' existence—with surprising ease, a determination that sprang from a sheer desperate need to live.

Today, fastening her coat against the chill, she observed the passers-by with a curiosity born of long gestation. Here was a young girl wearing a white twill jumper, a green hippy skirt, and (despite the cold) thongs with plastic yellow daisies on them. The girl's long blonde hair swayed as she walked along; she had a big blue plastic bangle on her left wrist, and a silver ring on her right fourth finger. When she heard girls like this in the mall saying things to each other like, "That would be the bomb!" she couldn't understand what they meant.

She noticed a liquid amber leaf lying on the pavement and picked it up. In this new place she was rehearsing a new way of being. She believed transcendence was possible, and usually could be found amongst the detritus of people's mundane lives.

Elizabeth caught sight of herself reflected in a shop window. The eyes were attractive, but somehow closed in. The hair, mousy and a little unkempt, carried a streak of undisguised grey at the temple. The mouth was a bit downturned, a little sour.

She looked away. There were certain things that weren't so easy to shake off. Her past experience still stuck to her like flakes of burning plastic, scarring deeper.

One night she dreamt she was wandering past the retirement block (a place she has heard referred to by locals as "Dementia Towers") and towards the orange hospital which loomed on the hill. In this dream, everything seemed salient, events simultaneously particular and universal. Skirting the hospital grounds, she searched for a way in. The grounds seemed populated by indistinct figures who kept their distance, but she was unable to locate an entrance.

A yearning, so intense as to be indescribable, overcame her; she longed to be washed clean. Rounding a corner she was confronted by a gigantic chrysalis, slowly revolving before her. Its covering was blackened, shrivelled up; the pupa inside was dead.

She jerked abruptly out of her nightmare. For a few moments she lay still, then got up to make tea. She couldn't connect the dream with anything, wouldn't think about what it meant: done with all that! Hot, fresh tea, was what she needed.

That morning, back at the mall, she watched the shoppers again. She moved in an instinctual way towards the open-air tables outside the coffeeshop. "The point being," said a woman dressed in a red power-suit, gesturing to her smartly-clad companion, "these things are negotiated in different ways." At another table, she overheard two men talking about wealth creation schemes.

Suddenly she felt dizzy. Everything was a tissue of dreams. It didn't make any difference that she had moved here. She didn't understand anything, least of all her own life. Abused, exploited: those terms she knew well. Dad had finally died, years after what he had done to her, so that should make it all right, shouldn't it? Mum, racked by guilt and a belated desire to protect her daughter, had taken too many years to die, and Elizabeth had sacrificed her best years looking after her. Yes, she had been exploited.

She sat down heavily on a bench next to some kids who were squabbling loudly over whose turn it was to text their mate. What she had wanted most was for this place to disclose new possibilities. She tried to imagine what it must have felt like to be the caterpillar as it transformed into the imago, before finally emerging as the beautiful black butterfly, her summer companion. But her vision filled with the image of the dead chrysalis, slowly twirling on its silken threads.

She looked around, baffled, aware that her crisis had followed her. What did they say? "Wherever you go, there you are."

Her body folded in on itself, her arms wrapping tightly around her chest. She rocked there, lost, silently crying. No-one approached or offered to comfort her.

After a long time, she got up and shuffled slowly towards the place she now lived.

# DR NADURNIAN S GOLEM

*"Why did I decide to add to the infinite*
*Series one more symbol? Why, to the vain*
*Skein which unwinds in eternity*
*Did I add another cause, effect and woe?"*

– Jorge Luis Borges, "The Golem" (tr. Anthony Kerrigan)

## 1. Nocturne

I had no intention of killing anything that evening.

However, given the circumstances, I had to kill the golem.

The golem had knocked for admittance and now stood on the porch. When I peered out cautiously through a furtive vent in the blinds, as was my wont (so few people came to call on me—if someone did, it was cause for suspicion), I could see it standing there, chalky-faced. Even trying to stand motionless, it still jerked about clumsily, as if it felt uncomfortable in its own body. Attired in the ill-fitting dark suit with which Nadurnian had clothed it, it looked more ill at ease than ever. Sweat trickled from its brow.

*What a nuisance*, I thought.

I opened the door to let it in, and it blundered past me, knocking a vase to the floor and smashing it to shivered fragments. I was suddenly afraid, for this was how the creature had begun to act when last I sighted it at Nadurnian's; evidently it was still in a state of blind rage.

Sweeping its hand across its face, it knocked its black spectacles off. A look of murderous rage appeared in its eyes, and it swept everything violently from the surface of my sideboard. Artefacts tumbled and broke. Then the creature advanced on me, its intent only too apparent. It placed its meaty hands around my throat and proceeded to try to strangle the life from my body.

The empowering hexagram with its word of truth (which I assumed to be in place on its brow) was not visible, presumably hidden beneath its sweeping hair. In any case, I did not know the exact banishing ritual to disempower this particular homunculus. Classically, of course, if one were a rabbi using the magical Hebrew letters to impart life or death, one would change the Hebrew word '*emeth*' (truth) by rubbing out the initial 'e' to make the word '*meth*' (death), resulting in the creature's immediate demise. Or, one could walk around it in the opposite direction, reciting the magical formulae in reverse order. Or, one could simply command it to return to its dust.

But I was far from being a rabbi. Besides, Nadurnian himself was unlikely to have been such a classicist in this regard, and in the heat of the moment, I decided I could not rely on the conventional methods of dispatch.

In any event, a ritual knife that I happened to have lying handy was sufficient to stop the hulking creature in its tracks.

I stabbed it through the part of its body corresponding to the heart in a human. I had no hope of pushing its bulky body away from me, but as I tugged the knife out, was careful to step out of range as the creature toppled. I recalled certain legends of medieval Prague at the time of Tycho Brae and Kepler, and I certainly did not wish to be crushed by this brute. In fact, it fell not forward onto me, but back, where it struck against the wall and lay still. Its eyes became cloudy, and then seemed to turn into deep whirlpools, hinting (even in their dying) of distant and malefic orders of entity. The last of the life-energy seethed in them and then was gone. A small amount of reddish-black fluid leaked from the wound I had given the thing, soaking deeply into my plush, expensive carpet.

Breathing heavily, I sank in the armchair to consider this unexpected turn of events. *Damn Nadurnian!* I was sure he was responsible. I would have to go in search of him. I did not take kindly to magical wars, but sending out an avenging golem was a deadly insult not to be ignored. For a time I gazed deeply at the whirling patterns of the wallpaper in my sitting-room. Why did it remind me so of the wallpaper in Nadurnian's inner sanctum?

## 2. Inner Secret

One evening of the year before, as I walked through part of the city via a tangle of drab alleyways where I had not ventured previously, my eye was attracted by a cheaply printed black-and-white handbill taped to the outside of the stairwell door of a shabby tenement building. It read:

**DR NADURNIAN'S DISQUISITIONS
ON THE TRUE NATURE OF REALITY**

A brief programme of weekly lectures was appended beneath: *The Shadow Form and Its Impact* was one; *The Spectral Carnival: Intimations of the Zombie Body* was another. These topics immediately piqued my interest. Too rarely did anything in this city of mundane realities come forth to excite my jaded senses. "All disquisitions at 7:30 sharp. School of the Inner Secret: Dr Nadurnian, Master."

All lectures were being given on Tuesdays, and as it happened, this was a Tuesday. Tonight's lecture was entitled *The Animate and the Inanimate: A False Dichotomy*. I was suddenly seized with an intense desire to attend one of these lectures and to discover more about this mysterious Dr Nadurnian. It was approaching twilight, and I had nearly an hour to kill. Around the corner I found an inexpensive café where I could bide my time and ponder before returning to attend Nadurnian's 'school'. Of course, I was sceptical about what this Nadurnian would really deliver—probably some ill-digested mishmash of credulous and speculative nonsense. Still, something black and spidery, something embryonic and unformed, seemed to reach out to me from the tattered handbill—an obscure promise of genuine dark lore—which, I had to admit to myself, I craved.

# 3. Dr Nadurnian

After a certain period of regularly attending and observing Nadurnian's bizarre lectures, I was able to appreciate their normal pattern. There were never more than a few people in attendance—idly curious and nondescript entities, who wafted in off the streets at the commencement of each "disquisition" and who straggled out again when the disquisition reached its end. Sometimes they would leave before Nadurnian had finished explicating the thesis of any given talk.

I well remember one lecture, perhaps the fifth or sixth such I had attended, which Nadurnian had entitled *The Masks Upon the World*. He was holding forth from the front of the upstairs space which he referred to as his 'lecture room'—an overly formal description, given that its wallpaper was peeling and it held only a couple of rows of unstable folding chairs. Closed doors off this space suggested that Nadurnian's own living quarters lay beyond.

"There are hierarchies beyond hierarchies, and hierarchies within hierarchies," he was saying. "The patterns and colours of the world *behind* the world do not cease whirling merely because we are incapable of observing them, or unwilling to believe in the possibility of their existence…"

The blackboard was covered with the usual abstruse alchemical signs and disjointed phrases—the term 'la symbolique', for example, which I recognised as a borrowing from Schwaller de Lubicz. Sketches of formulae for Mandelbrot sets and Fibonacci sequences wove through the chalked sigils and meandering handwriting.

Over the course of several lectures I had begun to sense the general drift of the thesis he was expounding. In essence, each of his apparently disparate topics was connected by a discernible underlying viewpoint. It was Nadurnian's contention that the world, as we normally perceive it, is but a thin, transparent veil. This veil barely disguises an evil on an order unguessed, unsuspected, undreamed of by most people. Behind the surface appearance, he hinted, things are not what we assume them to be. He seemed to be suggesting that in places this veil, or mask, has worn thin, and that the seeker finds himself (in such places) almost upon the threshold of some stupendous discovery.

I was fascinated by these dark hints and portents that he threw out, although I noted that he did not comment upon the phenomenon that the anticipated 'stupendous revelation' is an infinitely receding one, never to be grasped—a phenomenon I had often remarked upon in my own experimental work of this kind.

On this occasion a listener rose noisily, pushed his chair to one side, and made his way out of the door that led onto the stairs out of the building. The few remaining attendees exhibited expressions of indifference, or gaped slack-jawed with lack of understanding. Nadurnian stared for a long moment at the back of the departing one. I had the sense that, had he not been wearing dark glasses, one might have said that he 'glared' at the vanishing back. Then, with a shrug which seemed to say "how indeed could one so dense begin to appreciate the subtleties of the secret knowledge?" he turned on his heel and began pacing and expounding anew, pausing only long enough every few sentences to scribble wildly upon the blackboard some arcane diagram, or disjointed but portentous phrase, which he hoped would illustrate or illuminate his further points.

By the end of each lecture (I should note that I thought his term 'disquisitions' somewhat pretentious, and at first had thought this symptomatic of the pomposity with which future teachings might be presented), the blackboard had become a tangle of chalked scrawls, like a webby jungle through which phrases like '*Ain Soph Aur*' and 'supra-rationality' could faintly be distinguished amongst the weaving and overlapping scribbles. The few apathetic listeners, who gave no sign of having understood the least part of what Nadurnian had said, would get up and shuffle out, leaving Nadurnian to lean or slump against the blackboard. Despite his immobile features, he always appeared physically and emotionally exhausted by these esoteric tirades. I could see that the disquisitions exhausted his vitality.

## 4. Black Gnosis

'Following another lecture, this one entitled *The Gaze of the Golem*, in which Nadurnian expatiated upon certain references in the *Old Testament*'s Psalm 139, I determined to speak personally with him. I did so as soon as the lecture was over, and he appeared to welcome my approach. The topics I have already mentioned were just a few of the panoply of subjects upon which Nadurnian had knowledge to impart, and I soon realised he was struggling to elucidate a theory so complex that even if he lectured nightly instead of weekly, he would merely start to approach a beginning of an outline of it. He appeared to be struggling against time and destiny, and in some obscure way, against himself, to complete the iteration of all facets of his overarching theory. He seemed almost afraid that he would be cut off before all the pieces in his metaphysical puzzle could be laid out coherently—though I had no idea why he cared, when his listeners were too patently disinterested, or too unintelligent, to grasp the faintest suggestion of the meanings at which he pointed, of the connections which he drew.

I myself was not without the capacity to appreciate the—shall we say—outré speculations of this esotericist. I recognised him as not merely a student of the Gnostics but as representative of a rare combination of heterodoxies, a seeker whose number in the population at large must be infinitesimal. It was this rarity, based upon the peculiarly recognisable blend of obsessions which formed the kernel of his theories that led me later to suspect and finally to realise for certain that this so-called 'Dr Nadurnian' had been known to me, in years past, by another name, another identity altogether different.

## 5. Dead Dreamer Wakes

Entering the tenement, which was apparently entirely empty of tenants other than Nadurnian himself, I ascended once more to the second floor where I had been coming privately now for some time. Nadurnian, having recognised that my continued attendance at his lectures indicated my deep and abiding interest in these matters had, as it were, taken me under his wing, and was tutoring me in his private quarters as a special student of his particular brand of mysticism.

In his sitting-room Nadurnian sprawled lumpenly in a large, over-stuffed armchair, which, engulfed in shadows, dominated one side of the room. The room itself was decorated with wallpaper of a whirling pattern strangely sympathetic to the tenor of Nadurnian's outlook.

The 'Master' never removed his dark glasses in all the time I knew him. I thought this an affectation and a cheap psychological device of intimidation, but to myself acknowledged that it was, nonetheless, effective. Though I had grown closer to him than anyone else, I was never permitted to see his eyes; the glasses lent his speech an air of mysterious and distant authority. When delivering his monologues his face remained impassive, the glassy blackness of the implacable sunglasses suggesting the blackness of infinite space. As to Nadurnian's place of origin he never let slip the slightest hint.

Typically, in these sessions where we sat together, Nadurnian's voice would drone, occasionally lapsing into silence, when I would then venture some remark or other. I thus inevitably revealed certain of my own mystical interests; and Nadurnian must have gained some insights into my own progress in investigating those persistent and pervasive hints that behind the surface appearance of the flesh, beneath the dermis of the phenomenal world, there stir restlessly utterly alien and inimical forms of existence whose unthinkably stupendous purport is only revealed in allusions and half-glimpses.

On one occasion Nadurnian showed me his copy of the forbidden *Psalms of the Silent*, a book without a living author. On another, he paged through a copy of Jakob Grimm's *Journal for Hermits* (1808), a work containing certain legends of artificial creatures created by magic. He himself had penned various tracts, containing his typically powerful mixture of densely laden myth, speculation and the excavation of strange mysteries. One was *Technicians of Profanation*, and another, *Dead Dreamers Wake*. I read the latter while in his presence and must confess that I found it singularly suggestive.

Due to the access which these private sessions with Nadurnian afforded me, I had the opportunity to observe him at close hand. We shared an intimacy with each other, but also, I believed, with spheres of a desolate order, consumed with light and darkness, a realm of secret doors into monstrous houses where few have trod. I was able to glean fresh insights into the subject matter of his talks, based on everything from the way he performed certain actions, to the furnishings of his private domain.

For instance, he would often let his hands lapse into yogic mudra, and by observing the positions of his crossed fingers in relation to each other as he spoke, I found the meaning of his statements infinitely multiplied. Each phrase became pregnant with multileveled meaning. His smallest gestures, replete with significance as they were, became rituals of the greatest, of the most absorbing fascination to me.

If there was, in all this, the conventional appearance of a student-guru relationship, this is certainly the type of relationship that Nadurnian must have fondly imagined existing between us. Whereas in fact, for my part, while convinced of his illuminated status, and while giving every outward sign of being rapt and awestruck by his personal presence, I was content to stand aloof within myself.

The exact rhetoric of Nadurnian's discourse would be difficult to reproduce. However, certain themes recurred like dark sub-chordings in the strange music of his disquisitions. These supramundane speculations were founded (if one could judge by his authoritative tone and the sense of authenticity he conveyed) on the most closely-reasoned analysis. As in a dark symphony, or some hypnagogic Tarot of shadows, the wanderings of his argument formed themes, expositions and especially recapitulations. He returned time and again to the idea that humanity is being overwhelmed with the horrors of the pulsings that lie beyond, of the poundings between the stars, and of the true 'world-face' that humanity is ill-prepared to behold. Identity itself, he often suggested, is mutable, subject to strange fluxes and transformations.

At times he would make references to odd places and entities, some of which I recognised from my own studies, but many of which were wholly unfamiliar to me—'Nethescurial', for instance, or 'the night schools', 'the theatre of Abominations', or 'ZIM, the thirteenth Aethyr', or again, 'the Qabalahs of Besqul' —but from these oblique references I recognised that he had worked long years amidst the mysteries and had peered into obscure corners of history, religion and transcendentalism widely separated in space and time. All these threads, of colours sombre in themselves, he wove into the conversation, persistently synthesising each scrap of arcane lore into his own complex theories. He was piecing together a horrendous fabric that implied a view of the world as the merest meniscus, like the skin on a dish of custard, which we are in danger of piercing accidentally at any given moment.

## 6. Golem's Gaze

One day, when we had come to know each other better, I made my way to his shabby and claustrophobic sitting-room to find, standing next to the armchair from which Nadurnian always held forth, the naked figure of a man-like creature.

Though catching me by surprise, I immediately recognised the thing as a species of golem. Indeed, I could hardly have called myself a student of the mysteries had I failed to recognise it as such, despite its uncanny resemblance to Nadurnian himself. It was a bulky, tall and imposing figure, which bore the traditional empowering hexagram upon its brow. On this first occasion, it neither moved, nor spoke.

Nadurnian spoke nonchalantly, indirectly of it from his armchair. "You know, of course, of the 261 Qabalistic gates spoken of in the *Sepher Yezirah*," was the only comment he deigned to make. But he volunteered no detail of the circumstances that had enabled him to produce this monstrosity. Indeed, in all my visits, I never observed any room with equipment or a laboratory where the requisite experiments might have been conducted.

Of course, I assumed the elemental Fire, Air and Water had been combined to produce this thing of Earth. But had the artificial life been infused into it by the Shem (the 72-letter secret name of God) being inserted on a piece of paper into its mouth, as the ancient rabbis had done? Had it grown red as glowing coals as Nadurnian circled it seven times with the appropriate incantations and permutations of formulae? I didn't know; all I knew was that the golem was there, palpable, undeniable.

And so, I deliberately conversed with Nadurnian without so much as mentioning the golem, as though I thought nothing of the fact that, next to his chair loomed this apparently inanimate duplicate of himself, fashioned from clay or from more dubious substances. Golems, I knew, were creatures without wisdom or understanding. Nor could they be permitted to speak. They are not human, and while they may make certain concessions to organic conventionality such as sleeping, they do not develop values, being essentially goalless.

I sensed the golem was inhabited by the energy from those realms of invisible yet powerfully impinging strangeness of which Nadurnian so often spoke.

In following sessions I began to notice the increasing resemblance between the golem and his creator. Whereas at first the golem's features appeared rough-hewn, they became increasingly smooth and immobile, as were Nadurnian's. Even the clumsy gait exhibited by the golem at first—in the early months it did not so much walk as shamble—soon smoothed out and began to resemble the more graceful movements of Nadurnian himself. The likeness between the two became more marked when Nadurnian put clothes upon his creature and went so far as to equip it with a pair of dark glasses not unlike his own.

## 7. Dead Waker Dreams

One night, some time later, I had a disturbing dream in which the golem figured. In this, I was in Nadurnian's sitting-room and the golem sat in the chair where Nadurnian usually reposed. It droned with a tone remarkably like that of Nadurnian. Behind the chair to the left stood Nadurnian himself, in his dark suit. His expression seemed more impassive than usual, but he looked more alive than his golem, which still, somehow, had a half-finished air about it.

That was all. But I awoke uneasily, sensitive to the play of shadows in my bedroom, and with a sense that this dream was somehow a colloquy upon Nadurnian's mysterious origins.

Of these origins it would be fruitless to speak since, frankly, almost nothing of them is known. I learned nothing about where he might have been born, what towns he had lived in, or his early associates. Even his 'School of the Inner Secret' was an exaggeration, for clearly there *was* no school—only Nadurnian himself, lecturing away in this inaccessible and rundown part of the city. As far as I could tell, he had never had a follower or fellow spirit before myself.

I tried my best to forget about the dream, and went about my normal business, which now included my weekly visit to Nadurnian's sitting-room for our private sessions.

## 8. Gnostic Blackness

Finally, we quarrelled. It was, in all likelihood, inevitable. Although the exact point over which we disagreed could have been anything, the seed was there from the outset. Nadurnian had a fixed idea regarding Da'ath as being the entry-point on the Tree of Life to the so-called Tunnels of Set. Instead of bowing to his infinitely superior wisdom on this point, as he would undoubtedly have preferred (for though spiritually endowed, he was not without, as I have indicated, a sense of his own self-importance), I accused him of being entirely too influenced by the Typhonian schools. In my opinion there were far more likely points of ingress to the Qlipothic spheres than via Da'ath, the 'false' Sephira of Knowledge. He disagreed with my impassioned interpretations of the Abyss and of the World of Shells and of certain ways in which I believed it was possible to progress through the

Atziluthic and Briatic worlds. Nadurnian seemed stung by my failure to fall into exact intellectual line with his own position.

I would rather spare the reader of this narrative the unduly technical details of our disagreement. Suffice to say that these disputed points tended to undermine the structure of concord we had built around our mutually-held beliefs, and Nadurnian suddenly felt his theories, to which he was deeply committed, to be under threat. Since I was probably the only one of his students who possessed sufficient understanding to make him feel threatened (and indeed, since I was his *only* student) the irony of this was not lost upon him.

He cast me out. Screaming that after all, it was *he* who had made a golem, he rained blows on my head and shoulders as he drove me from the room where but recently, we had enjoyed an obscure and esoteric communion. Raving of "the sky behind the sky," he screamed at me that I would not be welcome to return.

The golem had begun moving clumsily about the room behind him. Nadurnian's anger seemed to have upset it as well, and it began to fling volumes of Mircea Eliade and Talmudic tractates from the bookshelves that lined one wall, and to knock over the table with its freight of teapots and chased silver herb-boxes. As I retreated down the stairs, shocked yet somehow unsurprised by the vehemence of Nadurnian's sudden anger, I glanced back over my shoulder.

Through the doorway, I could see the golem's blundering form smashing furniture. Nadurnian continued to shriek invective and insults after me down the stairs, though he stopped short of hurling magical curses. He was red-faced with exertion and anger, but the ever-present black sunglasses still masked his eyes, making him resemble some red-faced insect. As I arrived panting onto the street and stopped to catch my breath, I thought I heard the door to the School of the Inner Secret slam shut.

## 9. Planes of Transformation

Now I had been confronted by the golem he had sent after me, sent to kill me in my own home. The golem was dead by my hand. But what of its creator, the mysterious doctor of the Black Gnosis?

Seized with an uncontrollable urge to confront the esotericist with the failure of his attempt on my life through his clumsy proxy, I immediately left the house, taking with me my ritual knife. Who could tell whether I might need to use it on Nadurnian when I found him?

Threading my way through the maze of crooked streets surrounding the region where Nadurnian's rathole of a school was located, I reached his shabby tenement and climbed the familiar stairs. At the top, the light from the stairwell cast my shadow before me as I advanced along the length of the passage leading to Nadurnian's sitting-room. Following my shadow form (which concertinaed and shortened as I approached Nadurnian's lair until, as I crossed the threshold it seemed merely a blotch at my feet), I entered, expecting to find Nadurnian anxiously awaiting the return of his murderous golem.

Instead, I found a hulking but husk-like figure, clad in an ill-fitting suit, sprawled against the far wall, engulfed by shadows. Its facial features were whitish and immobile.

I was momentarily confused. Had Nadurnian been killed by his own golem before the creature came to attack me? Suddenly uncertain, I kneeled down to examine the body, from which a small amount of reddish-black fluid was seeping into the carpet. Instinctively, I realised the body on the floor before me was *not* Nadurnian, but that of the golem; for now that I saw it, this body was more ungainly, identifiably more 'unfinished' than the body I had left on the floor of my sitting-room at home.

This could only have one meaning—the thing that I had killed, the thing that had entered my home intent upon crushing my life out, *was none other than Nadurnian himself*. The likeness between the doctor and his unvocal companion had become so close that I had mistaken the deranged esotericist for the golem...

As I raised my eyes from the golem's body, the whirling pattern on the wallpaper seemed to be moving, swirling in pulsations strangely familiar, and horribly like those pulses that Nadurnian believed throbbed at the heart of the manifest world. My vision went black, my senses reeled, and in that moment I felt my flesh, my animate or inanimate flesh (I could no longer tell the difference) inhabited by the forces which I had sought so long.

I collapsed onto the floor beside the golem's body. I remember thinking that there were now *three* bodies, of which mine was one, and I imagined I could hear Nadurnian's voice droning of the Hegelian theory of thesis, antithesis and synthesis. I could feel the synthesis taking place within me, a transmutation undreamed of by the alchemists. The pulsations, like tendrils, passed through my bloodstream. I felt the shocking interiority of the inner secret—the secret that I had, all along, been in the process of becoming.

## 10. Cadenza: The Mask Upon the World

Now I am Nadurnian.
Or I am his golem.

Or perhaps they are both, in some sense, the individual that in my previous phase of existence I thought was 'I.'

It is immaterial—a word I find especially apt for this situation. In any event, now it is *I* who give the lectures in this shabby and dilapidated lecture theatre with its pathetic rows of folding chairs, and its formula-scrawled blackboard, and its pitiful audience of unquestioning time-killers. I see the paramount importance of continuing the work, for it is my own work and, in some sense, always was.

These blank-faced fools that I lecture to…surely they must see that the inner secret is encapsulated in my flesh? Surely they must perceive that I am inhabited by the energies of which I, Dr Nadurnian, speak? They are all themselves golems, clay men and hollow men and straw men who will not truly come to life until my creative word invades them.

*I am Nadurnian.*

The hallucinatory Logos is here. I will continue, as I always have done, to speak of the Mask upon the world, as the Mask trembles and threatens to slide aside, as the stirrings in the abyss continue, as the thrummings animate the earth and the insectoid puppets that look out from behind humans' eyes continue to walk upon its surfaces. Those who have eyes to see, let them see. The soft black stars have come. I see them above the housetops throughout the city. But of them, I will tell in one of my *future* disquisitions on the true nature of reality…

# "BY THEIR FRUITS..."

*"I need a lover like any other, what do I get?"*

– The Buzzcocks

When it seemed to be over, Fowler, panting from exertion, made himself change. He unpacked the clean dark suit and blue tie and the fresh white shirt from his overnight case, replacing them with his soiled clothing, which he wrapped in a plastic bag lest it stain the case's lining. He wrapped the messy hatchet in a piece of towel, then hefted it in on top of the bulky plastic bag and snapped the overnight case shut.

He dressed in the bedroom's *en suite*—washed his hands, shaved, brushed his teeth, adjusted his tie, fought down the urge to be sick. He'd done what had to be done. He hadn't flinched from the task at hand. Surely the worst was behind him. He wished it had gone more cleanly, but he could hardly have wished it to go more quietly. She hadn't cried out at all—had hardly had time. She had fought him, despite the terror in her dark eyes, with more strength than he had thought she possessed. Nonetheless, an unvocalised curse had seemed to invade his mind from hers, an impalpable threat whose words had not taken full shape. He was glad that he hadn't quite caught the phrase. Had it been "You'll *regret* this"? That seemed weak and inappropriate. In any case, he couldn't be sure, and he was prepared to put it down to imagination, or stress.

---

He didn't look back as he walked out of the front door of the flat, the overnight case clasped in one trembling hand. He would not acknowledge the events of the last hour, even to himself, except insofar as he was glad to be rid of her influence. He felt safer when he snicked the front door shut behind him. He heard the hum of the lift down the hall, the reassuring throb of road traffic outside. He tried to block out the memory of the events in the bedroom, where what was left of Marion still writhed feebly in the murky light.

On the bus, heading back for the city, he forced himself to remain calm. Blobs of light from shops and houses seemed dissolved by the darkness which welled up outside the windows.

Despite himself, Fowler began to nod. A sound—gentle, yet disturbing, impinged on his hearing. *Splat…splat…*

The man next to him, nearer the window, drew back alarmed as large drops of blood spattered against the window…*splat …splat …splat…*

Fowler opened his eyes. Then he closed them again and drew his hand over his brow, which was damp with sweat. He re-opened his eyes and cast a nervous glance at the window as passengers began to mutter amongst themselves. It wasn't blood that they'd seen, only rain—fat, heavy drops of rain, each soft impact making a *splat…splat …splat…*

Fowler's reflection in the window seemed awash with subdued panic. He tried to shut what he had just done from his thoughts, for the passengers might sense them.

He tried to forget all that blood—*her* blood; tried to forget the soft '*splat*' each time a drop had fallen on the bare floorboards. Already, he was managing to feel distanced from that scene. No, the person who had entered her flat to bring their affair to its bloody culmination was not himself, but someone else—someone he had known a long time ago. Now he was—he *had* to be—Fowler, the happily married businessman. He had to prevent himself from thinking about the damned curse that Marion had communicated, mere moments before the final hatchet blow severed her throat; had to prevent himself from understanding what she meant by it.

It became easier as he neared home. He almost felt what he had hoped—that because he had destroyed her body her words could no longer touch him. He jostled his way off the bus when it lurched around his corner and splashed through the dim pool of light at the bus-stop towards his house. The fat drops of rain had turned to drenching downpour. He fought to keep out the memories threatening to flood over him. By the time he had reached his front door, he was soaked.

Janet hadn't yet returned from dinner with her Arts Centre client. That was good. He shrugged out of his heavy coat, leaving it dripping on the hall coat-stand, a cast-off, limply sagging figure. In the comfortably furnished living room he crossed to the fireplace, put the overnight bag down on the soot-encrusted hearth and lit the fire, coaxing it into life. Anything that could remind him of Marion had to be destroyed. *Logic.* He mustn't give in to the half-formed fear that now he'd let himself go he would never regain control.

First to go was the plastic bag of soiled clothing. It caught alight almost immediately, hissing and smoking. He prodded it with the poker, making sure the fire consumed everything. When it was ash, he unwrapped the bloodstained towel from the hatchet and threw it into the flames, which surged smokily around and through the damp cloth. Hatchet in hand, he climbed the stairs to the spare room.

Inside, he strode to the old locked dresser where he'd hidden the bulging bundle of Marion's letters and cards and photos so that Janet wouldn't find them. Unlocking it, he withdrew the elastic-banded pile, bundled them up, and replaced them with the hatchet, which he closed into the drawer and locked. He would dispose of it later. The memorabilia of his times with Marion, good and bad, must be consigned to the flames.

Back downstairs, as he tore the letters and things to shreds and flung them on the blaze, he tried to avoid looking at them, to avoid the pain of confronting the past; but the flames caught one shred of photograph and whisked it right-side up. Out of the smouldering ash, Marion's face gazed up at him for an instant, all her contradictory charms displayed — that look of bruised innocence, the pouting lips and dark, sullen eyes that had simultaneously enticed and frustrated him. Then, a quivering tongue of flame obliterated her features, and in a few more moments the only tangible evidence that connected him with Marion was gone. Except the hatchet, of course.

He didn't know how soon her body would be found. He tried not to care. The next day he studiously avoided reading the papers. He retrieved the hatchet while Janet was on a long phone-call with a friend, wiped it down with old rags from under the sink, wrapped it in newspaper, then walked five doors down and across the road, where he buried it halfway down in the detritus of a neighbours' rubbish bin. It would be gone with the rubbish collection next morning. After that, he returned home and involved himself in some pressing household chores. The rest of the day he lounged around the house, conversing desultorily with Janet.

By the following day, whatever tenseness or apprehension he felt had begun to fade. The police had nothing whatsoever to connect him to her murder. He had always been careful never to be seen in public with her, and they had never been photographed together. He almost began to believe that on the night of her death he had been here at home, warming himself in front of the fire because of the rain and cold — which was what he planned to say, should he be questioned.

Several more days passed without any official knock at the door.

He assumed that by now her mutilated body must have been found and buried.

A week after the killing Fowler sat bolt upright in bed in the small hours close to dawn. The room was steeped in dimness. Shadows pooled in the corners, dissipated only a little by a watery shaft of light which struggled through the window. Janet lay huddled in the blankets beside him, her blonde hair obscuring the side of her face.

Fowler sat up uneasily, eyes glued together, hair rumpled, the images of a half-remembered premonitory dream fading rapidly in his still-sluggish mind. He rubbed his eyes, peering around the room. He thought he could hear a vague sucking noise, which might have been the drains, but sounded more like something licking its chops. The noise ceased so quickly that Fowler was immediately unsure he had heard it at all.

There seemed to be a dark stain on the floor. Dark red blood fell in slow motion with a quiet '*splat*' in his mind. He stilled the thought, yet the stain spread liquescently, moving with ominous slowness towards the bed, to lap around its feet. Fowler disentangled himself from the clinging sheets, but by the time he had put one foot on the floor he realised that the dawning sun had gone behind a cloud; the stain was a shadow.

He felt sick, and barely managed to down the scrambled eggs and soggy bacon that Janet dished up for his breakfast.

"Get outside of that. You'll feel better," she said cheerily. She whistled a tune as she made them coffee.

He was not looking forward to going to the office this morning. His mind wandered as he got off the bus and trudged the concrete paths that led to the legal firm where he worked. He passed a disused theatre; one wall was plastered with peeling posters which flapped or clung desperately to the wall like reluctant suicides.

As he entered the Mills Robertson building and turned to enter the corridor which led to his offices, he glimpsed someone he thought he recognised in the middle distance. His heart leapt. Then, it started to pound, as he realised this dark-haired girl worked in his own office building and was dismayed to realise he had mistaken her for Marion.

It distracted him. At the office nothing seemed to go right. His bleary eyes gave his workmates an excuse to rib him.

"Had a big night of it last night, eh?" grinned Robert. "Janet been giving you a bit of a workout, eh mate?"

Fowler could only groan and bury his head in his paperwork, which lay in drifts about his desk. There was a slimy taste in his mouth, and his stomach refused to quieten; it kept growling at him.

"Leave him alone, Bob, he's just under the weather this morning," said Margaret in his defence, flashing a sympathetic look at Fowler.

He returned the look. Her raised eyebrow seemed to indicate that there might be better ways of showing his gratitude, but surely she couldn't be implying that he should ask her out? After all, she couldn't know what a joke his marriage was. He pretended not to have noticed Margaret's come-on, and bent his head back to his legal brief. It dawned on him that this was not the first time his mind had strayed to Marion that morning. He allowed his thoughts to drift back over their relationship.

Fowler had first seen her playing at the Guitar Lounge, a small club, the sort he had rarely ventured into. That night, however, he was in search of adventure, feeling jaded in his relationship with Janet. Marion had struck him instantly as the embodiment of his deepest desires. She was simply dressed, her long dark hair falling over one shoulder. As she played and sang, she seemed childishly unaware of the provocative effect that her body had on the men in the audience. She and her music were full of idealistic notions about people and society. He, though less naive, thought her soul as impossibly beautiful as her body.

The men were drawn to her; he could tell from the way they watched her. He, too, wanted her immediately, but before he had even spoken to her, he swore a silent oath that he would protect her from the depredations of other men. She seemed vulnerable, and whenever he was away from her, his inevitable mental image of her was of a dark, lustrous fruit that had been roughly handled.

It had been a passionate affair, one that left both of them breathless. No sooner had Fowler approached her, it seemed, they were back in her flat, in her room. She poured out her story of her love for her previous boyfriend, who had betrayed her. For some reason she seemed to trust him. Fowler ached for her, and when he was with her, he was able to forget the drabness of his life with Janet. His half-hearted protestations that he was married and that they couldn't embark on a full-scale affair died on his lips as she kissed him. He had it bad.

After that first tempestuous encounter, Fowler gave himself wholly to Marion. He thought they were giving themselves wholly to each other. Their sex together felt like an explosion of love and tenderness and violence that until now had been repressed in both of them. He was blinded by her, seeing everything through her eyes—or so he thought. He easily excused her wilfulness because of her beauty, her selfishness because of her intelligence.

Yet Fowler wanted to possess her, and he couldn't. The more he tried to pin her down, the more she withdrew. He suffered humiliations just to be near her. Eventually, he realised that for all her platitudes about caring, she was concerned at heart only with herself and with what she could squeeze from the moment. Once, in a jealous rage, he tried to accuse her of flirting outrageously with another man. But when he saw the mixture of hurt and contempt in her eyes, he felt as though he had kicked a small puppy, and hated himself for it.

His uncontainable lust for her ruled him. When he had felt her slipping from his grasp, something began to snap. One night, nearly a year after they first met, she confessed her increasing reluctance to have him touch her, and that she had only used him to get over the man before, the one she had really loved.

Fowler had gone to pieces. He raged, knowing he was destroying the relationship. She refused to see him.

He moped around, trying to take solace with Janet, while simultaneously disguising his adulterous relationship. Janet, deeply immersed in her own life and pursuits, had apparently noticed none of it. In private, he raked over the embers of his affair with Marion until his brain felt fit to burst. He gradually realised that if the moment had offered comfort, Marion had taken it. If the moment had threatened her—or if a situation did not offer her what she sought—she would abandon it. Now, she had abandoned him. He told himself that she did this blindly, as a moth seeks the light, or as a leech sucks its fill and then moves on to another host— unpleasant behaviour certainly, but one cannot blame such a creature, he thought, for acting according to its nature. It knows no better.

The mistake had been his—to have envisaged her as a butterfly, or as the Rose without a Thorn; to have created her in his idealised, romanticised image. He had thought her infallible. In one of his love letters he had compared her to a rough gemstone. Secretly he believed he could polish her to perfection, faceting the gem to bring out the inner brilliance. What arrogance! He came to the agonising conclusion that she was an altogether cheaper sort of jewel, a gaudy sparkler which has no true heart and in the darkness is lost.

The verse he had written her now seemed hollow, a record of his own self-deception. The times they had treasured together, their lovemaking, returned to mock him, making his relationship with the dull Janet more stifling than ever. He grew distraught and depressed by turns. Marion remained as she had always been—alluring, yet ever more unreachable. His love for her became morbid. The exotic fruit, for him, had become rotten deep within, as though worm-infested. He wandered the streets, contemplating ending it.

His sleep was racked with twisted memories and also dreams which haunted his waking hours. One night, he dreamed he was weeping, pouring out a guilt-wracked confession of—something—to friends, to former employers, to everyone who ever knew him. Faces leered at him. There was one face more sensual, more attractive than the rest—a face with dark, sullen eyes and a kind of hurt, childish expression of sadness. He moved towards her, engulfed in a rush of torrid eroticism as he kissed her. She was his perfect vision of womanhood, his bride-to-be. Then, he was carrying her through a church down an aisle of white fungi, which wavered and pulsed. Before he reached the altar, she had slipped out of his grasp. Had he dropped her? He wasn't sure, but suddenly the ground beneath his feet was wrenching itself apart, and her recumbent form was receding, falling away...

When daylight roused him, his jealous anger was at fever pitch. He planned everything in a fury of dejection—bought the hatchet from a hardware store in a distant suburb where he was unknown; bought the overnight case and the spare clothes—and the very same evening travelled to her flat. Janet did not even have to be informed; she had gone out to an Arts Centre function where she would be hobnobbing until late with patrons.

Fowler knew that if he could kill Marion, his suffering would end. A pawn in the hands of his own uncontrollable passions, he decided that if he couldn't have her, he would ensure that *no-one* could.

Marion did not even question his motive for returning. He knocked at her front door. She opened it. An expression of mild surprise crossed her face, but she did not seem displeased to see him. She was, incredibly, naive enough not to realise the impact her rejection had made on him.

"Russell, come in," she said.

"Thanks."

"I see you've brought your overnight case. Were you thinking of staying?"

"I thought I might," said Fowler. "Let's have a drink."

They found their way to the bedroom more through habit than desire. He picked up the overnight case on the way in, clicked it open unobtrusively. When she turned away, he was on her from behind with the hatchet in hand. The first blow laid her head open like a split melon. He closed his eyes as he landed the next savage blow between her neck and shoulder, and had to tug to get the blade out of her body. She fell onto the bed, twisting face upwards as she fell. Blood gushed from the wounds, which gaped like slack red mouths. Her eyes flickered half-shut, reminding him of how she had looked when they made love.

Hate suddenly possessed him. He hacked, and hacked, and hacked, destroying and rending her beautiful limbs. In minutes, the bedclothes were sodden with blood. She lost so much that before his fury was spent, the blood flow was slowing.

Time lost its meaning for him. All he could hear was the slow 'splat'…'splat'…as the blood dripped from the bed to the floorboards. Suddenly afraid she was still capable of screaming, he ensured his last blow severed her throat. It was then that her curse blossomed like an evilly-spotted fungus in his head.

He staggered from the room. His ragged breathing calmed gradually, and he began to change his clothes in the bathroom. From rage, he had cooled rapidly to calculation.

Now Fowler left his workplace, his skull pounding. He felt stalked by something as he stumped home, but he was too tense to look around to see who it might be—perhaps that girl from the office who resembled Marion. Well, he wouldn't give her the satisfaction of turning around. He heard flesh rub against flesh, but perhaps it was only in his thoughts. *God.* He almost wanted Marion back—but it was way too late for that, and he instinctively felt it fatal to pursue that train of thought.

Unexpectedly, for a brief while, his life seemed to run normally again. Since the affair with Marion had reached unbearable pitch, solved by her annihilation, he was almost glad to be alone again with Janet.

For some months he pursued the usual round of engagements—dinners marked by innocuous small talk with mutual friends, the occasional tennis match at which Janet never failed to thrash him, fundraising activities for Janet's Arts Centre where she worked part-time as Public Relations Officer. He even managed to make love with her a few times, taking refuge in his masculine ability to remain emotionally uninvolved in the act.

If Janet had noticed any change in him during or since the affair with Marion, she gave no sign of it. Her unquestioning faith in his fidelity sometimes surprised him. He assumed that her work provided all the stimulation she needed, and that his indifferent lovemaking deprived her of little. She was, to all appearances, happy with her life. He tried to be the same.

But it wasn't long before Fowler grew to feel again that their marriage was a mere shell, shallower now than before he had sought comfort in Marion's arms. Janet began to seem more colourless, yet more complacent and dispassionate. Newly sick of the dull routine, his intentions of injecting a new vigour into his relationship with Janet grew thin. Fowler's mounting dissatisfaction paralleled that of the year before his affair, when his boredom and restlessness had driven him to Marion like a thirsty man in the desert drawn to the cool of an oasis.

He arrived home one evening to discover that Janet had arranged a party at their place—another of the endless series of fundraising functions for her Arts Centre, he assumed.

The house was full of artists whose work was funded by the Centre. They were mostly a scruffy lot. Many looked nothing but skin and bone, most dressed in black or what appeared to be rags. Fowler thought anything would be better than to be stuck here, chattering about the latest exhibition, or last week's Arts Centre politics. He needed to be alone with his thoughts, instead of having to act the faithful supporting husband. He had a nagging sense that he wanted or needed to remember—something.

While a boorish middle-aged woman with an Elizabeth Bay accent droned on about her new fashion store, he forced a plastic smile. Over her shoulder, past the crush of guests, he glimpsed Janet going to and fro in the kitchen and emerging to refill glasses and pass around *hors d'oeuvres*.

"I didn't know they still *called* them boutiques," he forced out, hardly bothering to disguise his impatience.

"Oh yes! Well, the whole sixties revival is in full swing, you know," she said, with a look that told Fowler she faintly suspected deliberate sarcasm on his part. "The Arts Centre people seem to feel that it's a viable proposition. We're going to call it 'Granny Gets Hip'—a direct rip-off of the whole Haight-Ashbury scene of 1965, of course, but then the idea is to make money. We're reviving the sixties feel, but only in terms of fashion, not politics, of course; the whole peace-love thing was so naive, you know."

"Well, I'm sure you have the right formula for success," said Fowler, tightening his grip on his glass. He had begun to feel nauseous, and a headache pounded a tattoo in his temples.

"You must come to the opening," she gushed. "I imagine it will be much more exciting that going into that dull office of yours. *Everybody* will be there."

Fowler mumbled a vague promise to turn up, and abruptly excused himself to rush away to the bathroom. His stomach was fluttering violently, and his skin felt hot and greasy. Perhaps he had drunk too much? But he had only had two glasses of wine. He must be ill. He wasn't sure whether the strain of struggling against a half-forgotten traumatic memory was making him sick, or whether the sickness was what blocked his memory.

He heard the woman 'harrumph' behind his back as he stumbled to the bathroom. He hadn't meant to appear rude, but it was hardly his fault. If Janet hadn't expected him to attend this party, he would have been resting up in bed, losing his battered mind in sleep, instead of maintaining a brave face.

He was only just in time to abandon his glass on the handbasin, and yank up the lid of the toilet. Then his stomach convulsed and he vomited into the bowl. He gasped for breath. When he had finished heaving, he stood and wiped the sweat from his forehead, clearing his throat to rid it of the bile's sour taste. Then he gazed into the mirror above the basin while he washed his hands. His face was tired, pasty-looking. The flesh seemed somehow doughy.

As he turned his face away from the mirror, and switched off the light, he thought he glimpsed movement behind him. He glanced back, but all he could see in the now-dark bathroom was the pale rectangle of mirror, reflecting his defeated form slumped in the doorway.

He returned to the throng to give his excuses, but he was unable to interrupt, for the guests were singing now. Was it some special occasion that he didn't know about? Memories stirred like prematurely buried corpses; he dreaded what might happen if they burst through to the surface.

Janet looked contented enough, singing away, surrounded by her friends, who were waving champagne glasses and toasting her. '*Oh my God,*' Fowler thought suddenly, '*it's our wedding anniversary.*' No wonder she had chosen tonight. People were looking towards him, grinning. Their upraised glasses must be meant for him as well.

Now Janet was disappearing into the kitchen. She reappeared with a cake, and loud cheers resounded. A hand pressed between his shoulder blades, and Fowler felt himself thrust towards the gathering's centre. Before he could protest, someone put the lights out.

As darkness flooded in, he heard groping sounds. Then a match flared, and someone held the tiny flame to the candles on the cake.

Fowler clutched at his stomach. He felt wretched. The darkness was black mud, oozing about him. The candles gradually lit up, and he was able to see who was lighting them. A pale face floated above the cake—he thought at first it was Janet's, but it looked more like—

He felt the walls of his mind were about to give way. He was on the verge of remembering what he'd done, but confusion and panic gripped him. Why was *Marion* here? How *could* she be here? There was no mistaking that face, those sullen eyes, the full mouth that had often kissed his, but which was now twisted with hate. *You killed her*, Fowler thought. *Marion no longer exists. You — I — killed her. I wiped her out.*

He sobbed, finally realising — remembering — the fatal act. Mentally, he saw the hatchet coming down repeatedly, hacking Marion's soft flesh to bloody pulp. Dizziness made him sway.

Just before the mouth above the cake blew out the candles, it said something that Fowler suspected only he could hear. It was a throaty, betrayed kind of curse, in Marion's voice.

*"You'll rot for this,"* it said.

Fowler realised that it was the curse he'd tried to avoid remembering properly since the night she died. Then, the candle flames were snuffed out and amidst the incongruously celebratory cheers, he fell forward across the table.

Later, as he lay in bed, Janet, tucking a strand of her ash-blonde hair behind her ear, was saying that she hadn't realised he was so ill. For once, she was tending to him, caring for him. But in his feverish state, he hardly heard her.

He almost choked when she brought in a bowl of fruit, for the peach she offered him was bruised. He pushed her hand away.

Sullen-eyed, she undressed and climbed in beside him.

He felt no better, but to avoid talk, he read a book until drowsiness overtook him. His eyes began to flicker shut but oddly, despite his nausea, he found himself feeling amorous towards Janet. He was reaching out for her, reaching for her soft flesh, her warm embrace. He recalled being in the special place he had shared with Marion. Janet's naked body yielded to him, pressing close to his. She made a low murmur of encouragement.

As their bodies joined, her face loomed, filling his vision like a world. He felt detached and unaccountably sick again as her face began to change.

He drew back in horror.

It was not Janet with whom he was making love, but *Marion*, her face contorted with lust. As she bucked and thrust against him, her eyes closed, the cloying, sickly odour of rotting fruit filled his nostrils. Her lips parted to reveal a worm fat as a tongue, a worm that writhed, white and puffy, between her lips.

He jerked awake, dripping with sweat.

But the nightmare seemed not to have ended. He found himself out of bed, standing at the doorway in bare feet. All he could think of were Marion's words: *"You'll rot for this,"* the last word a protracted sibilant, hissed between her teeth with her dying breaths, her hacked-apart body in ruins.

Fowler's flesh hung heavily on his bones. What was happening? He looked around at the bed. Janet was sitting on its far edge, her back to him, a robe draped around her shoulders. He stumbled around the bed-end towards her. Perhaps if he confessed everything to her...

But it was too late, he knew, for that. As he put his hand on Janet's shoulder, he snatched it away again with a shudder of revulsion. Her flesh was spongy and moist to his touch.

God help him, he had to see her face. When she turned, in response to his hand's anxious pressure, he involuntarily fell back a step.

Janet's flesh was peeling away, sagging from her face and upper body in sallow folds and strips. Her eyes were dead, clouded like spoiled milk. Partly out of shock, with a kind of rare tenderness, he clasped her head in both hands.

The pulpy mass came away from her body altogether, with a mushy snap like a rotten cabbage being separated from its stalk.

Fowler gazed in blank disbelief at the rotten, maggoty object he was holding, as the rest of Janet's body toppled onto the floor. It wasn't when the mouth in the head dropped open that he began to scream, nor when he saw again that pale, lolling, grub-like tongue writhing obscenely within, nor even when he heard the detached, crumbling head croak in a harsh, hateful voice identifiably Marion's: *"You'll rot for this."* He dropped the head from palsied hands.

It was when he looked down at his own body and saw his own skin and muscle begin to discolour into ugly bruised tissue, begin to drop away from his bones like heated wax, and when his nostrils caught the reek of his fast-rotting flesh.

His screams were short-lived. Within moments he hadn't enough flesh to stand, and he fell, his brain seeming to dissolve into slime within his skull as he hit the floor.

The last thing he saw before vision and consciousness fled forever was the mouldy head that had been Janet's, upright but squirming on the floor in front of him—in the sockets of that detestable head, gazing into his with that wounded, sullen expression, were Marion's hurt-puppy eyes.

# WAVE

In the dream, they sat near a pergola shrouded with pink and red bougainvilleas. "It's been there a long time," she said. "Look how thick the stem is."

Cicadas chirruped in the eucalypt-thick bush edging the kiosk. Nearby, a kid at a plastic table slumped in his wheelchair, as stiff and immobile as a lump of driftwood thrown up by the ocean overnight.

In front of the kiosk, waves of hang-gliders like colourful giant boomerangs lined the grass. From the escarpment above, others launched and flew out over the sea, spiralling back like lazy multicoloured moths to land on the wet dark sand.

The kiosk girl brought their lunch—a caramel thick-shake, paper buckets of hot chips. Suddenly this was real, it was no dream. They bent their heads to the food, hungry now.

After the meal they walked towards the beach. The oppressive heat beneath the trees made him sweat. His breath rose and fell with effort. He took his sandals off to walk barefoot but the sandy track scalded him, so he put them back on.

The vista swam up before them: a stretch of white-hot sand. Ocean blue as night, immense as heaven, powerful as hell, sucked at the continent's edge—restless, heaving. It was so vast, so blind. Almost resistless, he thought. Girls in scanty bikinis lay on jags of rock thrusting up through the sand. The tide was out. Dark patches on the sand marked its phases of retreat. He felt its pull even from here.

"Come on," she said, tugging him forward, coaxing him along the open sand.

Had she forgotten that day when he had charged into the surf, wanting the slap of waves against his body: too eager after his illness. Within moments, he had been out of his depth. Now he shuddered, reliving the gut-gripping fear that had run through him when, unable to touch bottom, waves pounding over his head, he began to drift out of control. He mouthed again that panicked shout as he waved one arm aloft.

He saw again the fear on *her* face, too, as she had run along the beach, too far away to help. He swallowed, again tasting salt water; went down, once, and again, until a surfer had pulled him half onto his board, brought him in. He gasped anew as the lifesavers fitted the oxygen-mask over his face, the sand gritty on his skin as they laid him down. His body replayed its shock.

"Nah," he said, jerking out of his reverie. "Let's go back." Now he led her away from the water's edge, away from the beach. They walked the bluebottle-strewn sand fringing the lagoon. Squealing kids played touch footy in the sun. It was comforting to feel solid ground underfoot, to know things would not slip away beneath.

Like a giant swell against the napes of their necks, the increasing heat struck him as they reached the car. He held her hand more tightly.

"Let's go home," he said.

The wave in his dream hung overhead, waiting to break.

# THE GUARDIAN

The tiny spacecraft skimmed over the mysteriously silent city of Aurora. The streets between the spiralling, sculptured-crystal dwellings appeared deserted as the craft touched the ground, sank a little and came to a halt. The two Servants of the Guardian the vessel carried had returned from an expedition on their sister planet.

Hurriedly searching the empty streets, their consternation turned rapidly to fear, and the Servants found only an old man sprawled in unnatural sleep on the chalcedony walkway of his house. Everyone else was gone. As they lifted his head, he awoke. He told them of the sky turning deep crimson and seeing his companions fall where they stood, until he fell also.

Up on the mountain, which cast its shadow over the city, stood undesecrated the great stone serpent the Servants knew as Dragoram, the Guardian—their wizard master. Around its head hung the golden glow after which the city was named. The Servants moved slowly up the mountain.

Once there, the first, Vernis, spoke to the spirit within the stone. Receiving no answer, he spoke again. Slowly, the mind of the wizard within freed itself from the enchantment of evil sorcery which was woven over the city.

The Guardian looked upon the city of Aurora from which all but the old man had vanished. The wizard's mind spoke to the Servants. He told them that the city's inhabitants were nowhere on the planet. He then commanded the second of the two to place the jewel.

Roland took the pendant from around his neck and carefully placed it into a socket in the throat of the stone serpent statue. The stone quivered, then moved as it came to life, slowly uncoiling its fantastic length.

Dragoram launched his mind from the stone into the void. A pulse of familiar thoughtwaves reached him, so strong in force that it could only be the collective consciousness of the Aurorans, and he focused his attention on the source, tracing it with all his concentration and energy. He determined its origins to be a planet in a star cluster hundreds of light-years away—Sardon, the Planet of the Black Crystal.

The instant of his return, he ordered Vernis and Roland to prepare the craft.

The ground rumbled as they rose into the now-misty air. Night fell as the craft left the atmosphere. The planet shrank into the backdrop of white, silver and violet. They passed light-years of planets and stars and novae. Clouds of magnetic gas enveloped them as they reached an amazing velocity.

The three conversed telepathically. Sardon lay in the uncharted wastes of the Korgian system. Little was known of its people; but intragalactic pirates and traders had been heard to speak of a priceless black Korgian crystal of immense proportions. This crystal was supposed to whisper to its owner the dark secrets of power.

After hours of blasting through space, the ship reached orbiting distance of the planet. The Guardian and his servants, after surveying the surface of the globe, observed that there was only one landmass, the rest being covered by seas. Easing the controls allowed the craft to land rapidly, and the three alighted.

The Servants wore body armour, and the Guardian changed his form to that of a panther for ease of ground movement. He felt the nearness of the Auroran people. They set out over the arid landscape towards the only visible landmark, a jumble of tottering ruined buildings.

As they approached, they saw a few, ragged, shambling figures wandering among the fallen stones and rubble. A tall, skeletal man clad in greyish tatters was the nearest.

The Guardian probed his mind, then those of others and found that the people had been driven insane by some force as yet unknown. But here and there he caught fragments of intelligible memory. The Guardian paid close scrutiny to these and other apparently random thoughts, and by mental effort pieced together what must have happened.

Roland and Vernis were astounded as he told them of Myrania, the Scarlet Sorceress, known also as the Vampire of Souls, who had been banished years before from the temple for slaying the High Priest with sorcery. She had sworn retribution.

It was only when the people of the city began to die one by one in the same manner as had the High Priest, that the city realised Myrania was still alive and seeking vengeance. She had created beneath Onyctia an impenetrable castle where she drew sustenance by killing off her enemies. It was held that she devoured their flesh and the blood drained into the moat which surrounded the castle.

Soon after the slaughter began, buildings in the city crashed in ruins. It appeared Myrania had found something which gave her added power—something which was thought to be the evil Black Crystal. This she had shaped into a room of lustrous mirrored surfaces so she could admire her beauty while it whispered to her the spells of destruction she needed. But the crystal needed to be supplied with souls to carry on its evil pseudo-life. Myrania took less flesh and blood from the Onyctians, but more and more she sucked their souls from their bodily shells, leaving the bodies empty husks and bringing the city to utter collapse.

It was only too obvious, maintained the Guardian, that the people of Aurora had been taken to supply the Black Crystal with her more evil nourishment. But with what object, he did not know, for plainly Myrania's revenge against the city was complete. Perhaps she planned to extend her power still further.

Roland asked how they should find this sorceress. One city on a world may not be a great area to explore, but for three individuals, it would take time. Vernis suggested that the best point from which to start would be the temple, if it still existed.

The panther crouching at his side lowered its head, and its great golden eyes flickered shut. The outlines of its body seemed to shudder, then started to flow as the shape altered. As fast as the Guardian could conceive of it, his physical body took on the shape of a *shangor*, the great winged mountain bird of Aurora. He cast his body into the air, his wings beating furiously; his eyes had the same golden glow as before. Almost at once, he spied the temple.

A huge edifice, formidable even in decay, it stood amid the surrounding wreckage like a sentinel from an alien world. The Guardian perched on a toppled pillar in the half-exposed courtyard.

At the back, partly concealed by fallen masonry and creeping foliage, the stone panel behind the altar gaped open, revealing only darkness. Dragoram peered, fluttering closer and flapping about what he now saw to be a hidden entrance. The gap was too small to admit any of them; he was sure it must be connected in some way with Myrania.

From the outskirts of the city, Roland and Vernis saw the circling shape marking the spot where they were to go. They made their way swiftly to the temple. Once at the crumbling monument which had obviously been Onyctia's focal point before Myrania was cast out, Dragoram directed them to clear away as much of the fallen wreckage from the doorway as possible. He landed and took on the form of the snake which he had used in his guardianship of Aurora.

Slithering across the opening and wedging his supple body between the sides, Dragoram heaved and strained. A groaning and grinding came from the stone; then, cracking along a fault, it broke in half, enabling all three to squeeze past. There was no doubt, as they started the descent of the dangerously slippery and slime-covered steps cut into the solid rock, that they had struck the trail of Myrania almost straight away. The rock walls, smooth and black, pressed in closely on both sides, and the staircase wound sinuously downwards.

At last they emerged onto a sandy bank which lay at the edge of a vast underground lake. Stretching away as flat as glass, the lake was blood-red. Overhead, the rock walls opened out into an enormous cavern. On the far side, where the walls once again closed in, there thrust from the deep red a jagged black island of rock. Framed by a halo of light from behind, spires and battlements proclaimed the majestic and sinister presence of the palace fortress atop the dark island. The three stood motionless, tiny figures on the shore. They shuddered as they saw the extent of the blood-filled lake.

Roland had an uneasy feeling that it was all too simple. How could they have penetrated this close to the palace without alerting the guards or protectors she must surely have?

The answer became clear within seconds. There was a menacing sound of rustling from the stairwell behind them. They whirled to see several wriggling white shapes come from the stairway they had just left. The bloated, white, fat bodies were surpassed in loathsomeness only by the featureless heads, with mouths dripping venom.

The rustling continued, and a few more of the things appeared. One reached Vernis and he stamped on it with disgust as it tried to squirm up his boot. The evil-smelling black liquid which burst from the body made him recoil in revulsion.

Roland shouted, his face paling. He pointed towards the stairwell. From the dark was pouring a flood of the things, tumbling over each other in wriggling heaps. Thousands of the dirty white creatures formed an advancing wave which covered the whole beach from side to side, and grew ever closer to the three.

Dragoram circled overhead.

His change of form had gone unnoticed by the Servants in their surprise. The edge of the wave reached them, and wherever the dripping venom came in contact with the Servants' armour, it hissed and seared into the metal.

Dragoram could see that their only hope was to retreat into the lake of blood, which was evidently not very deep. The two waded in, their distaste increasing as they broke through the clotted red-black scum on the surface. Wishing they had their master's protean abilities, as they watched him soar above the lake, they moved further out, leaving the deadly venomous worms impotent on the shore.

But what was to ensure they would not be attacked by some greater horror, while up to their necks in this stinking morass? They would have to take their chances. But despite the unpleasantness and discomfort, breaking through areas clotted and coagulating, they eventually gained the shore of the island.

Dripping crimson, their hair encrusted and armour caked with blood, they gazed up at the basaltic edifice towering over them. There was no sign of life.

Dragoram flapped noisily down beside them.

After a few moments of consultation, and when the Servants had recovered something of their composure, they decided to make their approach boldly and without any attempt at concealment. With Dragoram's sense of nearness even stronger, they wanted to rescue the Aurorans before any harm could come to them.

A broad, spiralling ramp of slippery, translucent rock was the only path to the top, and they took it, with Dragoram perched on Vernis' shoulder.

At the top, they found the tall, brazen gates which normally enclosed the courtyard standing wide open. On their guard every second, they approached the opening. Their footsteps clattered on the cobblestones as they crossed the threshold, their weapons at the ready. Surely she must have protectors or servants, more than a few, in order to maintain this habitation, and to have taken the inhabitants of Aurora. Who had piloted the craft which took them? At this range, the telepathy between the Guardian and the Aurorans would normally be operative, but some sort of block had been generated, undoubtedly by Myrania. She must have guessed she would be followed, as the attack on the shore also testified.

From the shadows of the courtyard's far side stepped a figure no more than half the size of either Servant. "There is only me," it announced, as if it had divined their thoughts, "apart, of course, from my mistress, Myrania." Squat, barrel-chested and heavily-muscled, the dwarf rumbled a greeting edged with threat. "Welcome to her palace, fools—here you die!" It unsheathed a sword as big as those the Servants carried, and charged them. Grotesque and awkward, it was fast enough on its feet. The sword swung down at Vernis, leaving a blazing arc of fire in its wake.

Dragoram fluttered aloft, and Vernis jumped from the path of the razor-edged weapon. Roland shot a thought as he swung his own sword at the dwarf. *He's using a daemon-blade invested with magical power. Even the two of us can do no more than hold him at bay.*

Indeed, for a few moments, it seemed that the dwarf could win outright. He was terrifically powerful. Only the combined skills of Vernis and Roland fended off his awesome attacks with the rune-hilted sword, and they were fighting for all they were worth. It was soon obvious that the dwarf had merely to exhaust them, let them become worn down, before slaughtering them.

But Dragoram had disappeared during the fight. Vernis knew he had gone for a reason. The bird, which had perched on a wall behind the dwarf, had become a huge spider with hundreds of glittering golden eye-lenses. Crawling down the wall, he approached the dwarf's back.

The sight spurred the Servants to greater efforts. They forced their adversary to retreat for a second, and suddenly he was screaming as filaments of thick, silky web shot out to pinion his limbs.

Panting, blood streaming from minor wounds, Roland grabbed the wrist of the dwarf, whose muscles strained in vain against the spidery imprisonment. The daemon-blade vanished into the air as Roland's sword clove through the skull. The corpse twitched for a few seconds and then was still.

With that, the mental block collapsed. Dragoram's mind suddenly rang with countless cries for help, and he knew that the hundreds of vaults beneath the castle were full of Aurorans. But the sorceress was the last remaining link. They must find her. And when they did, the Black Crystal would be with her. Whether that would be a point in their favour, or against them, was yet to be discovered.

Once more they convened to decide on a course of action. This time they would split up. The Guardian would try to find Myrania, Roland and Vernis would go the vaults and try to free the Aurorans or to await developments which would enable them to be freed.

Running now, for they had no way of knowing when next Myrania would choose to take souls for nourishments and power, they entered the castle proper. Perhaps she had witnessed the destruction of her chief protector and waited to destroy them. They must be even more alert and ready, despite their already exhausted state. Roland and

Vernis went down the marble stairway.

Dragoram, assuming the form of the panther once more, bounded lithely up the same staircase to explore the upper floors. Dragoram felt strange indeed as he climbed the staircase, which spiralled into a labyrinth of mazed corridors.

Now he was seized with a primitive fear; fear for his people, not himself. Dragoram moved with haste. He suddenly felt a presence; she was near. Almost the very instant of this realisation, a corrosive wall of searing pain swept through his being, then—blackness.

Roland and Vernis continued on their way through the winding corridors, becoming more and more lost. In a vaulted room whose sides were actually the facets of the huge Black Crystal, and whose mirrored dark surfaces reflected the movements of those within, a stone beast lay prone on the floor. Over the apparently inanimate figure, robed in flowing scarlet, stood Myrania, the Vampire of Souls; and in her hand she clutched the life-giving jewel from the panther's chest. Her triumph seemed complete.

She could tell, from her brief contact with Dragoram's mind, that his soul was worth more to her than those of the rest of the Aurorans put together. In fact, she had been surprised at the ease with which her offensive waves of mind-force had defeated the wizard. And now she possessed the glowing source of his life. All that remained was to feast on his soul.

Around her, the glittering surfaces of the Black crystal whispered and laughed, uttering secret knowledge and babbling mindlessly at its own power. She raised her arms to begin the conjuration. "I have you at last!" she screamed, and started to chant, using the age-old magicians' tongue.

Suddenly, her eyes caught those of the panther, which were smouldering with orange-golden light. Dragoram's mind was still aware within the inert stone. He held the sorceress captive with his stare, sending out a pulse of irresistible suggestion. Her features contorted with fear and slowly, she moved forward, completely overwhelmed by the Guardian's will, and replaced the jewel. At once the panther grew, rising high above Myrania's mesmerized form.

Until now, Dragoram had successfully hidden his infinitely superior power in order to enter the very lair of his nemesis, but now he unleashed his total energy and unspent fury. Simultaneously, he began destroying the mirrors and the Scarlet Sorceress. The flaming aura around his body, incandescent white tinged with yellow, seared and burned. The weird suspirations and whisperings of the evil crystal mirror-room faltered, and cracks ran through the walls, sundering them.

Dragoram felt the turmoil of Myrania's mind being torn apart by his own burning might. She struggled, but all her energies were insufficient to protect her from the staggering blast emanating from the enormous panther with the golden eyes, and her lifeless body crumpled to the floor.

Panes of the crystal were loosening from the roof and crashing to the ground around Dragoram. As they did so, the souls fed into them by Myrania returned to their bodies.

Dragoram, weary and drained, shrank in size. He could hear Vernis and Roland conversing not far away. Bounding towards their location, he emerged from the lightless maze of corridors into a room where the two men were discussing something over a great control panel. He told them the sorceress was dead.

They responded that the Aurorans were safe, and that this room was the solution to their suspicions. The entire castle was the craft which had transported the Aurorans to Sardon, which was why they had not found a normal spaceship. Touching controls, the Guardian's allies prepared the ship for return to Aurora.

A rumble of power began to build and the whole castle trembled. So slowly at first that it was hardly noticeable, and then faster as the thrust increased, the blackness of the castle seemed to run off, leaving it a gleaming silver. The lake changed to a brilliant white from the glare. Then within seconds, the light dimmed and the castle was gone, transported into the stratosphere of Sardon.

They were on their way back.

# UNCHARTED

Imagine this:

*Islands in a sea of blue. Brilliant sunshine. Yellow sands. The scent of coconut mingling with ozone. No sound except a gentle breeze rustling the leafy crowns of palm-trees. Cascades of colourful flowers with wide blooms like faces upturned to the sky.*

OK? Not too difficult? Then you won't have any trouble imagining the rest of what I'm about to tell you.

## 1. Ash

Adrian Ash considered himself a magician, so I suppose he was one. You remember him quoting Crowley in justification for having interests so diverse: "The Magician must build all that he has into his pyramid; and if that pyramid is to touch the stars, how broad must be the base! There is no knowledge and no power which is useless to the Magician."

Others know (as well as I) how interested Ash seemed to be not just in anthropology, architecture, and cognitive science, but also in artificial intelligence, linguistics, philosophy, psychology, all of which he referred to occultism on some level.

He was forever dabbling in obscure subjects, technical journals on which — *Metaphilosophy, The Journal of Bioethics* — littered his flat, as did texts on functional genomics, stochastic geometry, neurostereology. Mathematics was a particular interest: as long as I knew him, he was working on a paper to do with complex subvarieties of compact Hermitian symmetric spaces and Shubert calculus. When you tried to sit down on his grubby brown two-seater sofa, you had to push away sheets of paper covered with scribbled Schur polynomials and other complex algebra. He was interested in subjects I'd barely heard of—the foundations of probability theory (he was particularly taken with Richard T. Cox's work on inductive inference), convex polytopes, something called 'greedy dimension'.

I found it difficult to believe he could actually have understood these subjects in the depth required to work seriously in them. And indeed, from month to month he would blithely abandon one for another.

Ash was fond of the Suprematists. He had a reproduction of Malevich's most famous painting, *Black Square*, on his wall. His life, like the painting, was a work whose meaning and function was in constant flux.

He admired literary critic Northrop Frye, especially that unrealised project known as the 'Third Book'. He loved the fact that Frye's ambition for this 'Third Book' was for it to become no less than 'a symbolic guide to the entire universe'.

"It's friggin' incredible," Ash would say to me, knocking back another longneck of Little Creatures beer. The table was littered with bottles of this beverage, which we had emptied in the course of an afternoon of speculation and boozy camaraderie. Beneath the table, Ash's moth-eaten-looking cat slunk around, rubbing its head on the corner posts. "The work he envisioned contemplated the ways in which myth and metaphor are the keys to all verbal structure. What a concept, eh?" I could see he really loved this idea. Okay, he taught me a lot, his approach just seemed very scattergun to me.

He was, briefly, into functional architectures of the language system in cognitive neuropsychology.

"Bugger me! Did you know," he would announce with a sort of profanely magisterial nonchalance, on a hot summer night, as cicadas chirped outside, "that a group of neurons oscillating in phase can resonate with a group of neurons at a distance? These oscillations are the basis for neuron-to-neuron communication. Much like those cicadas, really." The burnt end dropped unnoticed from his cigarette, like a leprous appendage too rotten to stay attached to its body.

"Do tell," I said, flippantly. Tonight I wasn't really in the mood. To be honest, of late I couldn't absorb half of what he talked about. Not that I was stupid, mind. I was concentrating on other concerns that for me were closer to home.

I was somewhat adrift, had been for some time. Emotionally isolated from my family, I made sporadic attempts to show them what my life was like but these were rarely successful. Once, at my parents' place for a family gathering, I passed around a photo taken at a backyard party:

some of my mates. The photo showed a bunch of thuggish-looking blokes with tattoos standing against a fence in a backyard. Most clutch beer cans; a couple of them straddle the bikes they rode, Ash looming outlandishly taller than the others.

"Who are these people?" asked my mother dubiously.

"They're his *friends!*" said my sister.

I was vague at the best of times. I would never have my own phone number. I would take a VCR in for repair or apply for a credit card. "Your phone number, sir?" they would ask. "Oh—I have only just moved in." I had been two years at my current address; I just wasn't good at remembering, and couldn't organise myself to carry the number in my wallet.

I left Ash that night still talking, as though into a void, of the neuro-biological roots of cognition.

He was often wilfully odd. He would show up at my place wearing one of those knitted Nepalese hippy hats with the tassels, together with an immaculately dressed and appointed dress suit. In the streets of Petersham, he would wink at me, as people cast odd looks our way. "Confuses the fuck out of 'em." He would turn and make a graceful bow to the nearest trolley-pushing housewife, sweeping the Nepalese hat off his head in a courtly arc. Startled and embarrassed, the housewife hurried on her way, shoving the trolley piled high with oranges in net bags, detergents, bottles of soft drinks, cans of cat food.

At that time I saw Ash whenever I could. He would have on a pair of paint-spattered overalls he seemed to have forgotten he was wearing. Alternatively, he had deliberately put them on intending to dine out tonight at Rock Pool or Tetsuya.

Ash thought of these disparate interests as leading somewhere crucial. "I'm honing my craft," he'd say, when I periodically accused him of being a jack-of-all-trades, master of none. This perfected craft was a Platonic ideal, hovering in some realm to which the 'real' was but a faint counterpart.

"What, the craft of being a pretentious wanker?"

"You'll see," he said. "I don't muck about."

Ash had graduated from courses at small colleges and institutions most people had never remotely heard of, and had certificates in subjects that were as obscure. He didn't ever bother to frame them, but left them untidily rolled up and squashed flat between a book on

Vedic astrology and one on computational biology, or kicking about in one corner of the room amongst his ritual debris and trance drawings, spattered with hardened red candle wax from some Enochian working.

I unrolled one of them to read once: "Be it known that Adrian Ash has successfully completed the Certificate in Combinatorial Mathematics (special focus on hypergraphs & partially ordered sets). Antelme College, 1983." I hastily rolled it up again and dropped it back where I had found it.

In his later, magical phase, he often liked to dilate upon the particular hermeneutics belonging to Qabalah, the progressive filling of Jewish mystical texts with secrets and hidden levels of meaning, arcane dimensions which needed to be decodified. Given to extravagant speculation on such matters, he had written to Moshe Idel, the Max Cooper Professor of Jewish Thought at the Hebrew University Jerusalem about his insights, but never received a reply. But there was always something indiscriminate about his erudition. He was equally capable of quoting from memory the Chaldean Oracles or the Divine Pymander; and of indulging in flights of metaphysical speculation that would take one's breath away for scientific accuracy and rigorous logic; and then, incongruously, of launching into an involved and incoherent conspiracy theory involving everything from Atlantis to UFOs that tempted you to dismiss him as an idiot-fringe fool. The combination of outlooks was somehow unnerving.

## 2. The Enigma Coast

I had known Ash since we were both children. At my place after school, "Which sweet do you prefer?" my mother would ask, handing around the dish of cakes to me, then to Adrian. "Every decision you make, every alternative you choose tells you a little about how you see the world." It was a mantra she repeated often.

Adrian would snap up the chocolate brownies. I could never make up my mind, hesitating between the Greek sweet and the coconut slice. "Adrian sees the world more clearly than you, David," she said. She seemed to like his decisiveness about the cakes.

But when we ran out to play, it was on the endless sandy dunes of the Enigma Coast, a place we thought we had invented out of sunshine and air. Running flags up on poles and staking out ground, doing Robinson Crusoe, playing at being lords of our own domain, I knew that Adrian was at heart as dreamy as I tended to be. And why not? The world was magic then.

The Enigma Coast was our imaginary country, our own private

mythology. It was a place of long beaches with white sands, cool clear blue water lapping in and decorating the land with a lace of white foam before the tide sucked it back. From the promontory that jutted out into the sea, you could look back to the mainland and see flocks of colourful birds rising and swooping away among the thickly clustered stands of trees. The sky was a brilliant blue embroidered with swathes of fluffy white clouds that drifted slowly towards a distant horizon. A glittering necklace of islands led out from it into the ocean. It was a place where dreams come true, a place where you could be happy.

Back from the Enigma Coast, we would go into my bedroom and I would play records, old scratchy 45's on a little portable turntable my parents had bought me for my birthday. I loved that song from the *Wizard of Oz*, you know the one Judy Garland sings. "Somewhere Over The Rainbow…" It always seemed so sad to me, yet so appealing. Adrian liked it too, which is how I knew we were friends.

The only time I remember my childhood happiness being marred was when my pet rabbit died. I loved that rabbit. I would let it inside to hop around the floor, and my mother would clip its claws when they got too long. One night, after a freezing winter cold snap, I came outside to find it lying in its cage, completely still. The one eye that I could see—it lay on its side—was dull and glassy. I pushed it, and its fur was cold, and it didn't move. Something rose in my throat, and I ran inside, filled with a strange new knowledge, a knowledge of death. My mother dug a hole in the backyard and buried it.

After school, Ash had filled in a few years at university, while I held five or six different jobs during the course of which I attempted to make a reputation as a novelist. In the wake of the suicide of Ian Curtis in 1980, Ash seized upon his legacy, and became one of the host of gangling, anguished young dudes in dark grey macs, Doctor Marten shoes, suits bought in St Vincent de Paul, and very small lapel badges pledging allegiance to Pere Ubu, Echo & the Bunnymen, and Patrick McGoohan. That phase didn't last long, though. With Ash, nothing did.

He started to investigate magick in his university years, but at the time I put it down to another flirtation, a fad on his part. Rumour had it that he had once attempted the Abramelin Operation but had freaked out.

You remember Ash in the early years standing in the doorway of your room, rangy, energetic, restless, ghost of a smile on his face, anxious to be off to the next thing.

"I'm working, Ash."

It's August, and you have been ill, but a rain of words is coming out of you, and you want to get them all, get their rhythm down, capture the dance of them.

<hr>

Sometimes you walk down to the park, even though it is closed for 'work'. The cockatoos wheeling in the tops of the high gumtrees give you a sense of colour and vitality, flashes of yellow and white. This is the high point of the valley. The horizon on the other side can be seen sweeping around in a great tree-studded curve. You sit on the bench near the small wooden bridge, working on a bit of writing, giving it tentative shape. You can hear birds chirping, and from further up the street, the sound of someone having a concrete driveway poured.

Often these days you wake at 3.15 in the morning, the room dark and silent, your head full of words that threaten to slip away unless you put them down. Stretching kinks from cramped limbs, you get out of bed, switch the light on and scribble down the words that are in your head. Next morning, some of the phrases don't make sense—"dance of enigma." You wonder what you were thinking or dreaming that made writing this seem so urgent. But sometimes a sentence takes shape and is still usable when you resume work on the book in the morning.

"Never mind that," he says disingenuously. "There's an exhibition at the Object Gallery I want to check out. Jesus, Gunn, you can't work all the time. Come on, take a break."

I let the urgency in his tone persuade me. Only slightly reluctantly, I hit SAVE and close my file. "Bugger you. Let's go then."

After his final exams, he claimed to have led a party through the temples of Angkor, posing as a palaeobotanist. They looked at the headless statues of the Buddhas where the locals had decapitated the sculptures and sold the heads to the tourists. The young girls from Sydney University archaeology and Asian art courses had been "incredible—fuckin' amazing—so bright—so young," Ash said. The traces of the devastation caused by the Khmer Rouge—people everywhere with no legs, the poverty in your face—were balanced out by the laughter of the children, the water shining on their brown skin as they leapt into the waters of the Eastern Barai. That claim at least was verifiable—once at the bookshop where I later worked, I spoke to a student who had been in the party at Angkor. She remembered Ash as a bit of a sleazebag; the least amusing of his habits was a tendency to lech.

He now thought of that period of his life as an immature phase. Back in Sydney, he took up with a regular girlfriend, Sarah, and for a year or two worked as an electrician until he did his back in one day on a building site, pulling long wires out of a roof he was standing on. "Fucked that," he said ruefully to me afterwards. But it didn't stop him larking about. Once at the Royal Easter Show, Ash had a go at that game where you smash a sledgehammer down on a steel plate which sends another piece of metal up to ring a bell at the top of a ten-foot pole. He succeeded in ringing the bell first go. He looked around at me with a big stupid grin on his face, like a prize-fighter whose opponent has gone down under a blow that should have glanced off. "Well, dip me in dogshit," he said.

Today he wears a faded blue zip-up jacket with a red and blue logo on the breast. His plastic-armed sunglasses perch atop his head and he presses his hands flat together when emphasising a point, his eyebrows raised so far the wrinkle on his brow seems to go all the way back to the short crop of his hair. In the Pharmakon Pharmacy, picking up headache remedies for my migraines, Ash claims "I'm more interested in reconstruction than deconstruction."

We have lunch in the suffocating confines of a restaurant whose idea of stylish décor is flocked red wallpaper. We have not talked since childhood of the Enigma Coast, but somehow the idea of mythical realms remains a passion for both of us. These days, we talk of Autotelia, Tiwanabu, Kadath, Cahokia, Egnaro, Amarna, Calabash, Sobratha. Ash has favourite examples in literature; his copies of THE TATTOOED MAP and HIPPOLYTE'S ISLAND by Barbara Hodgson are thumbed to the point of falling apart, the bindings slack and the pages creased from re-reading. We share a particular fondness for the influence of *Le Grand Meaulnes* on John Fowles, and for the poetic collage-surrealism of the works of Nick Bantock.

At another table a man says to a woman "but obviously the more money we pay off, the easier it would be for us in the future." The smell of chilli from the laksa he is eating seems to fill the whole room.

You are constantly trying to shape your world, to make it assume some form that will have a meaning for you. You are never quite sure what makes you think you can change the world you live in, even when daily your aspirations are smothered by the unspoken accommodations you make—we all make—with the world.

## 3. The Forties

In your forties, you find yourself wishing your life was like this:
You have the perfect partner, who gives you the support you need

and accepts exactly what you have to give. Your finances are in order. Your stories are being published regularly and meeting with a favourable critical response in the right places. You always feel well and full of energy; things fall into place and you easily accomplish all your goals. Life throws up new challenges continually, but they are challenges you enjoy meeting. You live in a good neighbourhood and want for nothing. Friends are loyal to you. At social events you are full of an easy charm, leaving people who think, "I'm so glad I met him."

Instead, it is like this:

It's July in Bardwell Park. You have almost given up literary aspirations and you fill in your days with long stints doing data entry in anonymous offices, sometimes interspersed with bookshop work. Expert in several subjects which have taken you years to master, you nevertheless think: "So what—I can't boil an egg." You suffer from chronic tension headaches that make your days a misery, and spikes of migraine that make the tension headaches pale into insignificance by comparison. Your credit card is maxed out. You've had the odd lover, but nothing that's lasted. You can't seem to publish a book review let alone the work of art that you felt was in you ten years previously.

You are waiting for the bus to the city from Earlwood. Distant sounds of the railway, of the trains rushing through Bardwell Valley, the sounds echoing up the gumtree-covered rises to the main road. Our Lady of Lourdes Church tops the crown of the hill, looking with its white walls, red-tiled roofs and white plaster statues of the virgin, as though it has been transplanted here from the Mediterranean. The slightly-crazed man who is often on your bus in the morning walks up and down, waves his arms, shouts in unintelligible Greek at passersby: men wearing padded anoraks in two clashing colours they have bought in Target or Kmart, a young girl walking a dog.

The wind bites your face, the cold nips at your fingertips, numbs your feet. You watch curiously the green over-shirted council man, who today, as he does every morning, comes up Homer St with a pile of posters over his arm. With a look of weary resignation, a kind of suburban Sisyphus, he razors off the posters for concerts that have been taped to the telegraph poles overnight, adding each one to the pile over his arm. You imagine him doing this the length of Canterbury Rd and suddenly you don't feel so badly off.

You clamber aboard the bus, into its warmth, lodging yourself in for the journey. Illawarra Rd is a broken-spined reptile, snaking listlessly through the Canterbury suburbs. The bus bounces and crashes its way around the back of Earlwood, Undercliffe and Marrickville, jarring over speed humps all the way. The driver regularly brakes hard, so that you continually lurch forward in the seat.

A luxury car repair place features a BMW with its front smashed in. The bus passes blocks of flats with washing hanging on the balconies. The stuff people put out on the footpath—broken chairs, crippled TV sets, rusting birdcages, a bedside table of dark wood with the top missing.

A jogger passes along the banks of the Cooks River, whose greenish water looks chilly, towards the burnt-out golf club near Steel Park. The bus pauses opposite the abandoned petrol station, the tin walls of which are plastered with concert posters for System of a Down and The Whitlams. Holes have been smashed in the glass beneath the girdered roof with its flaking paint.

The bus fills up with people: an old woman with a woolly hat and wheeled shopping trolley; a Tongan woman with a small child, who bangs repetitively on the seat until he is "shushed" by his mother. Most of the people look so careworn that they remind you of refugees seen on TV. Old men: one wears loafers, grey slacks, and a white windcheater; his face is pouchy, the skin white-mottled; his nails are unkempt. Another has topped his white hair with a plaid golf cap; his hands are sinewy, age-spotted, heavily wrinkled near the wrists. A young woman with small earrings gazes out the window, her hair pinned back. There is a hubbub of five or six different tongues being spoken.

The bus carries on past the coinop laundrette, shops selling hot bread and kebabs. Stained white letters bolted to red brick spell out the name on the front of the Hocking Water Heater Co. A procession of shops jolts past the bus window: the fruiterer, the Indonesian restaurant, the Centrelink office with its dowdy exterior. Near the railway station stands the Marrickville RSL Club: "Sydney's Las Vegas" proclaims a large neon sign, which seems to be lit at all hours. Young men in hooded windcheaters cross the road to the orthopaedic shoe shop, the Hellenic Bakery, the tax agent, the Vietnamese/Chinese restaurant. Cardboard boxes of potatoes, oranges, and capsicums crowd the pavement outside the Asian grocery, where green tinsel hangs forgotten from last Christmas or early for this one.

A half-muffled computer-music quotation of a classic theme tries to escape from a mobile phone buried deep in someone's purse, as you pass a drycleaners, a medical centre, cut-price fabric shops with signs in the window declaring, 'All stock MUST go!' Further along, past the Vietnamese butcher, young girls hover around the door of the Astra Lounge, rolls of puppy fat protruding over their overtight low-slung slacks. Failure is palpable in the air that hangs about in the doorways of the discount variety stores, and the brightly lit shop window where a display of popular wedding stationery seems to merge indistinguishably with the cigarette ends and chip wrappers on the pavement outside.

The bus takes you through more suburbs slumping like wounded animals onto their knees, roads lined with dingy factories that make leather and PVA fasteners. Blurry glimpses fill the window: a lumberyard strewn with different lengths of wood, cheap goods stacked behind the bleary panes of storefronts.

At Petersham, palms stand in the front yards of blocks of flats. Traffic surges forward on Crystal St as a thin rain falls on the pavement outside a run-down motor repair shop. 'Sewer Sider' reads a graffito painted in wobbly white letters on the abandoned post office at Enmore Rd. The window of the Cat Protection Society is full of old shoes.

At the back of Newtown, near the Cellblock Youth Health Service, one middle-aged woman helps another, one of those black-clad and hooded widows of indeterminate European origin, to climb the rise. The woman in black uses her left hand for support against the walls of rough sandstone while her friend supports her beneath the right arm.

An ice-cream van is parked outside the Women's Hospital with its roughly hewn stone statues of mothers and babes in arms. And so, on to Parramatta Rd past the University to the day-job.

At lunch in the atrium of the Food Court at the Broadway Youth Hostel, above a multitiered fountain of greenish copper, surrounded by the bright glossy foliage of long-leaved plants, a skylight gives onto the open sky. Directly beneath the skylight is a painted frieze of fluffy white clouds in a blue sky, which always puts you in mind of the Enigma Coast.

Most evenings you watch videos of movies so formulaic they sometimes end without you being able to remember what they were about. Or you try to sort out the eternal clutter of your life, like that song by the Church, struggling like a fool with your junk and your jewels, before giving up and falling into bed in a kind of enervated stupor.

You train judo once a week to relieve the boredom of working in the city. Carefully folding up your *gi* after the training, you walk outside to see daylight fading, like good intentions.

# 4. Svetlana

Such is the salient paradox of being human, that moment to moment, our lives move from the expected to the unexpected.

You first see her when she comes into the bookshop, wearing a skirt with a loose-fitting flowered blouse. She has just a touch of colour in her pale cheeks, and her blondish hair, with light streaks of orangy-red, is a little tousled.

She has been a researcher at the Tbilisi University Press, exploring the origins of the Indo-European languages. Do you have in stock any books which would illuminate whether they originate north of the Baltic Sea, or around the North Sea coasts?

"Over this way" you say, delighted to speak to someone not criminally brainless when it comes to books. 'Elegant,' you think. While you point ahead to the shelves where the range of language books—actually far too limited to answer her specialised query—are displayed, you gaze after her, seeing how the soft curve of her naked back and shoulders would take the corresponding curve of your caressing hand if she let you place it there. You find yourself thinking: if her head were cradled in my arms, what shape would our bodies make on the bed's white linen? What seacoasts, what inlets and mountain ranges would our bodies trace? What evanescent cartography would be needed to decipher such a liaison?

You immediately ask her out for coffee. Over flat white with two sugars (you) and short black without (her), you learn she was born in Kanesh, the modern Turkish city of Kultepe. She has lived most of her life in Russia, and she loves the languages cognate with Hittite—Luwian, Palaic. She talks passionately of proto-languages and needs little encouragement to speak of her favourite speciality, Mitannian Indo-Iranian. In your mug, a swirl of milk resembles a chain of islands in a dark brown sea.

"There is every reason," she tells you, in slightly too-formal English, "for thinking that the original home of the Indo-Europeans is the place where wheeled vehicles were invented and where barley and grapes were first cultivated." This place she refers to as 'Hither Asia' by which she means Asia Minor—Northern Mesopotamia.

"Do tell," you say. Then you say something else about this, something that makes her laugh, and a moment later she sets her head slightly on one side, looking at you with assessment, appreciation. In that moment, there, over bad coffee, you are captured.

You want her badly. Leaning forward, you take her hand. "Learn lost languages with me."

To your surprise, she doesn't draw her hand away, but returns the gentle pressure. "Da."

Not long after that, you move in together. She has a post teaching at Sydney University and briefly, things in your life seem to flower. These are the times you treasure later, days when everything seems endless, every moment full of promise.

In Bardwell Valley the winter evenings are still and quiet. The stars are unblinking and hard against a clear sky the colour of dark blue silk. Gumtrees raise dark boughs to an occasional red flashing light traversing the vast expanse over the valley: incoming small aircraft headed for Mascot. When everything is so lucid, you don't stop to consider the incalculable consequences of small actions.

Sometimes when you make love, she sings softly some meters from an old Hittite song:

> Tkani nesy, Tkani nesy
> Prinesi, pridi
> (The dress of Nesa,
> the dress of Nesa,
> Put it on me, put it on me)

You love it when she sings to you. She is half-sitting, half-lying, leaning on one elbow. Streetlights run long fingers in through the window and stroke the wall above the bed. She raises one knee slightly and her thighs part to allow you entrance. You clasp her waist, drawing her to you, and as you fit together, the light in the room is suffused with a soft glow as though the universe is pleased with you, with the precise curve of your limbs, with the sounds you make, with the tang and musk of love that hovers in the air, with the scent of sweaty sheets and the way you touch her, your right foot caressing the instep of her left, your eyes drinking up the look in hers.

What unique terrains you make, like a union of two countries that have decided they belong together. Your fingers trace the country from the curve of her shoulder down to the hollow of her elbow, along the delicate inside of her wrist with its faint blue tracery of veins, and into the lined ways of her palm, a secret country all unto itself. You hold her and whisper in her ear, which reminds you of a shell found on the sands of the Enigma Coast, "I want to take you there…"

Out at dinner, eating Korean, I would have the Sam Gyep Sal. She would have whatever I chose, and we would share a bottle of white wine.

A man at the next table says, "No doubt some people think that's funny."

In the cool of the evening we walk along the harbour shore, serene and silent, drinking in the distance, bathing quietly in the rightness of it all. A red triangle of light on the bridge arches over moored boats that cluster in-shore. Moonlight glimmers on the water near a pylon; patches of gentle rippling light that seem special and bring us close.

She talks in glissando phrases of the importance of glottalized consonants to the identification of the original home of the Indo-Europeans, but once she starts discussing old Armenian and proto-Iranian she loses me. Instead, we joke about being full of wine and Mexican food, and at the heart of the time we spend, we are one with each other.

We make love often in those early days, the fragility of the bond between us seeming a large part of its beauty, rather than the warning it would seem in retrospect. You take her out, say to the party of a friend from work. At the yacht club the women all wear boat shoes, jeans and pearls. The men all wear polo tops and are braying about stock options. You look at each other and simultaneously burst out laughing.

Ten minutes later, in a taxi home, you are pulling at each other's clothes like anxious adolescents. Fumbling with the front door, you manage to get it open and you both stagger to the bed, throwing clothes to the four winds. Your mouths close on each other; she has the sweetest breath. Holding each other is exhilarating. "Da, da...like that..." At the urgent crest of things, "Oh, that's beautiful" she says, and "Push up, push up." Afterwards, as she lies on her stomach, you kissing her gently from the nape of her neck to that seductive little indentation that comes at the base of the spine, you feel as though you have fallen into each other, that everything else is outside of the ambit of the world shared by only the two of you.

At Earlwood there was a shop called 'Bizarro' which apparently made wedding dresses. Its two windows were lit up at night with normal, if elaborate, wedding gowns on display—floods of chiffon and organza or whatever. I had never seen the place open, had never seen anyone inside. I couldn't help imagining that it was run by Superman's evil twin. I couldn't imagine why else anyone would name it that. Svetlana loved to look at the dresses, which you could see framed in the shopwindow from the bus on the way home of an evening.

When I regard this piece of the past from the distant shores where I now stand, how brightly unreal, like the shop itself, it seems.

Yゆou don't see Ash so often in this period. I know vaguely that he has become a member of some shadowy sodality, for he has dropped dark hints about the group with whom he is working rituals. Lately he has not so much abdicated his earlier interests as put them to use in the service of magick.

When you do see him, he has acquired a haunted, but confused air, as if he is perpetually on the verge of discovering something but has forgotten what he is looking for.

As a child, he tells you in a rare moment when he slips into confessional mode, he had seen a rainbow, and tried to find the end of it. He had walked for what seemed like hours, only to discover that the end of the rainbow constantly eluded him; it was always just in the next street, or over the next hill. Then, as steam started to rise off the wet grass, the rainbow had disappeared. He had stumped home dispiritedly. He hadn't managed to find it this time, but he knew the treasure at the rainbow's end was there. Oh, it was there, he only had to get there quickly enough when the rainbow appeared again.

## 5. Ash the Esotericist

Memory's a profligate—flinging its coinage of moments to the winds, scattering them like a maniac scattering dust. Then it finds itself penurious, the real sequence of events leached away: Memory a tatty figure with holes in its trouser pockets.

Even so, what light can spark off those bits of loose change, those remaining images; what stories memory, despite its profligacy, can tell. Anyway, here's another part of the story, to the best of my recall:

You decide to introduce Svetlana to Ash. He rings to say he's broken up with Sarah.

We meet him outside the shopping complex bordering on Glebe Point Rd. The long ramp from the shopping centre is surrounded by faux-surrealist sculptures—huge gantries of rusting iron pierced by a couple of archways in which sit a colourful ceramic jug, some jolly figures with blue hair and a yellow hat. Someone's idea of urban sculpture, of bringing art to the impoverished urban masses.

Starlings perch in the ledges of the gantries, which overlook a basketball court and a small park with benches and a set of swings. At the bottom of the ramp, abandoned shopping trolleys cluster like small herds of iron sheep.

Ash looks used up. To hide your embarrassment, you suggest going for a meal.

"Want to get something to eat?"

"Fuckin' A," says Ash.

Svetlana screws up her face.

---

At Badde Manors, over foccacias, he tells us he's fed up. In the fight with Sarah, the telephone had been pulled out of the wall. He had a deep gash in his leg. "What really pissed me off was that she threw some of my stuff out in the street." He had picked up a broken vase. "Cut my hands to lace." He rubs his temple in a characteristic gesture. Today, he's been hanging about at the bus-station at Wynyard. Outside the Menzies Hotel, American tourists in their slacks and cloth caps were sitting on a raised stretch of concrete, waiting to board their tour buses: sights of Sydney, day in the Hunter Valley. He hates their complacency, their American-ness.

Over his coffee, he makes that other characteristic gesture of flapping the little sugar packet they give you nowadays to get all the sugar in one end before you tear it open. This whinging seems shallow for Ash, but I don't take his depression too seriously. After all, I'm not yet in retreat from a failed relationship. But his whinging is symptomatic of his descent. Svetlana can't stand him, and this is one of the wedges that start to creep in between us.

People like Ash are like souls out of time. They move from the centre of their life to the edges in great loping strides and back again, and never seem able to distinguish the shape their life is making.

---

A week or so later, he phones up to tell you he's going to perform an important invocation, and he wants you to be there. You hesitate. The bitter fact is that Ash now seems to have lost his taste, to have finally no criteria for distinguishing between the dross and the gold of his magical interests, ironic in one so interested in alchemy.

His makeshift bookshelves are built of old planks hastily piled up with, at the interstices, mud-coloured bricks salvaged from a roadside construction site. They accommodate his ever-burgeoning esoteric collection; erudite volumes by Crowley and Blavatsky shoved in indiscriminately beside the most sensational potboiling paperbacks by the likes of Cheiro and Zolar.

His gluttony for secret knowledge, apart from blurring his once vigorously asserted demarcation between science and magick, seems incapable of distinguishing shallow navel-gazing and traditions genuinely steeped in ancient wisdom. To Ash, it is all the same—the purple crystal that he bought at the New Age store is as likely a component of his rituals as the jumble of incenses and talismans that he works with willy-nilly.

The theory of correspondences drops into his conversations with ease, and his profound understanding of Hermes Trismegistus and Gnostic literature had enabled him to dispute with university professors who had made lifelong studies of the Nag Hammadi texts as to their findings. But his practical work is an orgy of syncretism—not necessarily a bad thing in itself, except you know he had not the faintest understanding of some things he worked with. He thinks the more he includes in the smorgasbord, the more magically effective it would be. I feel sure his commingling of inappropriate elements would make more discerning ritualists wince. There is a pervading sense of a shabby façade about everything he does nowadays.

"Come on Gunn, I need you for this."

Reluctantly, you agree to go over there.

---

From Wemyss St, looking towards Newington College, the black finger of the chapel steeple thrusts skywards, puncturing the hazy dome of grey-purple cloud raggedly rent by cerulean.

On the wall outside Ash's door, with its inconspicuous buzzer, is a graffito superbly unselfconscious in its illiteracy: "Brenda and Rebecca are ledgens." You let yourself in and climb up the dim stairs. Through the half-unlatched door of the downstairs flat, leaks the sound of someone playing the wrenching industrial pop of Marilyn Manson.

Adrian's lachrymose face reminds you of a piece of damp cloth, so worn through by use that the original pattern has become obscure and rubbed so thin that you feel a touch might cause it to fall to pieces. He resembles a patchy collage through which one can still glimpse his ability and youthful promise, simultaneously threaded and overlaid with the emblems of his own self-defeat.

He lights a cigarette with trembling fingers.

"Did you ever read Plotinus? *The Enneads*, you know. Great truth in those. Sticks out like dog's balls."

Painful, unfinished business lies between us. The ash at the end of his forgotten cigarette grows tremulously longer. You wonder when it will spill and softly scatter onto the floor, though it would hardly be noticed if it did. Trodden underfoot are smears of grey ash from countless previous cigarettes Adrian has smoked.

He casts vaguely about for an ashtray, lifting crack-spined books resembling pinned butterflies, like an ibis overturning old sandwich wrappings in Hyde Park in the hope of a bit of food. Not finding one, he abandons the search and stubs the remains of the cigarette out on the windowsill, which is already raddled with scorchmarks. He drops the butt on the floor, regarding it for a moment as if wondering how it had gotten into his hand in the first place.

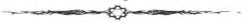

The whole room is littered with rubbish—in one corner, a dingy mattress is swathed with clothes, tangled up with the grubby varicoloured sheets. Trails of candle-wax cross the floor and the bed itself, and a thin covering of dust seems overlaid on everything, as does the overpowering smell of cheap frankincense and stale day-old cooking. This stuff lies like a sea around the dark island of Ash, who looks marooned in its midst.

Chalk has been used to draw, with no little artistic skill, a double circle in which Hebrew words and Enochian characters revolve. Immediately to one side of the circle is a small shrine consisting of a stele, adorned with Chinese candles and lion-dance ornaments. Strewn amongst the detritus of books and clothes on the floor are sheets of white paper covered in fine whorls and intense blotches of black ink, the residua of experiments with trance and automatism.

A bookshelf in one corner brims with dog-eared copies of works on Qabalah and magic; a mirror reflects the room's chaotic contents. Several knives and a sword lean up against a wall and amongst the other litter you can pick out charcoals and a censer, with incense sticks and beeswax candles, worn or burnt down to stubs.

A stack of old Zip disks totters on the bookshelf. Picking up a few and shuffling disconsolately through them like cards in a poor hand, you note they are labelled in scrawly pencil 'Watchtower Rituals,' 'Zones of Power,' 'Tunnels of Set.'

You have spent all day feeling on the verge of migraine, shielding your eyes from the glare that flashed up from the hot streets, cringing in half-dread, half-expectation that the edges of your vision will begin to flicker into the blinding aura of shimmering white light edged with rainbow colours that typically prefigures the headaches themselves. Sometimes when the aura has set in with a vengeance, and your palms have begun to sweat as though with tropical heat, you think you can recognise in those flashes of colour the startled flutter of exotic birds on the Enigma Coast. The bright shimmer of the migraine haze reminds you of the sun glinting off the water there, blinding in its brilliance.

Already on the edge of resentment when you arrived, you try to rally him. "Come on, Ash, it's no use sitting at home all day. Let's fuck off out, eh?" But this effort doesn't last long; you fail to disguise your irritation with him.

"Do you really imagine this stuff is helping you?" you ask peevishly, dangling between your forefinger and thumb a Cheiro book with the same distaste as you would have handle a snotty handkerchief. "Where do you think all this is getting you, for Christ's sake?"

Your lips pantomime his predictable reply. "Honing my craft." Yeah, right.

You catch a glimpse of yourself in the mirror. You see the way the upper eyelids have started to droop, the slight hollows at the outer orbits of the eyes: too much staring at the ceiling in the middle of the night. (Things with Svetlana are becoming strained). Age is having its effects: the grey in the hair that keeps on spreading, the flesh of your face becoming pouchy, sagging with neglect. You look away from the reflection.

"I'm going to *do* this evocation, so just *help* me, OK," says Ash. The only help you offer him is to stay, instead of leaving immediately.

He is swaddled in an ancient Tau-shaped white robe, made of a heavy wool quite unsuitable for Sydney's summer heat. It is dirty around the hem, and pale blotches of red on the front bespeak wine stains from some previous ritual.

He begins to perform the Lesser Banishing Ritual in that habitually dolorous voice of his, vibrating the Divine Names with a nasal quality that always makes you imagine his angels would appear clutching spray packs of Sinex to stop him.

After a bit—more gestures and theurgical carrying on from Ash—the room gradually becomes suffused with a mucoid greyness that struggles feebly to either block out the light completely or to transmute itself into something more solid. The space pulses with writhing energy, begins to boil with flakes of something like spindrift. Your head aches; you are unsure if the spatial dislocations that seem to be occurring are due to Ash's magic or what's in your own head.

Suddenly, you are startled by the faint cries of a terrified child; the more surprising because the noise seems to be in the same room, and you know no child is present. With a shock, you see that Ash's eyes have rolled back in his head. This frightens you, but the next moment you realise it is less a psychic possession than a kind of failure of spiritual concentration on Ash's part. Angrily, you shake him by the shoulders, and his eyes rolls down again. The flickering in the room trails away to nothing.

Evening settles in outside the window. Apparently, the ritual has failed. I say apparently, for later it becomes clear that whatever Ash has called up has not merely faded away without result; but at the time, the whole thing seems pathetically inadequate.

In the photo of him you took that day, Ash crouches on the floor in the Goetic circle, attempting to light the incense with a nearly expired lighter that kept burning his fingers. On his face, he wears an unreadable expression, faintly uncertain as though he has lost his nerve. His hair, what's left of it, straggles dispiritedly down one side of his head.

---

Some people would have been discouraged by their lack of result and moved on, dismissed this path as a blind alley, but Ash was different. Although his murdered hopes, like his hairline, kept receding, he kept trolling through his magical diaries like someone picking at a scab, trying to pinpoint the nature of his malaise, the cause of the ineffectuality of his rituals. Eventually, fraught with the need to find that something more, he took to carrying his notebooks everywhere he went, and scribbling feverishly in them about every stray event that crossed his path as though it were pregnant with mystic significance.

After the ritual, Ash told me he'd lost his confidence. Not too long after that, Ash himself got lost—just disappeared for a protracted period.

## 6. Ash's Descent

Sometimes you watch someone live their life and they're in a slow-motion fall, as if they've jumped out a window but haven't yet hit the ground. You watch their body twist and turn in the wind of events, spiralling slowly; and you want to be able to help them back to safe ground, but the leap they've taken is irrevocable.

Ash had his Psychogeography of the city, a complex of paths that he trod on his daily wanderings, as you have yours, as we all do. It doesn't seem to you to be getting him anywhere. He has gone from being outlandish to being almost thuggish.

Someone bumps into Ash.

"Am I fuckin' invisible to you?" he demands, wheeling on her. She looks shocked but says nothing.

"Oblivious bitch!" he yells at her retreating form. People turn their heads to look at us.

You are tempted to remind him of Seneca's view of anger—that if we expect things to go wrong we'll be less upset when they do—but Ash is fully into his riled up state. "Bloody stupid bitch!" he complains; but he is already looking in a shop window, eye caught by a shiny object on display there.

All night you toss uneasily on the bed, turning on the spit of your own misgivings, fears, and regrets. You've crossed the border into sleep, but the checkpoint guards have given you a hard time and the country you've reached is inhabited by people that don't seem to speak your language.

One morning you turn on the TV and watch a flooded Europe, houses and buildings destroyed, wide plains of churning grey water engulfing whole villages and towns, trees fallen, cars swept away. In the old city of Prague, they are blowing up boats that have come loose from their moorings and have been carried downriver, sinking them so they would not cause further damage to already damaged-bridges. You think of Ash as a bit like one of these boats, adrift from his moorings, carried by the uncontrollable flood of his desires towards who knows what destruction downriver.

That November, you hear that Ash has suffered a nervous break-down and has been admitted to Royal Prince Alfred Hospital.

You speak to Svetlana about it. You know she doesn't get on with him, but he is your friend.

"I thought we could visit Ash in the hospital," you say.

There is a silence. She stares past you, her lips compressed. She doesn't have to say, "I don't give a stuff about that bastard"; you can read it on her face.

In the end you go on your own. You pass the HK Ward Gymnasium where a sole runner does circuits, lap after lap, his running shoes slapping on the wooden floor. The glare of the sodium lamps in the carpark on the approach to the Disorders Unit illuminates in a kind of orangey aura various patients sitting on the balcony: a large, crop-headed girl in a white t-shirt chats to a man with a sports top, a bluish badly-drawn tattoo on his left wrist.

Inside, near a big painted poster of sunflowers that has been taped to a pillar, a couple, perhaps his parents, support a shuffling Greek man with his eyes screwed up in pain. At the drinking urn to one side of the ward lounge, an elderly woman with a bandaged head is struggling to get a plastic cup out of the urn's holder. A dark-haired girl with circles under her eyes shuffles in socks around the ward.

You hear Ash singing from the corridor. Following the sound, you find two or three guys with guitar and harmonicas playing a plodding twelve-bar blues. Ash, leaning in the doorway like a big scarecrow, is ad-libbing over the top. You watch him for a while trying to scramble back up the side of various pits he's dug for himself, and then go in to spend some time.

He is more closed in than you have ever seen him. His body seems folded into itself, like a despairingly clenched fist, his whole stance tense with pathetic and inexpressible loss.

"Sarah used to ask me what colours she should wear, what I liked to see her in," he says, fumbling through his pockets for a fag. "I always said I couldn't advise her, that I didn't know about that sort of thing. I could have told her to wear green—it would have gone with her eyes."

The regret in his voice is the first genuine human feeling you've heard from him for years. He stares down at his shoes as though in their scuffed and peeling leather he might scry some meaning in this dismal turn of events.

"You know what she said to me once? 'I believe in apple pies and warm beds and laughter.'" He clears his throat nervously. "I wish I could believe in those things too."

This time, despite your good intentions, you give him no help. It seems pointless. You don't know what he had hoped the ritual could give him, but he had evidently been disappointed. You stand up.

There is an awkward silence, broken only by the sound of a distant siren on the main road. Adrian looks up at you. He waves vaguely at the kitchen.

"There's some—Chinese tea in there, I think. You could make us a cup." He employs the wheedling tone he usually reserves for coaxing in his pet cat.

It is, for him, a propitiatory gesture, and for a moment you almost change your mind. There is another awkward pause while you consider making one last-ditch effort to help him out. But his next sentence changes my mind.

"You look like a bloody beagle with those pouches under your eyes. Why don't you cheer up, you bastard?" An expression somewhere between mockery and pleading has come into his eyes.

It's the last straw. Though you dimly know that faintly insulting vitriol is increasingly his only way of making contact, that the mere fact he is talking to you means that he is trying to reach you, you choose to detach his suddenly clinging fingers from your wrist and let him drop into the abyss, alone.

"Fuck off, Adrian. You've got what you wanted. It's not too late for me."

You push him back against the wall and stumble towards the door. "And clean this fucking shit up, why don't you."

Then you are out on the street without remembering making your way through the ward lounge. A drizzly rain is falling. On the way home, it plasters your hair to your face. The gusty wind hitting you every few seconds feels as though someone is slapping you in the face with a sodden sock.

What you don't want to face is that Ash and you are like one another, self and shadow.

## 7. The Limits of the World

When you saw Svetlana for the last time, it was approaching the turning of the year. All summer the sky had flung its harsh light through the streets and houses of the neighbourhood. Kids in sweatshirts wearing Raiders caps backwards had shouted up and down the street on skateboards and bicycles. Weekend cars full of people heading for the beach or the pool had crowded the air with the noisy repetitive thump and hiss of radio rap. The nights had been humid and interminable, alive with a cacophony of chirruping locusts and the caterwauling of mating cats.

Now June has set in like a pestilence. Under a still grey sky, trees bow their branches before a desultory breeze that seems to have silenced summer's birdsong. The cars and the kids seem to have disappeared. The days still have a little warmth, but the mornings are chill with the threat of autumn and emptiness.

That morning you ask her if she wants to go to a film later.

"No, I'd rather not."

You are quiet for a while.

"See you after work then."

---

That evening you arrive home to find a small piece of notepaper on the table in the living room. You can smell soap-powder and the curious musty odour of cupboards long unopened.

You pick up the note with one hand while your other hand goes nerveless and your satchel drops to the carpet, its contents spilling out: a diary, a notebook, a dog-eared copy of *Street of Crocodiles*, some headache tablets in a plastic blister-pack.

Svetlana has written you a letter, which reads:

"Imagine this. Life without you. Life without any of this. In fact, life. Forgive me, but please don't try to find me."

All her things, what few of them there were, are gone. You crumple into the nearest chair, clutching the scrap of paper, as darkness seeps into the afternoon like a stain.

You know, of course, that lovers are apt to come and go. They appear at twilight like beacons out of the fog, and they depart at midnight with your heart tucked under their arm. You know that. But each woman you have loved has been the woman a man dreams of in the secret reaches of his heart.

You sit for a long time in the loungeroom, trying your best to imagine where she might have gone. You feel as though you have been smashed in the face with a brick. A sound comes from somewhere deep within you, a sound you hope you never have to hear yourself make again.

In your journal, you will later write: "My arms went out, but she wasn't there to come into them anymore. For me, it is an immeasurable loss."

Towards the end of a relationship, couples will sometimes engage in ego damage-limitation negotiations, going through the same routines even knowing that things are drawing to a close. There was none of that here. You had no idea anything was wrong.

You're a victim of Pompeii, caught unexpectedly in the pyroclastic blast, dead in the midst of life. You're a rag doll, with stuffing coming out of the seams. But you're supposed to still walk around, make conversation, smile, log in for your daily work routine.

You pace the limits of your world, shocked at the prospect of having to be on your own again. You spend months just feeling your way, like a blind man. You examine in the minutest detail what you did, what you could have done differently, what it might have been that you did wrong, where the life that she wanted was missing. Like a kid with a dead rabbit, poking it, prodding it, thinking it might come back to life if you push it around for long enough.

Slowly, so slowly, it dawns on you that none of this makes any difference. You were together, now the season has turned, the borders have been redrawn. Even if she's still physically in Australia, she is gone, withdrawn again into her own mysterious country. You never bothered to phone the university; after all, she left of her own accord, there's no sense trying to track her down.

Someone lets slip in conversation that a friend who took some of her classes has heard she's returned to Europe. Other friends say of Svetlana, "You will forget her." You stare at them. They don't know anything.

You put Schumann's 'Carnaval' on the CD-player in the study where the light has begun to fail, and moving through the gloomy hallway to the kitchen, begin absently to prepare a meal. From the window overlooking the backyard you can see damp clothes on the line hanging motionless, like sodden shrouds. Over dinner, you watch television.

Imagine this, if you can: in a cancer ward in a local hospital, a small girl with a terminal condition lies in pain without the drugs she needs while radiation therapists walk off the job to strike for higher pay.

Or this: Thugs have broken into the home of a 65-year-old woman. Intent on thieving, they first kill her dog, then to make her reveal the hiding place of her valuables, cut off her fingers one by one with a pair of heavy-duty garden shears. She loses four fingers before she gives them details of her bank accounts and they take her entire life savings. The police have no leads.

Examples could be multiplied. Your dislike for this world deepens into a kind of wounded savagery. You are shipwrecked, high and dry, and at the same time afraid of drowning in oceans of night. You are trying to mount a salvage operation on your own life, but it seems increasingly useless. Of your hopes, there seems little left but wind and fading light.

At *randori* with your regular judo partner, you go for a *tomoenage* but don't quite manage it. You get up off your back. Your opponent is dragging on the lapels of your *gi* as though throwing you is too much effort, as if intent on simply dragging you to the ground with dead weight, a sloppy technique you have always despised. In the dance of the *randori*, hands seeking purchase, feet scuffing on the white mats, you are momentarily alive.

You lever your opponent off-balance with a shove to the upper body combined with a well-placed backward leg sweep that takes his right leg from under him. His right arm goes out and he goes down, breaking fall with a flat slam that sends dull echoes through the half-full *judoka*. Then you are at his throat with a needlessly vicious hold-down you know you can keep on for the requisite count to make you the victor. Standing, you bow each to each, keeping the code. Your opponent rubs his throat. You have won; but to yourself, in the midst of a vast personal transition you don't even begin to understand, you reek of defeat.

## 8. Enigma Coast 2

Memory's a patchwork coat, scenes here, snatches there, a laugh, the sweet essence of a kiss, the way the light fell when you first saw her, the sound of yourself coming, the tautness in your gut that time you had to speak unpleasant truths. More patches than original coat after a while, memory.

You can still see Svetlana. Once, cutting up the carrots for the soup, she made some quick deft strokes with the kitchen knife. You watched her from behind and slightly to one side as she tucked back behind her ear a loose wisp of hair. In the light from the kitchen window she looked strong and capable, and vulnerable all at the same time. This is how you'll remember her, you think, twenty years from now: her incomparable face shelled in light in a kitchen on a blustery, grey day.

One day, without warning, no trumpet or fanfare, a postcard arrives. The postage stamp, which depicts a glittering necklace of islands in a blue sea, overprinted by a fuzzy and only partly readable date stamp, is marked "Enigma Coast." Turning it over, you read:

"Imagine this, if you can.—A."

Ash has made it. Despite his blundering, his breakdown, he has stumbled through. So it is possible after all!

Suddenly you notice that the letters of the word 'imagine,' jumbled and arranged differently, make the phrase 'I, Enigma.' You are on to something! *My God*, you think, *why didn't I ever notice this before?*

You head for Ash's flat. The doomed streets of Marrickville seem choked with heat and lassitude, the houses etiolated and vacant-looking. The sluggish air crawls wearily over the pavements like a stray dog, nosing amidst old chip packets and rattling crushed Macdonald's shake containers.

Approaching the dark bulk of the flats, taking the stairs from Old Canterbury Rd to his doorway, you begin to feel as he had when chasing that rainbow—that you might keep walking towards it and it will remain elusive, just out of your grasp. But suddenly you have arrived, and the doorhandle is firm under your hand and you go in.

The room is more madly chaotic than before, an *omnium gatherum* of artefacts in disarray. Even the makeshift bookcase has tumbled down, spilling its contents—Weiser paperbacks on Tarot, loose-leaved notebooks that Ash always began to fill with occult formulae and never finished, vials of essential oils—like a rubble-strewn fiord of utterly random secret wisdom.

A copy of Greil Marcus's *Dustbin of History* is lying open on the desk. A phrase has been highlighted in yellow fluorescent marker pen: 'Defeated, revolution turns to magic.' Looking around desperately, you notice for the first time how many things in Ash's room have 'Imagine' in the title—a copy of *Imagination Dead Imagine* by Samuel Beckett, a copy of John Lennon's *Imagine* album. A light goes on in your head, and you leave without touching anything, thinking that you might have found a key.

Over the next few weeks, you haunt libraries, search the net, for references to Enigma. Nothing relevant to your search reveals itself. You realise the clues are more—well, enigmatic. You read dozens of books that have Enigma in the title—books about the cracking of the wartime code, and so on. They don't help.

The Enigma Coast eludes you. At Bardwell Park station, the flags above the RSL Club flap morosely. In the hamburger bar, businessmen are ordering lunches. Mirrors in wooden frames adorn the walls and a large-bladed wooden fan the ceiling. You finger, shaking, the lines of streets in street directories; you find significance in the adjacency of certain alignments of painted lines in the roads around Sydney University, certain junctions and confluences. You wander stretches of railway tracks, searching for the way in which their trail could lead to the goal. You live your days according to strictly delineated parameters designed to help you find the secret.

Two years later, you are sitting in a café in Soho. You have fetched up here via a 'holiday' in Isfahan (long-service leave, they couldn't deny you), a long spell of inactivity in Barcelona (where you became afraid you were going to think yourself to death), and a longer spell of listless indifference in East London.

In the mornings when you get up, landlocked into a hostile self-abnegation, you avoid the mirror's pitiless gaze, its treacherous infinite regressions, and shrug on whatever clothes are lying crumpled across the foot of the bed. You check your email, which forwards whatever messages you receive via an anonymous remailer. Lately there have been few messages. You decide to go out.

A Flying V makes its way along the pavement—a woman in a yellow anorak and her two children, woman leading, the two little girls trailing behind at the extremities of each of her arms. You follow them, seeing some hidden meaning in their postures, in the invisible trails they leave behind them. Two blocks along, the woman turns and yells at you to go away, now pushing her children on protectively ahead of her.

Finding yourself in Foyle's bookshop, unsure of how you got here or how long you've been roaming the streets, you catch a glimpse of a travel guide being replaced in its shelf by a tourist couple. They wear bulging new Caribee backpacks, jungle green with yellow ties attached to the numerous large silver zip-tags.

Squeezing past the travellers, you snatch up the guide, whose cover blazes its title: *Lonely Planet Guide—Enigma Coast.* Shaking, you leaf through the pages. On p. 141, there is a photo of a man leading a party up a steep incline, his face partly shadowed by a broad brimmed hat. It looks like Ash! But then you can't be sure. In something resembling panic, you drop the guide on the floor and run out.

When you return minutes later, realising you need to buy the guide, it's nowhere to be found, and does not appear on the Lonely Planet catalogue or the Global CDROM database when you ask the bookseller to help.

---

A couple of weeks later, you are on an impulsive plane trip to Dresden, thinking, God knows why, that you could help in the restoration of the artworks damaged in the floods. Turning the page of the in-flight magazine, you are confronted with an article: 'Joys of the Enigma Coast' by Adrian Ash.

It's all there—the waving palm fronds, the white sands, all described with the turns of phrase favoured by Ash himself. This time you keep the magazine, stuffing it into your travel bag. You check the copy in the seatback next to yours, and the article does not appear there. Shit! Perplexed, you pull the copy out of your bag again, leafing through— the article is gone, as though it were never there.

---

In the hotel in Dresden, staring out the window, you nervously watch the city gather, watch it draw itself up like some great dumb beast stirring restlessly in a half-sleep, and you think of Ash, and of Svetlana. You catch a glimpse of yourself in the reflection on the window's inside—gaunt, dark circles under the eyes. You have tried to become absorbed in the restoration work, but involvement, like a solution to Enigma, eludes you.

Sitting on the edge of the bed, you stare at the wall. The air of defeat you carry has been with you so long it is almost a badge of honour. You know that the way to get on with life is to find new doors and step through them. Why then do you insist on picking over the bones of the relationship, pulling them out of the ashes to re-examine their charred surfaces? More restless nights follow, interspersed with increasingly erratic days of wandering the streets.

In elliptical conversations in bars, at bus shelters, you suspect people of discussing the Enigma Coast. A man with dark eyebrows and a brown-skinned complexion is leaning close to a young man in a blue and grey chenille pullover, and black track pants, with the haircut favoured by such young men—very short around the back and sides but sticking up like a cockatoo's comb on the top. The young man has removed his bug-like earphones to listen to what the old man is saying. You strain to catch it and random phrases drift across to you—did he just say, "the sunlight there is never cold..."? But when you focus on the conversation, the topic has already changed to something else.

Time passes. You are faintly conscious that your years, that limited span, are slipping by too fast; yet each hour of each day inches forward with agonising slowness.

## 9. Over the Rainbow

One day, without realising how you got there, you are blundering about on a refuge island at a crux of streets near Trafalgar Square. Your face upturned towards the sky, you are stretching towards it, sure you can reach the fluffy white clouds that drift towards the distant horizon. You wander into the path of oncoming traffic, still gazing up. Sounds are coming out of your mouth. Shoals of traffic are banked around you, angry drivers honking their horns.

After a while, you are dimly aware that someone is leading you away by the shoulder. As they do so, they hear that you are singing, with a catch in your voice, over and over again, "Happy little bluebirds. If they can...Happy little bluebirds."

Or, if you preferred, it could end like this:
Svetlana is back in Kultepe, continuing her studies. She hasn't thought of you since the day she left you. One day, marking up notes on a lecture to be delivered, she receives a postcard. In the uncertain light

of her room, she can faintly make out the partly obliterated postmark:
"Enigma Coast"

---

Carefully turning the card over, she reads, as a tingle of fear passes up her spine, in handwriting she recognises as yours:
"I made it. Can you imagine what it's like to be here at last?"

---

Which ending do you prefer? This, as my mother would have said, will tell you a little more about how you see the world.

# AUTHOR'S AFTERWORD
# TO "UNCHARTED"

Kurt Vonnegut has written that "you cannot be a serious writer of good fiction unless you are depressed." Certainly "Uncharted," which felt as much like an exorcism as it did a stylistic breakthrough while I was writing it, arose from a besetting sense of futility, and from the particular sense of being at sea in uncharted regions, the sense of a passage through pitch-dark places that constituted my very own mid-life crisis. How, I wondered, could I mould something positive from raw materials so unproductive, so unpromising?

I had begun the story in 1999 as 'The Secret Books,' a tale featuring only Ash and the narrator; but I greatly expanded and rewrote it in 2022. Direct influences on this version included the failure of my marriage, the severe anorexic condition of a close friend. And various of my own (positive and negative) experiences with ritual magic (both as a 'solitary' practitioner and a sometime member of esoteric groups. That Ash's initials (A.A.) are identical with those of a well-known magical order founded by Aleister Crowley is only one of the reverberations with which the story became imbued as it grew.

The pervading literary influence is from M. John Harrison (though one of my early test readers found the tale—to my delight!—reminiscent of Iris Murdoch, Milan Kundera and Robertson Davies!) and in that sense 'Uncharted' is an homage to him. I have deliberately derived elements of my story from the way specific tales and themes of Harrison's have haunted me—the rumoured country becoming obsession ('Egnaro'), concern with map and ground ('The Gift'), cheap, ineffective urban magic ("The Incalling'), eccentric loser friends ('Anima'). I confess to a more generalised influence from all his work, especially the period from *The Ice Monkey* to *Travel Arrangements*; the phrase "occult power of apathy," which occurs in my story was once used by a perceptive critic of Harrison's work. Harrison's books—his eye for detail, his compassion for characters caught in various forms of failure—have changed my whole way of thinking about writing, and continue to be a benchmark for what I am trying to do in my own fiction.

The work of such authors as James Sallis (novels both gritty and poetic) and James Kelman (worker in urban Scots settings of the grimly humorous seam best mined by Samuel Beckett) also influence my story's tone. I can also hardly fail to mention Borges, with his texts that are not what they first appear to be, as a general inspiration. I am grateful to Terry Dowling for allowing me a small tip of the hat to his work, with a mention of his Twilight Beach, to which the Enigma Coast may be faintly akin.

Yet, influences aside, that tale and its style derives from the intensely personal. I am not Gunn, but like him, I have played judo, worked in bookshops and suffered chronic migraine headaches. (Playing with anagrams of the word 'Imagine' and realising that 'migraine' is an anagram of 'imaginer' was but one bit of fun I had with wordplay in the tale). I am not Ash, but like him, I have gazed into the abyss so long I sometimes wonder whether the abyss is staring into me. More obviously, I am not Svetlana, but like her, I have an abiding fascination with languages. I suppose all writers invest their various characters with aspects of themselves. At one level, Ash, Gunn and Svetlana represent to me the three terms of an equation, a Hegelian thesis-antithesis-synthesis of beings fated to revolve interminably around one another: neutron, electron, positron. But I like to think their entanglement is also very human.

I hope the tale raises some questions. Does Ash, for instance, actually exist? (I'm not saying that I think he doesn't, but I hope the story offers various readings, of which this is one). What is significant in that the last time we see him, he's suffered a mental breakdown? And what does this imply regarding Gunn's ultimate fate? The author is rarely the one best placed to answer such questions.

'Uncharted' is a tale I was impelled to write. It is an attempt to fuse the child's sense of infinite possibility with that of adults who must also struggle with the eerie banality of their own real lives; to examine the tensions between (on the one hand) the desire to escape into the ideal and (on the other) the imprisoning nature of the material world. Experimenting with the point of view, and using an unreliable narrator, were techniques I found useful to this end.

I leave it to the reader to decide whether the attempt succeeds; making such a decision, as the narrator of the tale implies, may well say more about the reader than about the tale itself.

'Uncharted' was nominated for a Ditmar Award for best Novella in 2004.

Oh, and by the way—I'm all better now.

– Sydney, March 2004

# THE SQUATS

The afternoon heat struck Templeton as soon as he emerged onto the main street from the small terrace house into which he had moved the week before. On the corner, a telephone booth was a box of light. Its occupant, a fat man whose clothes looked several sizes too small for him, was trying to fight off the glare, but his streaming face showed that he was losing.

Templeton crossed the road, passing the car repair shop, the old boarded-up Film Institute building, and more terraces that climbed the hill in staggering rows.

Next to the Italian restaurant was a small convenience store where he bought milk and coffee and cigarettes. Through a doorway behind the counter, men could be seen playing cards and laughing loudly. In one corner a young autistic boy was sitting hunched over a steaming cappuccino, 'stimming' with one hand and raising his mug with the other.

A child with eyes black as currants watched Templeton incuriously as he left with his purchases; perhaps something in his manner revealed him as a recent arrival to the area. He shrugged and crossed to the general store.

A couple of local bogans were talking over-loudly as they riffled through the daily newspapers on a rack near the door, the concept of speaking *sotto voce* completely foreign to them. One, a pudgy, pale-faced bloke with a blue-and-red cap, suddenly turned to his mate and said, "We might just have a party at my place and get blind!" His friend, wearing shades and cargo pants, yet girly-looking with a curly haircut shaved up at the sides, guffawed. "Aaw, that'd be heaps good, mate!" A smell of stale body odour came off him that made Templeton wrinkle his nostrils. Every few seconds the guy's head jerked in a tic to the right. At the nape of his neck on either side, two long bands of hair flowed down. The hairs at the bottom were the longest. It made Templeton want to get out a sharp razor and shave his neck clean.

Once Templeton had bought meat and vegetables as well, he turned for home.

He thought about his band. They were becoming quite popular around the inner city, frequently playing shows for free—or for whatever money they could squeeze out of the recalcitrant club owners. It was *his* band, of course—he was the one who'd always wanted to sing on stage, who'd always loved the feel of an electric guitar and the sound of feedback, when his school friends were chatting up girls or getting their first motorbikes. He'd formed Temple of Light to play his own songs, and that's what they'd done. The other guys were competent musicians but never seemed to have any real drive or inspiration—and that's the way Templeton liked it. It meant he could tell them what to play and how to play. He had had plenty of girlfriends since the band became an attraction at local pubs—but none of them ever gave him the same feeling as blasting out the first chord of the night on his Telecaster.

Above the rooftops a giant crane and wrecking-ball seemed to threaten a building with destruction, except that it was poised motionless; it would not strike until the workers returned to give it life at the beginning of next week. A flock of cockatoos was blown like raucous confetti across the sky. Spiky sunlight glinted off the windows of the buildings which stood near the international hotel. Templeton found it hard to comprehend how such luxury could exist alongside the grit and squalor of the area he was walking through; it was grotesque.

He passed the squats. A litter of paper rubbish flapped about his ankles; as he strode through it, the pounding of drumbeats reached his ears. Perhaps there was another band living in one of the shoddy terraces, which reminded him of pictures of shelled cities in wartime he had seen in his high school history textbooks. An unpleasant odour wafted across to him from the buildings—an odour like unwashed flesh, or lingering sickness. Greyish strands of mould or dust streaked the outsides of many of the terraces. Some looked scarcely inhabitable, their tiny front gardens strewn with rubble. The sound of the drums faded as he reached his own street and stepped into the shadow of what he now thought of as his own row of terraces.

Having put the food away in the kitchen, he stood in the bedroom at the top of the narrow stairs, planning how best to arrange his scant furniture now it was moved in. His yellow maple-necked Telecaster, the instrument still a source of pride to him, leaned against his little black practice amp. It had taken nearly a whole year of saving his pay to buy the guitar. He idly noticed the manhole cover in the ceiling above the bed.

The sound of footsteps from the street reached him. Surely he couldn't have a visitor already? He hadn't even told any of the band his new address yet. He went to the window, which overlooked the narrow lane where his new home struggled for space amongst the other terraces.

Opposite, the children's day-care centre was deserted; barbed wire topped the heavy mesh fence surrounding its yard, which contained seesaws and swings. Amidst an uncompleted mural of native wildlife, a platypus appeared freakishly albino—the colours were yet to fill in its outline. Beyond the leafy trees in the yard, he glimpsed the blackened chimneypots of the row of terraces in the next street. Here and there TV aerials on slaty roofs thrust thin limbs at the grimy air, like metallic plants in inhospitable soil.

He couldn't track the source of the footsteps until he glanced sharply down. Someone was standing, or stooping, outside the door of his neighbour's house. All Templeton could see was the top of a head, which looked plastered with sweat. He could tell the figure was tall, though, for when his neighbour, Mrs Donald, opened the door and began to speak to her visitor, she had to raise her face and tilt her head back against the back of her wheelchair.

Templeton withdrew slightly so as not to be thought spying, but not so quickly that he missed seeing the man pass a crumpled wad of money into Mrs Donald's shaky hands. Words drifted up to him. "Too overcrowded there, is it, love?" quavered Mrs Donald. The black-coated man grunted assent.

Templeton sat down to contemplate the surroundings. The suburb was not well off, but then neither was he; his job in the bookshop paid only meagre wages. At least here he'd get a chance to devote himself to his music—now that he had a proper place to himself, perhaps he could even use it sometimes as a rehearsal space for the band. Of course, he'd have to check whether sound travelled through the walls in this place. If he was able to hear his neighbours playing live music, as he had, it was a fair bet that they wouldn't take kindly to Temple of Light's bass and drums thumping at high volume.

His terrace was in one part of an L-shaped street. If one went to the street's end, it curved right, bringing one immediately to 'The Compound.' Well, that's what some graffiti artist had labelled the row of squats. The terraces there were due for demolition according to local government notices hammered crookedly up on the telegraph poles on that side of the street. Outside, the pavement was littered with rusty cans and empty bottles beneath gumtrees moving unsteadily in a fitful wind. Sun-faded curtains hung in a few windows, were half blanked-out by dingy blinds, or grinned jaggedly through sharp teeth of broken glass. Some were covered over with pieces of two-by-four or chipboard.

Passing the squats last week, in the furniture van on the way to moving in, Templeton had noticed the crumbling walls, the coloured slogans that daubed them, the webs of graffiti that seemed to cling to the whole row of houses: 'It's like a jungle sometimes.' 'Bela Lugosi's dead.' 'The Cramps.' Peeling posters proclaimed, 'No Freeway Through This Area.' He could imagine the tenants—the squatters—putting up violent opposition when the time came for them to be evicted. Not a place that he'd care to inhabit— yet he supposed that he, too, would fight to protect his living space if he had to.

He decided to go out again. Arranging the furniture could wait. He pondered his new residence as he descended the narrow staircase. The high-walled, concreted backyard was somewhat too akin to a prison exercise yard for his liking, but the house itself would be quite liveable once some painting and mending had been done. He could get his friends in the band to help him if they were to practice here. He crossed through the small living room and out onto the street, closing the door behind him.

As he passed Mrs Donald's, he noticed the scrawled sign *Rooms to Let* in her front window. He was sure that hadn't been there when he first viewed his place a couple of weeks ago. And what did she mean by 'rooms'? He couldn't imagine anyone letting more than one room in a house that size, for he knew it to be exactly like his in layout. He paused momentarily to gaze vaguely at the sign.

As he did so, Mrs Donald's face, framed by wispy, grey hair, appeared in the window next to the sign—she was taking it down. She offered him a thin smile, then vanished. Of course—the black-coated man who had come to her door was a lodger or fairly soon would be. It seemed that as well as Mrs Donald, whom he had met in passing, he would have a new neighbour. What was it the real estate agent had said about the old woman? "You won't have any trouble from the lady next door—she's quiet as a mouse. Lived in that house for years. Never married, though; her being disabled probably has a lot to do with it, poor thing."

As he turned the corner towards the squats, he glanced back. A gangling, black-clad figure was entering Mrs Donald's house. Templeton recognised the man who had rented the rooms in her home. He was tall, with stooped, hunched shoulders—and so thin that his spindly limbs looked barely able to support his body. Someone shuffled forward in the hallway to close the door after him; it must have been Mrs Donald.

As Templeton passed the squats, a couple in one of the down-at-heel terraces could be heard loudly quarrelling. "Shut ya face!"

Returning after dinner out at a cheap fast-food place, Templeton rearranged some of the furniture in his room. Rock music blasted from his sound system. He kept one ear tuned for useable riffs—although after half an hour the sameness of the music began to pall. Tony, his keyboard player, had gone down in his estimation for recommending this tepid album of rehashed ideas.

Darkness banked against the windows, thickening. Exhausted from the work of moving his bed, his bookshelf and his musical gear into places where they looked least ungainly, Templeton felt drowsy and ready for bed. As he switched off the light, darkness poured into the room, and into his mind. His eyes were already closing, and as well as darkness, there was dust.

Everything was thick with dust. It seemed to clog his pores and seep through his mind. He was stumbling through a confined space that seemed filled with floating debris. The air was close and hot, bearing in on him. He strained to make out the details of the space in which he was tentatively moving. Beneath his bare feet were boards, which felt rough despite their dusty coating.

Gradually, his eyes became accustomed to the gloom. Dark walls surrounded him. In one corner, he could make out a shape, which slumped half against one wall and extended a little way across the floor. Was it a human form? He was uncertain whether to move towards it or to move hurriedly away. Wherever he was, something was wrong here.

The shape did not move. Perhaps someone had been hurt—he should try to help. Warily, he advanced. Greyish tendrils swayed in the air, floating towards his face. When they touched him, clinging to his mouth and cheeks, he awoke screaming.

He found himself halfway out of bed, scrambling for the light switch. For frantic seconds, he feared it would not come on, but suddenly his bedroom was flooded with welcome light and he sank onto the bed among the rumpled sheets, panting with exertion.

Tony rang him at the bookshop next day. "John's left the band," he said.

Templeton was pissed off. "Ah, shit." John was the drummer, and while time-keepers were a dime a dozen, getting a new one in meant delay while songs were rehearsed. "I had a bad feeling about John. Did he want to talk about it?"

"Nah, he's done the bolt. Reckon's he's off to Melbourne."

"That's seriously fucked up. He knew we've got that gig at The Vanguard next week."

"Yeah," said Tony. "We're gonna have to cancel."

Templeton sighed. His supervisor was glaring at him, gesturing towards a stack of bestsellers that needed changing over in the front-of-store racks. "Can you let the guys know we need to meet? My new place, tomorrow after 5." He gave Tony his new address, hung up and got back to stacking bestsellers.

**B**ack home after work, he made himself potato chips and beans on toast, then went upstairs to play a new riff he had an idea for. Having the Telecaster in his hands always felt good. He noodled around for a while with the riff and scribbled some lyrics; something was shaping up. By tomorrow he would have a new song. "Fuck John, anyway."

He found himself looking up at the manhole cover. Picking up a torch from atop a couple of yet-to-be unpacked cartons, he climbed up on the bed and pushed the flat covering away. A black opening was half-revealed above his head. Steadying himself against the wall, he climbed onto the chair and thrust the torch into the opening. The light feebly illuminated the walls. Without thinking about why, he was clambering up into the ceiling. As his head and shoulders came into the dank space, a shudder of trepidation passed through him.

The torchlight fell on—of all things—a detached bicycle wheel. What it was doing in the roof, he could not faintly imagine. Roughly-hewn beams crossed the space. The boards which made up the ceiling were so poorly fitted together that cracks of light were visible. He swept the torch's beam around the space. The roof met overhead in a tight angle, at the centre of which the brick chimney rose. A few old bricks were scattered around and towards the back of the space lay two jagged pieces of corrugated iron. Nothing rustled or squirmed; yet he sensed that something had been here.

He pushed himself further up, right into the roof. There was room to stand, slightly hunched. Still he swept the torch around—the corners contained nothing unusual. But the chimney concealed the far corner from his view. Carefully, so as not to trip over a beam, he moved around the old brickwork.

As he rounded it, his heart lurched. In the far corner a lumpy shape sprawled motionless. Wads of greyish substance spilled from its split skin onto the dusty surface of the attic floor.

Of course, it was only an old mattress, falling apart at the seams. There was no bedding, just the mattress itself, steeped in dim light.

A feeling of panic seized him, although his mind told him it was illogical. He backed away towards the trapdoor, stirring a cloud of dust. There was no reason why a mattress should not be here; yet as he moved back, he saw something else. In the wall which connected with the attic of Mrs Donald's house, a ragged door-sized hole had been knocked through the bricks. The attics of the two terraces were connected.

He realised intuitively that the spindly man who had moved in next door had been sleeping in this space, above his head.

Faintly remembered noises now made sense. Templeton felt his flesh crawl. Did Mrs Donald know of the space extension? Probably not; Templeton remembered her arthritic hands, her old-fashioned wheelchair. To have had to climb her own narrow stairs to investigate the man's rented bedroom would be more than she could manage. The tenant must have done this himself.

Templeton scrambled back down through the manhole, switched off the torch and sat on the bed to think. *Fuck this.* He did not like the idea of the unknown man prowling around above his head. Why couldn't he stay put on his own side? He would have to tell Mrs Donald what was going on.

* * *

The next day was Saturday, and Templeton slept in.

Outside the terraces children squealed and shrieked, a high-pitched raucous noise that felt as though it was cutting through his brain like a knife through cheese. He gave up trying to sleep longer and got up.

He took a quick look through his bedroom window and onto the street below, in time to see the spindly, hunched man shuffling towards the curve at the end of the street where a weedgrown patch of ground prefaced the row of squat terraces. Did he have friends or family there? Templeton thought maybe he had even been living in the squats before he somehow came into some money and was able to pay Mrs Donald for a more stable place to live. He shook his head and went down to make breakfast.

He scribbled some more tentative song lyrics for Temple of Light's first album, as he fondly imagined it, until lunchtime. Then it was TV, until 3:00 o'clock, which would be the band meeting with Tony and Phillip, their bass-player. Tony rang at 3.15.

"Ah—mate—Phil's busted his wrist skateboarding. I don't reckon there's any point meeting today."

Templeton swore. Sometimes the world threw you shit just when you were making it. "Which wrist is it?"

"His left."

"Well, at least he can still play bass."

"Yeah. He's just not feeling up to a meeting today. I reckon we cancel the gig and regroup next week to talk about getting a new drummer." Tony's tone was apologetic.

"Yeah, well I've got some new material. I'll have it whacked into shape by then, so the three of us can try it out. You and Phil can bring your instruments over here a week today for a jam."

"Sounds good mate. See ya."

Templeton killed the call, put his mobile phone down, and said out loud, "This bloody music business is killing me." If Tony had had the decency to turn up to resign instead of just scarpering, Templeton would have hit him with some of his patented razorblade cynicism. But as it was, he just had to swallow the circumstances.

He decided to go next door and talk to Mrs Donald about her new tenant. The guy sure had a nerve opening up his living space like that, intruding where he wasn't wanted.

He knocked on Mrs Donald's front door once, twice. There was no answer. On the third try, the door swung open. Templeton entered gingerly.

"Hello? Mrs Donald?"

He put his head through into the loungeroom off the narrow hall. Greyish furniture, dull walls bespattered with what passed for blotched wallpaper but looked more like simply stains of age. *Poor Mrs Donald.* Being confined to a wheelchair, she was probably on the National Disability. No doubt she had no funds for decorating or making the place more presentable.

There was no answer to his calls. Maybe she was through in the kitchen making a cup of tea. Templeton was determined to have it out about the hunched man's intrusion into his space. Mrs Donald was probably pleased to have the extra cash a tenant brought, but the man's behaviour really was too much. Templeton would demand that the attic wall between the two terraces be bricked up again.

As he entered the kitchen, a sour smell snatched at his nostrils. Had

Mrs Donald come to some harm? But it was only a carton of milk that had gone sour and been left standing next to the sink.

Templeton considered a moment. Should he go upstairs, see where the spindly man had his bedroom? If he was in fact using his bedroom, given the mattress in the attic space over Templeton's own sleeping area. He felt angry on Mrs Donald's behalf. The newcomer was taking advantage, knowing that Mrs Donald could not mount the stairs to check on what he might be doing up there. He decided against going up. Not his style to go poking about where it didn't concern him.

Retracing his steps to the front door, he looked out along the street towards the squats. He stepped out and closed Mrs Donald's door behind him. At the street's far end, he saw a hunched shape, shrunken with distance. It was the spindly man, blackly bent over something he seemed to be pushing. Templeton suddenly realised it might be Mrs Donald in her wheelchair. The tenant was apparently taking her towards the squats, for what purpose Templeton couldn't imagine. He closed Mrs Donald's door behind him and set out to follow them.

He soon caught up. The spindly man had Mrs Donald in the chair. Templeton could see the old woman's grey, wispy hair. Her head was lolling slightly to one side and she was waving one of her arms; she seemed to be protesting feebly.

The black-coated tenant crossed the road, passing a couple of the squatters who had emerged from one of the crack-walled, peeling terraces and were kicking debris around on the footpath. They started to move off. Maybe they were going to meet their dealer, for Templeton heard one say, "When we get back we can listen to Tool, and spend the afternoon doing cones." His mate said "Yeah! Eat a apple afterwards, ya get trashed!" As they trailed away up the street, the first one's reply was just loud enough to be heard. "Ya might as well just smile through a bong and lick the resin!"

Templeton watched the tenant push Mrs Donald's wheelchair into the ground floor stairwell at the closer end of the row of squats. He was furious.

About to cross the road to confront the spindly man and demand of him what he thought he was doing, Templeton glanced up. He noticed for the first time that along the top row of windows in the squats, every single one appeared to be curtained with the same dirty white-coloured fabric. But just as he regarded it, the whiteness at the last window, at his far right, stirred. It seemed to move from his right to the left, leaving that window a square of blackness. *Odd.* The next second, the second window from the right went black. The overwhelming impression was that through the windows, he was seeing not curtains at all, but something very long and swollen, of a dirty white colour. Something *alive*.

His mind lurched. *That was scarcely possible. The thing would have to be huge.* He was questioning his own senses when the third window from the right went black. The thing, whatever it was, was sliding along the top floor of the squats, from right to left.

He shook his head, and marched across the road, into the gaping stairwell where Mrs Donald had been wheeled. As his eyes adjusted to the dimness, he saw her there, still feebly waving her arms from the wheelchair. Of the spindly man, there was no sign.

Templeton took a step towards the old woman, raising his hands reassuringly. "I'll take you back," he said.

As he did so, something appeared, partly obscured by the shadows, on the landing at the top of the first flight of steps leading up from the stairwell. Its size must be enormous, for he saw to his dismay that the thing was opening a mouth that stretched almost as wide as the stairwell itself. As it slithered further into view, its dirty white body writhed convulsively, and Templeton could see that the long body continued behind it, up the stairs and no doubt halfway along the upper storey of the squats. *Good God!* That black-coated man, who had come to Mrs Donald claiming the need to move due to overcrowding in the squats, had not been lying. Christ knows what foulness he had roused in some fever of obsession, or from where. But he must have been responsible for knocking through all the upper walls of the attic rooms here, just as he had knocked through the wall in the attic room between Templeton's terrace and Mrs Donald's.

The thing splayed its paws. He heard his own outrush of breath as the thing moved towards Mrs Donald, its worm-ridden head nodding. Templeton felt sick at the thought of the old woman being wrapped in the thing's embrace.

As Templeton's sanity tottered on the edge of oblivion, the thing craned its head to Mrs Donald, swallowing her upper body in entirety, and bit down.

Suddenly Templeton saw the spindly man. He was kneeling in the shadows, his hands toward the thing, palms outward in what seemed a gesture of obeisance.

The gigantic ugly head moved back and Mrs Donald's lower remains were visible in the wheelchair like a bloody stump of rotted tooth.

The thing paused. Then it turned from what was left of the old woman towards him, the lopsided grin in the whitish face more visible as it undulated from the shadows. He faltered, terror gripping him as the figure reached for him. Templeton sensed that it was longing to wear his flesh.

He backed away, but before he could thinking of turning to run, one of the thing's rotted paws had his arm in its grasp and drew him inexorably in, its open maw filling Templeton's world.

# LEAVING TOWN

Ever tried shoving your life into a cheap suitcase at the last moment? It's no fun, no fun at all.

God save us from marketing people. You are preoccupied with what's happening in your own world and the phone rings. It's someone with a Bombay accent. "Good morning, is Mr White in?"

You know damn well they want to sell you something—a new phone account or hot water system. "No, he's not in," you reply.

"Oh, can you make decisions about this phone number?" You grow irritated quickly. You've already lost the thread of what you were trying to do.

"Look, I've got a child in the bath at the moment. Can't talk, sorry. Goodbye." You place the mobile on the kitchen bench. "Bloody hell."

The bed is strewn with clothes you're trying to pack up. You can't think straight about what else needs to go in. All you know is, you have to get out. You stand awkwardly at the end of the bed. You blunder about for a while, shoving more random items into the suitcase. Then you sit down heavily on the bed. Everything seems to have gone out of you, like the wind out of a heavyweight boxer who's been punched in the gut.

Later, you wander the streets of your neighbourhood, passing the other houses. You can see their residents in the late afternoon light, moving about in front of computer monitors and TV screens, black shapes watching 'Big Brother' or whatever other crap is distracting them from their real lives. You walk along Rowland Ave, one of those long, winding, heavily populated streets that connect Coniston and Mangerton. A street full of houses with garages where men work illuminated from behind like cut-outs, in garages full of old bikes, cardboard boxes overflowing with old children's books and toys, lengths of wire and rubber matting and half-empty cans of paints that will 'come in useful one day'. Where retired couples who left Sydney twenty-five years before bring each other Cups-of-Soup. You are taking a last look, because you don't intend to be back.

You drive over to the TAFE and wait for her in the open-plan food court. Orange moulded-plastic chairs are stacked up next to plain, serviceable, wooded-topped tables. A cleaner, wearing blue jeans, a blue short-sleeved shirt and a blue peaked cap, and a five o'clock shadow, mops up around the tables. A roof-mounted television faces an area of low uncomfortable lounge chairs, upholstered in a uniform cheap orange vinyl. "NIB can cut your physio, chiro, and optical bills in half for just $9.95 a week!" "The next programme is recommended for Mature Audiences—Some Violence"—followed by an old episode of the police soap *Blue Heelers*.

At the left-hand wall, a noisy group of teenagers play table-tennis backgrounded by a series of noticeboards plastered with ads and flyers. There is a blue vending machine with a red and yellow Smiths Potato Crisps logo, and two of the inevitable red machines filled with cans and bottles of Coke, and the Coca-Cola logo imprinted vertically on the side. Students—Asian, Middle Eastern—munch on chips from brown paper bags, or on hamburgers. There are Lazumba coffee logos on the metal barriers that separate the food court proper from an elevated stage area with a *trompe l'oeil* painting of a window punched through a wall of brick. Beyond this a lone seagull hovers in a cloudy sky over a cerulean sea and some purple mountain, fringed at sea level with a line of green trees running close along the shore.

Hospitality students, looking semi-professional in their white button-up chef jackets with double rows of black buttons, cross and re-cross the space. Metal crossbeams on the roof give the whole area the feeling of an indoor gymnasium.

You see her coming. She has pulled on a blue suede coat with dangling collar ties and a hood that makes her look like a pixie. Her hair is fastened on one side with a glittery clasp that gives her a girlish look.

As soon as she reaches the table where you sit, you are both arguing. You are so used to this by now that you hardly get upset at all. You hand her the keys to the house.

"I've packed my gear. I'm going to Nowra."

She stares at you. "That's a stupid idea," she says.

"Come on, you know it doesn't work anymore. I'm not sticking around to be stomped on."

She looks as though you've clubbed a baby fur seal to death. You lean forward to touch lightly the inside of her wrist. Of course, you don't expect such a gesture to mean anything now. She draws away from your touch.

Things are pulling out of shape. You remember the day she first let the front of her blouse be unbuttoned, closing her eyes slightly in anticipation of your touch. Everything since then has gone wrong. No matter how often you kissed her, no matter how tenderly you held her to you, your right hand cradling her head and stroking her soft hair, the death of her own ambition was present. You couldn't stand that.

You stand up. You leave. You don't look back to see the expression that is on her face. She is on her own now. She's had you and now she doesn't. Too bad for her.

A day later, you are sitting in a motel in Nowra. The cheap brownish carpet is strewn with your clothes.

*Spend enough time in places like this and your spirit will twist itself inside out*, you think. Of course, you're a bit depressed. It's only natural. But later, you'll go out and explore some of the coves and little bays which carve the cliff tops open like hunks of sourdough bread, their rough banks dotted with donkey orchids and hybanthus. These bright blooms will cheer you up. You will push your way past the bushes obscuring the little rough paths, and you will come out into your new life.

Leaving town has been the best thing to do, even if you will always dream of the muted light wavering formlessly in the hollows of her clavicles.

# THE MORSELS

Tom Burton was walking back with Duke along the riverside. The dog trotted along beside him, its head enveloped in the clear plastic cone. Tom was enjoying being outdoors on this sunny day. The looping course from Manningtree back to Dedham was his regular route on afternoon walks with the family pet.

He strode briskly beside the Stour, the river that formed the natural border between Essex and Sussex. Plenty of noisy wildfowl were swimming about on its surface today. "Come on, Duke!" he called. "Nearly home!" The dog kept pace alongside. It was some time since they had passed Flatford Mill, which painter John Constable had made famous with his paintings of it. Tom didn't much care for Constable's artwork, but he and Joanne loved living here in Dedham Vale, one of the quietest and most scenic parts of England.

Duke's hip dysplasia had required an operation performed a week or so before, hence the device to prevent him worrying at his surgical wound, but today was the last day that the 'Beast', as he and Joanne fondly referred to their pet, had to wear the cone. Tom intended to take it off the animal as soon as they reached their cottage in Dedham. He knew Duke hated wearing it. At the vet's, Duke had blundered about the waiting room, shaking his head continually, vexed and perplexed by the impediment which enclosed his head, extending from his collar to just beyond the tip of his nose.

Turning off the path onto the main street, Tom saw cars were queuing up across the road—parents picking up their children from the school. He waved as he recognised a local couple he and Joanne knew quite well, but the Sterlings were too preoccupied with getting their young daughter and younger son into their car to return the gesture.

Tom and Duke traversed the village, with its butcher, café, delicatessen, tea rooms and grocer, and of course, *Spirit Visions*, Joanne's shop. As they entered their own street and finally turned up the path to the cottage, Tom was aware of the muffled quiet. Perhaps he should have bought Joanne a teacake for afternoon tea, but no matter. There was no sense dawdling in the village. He could always slip out again later and pick up something nice to eat, and to share with their daughter, Ngaire. He wanted to get back and let Duke enjoy the regained freedom of having the cone off.

Inside, he called to Joanne. "Home!"

She was bustling around, trying to make the best of the situation. Her father had recently passed away, and he knew it was getting her down, even though she and Michael had never gotten on. The funeral last week had been an added strain, what with having the dog in for the operation at the same time, and Joanne had attended her father's funeral in Colchester on her own.

She kissed Tom as he entered the family room with Duke trotting at his heels. "Hi. I've just got the kettle on. I'll make us tea." She returned to the kitchen.

He sat on the lounge and Duke settled on the rug, his special spot. Tom bent to the Beast and unfastened the collar cone, removing it. "You're all good, my canine friend. No more collar for you." Duke, instead of licking his hand enthusiastically, growled at him. "Well, you can just wait for your dinner, Beast, if you're going to be like that," Tom said.

Duke lumbered out of the room, probably to see what Ngaire was doing. She would probably be up in her room, doing her homework before dinnertime.

Joanne returned with their tea and they settled to drink it while discussing the latest affairs of the village. She heard a lot of the local gossip while at work at *Spirit Visions*. She made no reference to her recent loss, and Tom didn't broach the subject. He thought it best to let the wound alone, unless she felt like discussing it again later.

"Your turn to cook tonight," said Joanne. "I hope you've not forgotten."

He *had* forgotten. Of course, he realised—she had her choir rehearsal tonight, so he would be preparing the evening meal for them all, serving up his speciality, soupy lamb meatballs with fennel, couscous and spring greens for himself and Ngaire, and leaving enough that Joanne could reheat her portion when she returned home about 9.30.

"Give my regards to Ashley," he said. The choir master was a mutual friend.

"I will." She made sure she had her music bag organised, slipped her phone into the bag, and went out the front door, closing it behind her.

***

As he cooked in the kitchen, Duke came stumping in. He growled again, low and long.

"What's gotten into you?" said Tom. "Hey, I know, Beast. I haven't fed you properly. Here's a couple of tasty morsels. Have a couple of meatballs until I can put your proper dogfood down. And don't say you don't get spoiled around here."

Duke growled again, but as Tom threw two meatballs down on the kitchen floor, the dog snapped them up, slavering over the treat. Then he growled once more, lowering his squarish head.

"Yes, chum, I hear you," said Tom, "but you're going to have to wait for more until I serve us our own dinner." He was plating up the meatball dish for himself and Ngaire. He looked down as soon as the plates were full, but the dog had left the kitchen again.

He went to the foot of the stairs and called up. "Ngaire! Dinner's up."

His daughter called back. "Can you keep it on the hotplate for me, Daddy? Or no... just leave it there, I'll zap it in the microwave later. I've still got this ancient history homework to finish."

"Okay." She was a good girl to be working so hard. He ate his own dinner alone in the dining room, then watched some TV. He had some vague thoughts about re-hanging the front gate, whose hinge was broken. Joanne had mentioned it to him more than once, but it was something that could wait a few more days.

Tom was dozing on the lounge when he heard more growling, an unusually fierce, savage sound. It was coming from upstairs. And now there were screams. It was Ngaire's voice. *What the—?*

Tom jumped to his feet and strode to the foot of the stairs. "'Ngaire?" The screams continued, and now he heard a growling mixed with the sounds of terror coming from his twelve-year-old daughter. He bolted to the top of the stairs. The door to Ngaire's bedroom was wide open.

***

Shock stilled him for a moment. Ngaire, still wearing her school uniform, was on her back on the floor, writhing, flailing her arms. She was screaming. On top of her was Duke, growling and snapping. His teeth were bloody, and Tom could see that he had torn away part of Ngaire's scalp. Before he could move to help his daughter, Duke fastened his jaws on Ngaire's right arm. Ngaire screamed anew.

Tom yelled, throwing himself on the dog, thumping it with his fists.

"Get off her!" The animal seemed to have gone mad. His teeth were still lodged in Ngaire's arm and to Tom's horror, the dog wrenched his head back. With a tearing sound, the arm came entirely away from Ngaire's body, ripped from its socket.

Ngaire must have fainted, for she went quiet and still.

The arm dropped from the dog's jaws to the carpet. Duke was still slavering and ripping at her flesh. Tom was battering the animal for all he was worth, but the dog continued savagely mauling his child.

Tom frantically cast around for a weapon—any weapon—he could use to kill the brute.

There was nothing.

He grabbed the dog's head in both hands and smashed it against the iron frame of Ngaire's bed. The dog struggled; it was nearly as strong as he was. Spittle flew from its mouth, mixed with blood from Ngaire's wounds. Tom pounded its head against the iron bedframe again and again. Finally the dog's body went slack.

Tom sat back, panting. The Beast was dead.

He leaned over to Ngaire, who lay still, eyes closed. Her lacerated scalp was bleeding heavily, and she was losing a lot of blood from her ravaged arm socket. He had to ring the ambulance. Half-crazy, Tom stumbled downstairs to ring Emergency.

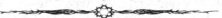

Two years had passed since Ngaire's death from her injuries. The dark shadow that had fallen over Tom and Joanne's marriage had taken a long time to heal, and even now there were things that remained unseen and unsaid between them. But they had decided to try for another child.

Tom reflected on how the villagers had all supported them after Ngaire's death. Really, they couldn't have asked for more understanding; but when it came to such a situation, there really were no words that sufficed.

He was in his studio, working. One of the ironies of their daughter's death was that Joanne had given up singing and that now he was finding new life in painting. In the last two years, he had sought refuge in this new creativity. Some of his landscape studies had recently been displayed at shows in the village, and one or two had even sold. He was experimenting with portraiture and other subjects now, and getting deeper into techniques he had not yet fully explored.

Joanne had expanded the stock of *Spirit Visions*, her shop in the village that now sold health and wellbeing books, crystals and Tarot cards. Tom thought the venture was more about her own healing than anyone else's, but he supported her in it, even though expanding the business had taken most of their savings. It was slowly starting to show a profit, but most of their income still derived from his dull council job in Colchester.

He applied oil-paint to his current large canvas, mixing the colours on his handheld palette. Various pictorial studies in different stages of completion were scattered around the small studio, which had only one window.

As Tom applied the paint, his thoughts turned to his relationship with Joanne. A couple of weeks ago he had found himself wondering if he and his wife were ever going to resume their sex life. Despite their tentative discussions of having another child, their lovemaking had been almost non-existent since the tragedy. Joanne was still in therapy with a local counsellor. He was seeing a clinical psychologist in Colchester, forcing himself to dig into whether he was responsible somehow for Ngaire's death. At night, he would cuddle up to Joanne, and they held each other comfortingly, but the likelihood of anything more seemed as remote as the small local cemetery where Joanne was now buried.

The small studio window darkened gradually as he painted furiously. He stepped back from the easel to regard the results in the large painting he was working on. He had lost all sense of time, almost forgetting where he was, so absorbed was he in the process of painting.

He had been seized with a compulsion to paint himself with the Rottweiler, Duke, by his side. It was providing some sort of catharsis, he thought. That's what the psychologist had said he needed, anyway. An expiation of his feelings of guilt about Ngaire.

The oversized canvas depicted him standing in the wilds of the Stour Valley, face on to the viewer. His own painted face was a mask of agony. Beside him was Duke, depicted as a red-raw beast, all its musculature showing, everything rough and exposed, especially its testicles, which he had painted like great golf-balls hanging in a purple sac, and its tumescent penis. He forced a grim smile. His psychologist would have a field day if she saw this piece.

He heard the front door open. Joanne was home from the shop. Holding his breath, he hastily turned the canvas around so that it could not be seen from the studio doorway should anyone look in. He switched off the light, slipped out of the studio door and locked it behind him before going through to the living room to greet her.

He supposed he ought to tell Joanne about what he was painting, but he was reluctant, in case she told him to stop. He didn't feel she would cope with confronting the image, either of the expression on his own painted face, or the terrifying figure of the dog.

"We put 800 pounds through the till today!" exclaimed Joanne as she came in.

"That's marvellous!" said Tom. "What was it, a coachload of tourists?"

"No, a single couple made all the difference," she said, putting down her things. "They bought up half the figurines in the shop! They wanted Goddess statuettes—something to with dressing a film set—so I sold them all but one of the Venus of Willendorf ones and several of the Greek and Roman ones—the Minerva and that large Diana. And then they wanted that gigantic Green Man that I'd despaired of selling— you know, the supplier sent it to us in error and wouldn't take it back. We're well rid of that one! And to top it all off they bought a bunch of Tarot packs and oracle decks for their friends back in London! We can celebrate tonight, my love. Let's have dinner out."

"Absolutely," said Tom. "Let's go to the Olive Tree and treat ourselves. We can take my car." He pulled on a jacket. It was getting autumnally cold outside and the signs of winter growing more evident. *Round about the time of year that we had lost Ngaire.* He pushed the thought from his mind.

They locked up and headed out. On the way out to the car, Tom thought he glimpsed movement amongst the trees in their front yard. His chest tightened, but it must have only been the wind stiffening.

The Olive Tree was cheerful and the food was fine. After their celebratory dinner and more than a few wines, they returned to their cottage ready for a good night's rest.

"I'm going straight to bed," said Joanne.

"I might just do a bit more work in the studio before I come up," he said. "Goodnight, love."

He let himself into the studio, which was steeped in shadow. Switching on the light he turned the big painting around, being careful not to upset the easel. His painting equipment was ranged across the old table—brushes of various sizes, satin medium and varnish, gum turpentine, acrylic gesso, tubes of oil paints and acrylic in a variety of colours.

Something about his current large canvas struck him immediately. In the foreground, the large figures of himself and Duke—the 'Beast'— menaced the viewer. But in the background, where he had painted in foliage around a tonal impression of the Flatford Mill, there was something else. He peered at the painting.

A figure like a tiny rag doll seemed to be standing there, propping itself with one arm against the mill wall.

His head suddenly felt clouded with images. He added some red to the flaring sky in the background sunset of the painting, but felt incapable of doing more than that tonight. After a few minutes he wiped and washed the brush before setting it down again. Darkness outside was splotching against the studio window, seeming to press insistently against the glass.

Turning on his heel, he switched off the overhead light and exited the studio, locking it as usual. As he climbed the stairs, his head was no better. It felt full of webs or gauze. It was probably the effect of the several glasses of wines he had drunk at dinner. *Time for bed.* Tomorrow he might feel more equal to the task of finishing the painting. A clear head would enable him to think about the last details of the composition.

He slipped into bed beside Joanne, who was already asleep, breathing steadily. *She deserved a good night's sleep*, he thought, *after all we have been through.*

He wondered suddenly whether their love life might resume soon. He felt strangely aroused but didn't want to disturb Joanne. His penis was rearing its head, stiffening more than the wind outside had. Perhaps he should masturbate in the bathroom. But that didn't feel right. He was sure their normal intimate relations would resume as time healed their losses and Joanne's shop picked up more business. Did he really want to cruel that by having a furtive solo sexual experience he wasn't going to share with her?

The idea seemed fanciful, and he let it go. He lay in a dreamlike state, willing sleep to come, and as the darkness engulfed his mind as well as the room, sleep overtook him.

The Beast gave every appearance of being friendly. It came to him and licked his hand, the perfect family pet. He had known all along that no animal could be so cruel, so savage. He must show Joanne, and Ngaire how placid Duke had become. He patted the dog and said, "Good boy, good boy." The dog panted and wagged its tail, very much the loyal animal it had been when Tom had first brought it home. Then Tom realised he was wearing a cone around his head, and he wanted badly to scratch his neck but was unable to. The itch was infuriating. He scratched against the cone, trying to rip it off his head, but it was slippery and so tightly affixed to his head that it wouldn't budge. "This can't be right," he thought, "but Ngaire will help me."

Just then, Ngaire entered the room. But when he asked her to help him get the cone off, she only showed him that one of her arms was torn off and that she couldn't aid him. The stump at the shoulder socket was bloody, and now he saw that a flap of skin on her scalp was hanging loosely down as well. As she raised her green eyes to stare at him, he awoke in a panic, drenched in sweat.

He sat up and hugged himself. *Jesus, what a dream*! Joanne must have risen early, because the bed beside him was empty. Rubbing his eyes, he got out of bed and padded downstairs in his pyjamas.

"So, you're up, sleepyhead!" said Joanne. "I'm off to the shop. You'll have to get your own breakfast." She pecked him goodbye on the cheek and went out the front door. He heard the car rev up and gravel crunching as she backed down the driveway, then the purr of the engine as she drove off into the village.

Silence fell over the house. It was what he wanted. He could get on with the painting. Still a little stunned from the nightmare, he sat in the kitchen and ate packet cereal with plenty of milk. *Normalcy, that's what I need.*

Joanne had obviously assumed he would take his own car into Colchester and go to his work as usual, but he rang in sick. He cleared away his breakfast bowl and dressed upstairs, then made for the studio.

Unlocking the door, he re-entered his private sanctum. He had forgotten to turn the painting around last night, so strange had he felt after seeing in it what seemed to be a figure he hadn't painted. It didn't matter, though; Joanne never wanted to come into the studio. She seemed to sense that he was best left alone when he was working, though she always praised his paintings when they were finished and he brought them out to show her.

Before him stood the large current painting on the easel. As his gaze fell on the image, a shock ran through his body. The picture of himself and the dog was bathed in sunlight, which penetrated the window like a blade. Tom himself felt penetrated, almost sexually so, as he took in the image. The expression on his own face in the painting was now twisted, not merely angry and wild, but with a tinge of the positively demonic. He had once seem a film called *The Picture of Dorian Gray*, and he was irresistibly reminded now of the painting of Gray, which aged horribly as he committed his sins in order to remain young. But Tom had committed no real sins that he was aware of.

He stumbled slightly as his eyes moved across to the figure of the dog. The 'Beast' was now even more bestial-looking, its muscles like thick ropes, its paws like massive clawed hoofs, its haunches like those of a gargoyle. Its expression was somehow simultaneously stealthy and predatory

Tom reeled. This was *not* how he had painted the figures. Had someone broken in here and tampered with his work? This was intolerable! A second thought followed hard on the heels of the first one. Had

Joanne been in here somehow and made these changes, to spite him for some obscure reason of her own? Tom's mind raced uncontrollably with the possibilities.

Then he noticed something else.

The small figure in the painting's background was larger than it had been. Now it was halfway between the Flatford Mill in the very rear of the scene, and the lush meadows of the foreground where he and the Beast stood. It had moved forward! It was possible now to see that it was the figure of a girl. Something about it seemed strangely amiss, for one arm was reaching out as though to touch the viewer, but the other arm was not visible. Tom desperately told himself the painter had depicted her with her other arm behind herself. But this was mad! *He* was the painter, and he hadn't painted any girl!

Blackness flooded in as he switched the light off. He backed out of the studio and banged the door shut without locking it. He simply sat at the table in the kitchen and put his head in his hands.

Could the delayed shock of Ngaire's death be producing hallucinations more than two years later? *Ridiculous!* he told himself irritably. A violent struggle was taking place inside him. Should he contact his psychologist? But it would be impossible to get an urgent appointment; she was always booked out for weeks ahead. Should he contact Joanne? He didn't want to worry her with his imaginings, especially not when she was in what her counsellor liked to call 'a good space.'

This was absurd. He needed to get outside into the fresh air, away from the house for a while. He stomped towards the front door, opened it, went out dressed as he was, and locked the front door behind him. He could drive into the village and visit Joanne at the shop. *No, had better not.* She would only ask a lot of questions to which he had no answers, and anyway, he would only risk upsetting her and spoiling *both* their days.

He decided to set out on the walk to Manningtree. Perhaps hearing birdsong would lift his spirits. Later, he could brave the studio again, maybe paint rapidly over those changes that had somehow crept into the image he had created from his subconscious. He was self-aware enough to realise that something neurotic was shadowing him. He knew his psychologist would see it all in terms of the Jungian self and the dark side of his nature. *Damn it!* He really didn't need to be seeing her; he could analyse himself if need be.

As he strode, he realised how tense he was and deliberately tried to relax, to force the image he had seen in the studio out of his mind. This really was peaceful country; it always eased his soul. Ironic, in a way, that Manningtree had been the centre of activities, back in 1644, of the notorious Witchfinder General, Matthew Hopkins.

Tom had once been to the library in Manningtree and looked up that story in order to be able to converse knowledgably about it with customers in Joanne's shop when he occasionally assisted her on weekends. They often got tourists coming through and asking about the local legends of Manningtree and Dedham Vale. Tom was only too pleased to be able to tell them about Hopkins' claims to have overheard local women discussing their meetings with the Devil, which led to their execution as witches based on his accusations. Tom had even convinced Joanne to stock for sale some DVD copies of the 1968 film *Witchfinder General* starring Vincent Price, and she had sold quite a few, even though in reality, the nearest locale used by the filmmakers for the Matthew Hopkins 'stamping grounds' was Lavenham, some distance away in Sussex.

These thoughts preoccupied Tom sufficiently that he felt better by the time he reached Manningtree itself. He passed the old Methodist Church on South Street, hurrying past since he was getting hungry. His father had raised him in the Methodist faith, and this church was the oldest Methodist church in the country; but Tom had no desire to practice the faith of his father, or of his ancestral fathers either.

At a café, he ordered a light lunch and took pleasure in lingering over it. Food tempered his experience back in the studio, and he ordered several coffees, letting the day dwindle into early and then late afternoon. He nodded idly at some locals, including some children who were playing noisily outside the café. For a while, he watched some of the small vessels on the Stour, lazily drifting, allowing his mind to be distracted from what he knew still lay in wait for him at home.

Leaving the café, he thought he had better face the return journey. It was only a three-mile walk back, but he wanted to be home before Joanne. The thought of re-entering the studio rose bitterly again in his mind. He supposed he must rectify whatever had gone wrong with the portrait.

The sun was sinking. Shadows trailed him as he strode the familiar eastern route home he always took. He was half-convinced he had been obsessively imagining or dreaming the changes he thought he had witnessed in the picture, perhaps due to his disturbed night's sleep. That nightmare last night had had a peculiar intensity.

He arrived back at their front door ahead of Joanne. He knew he was first, for her car was not yet parked in the drive. Banks of dark cloud swarmed across the setting sun's face as he hurried to open the door into the hallway. He would be relieved to get this over with. Mentally summoning up courage, he went straight to the unlocked door to the studio and opened it. He switched on the overhead light.

If shock had nearly overcome him that morning at the sight of the portrait of man and dog—and, God knew how, *girl*—he nearly floated out of his body with terror at the sight that now met his eyes.

On the easel the portrait still stood. There was the man—*himself*. The mouth was twisted horribly, the lips drawn back in a hideous grimace. There was Duke, otherwise known as Beast, like some gargantuan hellhound of legend, his eyes blazing red, drool slavering from the thick lips, maw wide open almost about to bite—except that between the powerful jaws dangled a severed arm and hand. *His daughter Ngaire's hand and arm.* And now, beside the dog, the hand of the remaining arm resting on the brute's massive head, was the full figure of Ngaire herself, dressed in her school uniform—identical to what she had been wearing the day she had been mauled to death. Her expression too, was vile—a malevolent light shone in her green glittering eyes.

Tom swayed back in horror, turning away from the easel and bumbled out of the studio. He fell rather than slumped onto the living room couch, clutching his head. Piercing shrieks of laughter from tourist children—or did they come from behind him?—seemed to stab through his mind. His head seemed to be dissolving the way he had hoped to dissolve the terrifying parts of the image that he had produced.

He sensed a presence near him. His body felt drained of energy, but he managed to look up. Believing what he saw in front of him was almost impossible.

He struggled to his feet, staring at Ngaire's form standing erect before him. "You're not real!" he sobbed.

But his cry didn't dispel the figure. Nor did it hide the fact that in Ngaire's good remaining hand she held a leash, with the red raw Rottweiler at the end of it.

Rationality had fled, and so should he. But he was rooted to the spot. Lockjaw silenced the scream he felt internally.

Ngaire bent to the Beast, whose flanks heaved and shivered with sinister vital energy, and undid the leash. Cords of reddish muscle stood out all over the animal's taut body. Its bared teeth were flecked with foam. Strings of saliva hung from the black lips and unspooled onto the floorboards.

Ngaire raised her good arm and pointed at him. "You will never have more children. You didn't protect me, Daddy."

He felt gutted. Perhaps he was about to be. He was as intensely aware of the scene before him as if it had come from his own painterly hand and mind.

Then the Rottweiler's paws were at his chest, knocking him down. The Beast lowered its head and sank its jaws into his groin, clenching its teeth, pulling, ripping, tearing.

Tom's scream came at last, like a long-postponed orgasm, as the Beast ripped his testicles from his body through his trousers. The man lay groaning. The last thing he saw before his mind shrank into unconsciousness was his daughter feeding his balls to the Rottweiler.

"Here you go, Duke," she said. "A couple of tasty morsels."

The Beast gobbled them down.

Joanne drove up outside the cottage, parked her car, and unlocked the front door. All was still and silent within.

"Tom? Are you in the studio?"

Rounding the lounge, she saw his body. He had bled out completely. Gasping, she kneeled to examine him. Her hand flew to her mouth as she found he was no longer the man she had married.

In fact, no longer a man at all.

# CEMETERY ROSE

*"Far safer through an Abbey gallop,*
*The stones achase,*
*Than, moonless, one's own self*
*Encounter in some lonesome place"*

– Emily Dickinson

It didn't begin as a terrifying experience. Ray Kilworth wasn't the sort to be easily frightened by things as insubstantial as moving shadows, or by wind shaking the dry leaves on the huge trees in the cemetery, or even by the proximity of hundreds of long-dead corpses.

He had photographed everything in his day. Buildings for architecture magazines. People for fashion magazines. Even flowers for gardening magazines. Once, everything had been luminous with its own inner glow. And he had been—still was!—a photographer who read poetry, who saw photography as a poetry of light. (How wonderful, he still thought, that the Lumiere Brothers, so prominent in the invention of the motion picture, had a name meaning 'light.')

But right now, he was at his studio, snapping a model for a fashion spread. Right now he hated this job; the game was no longer to his taste.

"Where do you want me?" she asked, with disarming frankness.

The 'Guess Where I'm Pierced?' t-shirt she had on had already told him she wasn't shy. But he wasn't in the mood for womanising. He'd done that in the past. Getting too involved with his models had led to his marrying one of them. Which had ended badly. Ray Kilworth, brown-eyed, reasonably muscular, attractive and sure of himself, had believed he could settle down. Of course, he hadn't done that, had he? He had persisted in sleeping with other models on the side, so inept at disguising his infidelities that his marriage had gone on the rocks in record time.

Lately he had been frustrated, trying to unravel the knot of his own misdeeds. The woman flaunting herself in front of him was getting on his nerves.

He took a final couple of shots. "OK, that's it. Out you go."

She looked disappointed. "You coming?"

He gave her a surly, "The shoot's over. You can clear off." He let the silence develop.

She snatched up the jacket she'd taken off earlier and flashed him a dark-eyed, angry look. "Well fuck you too, Mr Bigshot." She clumped off down the stairs.

He laughed. It was an ugly sound even to his own ears.

Nick, a small guy with a ponytail and a battered leather hat who hired the models, came into the studio. He was at pains to let Kilworth see he was amused by the exchange he had just overheard.

"You got rid of her in a hurry," he smirked. "Changing our ways, are we?" He scratched at his crotch.

Yeah, that's attractive, thought Kilworth—about as attractive as your grandmother doing a lap dance. He couldn't talk about his more artistic aspirations with Nick, who frequented karaoke bars and football games. He drummed his fingers impatiently on his camera case. "I've got a private project to get on with," he said, packing up his gear. "Out at Rookwood."

"Doing a spot of necrotourism then, are you?" said Nick, still smirking. Kilworth felt like wiping the smirk off the little bastard's face, but realised it wasn't worth the bother. He just wanted to get away.

"Necrotourism? Yeah, mate, you could call it that. See you later, eh?" He headed out, driving back home to Berala.

***

Later that evening, he put down his copy of Blake's *Songs of Innocence and Experience*, and gazed absently out over the back garden. The small plot of stony ground boasted some weeds and a spindly, leafless tree that grew up beyond the height of the shed roof. The shed he had converted to a darkroom.

Kilworth knew photography, if he knew anything: its sights, its sounds—its smells, even. Expert in pre-digital techniques, he was particularly proud of his albumen prints, his way with a chemical bath, the fine effects he could produce by using collodion negatives. Although the process was slow, he liked the warm image tones he could obtain by using printing-out paper. He even occasionally used calotypes, fond of the light-diffusing effect of the paper fibres. When he was really bored, he would make simple carbon prints. He did his burning in and so on all by hand; digital was okay, but too clinical for his taste. He was adept at bringing out the finer shades of his ideal image in the developing tank. It was old-fashioned, but something about the mystery of it felt right to him, the way the latent image would come up like a shimmering ghost.

For the last two years, eager to escape the confines of a soul-crushing suburbia, Kilworth had been working on a book he intended to call *Great Key Grips of the Twentieth Century*. It had started as a joke, although there was, he thought, an astounding ignorance on the public's part about the essential role played by the key grip in modern cinema. Most people didn't even know what a key grip did, or his relationship to the construction coordinator on a movie, let alone that he sometimes operated as a backup to the camera crew or helped out the chief lighting electrician (equally mysteriously known as the 'gaffer.')

Suddenly, the idea bored him. What had seemed a stroke of mild genius two years before now seemed self-involved, once again a joke and now an unfunny one. He planned, instead, to mount an exhibition or two; perhaps he would get a book out of that. Meantime, he needed some classy new material. He had a twisted, mad desire to do something really different. Something to make the photography world sit up and take notice.

Lately, he had become obsessed by the notion of photographing cemeteries. Someone had once shown him a book by New Orleans photographer Clarence John Laughlin. He had been struck forcibly by Laughlin's vision of the spooky old Southern house, his eye for the most surreal, ghostly, vine-draped trees. Another of his role models was David Robinson, who could conjure the warm sensuality from the cold marble women of European cemeteries. Sex and death—how opposite they were, and yet how close.

Now, a fresh idea popped into his head. Rookwood Necropolis: a ghoul's paradise, the world's largest nineteenth century cemetery, located within spitting distance of Sydney's Olympic Park precincts, and only a stone's throw from his own home. Something about the great sagging headstones and the creepy overhanging foliage fairly seemed to beckon him whenever he passed the place. The 'necropolis' (great word!—its meaning, 'city of the dead', shivered through his bones as he said it) was a sprawling, mile-square place as extensive as Sydney's CBD. Rookwood was vast, full of crumbling vaults and Victorian architecture, an Australian Highgate. Kilworth decided to immortalise in haunting black and white images, the silent world lying adjacent to the city's bustle. He even came up with a catchy title— *Crucifixation*. Now that was a winner. *That* would sell it.

---

The festival banners along George St flapped and fluttered in the chill air. The sky was the colour of dirty cottonwool, and the clouds blocked out the weak sun, reducing the streets to discouraging tracts of dull twilight. He was on his way to see his friend Alex Thornton, a specialist in the cultivation of rare flowers.

"Tell me about the Cemetery Rose," said Kilworth, leaning back in a chair opposite Thornton's desk. He had heard vaguely of a rare rose that grew in Rookwood Cemetery. He thought it might add interest to his shoot.

Alex smiled. "Sure. At Rookwood, the flower known as the Cemetery Rose is a damask-style rose so rare its species can't be positively identified. OK, it's not as rare as say a Blue Rose, or that fable of the rose-breeder, the true Black Rose. But it's rare—rare enough to be valuable. Rare enough to be worth photographing, Ray. Rare enough that if one could identify it, perhaps breed it commercially, there would be a lot of money to be made."

Kilworth liked the sound of that. "What's so special about Rook-wood?"

"Shit," said Alex, "the place is a virtual time warp! It contains some of the rarest specimens of heritage roses in Australia. Look, rose gardens in cemeteries generally are quite common, real Cemetery Roses less so. They are typically 'found' roses, in other words, roses not known to be widely disseminated. Look here." Alex had pulled a large rose encyclopedia from his crowded bookshelf. He pointed to photos as he flipped through, for Kilworth's benefit. "There are a couple of 'Cemetery Roses' in the U.S—the hybrid Tea rose (Bot: Chinensis), the Titus County one, which is dark red. There is a North Texas one, which as it fades, darkens to near black, but doesn't drop its petals. There's a light pink one, the Chester County. There's also a rose known as the Cemetery Keeper's Peach Tree Rose."

"Yeah? What's this about a Blue Rose?"

Alex chuckled, and shook his head. "A rose breeder's pipedream. Researchers have been trying for years to hybridise one, utilising transgenic technology. The details would bore you—how the genetic sequences encode flavonoid pathway enzymes, enabling manipulation of the flower's pigments. I've talked to companies in Australia and the Netherlands which have engaged in the technological race; all of 'em have patented technology to produce the Blue Rose but none of 'em have succeeded—yet."

"Fascinating," said Kilworth. "And you mentioned a Black Rose?"

Alex spread his hands flat, palms downward, a dismissive gesture. "Maybe one day we'll succeed in hybridising a Blue Rose. But the Black Rose is a straight-up myth. Oh, I've seen some that came close. There's Black Jade, a very dark glossy red variety with blackish highlights.

There are natural roses that start black in bud, but which open a shade of purple or deep crimson. But as for a real Black Rose—forget it, my friend. You might as well look for the Holy Grail."

It was late in the day when Kilworth walked briskly along Railway St, Lidcombe, past tawdry shops, the air of failure around their doorways almost palpable. Old-age pensioners moved across the pavement in that peculiar way that made you unsure whether to move left or right. He passed the monumental Mason's, its yard cluttered with granite and marble bric-a-brac.

As he neared Rookwood's East St entry gateway, the surrounding streets were crowded with traffic and crows cawed endlessly from the eucalypts. Once he stepped through the gateway, the hum of traffic and human commerce began to die down. *Welcome to the Necropolis. The Sleeping City. The City of the Dead.* Kilworth noticed the curious combination of sounds here, so unlike the normal ambient background of the city streets. There was the wind rustling through the trees, the subdued chirp of birdsong. The sound of road traffic had already died to a faint burr.

Many things were whispered about Rookwood. He had heard stories even when, as a child, he had attended school nearby. Kilworth had acquired a perverse fascination with the atmosphere of this place, the way brittle brown leaves would tumble between the graves in the dark.

He started walking through the extensive grounds towards the Museum. His backpack slowed him only a little. Kilworth kept his equipment light and simple. When in the field, he carried two Nikon FM12 cameras, each with a 55mm lens. In his backpack he stashed a 200mm telephoto and a 24mm wide-angle lens for use if needed. He liked to take all his photos with natural light and a handheld camera (no flash, no tripod). He had thrown in, as usual, four rolls of Kodak TMX400, and a couple of portable arc lights he sometimes used for night work. For this type of work he relied on good old-fashioned feel, the weight of the camera in his hands, the instinctive judgement of how to combine light, focus, depth of field.

Reaching the Museum's entrance on Memorial Ave, Kilworth glanced across at the Jewish section, with its well-kept lawns, and large well-kept headstones of black marble with elaborate inscriptions in Hebrew.

A group of family and friends, solemn and black-clad, surrounded a grave. Nearer one of the perimeter fences, another family had spread rugs on the grass, and were handing each other sandwiches. A thermos flask stood between them on one of the rugs. The place was obviously popular with some as a picnic spot. In the other direction, he glimpsed the cinnamon blur of a cat streaking across a pathway between graves.

Suddenly, a raggedy woman who seemed to appear out of nowhere, accosted him. "Roses!" she squawked, thrusting a handful of large blooms at him. 'Five dollars, five dollars!"

"No thanks!" said Kilworth firmly.

She looked disappointed, and wandered off.

He watched her try the family near the grave. She had no luck; they turned their backs on her.

Pressing on, he entered the historic 1925 Rookwood Crematorium, in search of the Museum of Funerary History. Unusual caskets and urns from around the world filled the place, but he was looking for something different—some information that would give him a focus for his photographs. He intended to look up a few local legends at the library first.

The sullen man at the office spoke little, directing Kilworth with nods and gestures to the area where he could find the information he sought.

In a volume titled *Legends of Rookwood*, he found various accounts of unusual happenings in Rookwood over the years since the eighteen-hundreds. William Davenport, a famous spiritualist, was buried here. Davenport was one of two brothers (Ira was the other) who had become a sensation due to their 'supernatural' powers—instruments played, bells rang, objects flew about. In Australia in 1910, the magician Houdini had visited Rookwood and made a point of restoring the Davenport grave. Another legend concerned the sketchy tale of a creature made of sticks, rags, leaves and earth that was reputed to haunt the grounds in the late nineteenth century.

Kilworth turned the pages, absorbed. Another nineteenth century legend told of a butler who had lived at The Gables, a Victorian-era house in East St opposite the cemetery. This butler, axed to death in 1865 by a guest at the house, was somehow linked to the rumours of a dark thin figure and his pet or companion, a spiderlike creature, who were said to roam the cemetery at will and who had frightened several gravediggers over the years with their nocturnal appearances. In the sixties, there had been incidents of vandalism associated with black magic ceremonies performed in the cemetery.

Kilworth began to feel cramped and uncomfortably hot in the Museum. He went outside and toiled along the nearest pathway. Clumps of grass grew wild and rank alongside the path, yet the plentiful roses seemed carefully tended. Apparently, a small team of gardeners and heritage enthusiasts were slowly restoring both the gravestones and the original plantings. Magnolias and camellias flourished amongst the lantana along the roads. In spring, Rookwood would explode with flowers, but there were hefty fines for picking any.

Dusk was coming on as he reached the florist shop, a small kiosk covered with flaking paint. A bored-looking guy, a reedy, Italianate fellow, hunched over the desk. The flowers in vases on the counter around him looked more tired and wilted than he did.

"Excuse me," Kilworth said.

"Can I help you?" The man kept his eyes fixed on the newspaper spread on the counter before him.

"Yes—ahh—I wanted to buy some flowers." It was the obvious pretext for querying the guy about the woman he had encountered earlier.

"Yeah," said the guy, his tone taciturn.

*Why are people so goddamned prickly?* thought Kilworth. As the fellow looked up, he found himself looking into a pair of eyes the colour of cold porridge. "I ran into a woman selling roses before," he blurted out.

The thin guy shook his head. "Don't have nothin' to do with her."

"I'm sorry?"

"That's Rose. 'Cemetery Rose,' we call her. Mad as a meataxe. Get your flowers here, nice and fresh. She's no good, sleeps in the bloody cemetery all the time." He rolled his eyes.

"So she's not quite the full quid, eh?" Kilworth tried to humour the man. He noticed that the guy kept the right side of his face constantly turned away.

"We got everything you want here. What you want today, sir?"

Kilworth looked around at the poor selection of flowers, trying to find a bunch that was fresh. "They look good to me," he said, pointing to a group of mixed colours.

"Sure. That'll be ten dollars." He held the flowers up to drain the water from the stems, gave them a good shake and started to wrap them in clear cellophane.

The booth at his back was dim, enveloped in gloom. Kilworth thought he caught a glimpse of movement back there. Something seemed to be squirming in the murk at the man's back. In Kilworth's mind arose an old darkness, somehow akin to this one. He fell back a step.

The guy cleared his throat noisily. "Any memorial ribbons with that?"

"Ah—no thanks, that's all."

The guy gave a perfunctory shrug. Again Kilworth sensed a slight movement in the dark, as though someone or something was lurking back there, just out of sight. It made him feel uneasy. He handed across a ten-dollar note, which the guy took and put in a change drawer.

"That Rose, forget her." Was there a tinge of threat in his voice, as well as warning?

Kilworth was already walking away. *Officious little shit*, he thought. As he continued down the drive towards the Anglican section, a light rain began to fall.

Seeking shelter, he was drawn to a skeletal-looking building surrounded by graves and palm-trees. It was the Anglican Ornamental Brick Resthouse. The rough red-and-white bricks of the walls, pierced by arched windows, were stained by graffiti: 'Stick loves Kathy,' 'Nazi Punks,' 'Danielle Woo here 8/7/87.' Typical teenager stuff, rebellious assertions of identity daubed in messy white letters.

He ducked inside the structure as the rain sheeted down. Dirt and dust half-covered the originally multicoloured tessellations of the floor tiles. In the roof above, he noticed as he glanced upward, was a wooden ceiling with a half-open trap in its very middle. He noticed more scribbled graffiti: 'Prince Vlad rules!' over a swastika. *Guess it was those Nazi punks again!* He shook his head, smiling slightly. The world was rich with mysteries but the graffiti spoke only of banality.

Kilworth noticed the dusk was thickening. He decided to camp out in the Resthouse, ignoring the dust and debris. Visitors weren't supposed to do this, but he didn't think he would be caught. *Maybe black magic really had been performed here in past years?* Not that he believed in such mumbo-jumbo. He had remembered to bring the arc lights and was equipped with a sleeping bag as well. It would be a great opportunity to photograph some of the tombs by moonlight; certainly more atmospheric.

The tarnished moon, a once-shiny coin that had passed through too many hands, hoisted itself above the trees. Light like pale ice spilled into the Resthouse and bathed the surrounds.

Shrugging off his heavy backpack, Kilworth made ready to get a couple of hours sleep. He stowed the camera gear between himself and the wall, pulled the sleeping bag around him and huddled down. The rain hissed down outside.

As the gloom drew in, he found night's ancient powers could still affect him. He was not abnormally liable to fantastic delusions, but here, in such a place, surrounded by the sleeping dead, the wind soughing through the trees, it was not difficult to find one's thoughts were easily disturbed by strange imaginings.

About an hour later, the moon had retreated behind a cloud, and the crumbling Resthouse was shrouded in darkness. Just as Kilworth was on the verge of falling asleep, he fancied he heard a muffled sound from above. It seemed to come from the trapdoor leading into the roof. He propped himself on one elbow, half-awake.

Moments later, a dark shape swarmed swiftly and silently down the shelter's inside wall opposite where he lay. Against the light from one of the arched windows, he glimpsed the bulk moving. Then he lost sight of it. A few seconds later there was a sound like a large leather bag dropping onto the ground. Gooseflesh prickled his skin.

*Screw this! I'm out of here.* Shadows danced and pulsed. Wriggling out of the sleeping bag, he grabbed his pack and set off among the tombstones in the drizzle. He wasn't sure what he had seen, but he wasn't hanging around to find out. In the uncertain light, he could not be sure that some shapeless thing was not following him through the trees.

---

He had calmed somewhat by the time he reached Necropolis Circuit. He took his camera out of his pack and took a couple of shots. It was a pity that the Mortuary Station No 1, which had once stood proud here, adorned by sculptured herald angels, was gone. From the museum library, he had learned it had been dismantled stone by stone and rebuilt in Canberra as a church. The original station would have made an especially picturesque image. He mourned its absence, thinking of the grand old days when the trains used to bring in the corpses from Sydney's Central Station, perhaps stopping off along the way to take on board another coffin, and finally reaching Rookwood, where the rail system was in constant use for offloading the corpses prior to burial. But even without it, more than enough of the original Rookwood remained to photograph for his book.

Suddenly, with a roar and a howl, something was upon him, knocking the breath out of his lungs, and his body to the sodden ground. It was a yowling, screaming mess of flailing arms and legs. The camera in his hand was flung to the full stretch of his arm, but as unexpected as the attack had been, he managed not to let the instrument smash.

*What the hell?* Catching his breath, he looked up to see what had set on him. It was the raggedy woman from outside the Museum. 'Cemetery Rose,' the kiosk florist had dubbed her. She had on a shapeless red skirt, and a red pullover two sizes too large for her scrawny body. Several long threads dangled from an unravelling spot over the breast. Over the pullover was a ratty-looking jacket, which may once have been suede, but was now rubbed into bald alopecia-like patches. Her shoulders were appallingly thin beneath the rags.

Mad eyes, she had. In her matted hair, full of tangles, and of leaves, was a red rose, full-blown; it lent her a strange kind of wild beauty. Kilworth and the old woman looked at each other. He caught a glimpse of her milky, rheumy eyes, but before he could call out, she gathered up her skirts and darted off between the graves.

"For God's sake!" said Kilworth. He stowed his camera safely in the backpack, then picked himself up and gave chase. He caught up with her quickly and grabbed her by the arm, swinging her around. "What was all that about, eh?"

Rose, by way of reply, proffered him a brilliant red rose from the bunch she clutched in one fist. "Don't go out there! Dangerous! Thing that crawls!"

He took the rose. She babbled similar phrases until, gradually, Kilworth was able to calm her down. She filled him with a mix of pity and revulsion. What had she once been? A businesswoman? An actress? A dancer? Beneath the blowsy surface, he could detect traces of beauty run to seed. Once she had been a rich wine, mellow and delicious. Now she was a corked vintage, cheap, nasty, past its prime. Her breath was rancid; she was human refuse, the cemetery's child. Looking at the flower in his hand, and up again at her, Blake's famous lines ran unbidden through his head:

> *O Rose, thou art sick!*
> *The invisible worm*
> *That flies in the night*
> *In the howling storm*
>
> *Has found out thy bed*
> *Of crimson joy.*
> *And his dark secret love*
> *Does thy life destroy.*

"Secret! Show you!" she cried. She pointed towards some trees nearby. Something in her manner convinced Kilworth she was worth taking seriously despite her dishevelled appearance. He grasped both her hands in his.

"Rose," he said, "you *must* show me."

The pressure of her hand on Kilworth's arm overcame his disgust at the stench of alcohol on her reeking breath. She gave him a crooked, autumnal smile and urged him forward through the nearby graves. "Black, it's black!"

"What?"

"You'll see," she leered. She let go his arm and stumbled ahead, and merely looked back now and again to make sure he was still following. He was trying to trust her, but the florist's warning still lingered. Kilworth wasn't too sure why he followed her at all, but something about her secretiveness piqued his interest.

She stopped outside a grove of trees and pointed. "In there," she said.

"Lead on, then," said Kilworth. He had, after all, come this far.

She pushed through the thick tangle of undergrowth, a smudge of darkness. He did his best to follow her, pushing overhanging branches aside. "What is it, Rose? Where are you taking me?"

"Black," she said. "You'll see!"

Kilworth stumbled after her. He could see she ached to share her secret. If this turned out to be nothing but a prank or a dead end…but some inner sense told him Rose had something important to impart.

The wind was rising, and the moon was bright as an arc light as they entered a clearing between the trees. Suddenly, Rose stopped.

Ahead of them, beyond a series of low-lying, unkempt graves, overrun and tangled with weeds, was a solid wall of brambly growth. Kilworth could see rose-stems weaving thick and green amidst the plant-life, everything dappled by the pale moonlight struggling through the surrounding foliage.

Rose pointed, hopping excitedly from one foot to another. "Look, look!" she cried. "Look there!"

Kilworth peered into the growth, still uncertain what so excited her. For a few moments he could see nothing unusual, just the same flowers and shrubs he had observed throughout the cemetery. There were many blooms here, growing in profusion. He suspected this was Rose's private harvesting area for the blooms she sold. Perhaps there was something special about the soil here—some unusually productive and fruitful combination of nutrients—for the growth did seem especially luxuriant.

Then, as his vision adjusted to the half-light, he began to discern a bloom which looked different from the rest. It was a rose, a rose that looked very dark. If it was red, it was the darkest red he had ever seen. He blinked. *My God!* It wasn't a dark red at all, but of a hue so deep it could only be described as black. He took a few faltering steps forward.

Rose could hardly contain her excitement, dancing and pointing. "Black, black!" she cried.

He stared at her, astonished, before returning his gaze to the bush where, he now saw, a whole cluster of black blooms adorned the shrub. He was stunned. It really existed! He was no rose expert, but he knew how rare, how impossibly rare, this sight was. With mounting excitement, he gazed on the beautiful blooms. They were black as midnight, black as dead suns in the infinitude of deep space.

Alex Thornton's words returned to him: "The black rose has long been thought an impossibility, but people are fascinated by the idea of its existence. Like the ghost orchid, like the white tiger, its perennial allure consists in its rarity." The rose, Thornton had explained, was already considered one of the most beautiful of blooms, in fact a metaphor for Beauty itself; a pure black version would be considered a paragon, a superlative, some kind of floral quintessence. Kilworth could see why—the bizarre beauty of the blooms before him awed him into silence.

An inexplicable chill came over him. He had found the Holy Grail. Immediately, though he knew he could get rich out of this, simultaneously he anticipated the problems which would flood in with the discovery. Other people would try and get control. They might even want to harm him to get hold of such a rare find as this. He had to keep it secret. Rose was obviously not in her right mind, didn't realise what she had here. Why had she chosen to reveal it to him? He didn't know, but he was grateful to her.

He clasped her arm. "Thank you, Rose, you've done the right thing."

She smiled crookedly. "Black, black!" She was still excited.

"Yes, black," he said. "Now, we mustn't tell anyone else about this, do you understand?" He slipped a fifty-dollar bill out of his wallet and crushed it into her grimy fist. "Here. Go and get some good food, get yourself something nice, OK?"

She looked at the money, slow wonder dawning in her eyes. Fifty dollars was more than she sometimes made the whole week selling flowers to the mourners. Her expression changed to one of low cunning and she hastily stuffed the money somewhere inside her rags.

He wondered what he could do. What did he know of hybrids, grafting, cross-fertilisation? But perhaps he could take the rose, transplant it to his own garden, where he could keep watch over it.

Pulling his camera from his pack again, he tried to capture an image of the bloom in the exacting light. The Cemetery Rose, the true one, pure velvety black, was inexpressibly beautiful. He took his time over photographing it. Once he had it in shot, he used several rolls of film, capturing in extreme close-up the petals in all their delicate beauty.

But soon the drizzling rain turned back to downpour. A sporadic rumble of thunder became a continuo as the rain turned to a howling storm.

He could do no more at present. Shouldering his pack, and ushering Rose back out of the grove, he mentally marked the spot so he could find it again. Rose wandered away through the graves, presumably to spend her money somewhere. He headed home, to think.

*I*t is night again. Kilworth is wandering the City of the Dead.

On the Anglican side of the cemetery, the Serpentine canal, empty of water, starts shallow, then becomes five or six feet deep as he follows it. Ornamental ponds and latticed summerhouses dot the area, and silent angels cast in stone.

*Kilworth has followed the dry culvert's winding path to the cemetery's Independent section, which is swathed in gathering night. He shivers, pulling his coat close. Large black ravens perch on the nearby tombs.*

*Stifling his nervousness, he comes to a building constructed of honey-coloured Pyrmont sandstone. Looming above him is the cemetery's largest monument — the incredible Frazer Vault, built in 1894 at a cost of five thousand pounds by Maurice B. Adams, architect. A masterpiece of high Victorian Byzantine Gothic, it dwarfs everything around it. Four French-influenced gargoyles perch high atop it, channelling rainwater away from the roof. Most of the narrow small-paned windows set high in the walls are cracked or gaping open. He hears the chittering of birds roosting in the vault's upper reaches.*

*This place might conceal anything. He imagines dried-out corpses piled up like cordwood against the inside walls. Misshapen, boneless things, swollen with putrefaction and mould, might wait patiently to drag someone like him inside with them. These thoughts arise easily. His heart is in his throat, and he is frightened, more frightened than he has ever been.*

*Remember when everything was new and strange? a faraway voice seems to say. Water pools in the crevices of the building, drips down the sandstone. He hears the tolling of the bell from St Michael's Chapel, a slow, deep note. He looks around frantically for shelter from the sound.*

*He ventures forward to knock on the vault's large bronze doors. They echo ominously. They groan. One opens with agonising slowness. He gasps. A thin white hand appears around the edge of the doorframe. He screams and keeps on screaming. Something sluggish, a blurred figure, which he can vaguely see has a shrunken, hideous visage, seems to be spilling from the tomb's opening.*

*As it squirms feebly towards him, he awakes, sweating.*

His throat is raw from screaming. He is in his own bed, at home in Berala.

Two days later, still haunted by the nightmare's vividness, but intending to fulfil his original plan of photographing the monuments, Kilworth made his way between the brooding, lichen-encrusted graves. He also intended to dig up the bush on which bloomed the black rose, but that was for later, when darkness fell. Dead dried leaves and twigs crunched underfoot on the cracked earth of the narrow, uneven paths. Large trees entwined their gnarled branches above the pathways.

In the old Catholic section, past Necropolis Drive, huge grey-blue cacti and straggling flowery shrubs grew out of many of the graves, taking their nourishment from whatever still lay beneath. He marvelled at the maze of headstones in sandstone and marble, at the bewildering variety of crosses, carven angels, Celtic decorations adorning the uncountable graves. Loose marble tiles and pieces of granite lay in a scattered chaos of tumbled masonry.

Many of the flatbed tombs were half-engulfed by earth, and subsidence had shattered or tilted many of the headstones, lending them a crazy air. Fallen decorative urns filled with faded plastic flowers littered the graves. Sundried brown grasses thrust up between the cracks on the tombs themselves and in the paths between them. Rusting iron railings with fleur-de-lys-topped spikes surrounded headstones whose inscriptions were almost entirely effaced by wind and weather. He shot a roll of film as he passed through the tombs, ejected it, put another one in.

A dry culvert, like the one from his nightmare, snaked its way across the grounds. Number One Serpentine Canal was brick-lined, perhaps two and a half feet wide, and several feet deep. The thought of what might have been at the Resthouse, and what might be capable of concealing itself in those culverts, made Kilworth shudder involuntarily.

The black rose filled his thoughts, its beauty like a black brand on his consciousness, its very existence as subtly alluring as the siren's call. Yet for now, he had better persist with his plan, and photograph more of the monuments.

Wandering on, Kilworth gazed bewildered at still more concrete pillars, which boasted tortured figures of crucified Christs, and multiple versions of supplicating Marys. Many of the headstones here were rusty with red oxidation, above cracked black-and-white tessellated pavements. *Atmospheric, yes.* He snapped off shots here and there.

A little further on, he came to a church, the Chapel of St Michael the Archangel. Buried all around were generations of priests, their white marble headstones topping greenish lichen-covered stone graves. Not far away, lay a lawn with a myriad of small memorial headstones. The chapel itself had large, distinctively-shaped wooden doors, and many stained-glass windows, the most impressive of which was *rose-shaped*. Roses seemed to be haunting him. Two statues of angels adorned the peaks at the front, and a large cast-iron bell topped the building. He felt he had been irresistibly drawn here.

The inscription above the door proclaimed, 'It is a holy and wholesome thought to pray for the dead that they might be released from sins.' This conjured up a vision in Kilworth's mind of various unprayed-for dead, still locked in their sins and writhing in their graves, straining against the encompassing shrouds and coffins that constrained them. He ran a hand across his fevered brow. Altogether, his thoughts in this place had begun to run amok.

He made his way to the grove where the black rose grew. Its cloying scent filled his nostrils as he dug around its roots, placing it with infinite care in the sack he had brought with him. He was careful to avoid the large thorns that ran like sharp vertebrae along the plant's thick green stems. Bundling up the sack over his shoulder, he made his way out of the trees.

Enough for one day. He would take his booty home. After a half hour of walking he came to the cemetery's perimeter gate and went out. Something weird seemed to be happening to his mind.

Next evening, he returned to the chapel. Although he carried his camera, the original purpose of his photo-shoot seemed to have evaporated; the cemetery itself, the Black Rose in particular, had begun to obsess him.

As he drew near the chapel, some tall shape seemed to be obscuring the building's front, for he could no longer see the distinctive shape of the door which he had observed on his earlier visit. He peered through the gathering gloom. The shape was a dark, pale-faced figure, lolling against the chapel's nearest wall. Above it, steeped in dimness, something seemed to scuttle from the roof and drop to the ground near the tall figure's feet. Fellow necrotourists? He thought not. Had he seen them before in his nightmares? He stopped in his tracks, heart pounding.

Maybe, he told himself, he was seeing things, his mind playing tricks. The human mind wants there to be an order in everything, and so it creates patterns in chaos, patterns where none exist. It tends to interpret a dark shrub as a crouching thing, to see a pile of rubbish half-visible in the windy twilight as a prostrate body writhing feebly—one explanation for phantoms. Or so he rationalised, listening to his own scratchy breathing in the dusk.

Dismayed, he cast quick looks left and right, unsure whether he was more afraid to see the figure moving, or not to see it.

He arrived at a horrible realisation: something that wanted to catch him in its lethal embrace had been waiting for *him*, and for no one else. A shiver passed through him and his skin went cold. He began, slowly, to back away.

He had not yet seen the figure's face, but his imagination began to give it one. It was a face composed partly of darkness, held together by shreds of flesh, with two eyes the colour of cold porridge, above a mouth with all the compassion and softness of a lamprey's.

Then, it stepped out into the half-light. Glints of strange fire seemed to play around its head.

At its feet, something smaller scuttled and hesitated, scuttled forward again, disappeared into the long grass. Kilworth suddenly understood that in the unspoken hierarchy between these two, the thin man was in charge and the creature was its familiar. This was the creature he had sensed moving in the back of the florist shop, and which had been roosting in the trapdoor of the Resthouse when he had camped there.

He felt something slither past his leg, something with vestigial limbs. He glimpsed it—something shiny, anthracite-black, spiky with tufts of hair or fur. As he thought of the thing touching him with its clacking legs and its body furred with coarse hair, it felt as though fingertips were lightly walking up his spine.

A religious man might have called it a blasphemous abnormality, but Kilworth had no such facile response. For him, such things resisted interpretation. It dawned on him that nothing he could do would save him, for he believed neither in the possibility that these creatures could really exist, nor in the efficacy of any supernatural gimmick he might level at them.

No, he was alone with them. Out here, 'safe' and 'familiar' were meaningless terms. If the creatures existed in the face of all his well-reasoned scepticism, then the world was upside-down and he was doomed. They represented something unimaginable.

Moments later, backing away, he heard a dry rustling coming from the canal. There was a slithering, and a staccato scrabble of its claws on brick. He mustn't be fooled into hiding in the culverts.

Trees partly obscured the view, making it impossible to see back towards the chapel. Caught between the Scylla of the thin man and the Charybdis of whatever the smaller thing was, Kilworth was unsure in which direction to run. He was desperate to cry out, but the wind stirring in the trees made a continuous "shhh" as though warning him to keep silent.

Fear welled up in him. He turned, frantically casting around for a haven, and darted across behind a large gravestone. Leaves crackled beneath his feet, twigs snapped with a treacherous loudness in the silent graveyard. What terrified him most was the thought of all the ground he'd have to cover between here and possible safety. His mouth tasted of iron, and he tried to lick his lips, which had gone dry. The lights outside the Necropolis were but a feeble glimmer from here. Rookwood's gates were locked at dusk, and he had long ago missed the 3.30 bus out of the grounds, the last one for the day.

Breathing hard, his hands clasping the rough headstone, he ventured a look back towards the church through the obscuring vegetation. Squat gravestones, mottled with moss and darkness, dotted the ground between the small depression where he crouched and where the figure had been. But now, it seemed, the figure no longer lolled there.

His heart quickening, he saw it again. It was silently advancing towards his hiding place. As it approached, Kilworth could faintly make out the line of sutures stitching the flesh—if it *was* flesh—of the man's face. The sutures ran from the temple down the right side of the face and along the neck, disappearing beneath the black cloth of the buttoned-up suit. In its terrible eyes there was no spark of humanity, only a dull intelligence that enabled it to seek, to exert control over its inhuman companion, and to keep hunting until it got what it sought.

Kilworth rose from his concealed crouch, his knees already aching and his stiff back protesting. The thin man was only a few paces away. Kilworth seemed hypnotised to the spot. The strength seemed to have left his limbs, and his breathing was muffled, uneven.

The thin man reached him, and placed its hand on his shoulder. The gloved hand seemed to have been shredded to rags of cloth.

Kilworth shuddered, jerking back as he realised that the ragged threads trailing from the hand were not cloth at all, but flesh...

The thin one spoke. "The Black Rose is...ours." The voice was guttural, like a death-rattle in the throat of a dying man; yet sibilant, like wind in autumn leaves, like the fluttering wings of a trapped bird beating itself against a windowpane.

Now its fingers were about his neck. There was a slashing movement. Kilworth felt as though his throat had been cut from ear to ear. With trembling fingers, he felt gingerly at the nape of his neck. Blood was trickling from an open wound, and he felt it wet and sticky on his fingers.

In his shock, he dropped the camera. He tried to cry out, for help, for anybody at all, but fear choked his voice to a whisper. He jerked away from the thin man's grasp and bent to the ground, fingers instinctively searching for his precious camera. Shivering with dread, he felt around on the humid earth. He held his breath.

Then his hand fell on a smooth surface. His fingers sought purchase but found none. In the semi-darkness he could not see the whole shape, but clutched what felt like the camera's outer casing. As he drew his hand closer to him, however, it slid along the thing and he realised it was long—far longer than the camera would be, even had he grasped it by the lens. And what he clutched between his fingers was thin, as well as long. A horrible suspicion formed, and just then he felt a weight at the other end of what he was grasping jerk slightly. His fingers slid over a joint, and a cry of disgust escaped his lips as he realised he was grasping, by one of its legs, the revolting creature he had glimpsed before.

With a shock of repugnance, he snatched his hand away. Judging by the size of the leg he had inadvertently grasped, the thing's body was the size of a large cat. He kicked out, had the satisfaction of feeling it connect with a dull thud, and half-saw the thing roll away from him. In the grasses around the nearest gravestone, he saw a tangle of legs sticking up, waving about. The thing must have landed on its back and was struggling to right itself. Sour bile flooded the back of his throat.

Next moment, the creature was up again and sprang violently forward against him, landing heavily on his chest. He tried to beat it off with his hands. It emanated an overpowering odour of filth and decay, and the furriness of its body as his hands brushed against it sickened him.

It dropped into the grass again, and he hastily backed away, keeping his hands up protectively in case it should leap at him again. Wind shuddered the fallen leaves and raised ripples on the surface of the ornamental pond.

Suddenly, as if from nowhere, Rose appeared. He saw her pick it up, that thing, briefly cradle it in her arms like a baby, the tattered folds of her old red dress swathing it from view. Then, viciously, she flung it against the bole of a nearby tree. He heard a dull thud as it slammed into the tree trunk and fell to the ground. He could only hope she had killed it.

The thin man turned towards Rose, momentarily abandoning his pursuit of Kilworth.

Kilworth gasped in terror, adrenalin pumping through his system. He would run while his persecutors were distracted. He could make the fence if he ran now. In that slim hope, he put his trust. He ran, full tilt, panting, gasping, hurtling across graves, thumping down aisles of trees, his clothes catching in overhanging branches.

He was nearly there. The wire perimeter fence loomed ahead. He hunched over for a second, with a stitch in his side, gasping for breath. He listened. There was nothing, save the night winds in the foliage. But then, he sensed the thin man behind, vindictive, implacable, giving chase.

He hurled himself up and over. Just as his body was three-quarters across, he felt a shooting pain through his ankle. A hand had grasped him and was pulling him back into the cemetery. Almost out of his mind with fear, Kilworth shot a quick glance back over his shoulder.

The thin man's grin was fixed, the porridge-coloured eyes and the lamprey mouth set in hideous intent.

Kilworth jerked his leg violently, and felt his foot slip through the thin man's hold. With a surge of terrified triumph, he made it over the fence, dropping to the ground outside. He felt the thin man fall back, flopping against the inside of the wire fence. Something told him the thin man was unable to leave the grounds.

Kilworth fled home in a panicked frenzy, limping on his wounded ankle. A trickle of blood still ran from the wound the thin man had inflicted on his throat.

He spent the night sleepless, tossing on his bed, his throat bandaged. What would they do to Rose? He was sure they would harm her. But in his cowardice he stayed away all next morning, then for the rest of the day.

After that, he went into the studio for a few days running. But, unable to concentrate at work, he began to face the irresistible compulsion to return to Rookwood. By the time he had steeled himself to do so, it was a week later.

He had to find out what had become of Rose.

As he entered the cemetery that afternoon, for the last time, the shadows deepened, thickened. As he approached the grove where the black rose had grown, he slowly became aware of an overpowering smell.

Then he found Rose, what was left of her.

Her body was lifeless, her raggedy clothes thick with congealed blood. The smell of death, of decay, rose up to meet him. The body was slumped against the trunk of a tree on a weedy patch of ground. She was virtually faceless, her eyes and cheeks destroyed by maggots. Kilworth knew maggots move away from light. They had clustered in Rose's hair.

He saw the hair stirring as they teemed at the back of her neck. Her mouth stretched open in a distorted rictus, the lips peeled back to reveal the crooked teeth. Dried blood ran into her mouth. There was no longer a nose, and the little flesh remaining on her head was discoloured. The eyes were the worst, for they were nothing now but sightless pits filled with maggoty cast-off.

Kilworth reeled back and stifling a gag reflex as his nostrils caught the body's full reek, his mind frantically seeking to obliterate the reality of the old woman's death, taking refuge in Baudelaire's lines from 'The Carcass' in *The Flowers of Evil*:

> *The flies buzzed and droned on these bowels of filth*
> *Where an army of maggots arose,*
> *Which flowed with a liquid and thickening stream*
> *On the animate rags of her clothes*

For a few moments disgust filled him, and sadness for Rose and her pathetic end. Part of him, truth be known, had known she would be dead when he found her again. Then anger kicked in. Gnawing uncertainty of soul became need to take action. What kind of sick twist was he, to have allowed this to happen to her? Those who had caused her death would pay.

He turned away, sickened, as a mass of maggots dropped from her ruined head to the ground and writhed on the path before him.

Suddenly, just as he saw the trail of thin black slime leading to the tree bole, something dropped from the canopy of foliage above and crawled toward him. His nostrils quivered at the thing's stale animal odour. It surged forward, legs clacking. Kilworth's vision was teared up; the thing seemed to be twitching, lurching towards him as though wounded.

He knew what he had to do. Snatching up a broken-off piece of headstone from one of the graves, he hefted it in his hand and waited.

It appeared out of the long grass, poised to leap.

He hurled the heavy piece of stone at the thing. It hit with a sickening thud, immediately followed by a sound like a stick of celery being snapped in two.

The creature slumped to the ground. Its legs twitched a couple of times and then it was still.

The killing of the thing was small recompense for Rose, he felt, but it was the only kind of justice he knew how to dole out.

He was in the old shed, in the makeshift darkroom he had rigged up, surrounded by trays, and containers of fixative hypo. He was bringing up a print in his signature style. The hues looked dissolved in darkness. The image, which showed the Black Rose, drifted slowly into sharp relief. In the background was a shape, blotchy and unfocussed: the thin man.

Kilworth took the print and set it on the patio table to dry. He sat back in the old chair there, the one with the rain-stained plastic cushions. The sky, which seemed to tug at him convulsively, as the light drained out of it, was staining the evening with blackness.

The exhausted light gave him a distorted view of the back garden, which overlooked Route 45 Olympic Drive. Crumbling leaves lay strewn across the cracked cement of the back patio. Weeds and grasses, dotted with blown dandelions and dried-out stalks, filled the yard. Near the brick back fence, its ragged top edge like some ancient battlement, weeds rose so tall he could barely glimpse the wire enclosure he had erected to house the Cemetery Rose. *The Black Rose.*

Here it was, now his own, replanted, fed with rich dark humus. Its macabre beauty brought him a perverse pleasure. He would foster and feed it, nourish it with his own noxious desires. It would grow and prosper, and when the time was right he would know what to do. Perhaps the thin man would help him.

*Humans*, he thought. *We sleep in the dark, we rut in it, but not until we encounter true darkness do we begin to comprehend its nature.*

His mind was seething. Yes, he would feed the Black Rose, and it would feed him, and then there would be an accounting. A black flame, all-penetrant, would burn through him before he went out again to exact his vengeance on the world, a world that would finally sit up and take notice.

As he stood and advanced towards the Black Rose, which seemed to strain eagerly towards him, he was already on the verge of disclosing to it all the details of his own inner delirium.

Then came a sound that was ugly, even to his own ears. He began to laugh, and was completely unable to stop.

# WATER RUNS UPHILL

*"She's a witch, mutters magical cantrips,*
*can make rivers run uphill…"*

- Ovid, *Amores* I:8

It was one of those muggy evenings that come late in November. The sea was lapping against the harbour wall, under a pumice-coloured sky, like a cat licking up water from its drinking bowl. An area of low pressure had crept in from the east. Perhaps I'd started to doze, because the black-clad waitress tapped on my table where my glass stood empty.

"Anything else?"

"Lemon, lime and bitters," I told her. Couldn't she remember? It was all I'd been drinking. The sky, out over the Five Islands, was going a murky orange, the kind you generally only see when there's a distant bushfire.

The waitress returned to the bar to get my drink. Heat reflected into my face off the metal-topped tables. The chairs were those rickety aluminium tubing jobs, so uncomfortable to sit in that you feel like an intruder simply patronising the café. I imagined the owner watching through a secret spy-hole from behind the bar. Maybe he would be getting his jollies, timing each paying patron on how long it took us to feel so uncomfortable we would leave, so that different customers could come in to replace us.

I wished I had some gum, something to chew on, to take my mind off things. A few young girls were sitting around a nearby table. The conversations I overheard amused me. The girls were different from me: the way they tossed their hair, laughed loudly, talked over each other.

Earlier that day I'd decided to go up Mt Keira. The weather had been dicey at first, and I feared rain, but by the afternoon, the sea breeze had cleared the clouds. The mountain formed a shape against the sky like a pushed-in hat. The piecrust indentations of my old Volvo's steering wheel were hot and sticky under my knuckles. Trees dotted the streets, lush grey-olive foliage interspersed at intervals with the startling purple of jacaranda trees in full bloom. Along the edges of Mt Keira Road and the winding route to the lookout, I passed native grasses, yellow tea-roses growing wild, and acacia heavy with new growth.

As the afternoon wore on, I'd gone for a walk along the track that led away from the lookout's teahouse. The profuse undergrowth was full of yellow cassinias and straggling mint bush, wild honeysuckle and orange blossom. Scrubby paperbarks and tall Norfolk pines formed a shadowy canopy overhead. A little brook trickled slowly between the trees, heading down the mountainside towards the sea. Cockatoos shrieked and squawked as they flocked across the valley. But after a while I'd grown restless and bored, and drove down to spend time at the harbourfront café.

Now I was taken by the urge to go out to Toothbrush Island. Simultaneously, I knew I never would. The waitress returned with my drink. As I sipped it, I wondered: had the First Nations people ever made it out there in their paperbark canoes?

My mind played back a scene from the year before. I'd been at the Chinese herbalist at Kiama, waiting for my partner Val's acupuncture session to finish. The pungent herbal smell, reminiscent of marijuana, filled the small waiting room with its cane chairs and glass-fronted cabinets full of Pe Min Kan Wan, Xiang Sha Liu Jun Wan. A model of a human body marked with meridians sat atop one of the cabinets; there was the obligatory golden Lucky Cat atop another. A kids' toybox—a yellow plastic crate—filled with plastic cars and battered board books sat in one corner.

"How was it?" I asked.

"More work needed on the spleen." Okay.

At the Out of the Blue Café, we had date scones and coffee. Why were there so many small troubles, things we had to try and resolve? We lacked energy, since our health was poor. It turned out hers was far worse than we thought.

I remembered the days twenty years before, when, newly married, we had belonged to the fabulous in-crowd. Nothing could touch us then. *Now look at me*, I thought morosely. Belly straining at overly-tight pants. Unsightly bags under the eyes, chronic pains in various parts of the body. Where once I'd woken up fresh as a daisy in the morning and bounded out to greet the day like a young gazelle, now I awoke in a stupor, staggering out to breakfast with a headache and a stiff neck. It didn't seem to matter that I went to bed early or tried to treat myself kindly. It was the entropy—things running down, the body groaning at its continued use through the years.

These days, indulgence took precedence over duty. Any notion I had back then of being responsible had died with my marriage. Now I passed my days in a cloudy fug of smoke, sometimes drugged, often drunk. I kept strange hours, immured in my own indolence.

Another, more interesting woman sat at another table. She was a slender blonde with sensuous lips, pale creamy skin, dark eyelashes, long flowing hair. I fantasised about her: young enough to be into bands like the Kooks and the Arctic Monkeys. Occasionally, I thought, she listens to skate music—lo-fi, blunted beats over deft guitar melodies and solid bass foundation. Probably got a boyfriend the same age.

She didn't so much walk up to me as undulate in my direction, until, before I knew it she was right there. She had on a powder-blue dress, light and summery, that left her shoulders bare. Small pearl earrings. Tight black stockings that showed off her shapely legs. Bright red shoes. Around her neck was a string of dark wooden beads and on her right forefinger, a chunky amber ring. I had, at best, a cloudy knowledge of fashion, but I liked what I saw. Mildly startled that she had approached, I was aware of the faint scent of cinnamon wafting off her skin, the round smoothness of her shoulders.

"May I join you?"

"Of course." I tried to kid myself I knew all about her as soon as I saw her. Her lips would taste like luscious wine, her kisses would be intense. Her pale skin gave me a blissful amorous frisson.

I was sick of my life, of moping around. For some moments, I honestly thought about getting this girl into bed. But something in her eyes set me on edge; her look was so direct I could hardly face it. She lit up a cigarette. I took this as my cue to speak.

"Can I get you a drink?"

"What?"

"I'd like to buy you a drink. What'll you have?" I was as direct as she was, not wanting to say anything contrived.

She gave me an appraising glance, then; unclenched her hands, which opened like twin blossoms unfolding. "Daquiri."

I gave her my most winning smile, nodded to her unvoiced question. "I'll get myself a whiskey." I motioned to the waitress, who brought us the drinks. She gave me an odd look, which I took to mean she wondered why I had switched my poisons.

I noticed while we talked that she gestured with her hands a lot, using them like elegant wedges to emphasise her point. She spread them wide, or clenched her fists, and talked wide-eyed, enthusiastically. I imagined making love to her: the way her arm might tighten around my waist, the probable darkness of the tangle between her legs. I played deliberately with the notion of taking her home, willing myself to feel alive again. I managed to picture her opulent hips poised in provocation. I thought of her cool eyes, her liquid fingers, her nudity glittering with sweat as she seduced me.

"I feel like cutting loose and getting smashed tonight," she said. She smiled. I smiled back. It was all possible.

We continued talking the small talk that strangers often do when meeting for the first time. But something about her was injured. Oh, there was electricity there, we both sensed it, and we would play the game for a while. But something about her reminded me of old injuries of my own. The time I'd cut my wrist on a broken glass while pushing it into the wastebin and needed stitches at the hospital. The car crash I'd once been in on Gladesville Bridge: coming up over the bridge's crest, blithely laughing and talking with friends, when—wham!—just over the crest, our car collided with a vehicle that had stalled, and I walked away with whiplash. This girl was attractive, but I sensed she could be bad news. Inside, I was already drawing back. I noticed too, that her eyes were almost colourless. It wasn't a good sign.

Suddenly, not wanting to encourage her further, I began to pretend distraction. Before long, I was letting the silence develop. I couldn't do this. I had to rescind the illusion that anything could be the same without Val. Anyway, this girl must have some surreptitious motivation. I was no longer young and attractive.

The conversation faltered badly. She made an excuse and walked away.

*Chalk that one up to experience,* I told myself.

---

Back home, I sat listening to the evening sounds. A possum dropped on the roof with a thump. Bushes scratched at the window. There was the "fark, fark, fark" of great glossy black ravens perching on the high TV aerials. Cats loped across the road in the gloom. Raised voices carried from the housing commission flats opposite— another blazing row in progress. I looked out the kitchen window. Against the clouds' undersides blossomed a red haze that was less sunset than reflected flame from the steelworks.

I set up my camcorder on its tripod and replayed a tape of some of the old home movies on the TV. There was Val, with me and some of our friends, gathered around the barbecue equipment. Plates of sausages, onions, and rolls, Val's delicious terrine; glasses of red wine. I could almost savour the tantalising aroma of the special rice concoction that my friend Bruce always made at such occasions. Good days, despite Bruce's insistence on wearing shirts so loud I had to block my ears. Val: red-haired, fierce, independent. How could I do anything without her in my life? Here she was packing the station wagon: folding chairs, tables, picnic blankets packed up safely for the return trip.

Here was more footage: me escorting Val at the opening of her play. She was wearing a black feather in her hair. A friend must have taken that using our camera.

In another shot, we were drinking beer outdoors at the pub at the seaside town of Thirroul, Bruce's band pumping out R&B. The escarpment rises above, grey and green jutting against a cabbage-coloured sky, water sluicing down through the valleys and rifts, old miners' cottages staggered against them. Where, I wondered, did D. H. Lawrence get the internal reserves to cope with Thirroul in the 1920's? I'd visited 'Wyewurk' with Val, the Californian-style bungalow Lawrence and his partner Frieda had lived in—a wintry shack where he cooked up the plot to his Australian novel *Kangaroo*. Frieda had been independent, a free spirit, yet loyal to Lawrence. I thought of Thirroul now, a cluster of shops about to be gentrified and commodified out of existence. The film showed a few shots here of Sunday lunch after Sedition by the Sea lectures in the old Railway Institute Hall: dusty portraits of Labour Party once-greats on the walls, where Val and I had gone in our activist days.

I remembered Val's voice: it was hot lemon, honey and vanilla when you've just come in from the rain. On the still-running film, she turned to the camera and smiled, her teeth pearl-white, a strand of her auburn hair blowing across her face. The last scene was a holiday we'd taken, the spray from the waterfall behind her flying up into the air in a drift of rainbow-coloured droplets that the sun caught.

The film ran out. There was no footage of the hospital, where Val had lain for months as the cancer took her inch by inch. No footage of that, or of the funeral. No-one had filmed me either, as I grieved afterwards. I was glad our collection showed only the good stuff.

I switched off the camcorder and sat. The TV's blank screen stared back at me. My hands grew clammy. I hugged myself against the sudden chill in the room, drew my ratty black bomber jacket closer around me.

I cooked. I watched a TV programme about a woman who taught people how to train their dogs better. After that, there was the news programme: the usual stuff about children being forced to work in the copper mines in the Congo, about twenty-six people having died today in suicide bombings in Iraq. I walked around the room, picking up things at random, putting them down again. A clock chimed eerily in the silent darkness. Got to get grounded, I told myself. But I couldn't help remembering a time before the Net, before Ebay, before Google, before Amazon. It was a primeval time of typewriters and liquid paper. A time when we had both been speechless with passion, in bed and out of it.

Where was the pulse, the clamour, now? I closed my eyes and thought of kissing Val, her lips bee-sweet. Faint rainy noises, muted by the walls, came from outside. The room had gotten dark. I got up and switched on the light. I looked at the grease and dust on the surfaces of things, the kitchen cupboards with their shabby paint, some swinging open because their latches were broken and I could no longer be bothered fixing them.

I got into bed and pulled the blankets over my head. I lay awake most of the night.

But I must have dreamed at some point. In the dream, I was out in the street. I saw myself turn up my coat collar and quickly walk away from my house. I felt on the cusp of a revelation. A cloud passed over the moon. There was an extraordinary feeling that it prefigured something important, but what?

Next day, I set the camcorder replaying the film's last scene, looped to run endlessly backwards. On the screen, behind the face of the woman I had loved, water ran uphill, flowing from below to above. Time ran in reverse.

But it couldn't be like that for me. I packed a suitcase, got in the Volvo, and headed out of town and away from the coast for good.

# THE LAST TOWN

Two young men came through the gateway into the cobbled market-place of the Last Town. The one was tall and fair, and the other squat, dark and sombre-featured.

They made their way among the bustling buyers and sellers of goods, and as they went a hush fell upon the crowd. All the people looked towards the strangely attired pair as they took up a position in the centre of the marketplace. The golden-haired youth began to speak.

"I bear a message from the gods," he said. "Just beyond the hills there lies serene a land of beauty where no sorrow may exist. No man has yet beheld its grassy meadows, or walked its shady paths, or worshipped at its graceful shrines. It may be yours; you may dwell within its faery vales and groves for all your lives, playing by day among the fragrant flowers and sailing the peaceful moonlit waters by night. And when you pass away, your souls shall find rest in the house of the gods—you have but to follow me there."

He gazed expectantly around the marketplace at the emotionless faces of the men and women and children, but no-one stepped forward. He lowered his head in silence and the dark young man began to speak.

"I tell you this. Far away across the desert towers a black marble city, whose streets are fortune-paved and lined with pleasure-halls. There can you achieve power and wealth, within the city's shadowed temples make obeisance to whom you choose and in its onyx palaces, feast at will upon forbidden fruits. Your ambitions and lusts will be fulfilled while you live—but I am bidden to warn you that upon your deaths, your souls will find eternal damnation. To dwell within the city of your desires you have but to follow me there."

He gazed around the marketplace, and the people threw down their belongings and chorused as one, their faces distorted and gleeful,

"We will follow you!"

The expression of the dark man was sardonic as he turned to the other. The fair youth said with ineffable sadness, "I had great hopes for these people, but without a second thought, they—"

"They follow me!" exclaimed the dark man triumphantly. He beckoned to the crowd, which strode eagerly after him out of the town gate and along the road into the twilight. And behind them fell into place those who had been waiting without the walls, until the road was filled with an enormous throng of people, following the dark man over the black hills in the distance. The procession lasted what seemed to the fair man an eternity, but finally he watched the last part of the mighty crowd vanish over the crest of the range of hills.

And then he hung his head and wept for the foolishness of the people of the Last Town, and of those who had followed them—the people of the other towns of all the world.

# THE INFESTATION

Soon after you enter the house, you know you've made the right decision. From beneath the floorboards in the dark corner under the kitchen stairs, you can see out without being observed by the inhabitant. You feel warm and safe, and there are mouldering scraps of food for you to devour. Beyond the tattered strips of linoleum, which hang down into the hold where the floorboards have rotted, you can see the dingy kitchen—its yellowish walls, its grimy gas stove, a large refrigerator with a faded poster adhering to its door.

You are not sure why it is that you can identify these things by name, but then, there are many things of which you are not sure—how you came into being, for instance.

Your mind goes back, melting like shadows into the recent past. You cannot identify the moment when you first realised you were alive, but you can dimly recall your place of nurture. It was the decomposing body of some small animal, perhaps a rat, somewhere in the maze of littered alleyways behind this house. You remember your two siblings alternately tearing at the semi-liquescent organs of the rat and chewing at the festering innards of your parent, who must have died giving birth. You remember joining them in their feasting, feeling stronger hour by hour; you remember turning on them because they were smaller, devouring their living flesh with relish; and you remember extricating yourself from the carcass and scuttling along the badly lit alleyways in search of shelter.

Then you found the house, cockroaches swarming over the rubbish bin at its open back door. Pausing only briefly to swallow up a few of them, you entered the kitchen. A table loomed above you and your still-rudimentary limbs slithered on the grubby linoleum. Almost before you realised it, you had crept under the stairwell, and through the hole in the floorboards, to rest on the dank earth beneath.

You are jerked out of your memories by a sudden thudding of foot-steps on the boards above you, and you shrink down further into the darkness. You can just make out the inhabitant's form moving about the kitchen. There is the sound of running water and the clatter of plates being put away. You glimpse his form again; he seems immense. Your instincts tell you that he is attempting to clean up the kitchen and you are afraid.

The harsh sound of bristles against the linoleum comes sweeping towards you and then a shower of grit and dust and food particles rains down on your head. The man is not thorough in his cleaning; you realise he must be in the habit of sweeping the rubbish from the kitchen floor under the stairs and into your hiding place to save himself the bother of disposing of it in the bin outside.

You feel better. You are aware, again perhaps by instinct, that these humans are a race apart, that they do not see beauty in soot and slime; always they are attempting to sluice away the grease, to rinse away the dirt that is natural and necessary to your existence. But the man is lazy, or tired, or both, and his laziness is to your advantage. As you greedily swallow the food particles and the small sheddings of human hair and skin, you are thankful that the inhabitant is allowing you to gain a foothold in his house. Only the danger of a too-early discovery on his part appals you.

The man tramps up the stairs and does not re-emerge. You presume he has gone to sleep, and venture out into the kitchen. You are determined to make this house fit for yourself to live in. You make use of everything you can find to provide sustenance—a dribble of spilt sauce, a few drops of mouse excrement. You are growing little by little, accumulating strength. The failing light in the dingy room pleases you.

As you begin to regurgitate wastes, you reflect that your way of life is becoming less precarious as the minutes go by. You feel that your territory is expanding. Returning to your hiding-place beneath the stairs, you feel the need to sleep, which comes only every few days, and your mind drifts away.

When you awake, it is because of the noise the man makes return-ing from work. You are larger now, and he does not seem quite so enormous as before. Still, he is strong, and capable of hurting you if he discovers you. For the present you are content to bide your time.

The man follows the same pattern for several days and nights. You begin to know how he lives. He gets up early, eats breakfast and goes to work. Work seems to fill his days, leaving him with little energy for anything else. From some phone-calls you've overheard, you deduce that he works in a warehouse as a storeman of some kind. He comes home exhausted, his clothes covered in dust and grease, his face streaked with black, which he almost always washes off. Some nights he can barely stay awake long enough to prepare a meal. Sometimes he plays loud records or drinks beer after coming home. But always he seems too tired to notice that here and there, in corners and crevices, webs are appearing.

Often, in his hurry to eat, he spills a lot of food in the kitchen before taking it away to the other room to eat, and you do not hesitate to run out and eat what he has wasted. Soon you are of such a size that you live in a cupboard under the sink, which you have infested with a plentiful array of webs and waste matter, as the hole in the floorboards will no longer accommodate you.

You are becoming more confident. The inhabitant seems to have few friends. You think he will make a suitable host.

One night you manage to chew through a cardboard box of breakfast cereal and consume most of the contents. You have gotten into the habit of moving about freely while the inhabitant is asleep. So far, he has not even suspected your presence.

When he comes downstairs, half-awake, to eat breakfast, the expression on his face is not pleasant to behold. He all but drops the packet in disgust when he sees the sticky yellowish trails you have left among the remains of the cereal. He mutters to himself and, gingerly holding the packet at arm's length, disposes of it in the waste bin outside. He looks around the kitchen, seeming to notice for the first time that in places the walls are adorned with grey strands of web, and in some places, strands of the mucous-like substance you secrete after a full meal.

You hear him using the phone in the front room. You know the first person he talks to is his boss, by the subservient tone he uses to explain he will not be going to work. Then he dials another number. You hear the words "exterminator" and "infestation" and realise he is going to try and rid himself of your presence.

But you are cleverer than he is. While he is still in the front room, you scuttle up the stairs and hide beneath his bed. You have plenty to keep you busy, as the dust beneath the bed is rife with smaller edible life-forms, and you start webbing and regurgitating until the space beneath the bed is as heavily infested with filth as the kitchen cupboard.

Later, you hear voices and the sounds of spraying from downstairs. You hear them discussing the 'infestation'. The exterminator seems puzzled at its cause and extent; the man who lives in the house does not seem satisfied by the exterminator's hesitant explanations. Eventually the exterminator leaves; the sound of his van retreats into the distance.

You are not disturbed about the spraying, for you know, as if by instinct, that it will not affect you; in fact, you believe it might flush out other life forms that you can eat. When the inhabitant goes to sleep, you crawl out from under the bed and scuttle back down to the kitchen. In the cupboard under the sink, though the webs have been cleared away, there is a dead mouse and some other appetising morsels. You feel vindicated. You gorge yourself and then begin to redecorate the kitchen. After some hours, it is bedecked with webs and you feel comfortable again.

As the inhabitant enters the kitchen in the morning, he wrinkles his nose. You realise that your odour must be offensive to him. You are bigger now, but not yet of a size to risk an open confrontation. He partakes of a hurried breakfast, as usual, and departs without shutting the back door of the house.

You make your way into the alleys behind the house and find a cat pawing at a wastebin overflowing with rubbish. It hisses as it senses you coming, but it is not quick enough to avoid you, and you sink your teeth for the first time into living prey. It tastes good, and you linger over the meal, only making sure to try and return to the kitchen cupboard before the inhabitant returns.

You are halfway across the kitchen when he shows up unexpectedly early. Despite your satisfying meal, or because of it, you have nearly slipped up. You scuttle for shelter, panicking. Then you are safe.

But something is different tonight. You can hear a girl's voice. From your cupboard you can hear her saying that a woman's touch is needed in the house. You are not pleased.

There is more talk, most of it inconsequential; then silence. After some little while, muffled cries and squeals come from the front room, followed by slow moans. Intrigued, you venture into the doorway between the kitchen and the loungeroom, cautiously, poised for flight should you be seen. But the inhabitant and his girlfriend are too busy to notice you. Their clothes are in a heap by the couch, and they are clinging together, moaning softly. You decide you must deter the girl from coming again—she will interfere with your plans.

You keep listening. Later in the evening they talk again and you overhear something that may be useful. Tomorrow is the girl's birthday and the man is taking her out to celebrate. He promises to bring her back to the house afterwards.

------

All the next day, you lie in wait. Instinct tells you not to spin any webs because you do not want to arouse any further suspicions on the inhabitant's part. He comes home after work, as sweaty and tired as ever, running his hands through his lank hair. Before he takes a bath, he puts something in the fridge—a large cardboard box, square, with a fliptop lid.

You seize the moment to run across the floor to the fridge door while he is looking away and get inside, crouching low down at the back. He closes the door, unaware of your presence. Delighted with your success, you immediately pry open the lid of the box. Inside is a layer cake, smothered with sticky white icing and filled with cream. On top are the iced words *Happy Birthday Susan*.

You hear the front door close as he goes out, presumably to meet the girl for their celebratory dinner. Immediately, you set to work devouring as much food as you have access to—food from half-opened cans, eggs, and fruit and vegetables of all sorts that are not sealed up in containers. Then you allow your bodily processes to take their course, regurgitating and defecating copiously. You feel pleased with your plan.

By now you are big enough to almost fill the centre part of the fridge and you think you can probably force your way out again. You do not like it in here now—it is too cold. But the fridge door is too heavy and you have to wait until the inhabitant arrives home again with Susan.

------

When they enter the house, you can tell by their voices, which are even more slurred than you would expect due to being in your enclosed environment, that they are drunk. You hear him telling her to sit on the lounge in the front room and saying he will be right back. You hear his footsteps approaching the fridge and ready yourself to spring as soon as he opens the door. Your aim is not to attack him, but to get away as quickly as possible to another room. You still need more size and strength before you can reveal yourself fully.

Suddenly the door opens and you see his face peering in. He gasps in shock as you lunge for the opening, but you are sure he has only a quick glimpse of your bulk hurtling past. You run up the stairs, which are less of an obstacle now, into the bedroom. When it is clear he is not going to follow, you risk a look from the top of the stairs to the kitchen below. His back is to you; he is cursing, looking at the inside of the fridge with its messily eaten remnants of food and overturned cans. Is he capable of distinguishing the mess you have made from that due to his own sloppy habits? Apparently not, for you see him pick up the box containing the birthday cake and return to the front room.

Although you cannot see what is taking place below, you can imagine it. There is silence—perhaps they are kissing, or gazing, besotted, into each other's eyes. Then he says something, no doubt presenting her with the cake-box, wishing her happy birthday and flipping back the lid of the box. You know that both their faces have screwed up with disgust at the reeking mess that lies within. The cake, festooned with thick strands of viscous, pus-like secretions, slides apart, spilling out of the box. Maggots wriggle in the soft white filling.

You hear her scream, and her shouted words are clearly audible. She has jumped to her feet and is screaming that she thought he cared about her when all along he only wanted to play a horrible joke. She screams that he is sick, that she never wants to see him again. His feeble noises of protest are lost in her furious, tearful denunciation of him; she cries out again that she never wants to see him again, and marches to the front door, slamming it behind her. He is left speechless. You imagine him slumping back onto the couch, staring in horror at the cake, his face going slack and his head sinking between his hands.

Now things are starting to go your way. After what seems like hours of sitting slumped in depression, he stumbles upstairs. His face is pale. Beneath the bed, you feel his weight as he tumbles drunkenly between the sheets, and soon he is snoring. You crawl out from under the bed and return to the kitchen. This time you are going to make it to your domain. You tear open all the cartons in sight, devouring everything inside. You start spinning webs and you keep on spinning them all night, regurgitating wastes without further restraint.

When he rises in the morning, bleary-eyed, you are crouched atop a cupboard in the kitchen, high up, swathed in webs. You are sure that he will not see you, so heavily is the kitchen clogged with your handiwork. Before he is fully awake, he walks into a web, which partly veils the stairs. Suddenly he is shuddering and clawing it from his face. He looks as though he is going to be sick, especially when he sees the kitchen below.

You have done your work well. You have secreted pools of fetid slime, crawling with maggots, on the table and the floor and the benchtops. The room is filled with dusty strands, which sway languidly. Trails of glutinous matter ooze down the walls; webs are everywhere, hanging from ceiling to floor, lying thickly across the chairs and the sink and the cupboards—even across the back door.

The inhabitant runs upstairs. You think your night's work is beautiful but you know that he finds it loathsome, vile. He returns, his expression mingled distaste and determination, holding out a coathanger, which he sweeps before him in order to make his way through the room. In the front room, he lets it fall to the floor.

Then he phones work to say he won't be in, evidently intending to try and clean the house again, but the boss apparently doesn't believe his clumsy explanations. He gives up in despair. He runs upstairs again, dresses hurriedly, and leaves the house again.

You are not sure whether he has gone to work, or to fetch help. It is of no consequence. He is past the point when he could have rid the house of your influence. Now you are in control. You invade the front room and commence making it your own. As your size is now considerable, it takes you less time than did the kitchen the night before. You do not stop until more than half the house is webbed from floor to ceiling. Then you venture out warily into the alleyways in search of a meal.

———⊙———

Your size is now something of a problem when out of the house, as you can scarcely conceal yourself the way you did before. But as you round a corner near a rundown tenement, a child runs into you. You have wrapped it in your embrace before it knows what is happening. You cannot afford to linger over this meal too long, so you hastily consume as much as you need, and drag the rest back to the house, where you leave the amorphous mass lying on the kitchen floor. Then you return to the top of the kitchen cupboards to await the return of the inhabitant.

He is back quite soon. He does not seem to have been out to work, or else he would have been away longer. Perhaps he has been walking around, trying to convince himself that his whole experience with you is a nightmare. As he opens the door, at least it is clear that no one is with him. Pus-like liquid drips from the webbing onto his shoulder and soaks into his shirt, but he does not appear to notice, so preoccupied is he with the almost impassable wall of filth before him.

———⊙———

You leap down from the cupboard, preparing to close in. He crosses out of sight to the phone, parting webs as he goes, his abhorrence obvious. Perhaps he has decided to phone the police. But the phone rings as he approaches; he picks it up, clumps of webbing adhering to his fingers and the handpiece. You can faintly hear, from where you crouch in the doorway behind him, a woman's voice on the line—is it Susan, having forgiven him, ringing to ask if she can come to see him? You don't care, for the moment has come to strike.

As he turns, phone in hand, and sees you fully for the first time, his stunned expression rapidly changes to a look of haunted defeat. His hair and clothes are covered with strands of the stinking mass of webs that he has waded through. He does not scream. He barely has time to raise his hand, attempting to use the phone as a weapon, before you are on him, your jaws at his throat, webs binding his limbs tightly to his sides.

Later—much later—you rest. You are satiated. The windows are obscured by webs, blocking out the harsh light. The house is entirely your own—deeply covered with excreta, thickly woven with webs. You feel the site is suitably foul to commence breeding. Although you have no direct memory of what you are supposed to do, your instincts are strong.

The inhabitant's body reposes on the floor, his veins pumped full of poison, his throat torn out and his chest half-devoured. You cannot wait for the body to rot. You start to gnaw your way into the body cavity in order to nest in its warmth. You realise, of course, that your life will end when you have given birth; but the time is right and the instincts cannot be denied.

You are satisfied that you will be leaving your children a worthy heritage. Perhaps more than one of them will live, and they will have the run of the whole house in which to grow strong.

Sooner or later a human will come. Perhaps the landlord will break down the front door. Perhaps the parents of the child you partly consumed will have the police out hunting for the killer, and they will be the ones who enter. Or perhaps it will be only poor, helpless Susan who comes knocking, hoping for reconciliation with the man whose body you are entering.

In any case, your children will find nourishment somehow. And they will spread. There must be many more houses to infest.

# DREAM STREET

On Dream Street, anything is possible.

⸻ ✦ ⸻

A huddle of crooked back alleys lined with small dusty-paned shops. Inside, aged shopkeepers sell desperate visitors mysterious objects that transport them to strange dimensions and times. Visitors return after weird adventures with their mysterious objects stuffed inside coat pockets, intending to return them to the wizened shopkeepers, but the shop where they bought them is no longer there. Dwarfish shapes crowd the avenue, and the fish lying in the middle of the road is smeared with blood.

The streets are lined with copies of Freud's *Interpretation of Dreams*. Visitors find themselves trapped in recurring hallucinations, revisiting Dream Street or the Enigma Coast over and over again. Or trying to visit it, and continually being prevented from doing so. They are just rounding the corner when they are diverted by an open suitcase whose clothes fly out and wrap themselves around the head and body. Buses that took you there once now take you somewhere altogether different, and you cannot return to where you want to go. When the conductor asks for your ticket, you pull out instead a crumpled parchment covered with unreadable signs, or you run away and try to hide, while all the other passengers stare after you.

You pass people on Dream Street with blank expressions. They are dreaming of falling indefinitely in the dark, or locked in lucid dreams of people being murdered, of lost children and floodwaters rising around the globe. Nightmare creatures crawl fretfully past you on the kerbs, insectoid beings battering their claws against the corners of buildings.

A bearded woman puts her hand on your arm. You pull away in alarm, only to roll down a slope that wasn't there a moment before. A phantasmal rain of gold coins falls around you, while for some reason spiders emerge from your coat and eat your legs. Your original purpose has not been forgotten, but this is nightmare logic and everyone you know and love is far away, involved in their own private rituals. Train-whistles blow in the distance. You stumble blindly through pockets of cosmic interference as girls in malevolent clown masks have parties to which you are not invited.

Dream Street is different every time, consistent only in its unpredictable variety. Expecting company, you find yourself standing alone on a bare stage, trapped in the glare of a single spotlight, knowing the audience expects you to deliver a speech on a subject of which you have the barest possible knowledge. You peer through the shop windows on Dream Street but they are all mirrors, reflecting back to you your own haunted and haggard face. Poets and homeless people besiege you, clutching at your sleeves. You are naked from the waist down, and somehow you have lost your briefcase. You can see it on the cobbled streets behind you, but carriages rattle past, blocking your vision, and as you pull away from the grip of the others, the buildings lining Dream Street change shape, subtly altering, and all you can hear is one voice crying over and over again, "the wind and the sea," and then, "the bones, the bones." Dream Street with its museums, its sedans, its movie theatres and its floating pumpkins has become eclipsed by silhouettes, and you are swept ineluctably along. Hollow-faced, you will roam here for untold years, the rain dimpling your flesh, ashamed of your public nakedness, crying, "I, Enigma." People point and jeer as you shrink through the shadows, tottering on the edge of oblivion.

*Dream Street.*

Twilight on Dream Street.

# THE HOURGLASS

*"The figure of Time, with an hourglass in one hand*
*and a Scythe in the other"*

– Addison

We were at Rob's because there was nowhere else to go. I mean Honey and me. We had to be together, no matter what it took, and what it took was getting out from where we were—leaving friends and family and taking off into unknown territory, just the two of us. It would be frightening, but at least we would be together. I could hardly wait.

Now here was Rob, my old school friend, looking pleased to see us though we had turned up on his doorstep with hardly any notice. No doubt it wasn't terribly convenient, but he had sounded eager to see us when I'd phoned to say we were on the way through his town en route to Longreach. He had been the only person I could think of that would still offer us any sort of a welcome; with everyone else, I'd burned my boats. Doubtless, he could tell from my strained expression that this wasn't a routine visit; but he was good at smoothing over awkward situations.

"David—and Honey! Come in, come in... How are you?"

He shook my hand vigorously. He was as darkly handsome as ever. Dressed in neatly pressed jeans and shirt, he looked healthy and energetic. I, by contrast, was pale and enervated. The last few months had not treated me well. I had to put the best face on things.

"Good, mate," I said. Even so, I hesitated—something about his appearance had changed but I couldn't put my finger on it. "You look different."

"Must be the moustache," he said, smiling broadly, his green eyes flashing. Sure enough, a dapper moustache lent a new maturity to his always-boyish good looks. I wasn't convinced that was the difference I noticed, but what the hell, now wasn't the time to pursue it.

Honey kissed Rob affectionately on the cheek. "Good to see you." She smiled. We went through to sit in the loungeroom, our first chance to relax since leaving Sydney.

Most of my friends hadn't liked it when I took up with Honey. She was fiercely outspoken, and that antagonised some people who evidently thought women should be less vocal. She was free and wild, and there were friends who seemed threatened by her refusal to adhere to what they considered 'proper' behaviour. That was *their* problem: Honey didn't give a hang what other people thought of her. She said what came into her mind, and she did what moved her. I guess that's what attracted me to her. She was a catalyst—love her or hate her, you couldn't ignore her.

Of course, I was attracted to her for other reasons. That she was beautiful goes without saying. The mischievous light of her brown eyes, and the gentle laughter of her voice, had me under their sway; and I was (I don't hesitate to admit it) powerless to resist her curvaceous figure, and (trite as it may seem) lips that I thought tasted sweet as her name. She was also a bright student, studying social work, and I didn't see how she could be any more desirable.

My friends worried that she had too much influence over me. In hindsight, maybe they were right. I treated her with an almost religious devotion, a sort of awed wonder at her beauty—the kind of sensibility that led the pre-Raphaelites to paint iconic images of their women—radiant, yet distant and almost holy creatures, not to be merely loved, but to be worshipped.

But then I wasn't capable of seeing how unrealistic my image of her was. She was the first girl I had made love to, and I had fallen for her hook, line and sinker, as they say. Right then, Honey was all I wanted and I was prepared to go to the ends of the earth to be with her—a wild, romantic notion to be sure, but I was full of those; and if that's what it took…

"Come through, make yourselves at home. Tea? I have a special Nepalese brew that you might like. I prepare it with salt and yak butter in the Tibetan way." Rob moved to the kitchen and started the kettle.

Rob's place wasn't really the ends of the earth, but it was halfway there, or so it seemed to me. Longreach, the hometown of Honey's childhood, was our planned destination; but when I realised Rob's was on the way we had decided to see him. Three hours' driving took us to his house, via the freeway from Sydney and up through Newcastle to the North Coast. I had spent years in the inner city, hardly moving beyond the tight cluster of suburbs comprising Sydney's grimy, congested heart, and this move to Longreach amounted to an epic journey.

In previous years, we'd visited Rob in Sydney at his inner-city terrace several times. That had been before he'd been away to Nepal; but when he had returned to Australia, he'd bought this house on the coast. It was a beautiful spot, rather lonely and relatively isolated (but I only thought that because I was used to having hundreds of people around me all the time in the city). The house itself was only minutes from a long beach with white sand.

During previous visits with Rob, I had been proud to be with Honey and glad that he liked her. She always seemed intrigued because he was handsome and intelligent, but I never considered Rob my sexual rival. He knew how I felt about her.

I was confident about that, particularly because of one night when we'd all gone out on the town. Funnily enough, it had been earlier that same afternoon that Honey had spotted an old hourglass in the dusty, crowded window of an antique shop on Oxford Street, and impulsively bought it.

*I gaze deeply into the hourglass; or does it gaze into me? Within it, I see all sorts of things as the sands shift; different things—some good, some bad. Today I had a glimpse in it (or was it a waking nightmare?) of an alternate world. It was a world where Honey had left me, had abandoned her ideals, had settled into hideous domestication with another man. Is that as horrible as the way it really ended—or is it more so? I can't decide; any world where she's not present is one that must be endured rather than lived to the full.*

*The doctor they send to my cell to 'observe' me, makes notes, tapping at his computer keyboard. For the most part, I ignore him. He wears a white coat, and I imagine that, framed in dark wood on his white office wall is a degree from some prestigious psychiatric school, but that doesn't impress me. He can't see through my eyes. His notion of reality, the template through which he restricts his view of the universe, is different from mine. His vision is closed, both to what I see in the hourglass, and even to what I saw on the beach. I don't blame him for his limited imagination, but I get irritated when he questions the validity of my reality just because it's different from his. He terms my constant fixation with the hourglass 'obsessive.' I don't care; there's a secret to which it holds the clue: "As above, so below." As sand trickles down from the top chamber of the hourglass to the bottom one, memories trickle through my consciousness. I turn the hourglass in my hands, as I turn the facts in my head. Bits of the past, of the events that led me here, pass through my mind in flurries and occasionally in floods…*

She had whispered hotly in my ear. "Wouldn't it be fun to make love for a whole hour and have that tell us the time—you know, how long we've got to go before we come?"

Her little joke was typical of her frank speech; as I've said, it was one of the qualities in her that turned me on. Before I could protest, she had rushed in and bought the thing, presenting it to me. The hourglass was made of silver, beautifully turned and filigreed; she was certainly, I thought, a woman of good taste in such things. I wondered whether we'd use it as she had suggested. The idea gave the rest of the afternoon a subtle undercurrent of pleasurable anticipation.

Later, Rob had taken us to a pub off Taylor Square. He was keen for us all to have a good time. Well, we'd been drinking heavily and Honey had gotten very drunk, which she was prone to do. If she was uninhibited sober, the sorts of things she did when she was drunk sometimes were too much even for me. She ended up lying in the road giggling, and it was all we could do to get her to her feet and struggle back towards Rob's nearby flat.

She had hung on Rob's shoulder all the way back, laughing, babbling. To be honest, it had begun to annoy me. Honey lived only in the moment, but I thought I could see the evening unfolding in my mind's eye and I didn't like what I foresaw. The alcohol was allowing her obvious attraction to Rob to show itself. I thought it odd and I was annoyed, even a little jealous I suppose, because while outwardly everything was fine, I felt insecure. You never knew quite where you were with an impulsive woman like that.

With some difficulty, we had gotten Honey up into the upstairs bedroom in Rob's small terrace and laid her out on the bed, assuming she would pass out. A few minutes later, I was talking with Rob downstairs; actually, I had told him that I thought I loved Honey; when suddenly she had stumbled out at the top of the stairs, almost entirely naked, mumbling to herself and trying to remove the last shred of clothing. She was apparently oblivious to her surroundings; there might have been strangers in the room—other friends of Rob's, for instance—but luckily, it was only Rob and me. Even so...

Well, I trusted Rob. Looking at Honey's voluptuous body being paraded in front of his eyes, another man might have turned the situation to his advantage, might have taken Honey up on what appeared to be a slap in the face to me. Not Rob. Not then. He was great. He had helped me to get her back to bed—his bed in fact—and because of the situation, he had offered to sleep on the couch downstairs.

Next morning when we awoke, Honey made love to me. No, I didn't initiate it; she seemed eager to use the hourglass as she had suggested. I guess it became our fetish, contributing an indefinable 'something extra'. I can remember as though it were only last night the softness of Rob's bed, the morning sun hot on my back as we pleasured each other. I can still see her long dark hair spread out on the pillow, the whiteness of her skin; can still feel her full breasts beneath my hands, as we timed our mutual orgasm to the rhythm of the last sands running through the glass at the end of the hour. The delicious satisfaction of lying back with her when it was over, sharing the bed as if it were our own, Honey telling me how good a lover I was. I had thought I'd always be grateful to Rob for that.

We had used the hourglass many times since that night at Rob's. I often found that in sex, time seemed to expand. Although the hourglass told us that it was only an hour, a similar span of minutes each time, sometimes when Honey and I made love it had seemed to last for days. Using the hourglass was a game we both enjoyed; as time went on, it had become almost an essential element in our lovemaking ritual, and eventually we would no more think of fucking without it in the room than of doing it with our clothes on.

We played other little sexual games—there's nothing like variety—but because the hourglass had been a gift from her to me, its use had always lent a special aspect to our lovemaking. We hadn't always been able to correspond precisely to the hour; in fact being rigid about it would have spoiled our enjoyment; but when we did manage, sweating and moaning in mutual ecstasy, to climax at close to the instant the sand ran out, it had been a thrill difficult to surpass.

My mind was racing with these thoughts, but Rob pouring the tea brought me back to the present. This was the first time we had seen his home since his return from Nepal, and the lounge was decorated with artefacts that bespoke his deep interest in the culture.

"What brings you?" Rob said, proffering two steaming mugs full of dark liquid.

I needed a caffeine hit, more so than usual; my nerves were pretty much on edge, and I was grateful for the jolt drinking the strong beverage imparted. There was a hollow feeling in the pit of my stomach—part excitement at the prospect of starting a new life, and part shock at the magnitude of the step I'd taken in leaving everything else behind. "We're going to Longreach. I've quit my job. I've quit the band. Honey's got a place there." I was blurting out everything without any logical sequence.

Rob looked concerned. I could tell he thought I'd acted hastily but he took it in his stride. "What about your flat? The people you were living with?"

"I've given my notice. We've got all our things in the back of the car."

"Hmm. Longreach? It sounds totally inaccessible."

"That's the general idea. Honey grew up around there. I just couldn't handle it anymore the way it was." My arm was around her.

She laughed, tossing her head back. "You're looking well, Rob."

"Thanks." He sat beside us. Being at Rob's was a relief. It gave me time to think. As for Honey, I sensed that for her this was another in a perpetual series of adventures. She was not out on a limb like I was. I'd given up everything to be with her, closed things off with my friends. To a lesser extent, she'd done the same, but I knew that if we should split, she could carry on. Whereas by effectively making her my world, I had gone out on a limb. Honey was the limb I was clinging to, and if anything should separate us, there was nothing between me and a long hard fall.

"By all means stay—take the spare room. Stay as long as you need to."

It was what I'd hoped he'd say. "Shouldn't be more than a few days, mate."

I looked around Rob's living room. There were more artefacts than I had remembered from his old place, testimony to his delvings in strange places. Numerous mandala paintings hung on the walls. In one corner was an ugly statue, which I recognised to be of the god Samvara, with his writhing snake and crown of five skulls. Here and there, yellowing yak skulls reposed on other pieces of furniture.

"What's that one, Rob?" I queried. Over the couch, a carving showed a god and goddess engaged in sexual intercourse of a yogic nature.

"*Yab-yum* icon," he said offhandedly. Rob had a way of always seeming knowledgeable both in book-learning and practical things. The artefacts were physical proof of his advance over me in terms of exploring other cultures. I had trailed in his wake in many of my interests. He would enthuse about something, which I would take up and pursue in depth; meanwhile, he had moved on. After taking his anthropology degree, he had taught in Japan for a year, and since we had last seen him had delved extensively into some of the darker Asian religions. His postcards came often at first, but then for a while less regularly. It seemed that from the non-dogmatic style of Buddhism and Zen, he had moved on in his personal explorations through Indian tantrism (hence Samvara) and now had become interested in the Bon-Po people of Kagbeni.

We didn't have to sit for long before Rob had us both helping with a brilliant meal he had been preparing before we came. He was great at cooking; I had always sworn I must learn to cook when I saw the enjoyment he got from it, but somehow I never did. I guess my head was too much in the clouds. Honey took to it with a will, since she loved cooking as well, although she hadn't made this meal before. Rob showed us how to combine fish, beef and kidney beans, which he had already left soaking in wine.

"*Matsya, mamsa,* and *madya,*" he explained. He served up the food on shallow bone dishes. "Made from the brainpans of human skulls," he said.

"Oh really? How—er—unusual" I commented, hoping that was non-committal enough. Truth to tell, I didn't want to appear unsophisticated. I looked askance at the dishes. Their age was indeterminate, but I couldn't help but wonder how recently they had been made. Was he gauging my reaction?

Rob delighted in preparing this kind of an unusual feast, but this surpassed anything he had done in the past. Over the excellent meal, Rob held forth on his recent travels, and was especially expansive on the subject of Nepal.

"It's a great part of the world—Kathmandu has got to be seen to be believed. But I spent more time in the small towns…Jogbani, Dharan, Dhaunkuta, Tesinga and some even smaller settlements along the Sun Kosi River. And the mountains—Kangtega, Tamserku, Amadamblam—spectacular! There's not much access to safe drinking water, in some regions there's a very low quality of life, and some extreme human suffering; more than one in ten children die before their first birthday."

"Oh, that's horrible." Honey had a soft-hearted approach when it came to the realities of world poverty. It was going to be an obstacle to her in social work.

"Well, it's a tough place; many's the time I had to suffer monsoonal rain and blood-hungry leeches. Also, the state discourages deviation from social norms; there's rigid state censorship; but it's surprising what you can get away with if you're determined."

I pressed him on this point but he wouldn't elaborate. He waved his fork, continuing with his lecturing.

"The good thing is the population is about half that of Australia, which is unusually low for that region of Asia. There are no current border disputes, low army numbers, no open wars. The people have quite high purchasing power compared to their income, and low foreign debt. They use traditional fuels like wood and animal wastes to provide more than half their domestic energy use, so they're a low contributor to global warming."

I couldn't help feeling these facts and figures he was reeling off were pretty superficial, not much related to his real interests. I was interested, but I sensed that he was glossing over his real purpose of his living there.

"Will you go back?" asked Honey, her brown eyes wide. I knew she was interested in travelling to exotic places herself.

"My main interest was in the religion of the Bon-Po," said Rob, "and I've learned nearly all about that I can."

"So what *did* you learn there, Rob?" I probed.

He smiled suddenly a rather frightening smile that seemed unlike him—well, not as I remembered him. But gradually, it began to dawn on me that there were many things about him that were not as I remembered. "Oh, all sorts of things. The Sherpas showed me the yeti scalp in the Khumjung Monastery, and the bony hand of a yeti at Thyangboche— for a sordid chinking of rupees, of course. I was able to greatly expand my knowledge of tantra. I participated as a masked dancer in the Mani Rimdu ceremonies—and in others less—wholesome. Have you—have you read Conrad's *Heart of Darkness*?"

"I'm afraid not." I felt stupid, uncultured.

"Ah. Well let's just say that I have a great admiration for Conrad's Mr Kurtz. It's just as difficult to explore—unknown territory—these days as it was then."

Did he mean unknown territory, as in Himalayas, the 'Roof of the World'? Or did he mean it in some more metaphoric sense? I didn't pursue it, but I made a mental note to read the novel when possible. It was often that way with Rob—catching up on his knowledge, realising months later what some fleeting reference in his conversation had really portended.

"Tell you more tomorrow—it's late, you two should get some sleep. The room's already prepared."

And with that, the meal over, Rob dismissed us.

We didn't mind. We made love again that night, the hourglass on the table beside us, within easy sight. The hiss of the night ocean's waves on the nearby beach, and the smell of spray, mingled with the sounds and scents of our lovemaking. Honey was proud of her small waist, which I could almost encircle with my hands. When my hands were on her body, I thought I was in heaven. For her part, she would compliment me on the things she could—I was by no means good-looking but she liked my strong arms and the way I kissed her all over. I felt cut off from the outside world; vulnerable, fragile; but I trusted Honey. I fell asleep with my arm around her, breathing the smell of her hair and her skin. Even then I had no idea what Rob had planned.

*I gaze into the hourglass and I see a vision of eyes, a giant pair of green eyes in the bed with us, looking up out of the mattress. They are wide open, they don't blink. Eyes the colour of Rob's. I blink my own eyes and when I open them again the vision is gone.*

*That afternoon, I go around behind the doctor, who is working with his laptop, in his long white coat. He is tapping, always tapping. There are symbols and pictures on the screen. One of them is shaped like my hourglass; I point at it and ask him what it's called. He says "It's-called-an-eye-con." He speaks very slowly and clearly, as though to an idiot. He thinks I am one, because I so rarely speak. Let him think that; it suits me fine, puts me at an advantage. Can he see the world in a grain of sand?*

*I say nothing, but my eyes widen. I watch the symbol. He clicks something under his hand, and the icon spins around. Watching it makes me dizzy. My head feels as though it's falling through a black hole. I go back to my table and pick up my hourglass, which is lying on its side. I run my hands over its smooth curved figure-eight surfaces, which remind me of Honey's body. The memories keep coming back...*

No matter how well you know someone, you can't see into their mind. I see now that I was too trusting, but how do you know that in advance? You can only learn it the hard way, and that's what happened to me.

At lunch next day, Rob spoke more of the Nepalis. Now he was thinking of writing a thesis on their fetishes and their primitive rites. Honey asked him a lot of questions.

"Got some great hash here, mate." We all smoked while we talked. This and the liberal amounts of beer he served up went to my head. I thought that I should have begun to feel relaxed, but in fact, I felt tense.

Rob gestured towards my glass. "Have some more *madya*—actually this variety is called *'chung'*. This is a really special experience; the goblet is made of a man's brain-pan."

"What is it with this guy and skulls?" I thought, then quickly silenced my misgivings. He was definitely weirder than last time I'd seen him; but I suppose prolonged exposure to another culture would do that to anyone.

He poured the beer into the bone goblet, passed it to Honey. She was normally queasy about things like that, and I expected her to refuse it, but to my surprise, she took the goblet and quaffed deeply, then passed it to me. The thing was cold and hard, an inverted skull whose black eye-sockets gazed blankly. I held it by its stem and decided, well, if they can drink out of this, so can I. I drained the beer, and it was surprisingly good. I immediately felt my limbs suffused with the alcohol, which I suspected was not some local variety but a powerful brew Rob had brought back with him.

Next, he held up a carved mask, black with silver-studded eyes and nose. Several long pointed polished sticks stuck out of it at odd angles. All in all, it was pretty hideous, I thought.

"One of their fetishes. It's an icon worshipped by the Bon-Po. The face of a nameless god in their culture; I believe him to be one of the Sri, the demonic vampiric beings of Bon culture in Tibet; but I believe he has actually had many names throughout history—he has affinities with the Greek Chronos, the Indian Kala, the Roman Saturnus Africanus. And he shares qualities with other gods too—the Iranian Zervan, the Indian Rudra, and especially Oya, mother/storm goddess of the Yoruba people.

He leaned across the table and picked up a couple more items, which he held up with what seemed a flourish. "Paraphernalia of the rites…a rosary made of human teeth. Wonder about that chair you're sitting on?" He was looking at me. "It's made of the skin of an adept."

Indeed, the seat, made of what looked like tanned leather bound across a wooden supporting frame, had a texture that was unpleasantly like that of human skin; but this seemed a little farfetched to me. I honestly didn't know how seriously to take Rob on this point. For a start, how had he managed to get all this stuff into Australia? Nevertheless, I was starting to feel distinctly uncomfortable. These Bon-Po people sounded damned primitive to me.

Honey seemed to be lapping it all up. Every time I would try to change the subject, she would bring it back. Now they were on about tantra.

"Tantra teaches that the hunger for orgasm defeats the possibility of real orgasm," Rob was saying. "There is a greater orgasm. The obsession with physical orgasm precludes having sex for hours instead of minutes. It's possible to become drunk on the energy of life itself…"

My attention began to drift. This was fascinating but I began to wonder what it all meant. Siouxsie and the Banshees were blasting away from the stereo: 'Entranced' from the *Juju* album. Honey was looking at Rob; she seemed almost entranced herself… The evening ended once again as Rob went to his room, and Honey and me to ours.

The following morning Honey seemed preoccupied.

"What's wrong?"

She frowned. "Robert came into the room last night."

"What, in here?"

"He was naked. He asked me if I'd go with him to his room."

I was incredulous. "You're joking! What did you tell him?"

"I said no, of course."

"Shit, I don't believe it!" But I could hardly blame him for finding her attractive—or her for being so. Thank God, she didn't take him up on it. As it was, I felt like punching him out. How could I have slept through it, anyway?

"Don't tell him I told you, David. I'm sure it won't happen again."

"Not bloody likely. I'll see to that."

"It's okay, David—it's just something that happened."

Not to me it wasn't. Had they slept together? Surely if they had, she wouldn't be naive enough to volunteer anything that would make me suspicious. But something about the way she said it planted a seed of doubt in my mind.

"We'll leave tonight. No sense hanging around here if he's going to behave like that. Let's get up to Longreach."

It took me a few hours to unwind. Honey persuaded me to say nothing to Rob, but now I was looking at him through new eyes. At lunch together, I was decidedly cool towards them both.

Afterwards Honey drew me aside. "You're the one I want. I hope you know that." She kissed me. I returned the depth of her kiss, and she yielded languorously as usual; I felt a stirring in my loins.

"Let's go down to the beach," I suggested.

It was twilight, the beach deserted. We made love unconvincingly on the damp sand and afterwards trudged the beach's length. Honey tried to get me to swim, but my reluctance was as strong as usual. Besides, it had begun to get cold.

"Come on, why won't you take a dip?" she teased. She went in, splashing about, waving and although it was the end of a bright hot day, I felt a sense of impending—what? She looked so small in all that water, for all her vibrant life and vitality; the ocean's immensity scared me. I was glad when she came out, dripping, and asked me to towel her dry. We walked back to the house.

That night, Rob cooked for us again. Once again, he prepared the fish, beef and parched beans, and we all indulged in huge quantities of dope and of a Nepali firewater, Rob called *rakshi*.

I drank it against my better judgement. I was making plans for us to be leaving, getting on to Longreach so we could get properly set up. I tried to tell Rob we had imposed on his hospitality enough, but he wouldn't hear of it. I began to fear he was angling for Honey. If he tried anything… My fears were not allayed by his continual conversation about the spiritual qualities of sex, interspersed with dark hints about the rituals in which he had participated in Kagbeni. As the evening wore on, Rob talked further of, "the tantric texts…the supreme religious observance of Durga…the Initiation of Death, following which the adept gains magical powers speedily in this Kali-Yuga…the left-hand path."

My head began to swim. I disliked the mental sensation as much as I did the physical one. I liked to feel on dry land, and now I felt all at sea. The smoke of the hash hung heavily in the room. Honey was sitting right next to Rob, her eyes lit up bright, hanging on his every word. Did she follow what he was saying? Maybe not all the ins-and-outs of the philosophy he was expounding, but whereas I was lost, Rob seemed to be getting through to her on a more basic level. There was a look in her eyes that she normally reserved for her hornier moments with me. Shit, I thought, is he trying to get her into the sack? He's really serious about all this sexual magic bullshit. Through the dope-induced lethargy, I couldn't quite summon the energy to change the course of the conversation.

Rob was trying to convince Honey to cut some of her hair off. They were both stoned, and she did it. Rob began to weave a bracelet out of the shortish locks she had removed with a pair of scissors. His intentions were becoming plainer by the minute. He was overstepping the bounds of friendship. I could have handled that if Honey had resisted, but she was going along with it.

Then the room was swaying, and I must have passed out, because when I came to, with a mouth so dry I could barely swallow, I was alone in the loungeroom. I faintly heard sounds coming from Rob's bedroom. For some reason my head was full of the word *maithuna*. Memories of what Rob had been saying welled up in my mind. "The five sacraments partaken of by the practitioners of tantric rites, are usually known as 'the Five M's'," he had been saying. We had partaken of four of them; *maithuna* was the fifth 'M'.

Raising myself on one elbow, I racked my mind to remember what Rob had said *maithuna* meant. But suddenly I realised—the sounds from the bedroom were unmistakably sounds of passion, and in Honey's voice. My chest tightened with an uncontrollable feeling of jealousy and rage. What the hell was going on? I asked myself—

rhetorically, because it only meant one thing.

I strode to the bedroom door, which was slightly ajar. Beyond the door, the room was more or less in darkness, but there was a faint, flickering glow. I pushed the door open.

The illumination from the candles was faint, but it was enough to show me that Honey and Rob were on the bed, fucking. Honey was sitting astride him, bucking furiously, her breasts bobbing, a look of unnatural ecstasy on her face. Rob was prone, almost motionless beneath her. His face was turned away from the door so I couldn't see his expression but I was sure it was one of victory. He hadn't seduced her by halves; she seemed totally abandoned. She panted heavily as she thrust, seeming desperate to reach orgasm. Entwined around her wrist was the bracelet woven from her hair, and on her breast was that damned rosary of human teeth.

"Jesus!" There was something savage and totally outside my experience here. It wasn't just the betrayal—there was something that scared and angered me, and sickened me much worse than that concept. "You bastard Rob, what the hell are you doing to her!" Although he wasn't moving, and she was, I sensed that she was in his power, hypnotised, drugged, God knows what...

I rushed forward, jerking his shoulder. His head rolled towards me and I drew back sharply; there was something wrong with his face. The eyes were too small and beady, the mouth was a silver slit in the black head, and long pointed sticks rattled as I turned him towards me. My God, I thought. He's wearing the mask! He's raping Honey and wearing the Bon-Po mask...I felt sick to my stomach.

He said nothing, but his hand came up and caught my wrist in a grip that threatened to snap the bone if I should persist. I cried out in pain, dropping to my knees.

Above me, Honey was screaming in short bursts that seemed to wrest themselves from her innermost being. Tears filled my eyes as I realised I couldn't stop what was happening. Rob's grip tightened on my wrist and Honey's gasps came closer together, louder, until they culminated in a cry commingling pain and pleasure such as I'd never heard. Rob pushed me away with his fist and I fell backwards, awkwardly, smashing my hip on some hard piece of furniture as I fell.

Honey fell too, panting, spent, her orgasm past, forward onto Rob's body. I tried to get up on one elbow, ignoring the pain in my hip. Rob was withdrawing from Honey's body, calmly, slowly. I gazed with horror as he stood, picking up one of those shallow bone dishes from his bedside table, and holding it beneath his penis, allowed his semen to spurt into the dish. From another dish on the table, he pinched up what looked like some sort of herbs and sprinkled them on the sperm, using his finger to mix them together with the sticky fluid.

*Christ! I'm going to kill him!* was the only thought in my head. I crawled across the floor trying to get up.

He turned back to the bed, and grabbed Honey's hair, pulling her head up, so she was in a kneeling position. He moved the dish in his other hand towards her mouth.

"No!" I screamed. I was on my feet, about to lash out and knock the obscene bowl from his hand.

Too late.

Honey's eyes were glassy. She received the edge of the dish between her lips. And then the fluid was in her mouth, a little trickling from one corner, which she licked away.

Rob laughed, a harsh alien sound; he'd been hiding the person he'd become ever since we had arrived.

I hit him then, a savage blow that carried all my bewildered anger. It caught him in the chest and sent him sprawling. He kept laughing, infuriating me, though he sounded winded, as he lay on the floor, the dish knocked from his hand.

I was enraged. I wanted to kill him, to smash his brains out. But I was more concerned with Honey. I turned to her. She was halfway out the door, still naked.

"Wait!" I ran after her. Rob's laughter, dark, sardonic, rang after me as I went. Then he stopped laughing and began a rhythmic chanting. He must have started to beat on that ritual drum, for its pounding echoed in my head as I fled the house in search of Honey.

He was insane. I couldn't fix that. I had to stop Honey. Surely she couldn't run far in that semi-drugged state? I heard the front door slam. Outside it would be dark; I had to find her quickly or she might wander in front of traffic. I was panicking. Ignoring the pain in my hip, which made me limp and slowed me down, I made it to the front porch. I couldn't see her; all I could hear was the wind and the pounding of breakers. I limped towards the street.

She must be heading for the beach. Maybe that would be OK, I would catch up with her there—as long as she didn't go near the water. It seemed to take me an eternity to make my way down the street and cross the road to the beach.

My heart pounding, I staggered on to the sand, climbing over the stubby fence that separated the sand from the rough grass that edged the road. She hadn't been gone more than a few minutes, I would catch her—but I was afraid of what had happened, afraid of what I might find. I had to trust that she had been in Rob's power; the thought that she might have betrayed our relationship consciously was shoved somewhere I wouldn't have to think about it. If I could just catch her, get her away from here... It had all been a mistake...

The sky loured overhead and the beach felt lonely and empty and huge and the smell of ozone was in my nostrils. Waves crashed on the shore. An irregular line of black seaweed glistened beneath the froth of the surf's edge. I sensed that overarching the sky above the beach was a force, some tremendous supernal evil.

Had Rob called it here? Could he possibly have any power over anything that felt so powerful itself—for I could feel its might in the shades of the dark sky, in the pounding surf, in the black clouds that swelled ominously above. Something or someone was going to hurt Honey. I ran, and ran. I had to save her.

There was a dark shape up ahead on the sand. A tremendous feeling of relief welled up in me as I recognised Honey. The sand was dragging at my feet as though trying to hold me back from the sight; I felt like a foolish marionette at the command of a puppet master infinitely vast and cruel. As I moved closer, the dark shape resolved itself and the relief was replaced anew by rage.

Honey's body was lying across the slight rise of a dune. She must have passed out. Her head was thrown back, her eyes closed, her arms outflung. Grains of sand trickled down between her fingers, joining with the myriad of grains that formed the dune. A slow, steady trickle of grains, moving with infinite slowness, one by one.

Everything seemed to be happening in slow motion. I wondered how many grains remained in her hand, and how many were already on the beach, and how long it would take for each and every grain she clutched in her outflung hand to make its way down onto the sand beneath her. I seemed to be looking at the stars too, and it was as though Honey held all the stars of the firmament and was allowing them to gradually twinkle out as they joined the universe of grains that formed the beach. Holding infinity in the palm of her hand. I lowered my head to kiss her beautiful throat.

When Rob found me, I was still supine on the sand, my hands encircling Honey's waist. I was still counting the grains. The trickle had slowed, but every now and then—it might have been once a minute or once an hour—another grain would dislodge itself from the palm of her hand and tumble towards the beach, sometimes taking a few of its fellows with it. When I had counted all the grains that dropped from her hand, I would count all the grains on the beach, I was telling myself.

I saw his feet but continued to stare idiotically at Honey's body. Her torn throat filled my field of vision, and the darkened patch where her blood had run down into the sand.

Rob was standing there, looking down. From one hand dangled the vicious mask with its slit eyes and clattering sticks. He said tonelessly, "Do you know what you've done?"

I didn't know what he meant. I couldn't read his expression; it might have been victory, or pity, or despair. I was incapable of judging. The world reeled around me as I tottered to my feet. The hissing of the breakers was in my ears, but above it I swear I could still hear those grains trickling, the susurrus of them, from Honey's hand. Rob's face loomed in front of me, and the susurrus became a roaring of blood in my ears. At my back, I could feel the overtowering shadow of the force that filled the sky, seething with a malevolence I couldn't comprehend.

---

The police found Rob on the beach, his body not far from Honey's. His skull had been smashed open. Gritty sand was sticking to the bits of grey matter that poked out through his bloody scalp.

The police think I killed them both. They say I had their blood on my mouth, on my hands. The court believed them. My friends testified against me; I had been acting strangely before I ran off with Honey, they said. No one listened to what I said about Rob's Initiation of Death or his evocation of a brutal, timeless god. Now I'm in this barred cell at Goulburn, and every day I have to listen to the doctor prate of 'emotional storms'.

---

*Now I sit here, staring at the hourglass. They found it at Rob's place, next to the bed that I shared with Honey. They gave it to me when I asked for it. How did she die? Why? Why? Each time I turn it I hope to know the answer to those questions by the time the grains run out. But I never know. And I turn it over again, inverting it, starting again. I loved Honey. I would never have hurt her, but no-one else could be allowed to have her. All I can think of is the sand and of Honey. When the grains run out, I turn the hourglass; although I know she's dead, there's a sense in which I'm keeping her alive.*

*The sand at the top gets concave like a little pit. The sand makes little flurries at the bottom as it trickles through, piles up, fills the lower chamber. The grains begin to pile up at the bottom, slithering over each other. I watch fascinated, unable to draw my eyes from the unpredictable movements. Worlds form and reform in front of my eyes, shapes and figures dancing in the restless shift of the sands.*

*They tell me it still only takes an hour for the top chamber to empty into the bottom. I don't believe them, for the things I see last sometimes for days. Whole chains of events, strange visions. When the bottom chamber is full, I turn the hourglass and the process starts again. If I ever stop turning it, Honey's life will have run out. The grains flow down, incessantly, from top to bottom, from Heaven to Hell. I turn it over. And over. And over...*

# Tales of the Cthulhuesque

# BENEATH THE CARAPACE

*"While the greater number of our nocturnal visions are perhaps no more than faint and fantastic reflection on our waking experiences—Freud to the contrary with his puerile symbolism—there are still a certain remainder whose immundane and ethereal character permits of no ordinary interpretation."*

– H.P. Lovecraft

In legend-shrouded Beremythos, Euchronium's great High City, spring breezes waft through the apartments overlooking the Via Marcato. They whirl loose petals delicately from the Pavilion of Garnet near the Gasworks Bridge to the riverside barge-docks with their pontoons and pelicans, with their heaps of spoil; from the decadently luxurious Promenade of Fools, to the secluded, haughty terraces of the Genolan Estates. The streets throng with bravos, tosspots and ne'er-do-wells. Fishing boats bob in the harbour.

At dusk shadows lengthen and the sun retreats behind the city's ancient verdigrised copper-domed towers. Then the Sensualist Mask factions patrol the streets, prowling the Plaza of Ingenues and pursuing their curious rivalries amidst the abandoned observatories. If you listen you can hear them, whistling their calls—now like the murmur of insects, now like the shrill cries of startled kestrels fleeing the grass in the windswept marshes and ill-omened moorlands which enclose the city on three sides.

The assassin and kidnapper Darius Chaeish surveys the city from a high balcony window. Verdant parkland slopes away beneath the ivy-covered tower in which he tarries. Light, imbued with the peculiar absent clarity often observable in the better districts of Beremythos, as though everything is actually as real as it seems—with no intervening distortions—dazzles off the streets.

*That*, thinks Darius, *is the confusing part. This light's quality leads us to think we can reach out and touch the piazza's stuccoed walls, feel their solidity, or hold up an orange with its stippled skin, the shadows in its little hollows, and experience it in all its fullness.*

Darius knows otherwise. Everything in Euchronium is mutable, insubstantial, apt to metamorphose when you least expect it, even on such a bright clear day as this, with the golden light dappling the iridium steeples and terracotta tiles of the huddled city roofs.

Chaeish frets in his high apartment, awaiting his orders. *Deep calls to deep*, he reflects. *The orders will come soon enough.*

———⬦———

Osvaldo Carotid was scratching his grandfather's foot with a nail. Grandpa Lenten, a short, weak-mouthed man, lay spreadeagled on a threadbare couch in the living-room of his house in Ghrynne, a town far from Beremythos. Osvaldo worked hard, scratching Lenten's feet with the six-inch long iron nail which always hung on a loop of twine beside the tattered couch. Lenten's soles were yellow, callused and horny with age. Having them scratched this way was the old man's favoured method of gaining relief from his perpetual itch. To Osvaldo, Lenten offered his usual reward: tales of old Euchronium.

Some children would have hated this chore. Osvaldo, nine years old with unmanageable black hair and a hunger for knowledge, loved Lenten's stories. He happily indulged the old man.

Sometimes, the shifting light illuminating his wrinkled face, Lenten would recount how his first workplace owned a python which the owner kept in the cellar storeroom to keep down rats, and how the snake once dropped unexpectedly onto his shoulder from above as he entered the cellar to fetch supplies. On other occasions, he would wax lyrical about far places he had visited, things he'd seen or done in the fabulous 'olden days.' He stressed Osvaldo's heritage. "Ours are an old people," he would proclaim. "It's all yours now, Osvaldo."

Osvaldo, eager to grasp the world through another's eyes, didn't know whether or not to believe his grandfather's tales. He believed that his farfetched stories clustered around nuggets of truth, though he suspected Lenten added colour and savour to the tales by stretching the facts. Grandpa was an easy man to dislike, unpopular even with the family—'a little man,' one of Osvaldo's uncles once spat. Osvaldo knew many of the adult relatives had no time for him.

Occasionally they strolled along the strada, and the boy would bend to pick up shiny bits of coloured wire or broken glass. "My little bowerbird," Lenten would laugh. One day, Osvaldo found a curious fragile object in the gutter and held it up wonderingly to his grandfather for inspection. His grandpa handled the object gently, examined it, and gave it back to Osvaldo.

"You may keep it, my boy. It's the carapace of a Golden Drummer." He explained that there were many species of cicadas in Euchronium, all with different names and colours.

Osvaldo held the carapace carefully, looking at the tiny, translucent cast-off casing in awe. Returning home, he placed the insect exoskeleton on a little side-table in his room, giving it a sacred place of honour.

Another day, Lenten was relating one youthful journey east to the great city Beremythos, and the wonders he found there, when he fell unusually silent.

"Go on grandpa," Osvaldo begged, scratching away with the nail and hanging on every word, "tell me what happened next."

His grandfather remained thoughtful for some time, then finally instructed Osvaldo to visit the ancient city for himself one day. "Primal secrets lurk there, my boy. An intelligent lad like you could go far. Seek the Lodge of the Lamprey," he said, concluding his tale.

Increasingly, Lenten's mind would wander, as he lay back gazing at the high ceiling: "Every adventure is an empty cup," he would offer; or, even more cryptically, "deep calls to deep, my boy."

"What does that mean, grandpa?" Osvaldo wriggled impatiently, grasping at understanding. He needed all the world's secrets, right then and there. But the old man would only nod sagely, then whisper: "The Lodge of the Lamprey."

As the years passed, Osvaldo's grandfather often ushered him into the library in the dusty house, pressing him to read widely. The old man would take one ancient tome at a time from the brimming shelves and gradually pile them next to Osvaldo's elbow upon the great oaken reading table.

"Read!" he commanded. "These books describe the elder times." Then he would run his fingers through his thinning hair as he shuffled away.

Osvaldo immersed himself in legends and stories of old Euchronium, reading from such fabled volumes as the *Res Occulta Viscerum Mundi* of Veneficus, or the mysterious writings of Ibn Schacabao.

One volume described how, in Ancient Earth, in places called Crete and Malta, the people had held bizarre rituals. Picture plates showed dancing women, each adorned with a bee-like insect head, and with layered skirts representing the bee's body. The ritual was, the author averred, some kind of Dionysian orgiastic rite. The priestesses wore wings and danced a weaving dance in adoration of the Great Mother. One plate showed a statuette from a Cretan temple shrine depicting the goddess in her golden, fully-winged majesty. Osvaldo stared at those pictures for a very long time.

"Of course, we have a similar tradition in Euchronium," his grandfather wheezed. "Not bees though—here we venerate the giant cicada—creatures like that one you found, but grown enormous."

Lenten willingly revealed more to the fascinated boy about the gigantic cicadas of the Beremythos region. "They slumber long ages below the leaf-strewn loamy ground," declared Lenten. "Then, in one glorious summer they burst forth—creatures twice the size of a man with great veined wings."

Osvaldo was inexpressibly captivated by this legend. Habitually, he gazed up at the sourceless lights of the blackly velvet night sky, dreaming of the future day he would find himself in Beremythos. He read avidly, feeling this should indeed prepare him for the curious customs of Beremythos; but no matter how much he read, there was always so much more to explore in his grandfather's library.

---

When Lenten died, Osvaldo's adolescence became miserable. His parents—his mother Cristobal and his father Icardo—died suddenly too, taxed beyond endurance by their harsh lives. Most of his aunts and uncles soon followed his parents and grandparents, and without siblings, Osvaldo found himself utterly alone.

Though Icardo had converted the old house into a workshop, Osvaldo inherited some of his grandfather's books. He hired a manager to help him maintain his father's business, but Skrote was a shrewd, mean-spirited man who only managed to keep the business floundering somewhere between success and collapse. He called Osvaldo "Carotid," and the boy understood the family name was now his legacy.

Wounded by all this, he lived as though a blow was about to fall on him. When fortune favoured him, it seemed to him ominous; surely something savagely unfair would shortly knock him down? When misfortune came, as it inevitably did, he felt a strange relief. Difficulties confirmed his feelings of unworthiness, breaking the tension of the eternal wait for another crisis.

To ease his unhappiness, and because he had acquired a predilection for quality, he became an immaculate dresser. With his glossy black hair he was, in truth, not unattractive. As time permitted, he roamed Ghrynne's streets in his yellow-and-black chequered waistcoat, distracting himself with dreams. The air, laced with light rain, would fall coolly at intervals from a sky the colour of zinc. The smell of wet, fecund earth, the trees alive with colour, the intoxicating perfume from sprays of almond blossom and mimosa filling the spring gardens—these things soothed him.

At these times, everything seemed ineffable: the shadows' softness in the gardens; the surprising swiftness with which dusk fell into night; the desperate, half-fulfilled longing which tormented Osvaldo when the sun slid from view. To attempt to rationalise these feelings would, he thought, be like trying to analyse the butterfly's beauty by pinning it down and tearing off its coloured wings.

By evening the starry sky's supernal magnificence tugged inexorably at his being, as though summoning him to distant realms of black winds, of immeasurable vastness. At night, abed in his small room, with his precious cicada carapace close by, he drowsed and dreamed anew. He yearned to shuck off his physicality, to lose himself in a coalescing flow of time; but at a loss how to accomplish this, he could only imagine the indescribable splendour of the cosmos. At times his grandfather visited him in dreams, repeating old sayings, and Osvaldo would awake, Beremythos in his head.

Above all, he dreamed of going there. Over time, he knew, the city had existed under many different names—called 'Vriko' by some, 'Amergine' or 'Kikihia' by others. Days ground by. Despite the unpleasantness of working with Skrote, Osvaldo often managed a smile as he pictured himself making his way, someday, into the High City. When he might be able to get there, who knew? But he felt it as his destiny.

Each evening he stood on his terrace, gazing at the mists wreathing Mt Infererra, and the bluffs and crags intersecting with the sky. The old landslide's scar was visible there, and above the horizon, where the sun's crimson rays drenched the escarpment, the void's blackness hung like a velvet robe over the land. Beneath him, the small town of Ghrynne seemed to kneel in silent worship beneath a moon riding high and higher like a silvery goddess. The evening air was heavy with scents of night-blooming jasmine and roses.

He loved the countryside, but his daily town life was suffocating. No woman in Ghrynne had charmed him, and his work duties became the definition of tedium. Many years passed before he found in himself the power to change his circumstances.

At last, before another winter stole his will, Carotid sold the business to Skrote. He also sold the family home, determined to leave his old life and its loneliness behind. He gathered up his inheritance and the coins remaining from selling his grandfather's books, and left Ghrynne.

———————◇———————

Now in his mid-thirties, Carotid found himself struggling along the coast road under a sky brilliant with both much-loved and unfamiliar stars. He had only a few possessions, a scrawny pack-goat and a leathern wine-flask to quench his thirst on the road. The glamour of the eastern ocean, as he imagined it, had laid hold of him. Twilight came on, heavy with gloom; the birds fell silent but he heard the ocean's roar upon the rocks beyond the hill, and smelled the salty tide. Ilexes and pines rose twisted and windswept against the frosty stars. And because his grandfather had urged him on so often through dreams, he trudged on—through the crackling, dry leaves along the dirt road, which soared up to where Algol winked and leered among the boughs; on toward a place lodged in his very soul: his people's ancient seat.

He understood how far his grandfather had travelled from Ghrynne in search of their family's ancient blood. Carotid, a stranger to himself even now, anticipated feeling ill at ease in the strange city where they spoke a high tongue which he knew only from book-learning. Beremythos would surely be a place of mysteries, and his yearning to understand continued unabated. Making his last camp in the dark on the high hill above the city, he settled down to sleep on his outspread cape. In the morning, he would arrive at the city proper.

Early next morning, he woke, ate a meagre meal of bread and cheese, shaved off his growth of rough beard, and tidied his tangle of hair with the aid of scissors and a mirror from his bag. Then, gathering his few things, he began his journey's final leg. Below, the morning sun rose like a revelation on his destination. Nestled in a broad, rich valley, the city spread itself before him, glistening like a handful of rough-cut crystals in the sun.

Beremythos! The moment he beheld the breathtaking vista spread out below—the cupola on the great Council Hall blazing with reflected light—a powerful emotional flux peaked within him, seemingly the high tide of his existence. In a flash, the past of Euchronium under its multifarious names swept over him, identifying him with the stupendous totality of all things. Something of his grief welled up and ebbed away in that moment. He drank it all in—from the harbour, its shores glinting with alluvial deposits, to the fortified town with its sky-reaching steeples, chimneys and quaintly-peaked roofs.

Descending the cityward slope, he sought the Quarrion Gate, as his grandfather had advised him years before. He passed hushed, smoking farmhouses with curiously-pitched roofs, and stone walls covered in bright yellow lichens. Walking on, he heard the signboards of ancient shops and sea-inns creaking in the acrid breeze.

A small terrier ran out from behind a bush, barking and snapping at his heels, but he stood his ground until it slunk away. He wandered along the banks of the bruise-dark, oily river which flowed to the harbour. There, a maze of cranes and dry docks, piers and transportation tracks crowded beside the waterways. Long cascades of flowers trailed the riverbank—inflorescences of wisteria, blackwattle, clumps of Little Kurrajong with its rose-coloured bell flowers, the orange-yellow of dryandras, and here and there, delicate pink blossoms unknown to him.

A guard of the Quarrion Gate, clad in the regulation city uniform of a red-buttoned tunic, visored helm and halberd, examined his papers, then waved him through. The traveller noticed the guard's livery was emblazoned with a cicada motif, which was echoed in the design of his ceremonial pavise.

As Carotid passed within the city precincts, he noticed a young boy and girl, clad in blouses and peasant smocks, playing across the street. Carotid's eye caught the girl's; she poked her tongue at him. He glanced hastily away. What customs might he breach simply by his dress or manner? His euphoria fell away and his habitual self-doubt returned.

From where he stood, Carotid observed curving bridges and mazy streets cutting between the buildings. Great oaks and eucalypts raised their branches, shading roads of cobbles, asphalt and marble. Multifarious small lighted windows gleamed in the new morning like earthly reflections of the cold unwinking eyes of the Name Stars, long since banished from the sky.

———◇———

It took Carotid all day to get his bearings, wandering those badly paved streets. In the end, he found the Lodge of the Lamprey not far from the Quarrion Gate where he had originally entered Beremythos. Its swaying signboard, emblazoned with a device of a sharp-fanged lamprey head, confirmed his destination, for had it not been there all along? A double flight of iron-railinged steps led up to its front door.

He knocked heavily with the ponderous iron knocker. The door swung open, revealing the landlord—a wizened elderly gentleman clad in a loose robe with slippers, who clutched a quaint lit candle, as though fireworms had not yet been discovered. The Lodge's antechamber was filled with venerable, dark cabinets, bookcases, heavy tables and chairs, a cavernous fireplace. Its ceiling had massive smoke-stained exposed rafters. Though not overtly sinister, the place's age and gloominess, and dusty smell, oppressed Carotid after his many days travelling under the stars.

Still, he paid the landlord for a week's lodgings. The man guided him to a suite of rooms, which while not large, were simply and comfortably furnished. Once alone, Carotid sprawled on the bed, his eyes feeling bruised and aching. He fell into an uneasy sleep, from which he awoke in the dark feeling no better. His room's small-paned windows were curtained in rich brocade, but nevertheless admitted slits of light when pulled to. Some unpleasant scent was sourly present in the air, like the slightly metallic taste of fresh blood licked away from a wound. Hunger nagged at him but he was too tired to eat this night.

Going to the window, and parting the curtains, he saw again the demon star—yellow-blue, unthinkably ancient Algol—now poised above the city's Great Hall. Not long after, back on the bed, he fell again into an uneasy drowse. Apparently, he was here to stay.

---

Summer came early in Beremythos. It grew relentlessly hot. On Mugwort Street, the flame-trees were flowering crimson and gold. The air shimmered. People walked slowly, as if tranquillized by the heat. As summer advanced, Carotid would sit in the Kaminski Cafe each morning, drinking espresso. The delicious smells of bread baking in the patisserie opposite mingled with the pungent odour of horseshit baking on the open road. At lunch, he swigged periodically from a bottle of Red Dog Bitter and cut into a softly-cooked fried egg which spilled like liquid sunshine across the plate. Gradually, as the seasons progressed, he became accustomed to a new rhythm of life.

---

He generally kept cautiously to himself; yet the most extraordinary thing happened: he met a woman at the café. Her name was Visandia. She was of the city's highborn, but as a painter and an artistic spirit, she lived in an insalubrious city quarter.

"It was your black hair first attracted me to you," she said. Within the month, they became lovers.

Once acquainted, they moved swiftly to intimacy. She fell in love with his simplicity and his almost foolish love of beauty. A few weeks later she moved in, setting up her studio in his rooms at the Lodge—the Lodge with its dark oak flooring, its fusty rooms and its hard wooden benches pushed back against the passage walls. Her auburn hair, red lips and pale skin delighted him. In her presence he forgot his youthful unease with himself.

The café was their favourite rendezvous. They often saw there the local celebrity actress and dancer Ione Jonak, who would sit, like a dowdy bird of paradise preening its plumage, patting her hair, touching up her makeup in the mirror of a handheld compact. She apparently drank nothing nor ate a thing! Carotid never spoke to Jonak, but he often admired a faded poster advertising one of her stage performances which adorned the café wall; beneath sprawling filigreed lettering, she danced in a swirling red gown.

Carotid discovered the Lodge of the Lamprey was no mere rooming house, but the official home of some occult order which apparently transacted strange business—business into which he was loathe to enquire. He occasionally heard furtive whispers amongst the townsfolk of a sect called the Evokari, who were commonly considered the Lodge's masters, and members of the High Council of Beremythos. More than this, he was afraid to know or ask, although his dreams were growing steadily more disturbing.

Though his nights were long, his days were delightful. Through Visandia's eyes, he began to enjoy the city. Summer descended. Amber-white light stacked up in slabs, glaring off the shop windows, making him squint as he moved along the ever more familiar streets. He kept his head down too, lest he should attract undue attention; curious looks were still often cast his way.

The Kaminski's owner, Silvis, a voluble man with a round bald patch at the back of his head, having discovered Carotid could play the tambour, offered to pay him to play there, and so Carotid was able to supplement his dwindling inheritance.

He found playing helped him think. Ensconced in the café's performance corner his hands moved absently along the instrument's neck, coaxing out unusual tonal chordings and polyrhythms. The patrons showed their appreciation for his playing by listening raptly. Carotid would enter a blissful state, allowing his fingers to produce aleatory resonances. Being appreciated by the locals made him feel more at home.

In the evenings, after heavy rain, the warm night air smelled of pine needles, of grevilleas blooming amongst copses of teaks; the breeze thrummed amongst wires and weathervanes. Gas flares at Port Alveraz lit up a sky devoid of stars. Carotid welcomed the smell of more rain on the wind, the promise of coolness and relief like a long drink of iced tea. In the all-night cafes and bistros, the aromas of onions and garlic, the delicious scents of seasoned meats cooking, tantalised his senses.

Packs of Demented Boys roamed the deserted, unpaved alleys, banging on the house doors with their long, painted cudgels, or tormenting cats in back alleys amidst the lingering piles of scaled and stale refuse. Their pointed shark masks cast rhythmical shadows against the colourless stone and clapboard of decrepit buildings. Women leading their children home in the dusk, their heads thrust forward against the wind, trod heavily; men shouted as they left the inns; the iron-belled buoys tolled in the harbour.

On such evenings, Carotid would accompany Visandia as she walked the cobbled streets. The air was always rife with the voices of larrikin gangs yelling at each other around corners as they toppled carts of fruit or threatened to knife each other over some perceived insult. Talking as they walked, the couple would take the long, liquid amber-lined road home; they went late to bed on such evenings.

One of these nights, plunged in darkness so liquid-thick that Carotid felt he was wading through it, he was abruptly aware how exposed they were standing in the street, but Visandia, smiling, seemed unconscious of danger.

"Have you ever seen a giant cicada?" he ventured suddenly.

Visandia shuddered. "Not alive!" she answered.

A grey cat sidled up to them, meowing. Visandia, bending, lowered her slender hand to stroke the soft grey down between its ears. The animal purred softly at the attention, then suddenly darted away around the corner of a boarded-up building. Both he and the creature sensed some trouble, even if Visandia did not.

<hr />

Towards summer's end, Carotid was sitting once more in his favourite café. Over the city bright morning dawned. Towards noon, patches of brilliant sunlight dazzled off the street walls. White-frosted bottles shaped like icebergs lined the shelves behind the Café Kaminski's bar. It was dim and quiet inside. Cloths in shades of russet and pearlescent grey covered the tables. Carotid drank steadily a glass of cool ale, in silence. Trance paintings decorated the café walls. The images they presented depended on the angle from which you observed them; Carotid loved this. In the corner, a string quartet performed Elgar's *Enigma Variations*, a suite of music he knew originated, like the musicians' instruments, from Ancient Earth, once thought to have been part of old Euchronium.

Carotid drained his glass and set it down on the table. Beads of moisture trickled down its side. He was daydreaming of Visandia.

Yesterday, as they passed by a field of late summer flowers, she had insisted on wading in amongst them. She danced a marvellous little dance of happiness, causing pollen from the dense flower-heads to fringe her skirt with golden dust. Something about her that afternoon reminded him suddenly of his childhood fascination with the bee priestesses. He pushed the remains of his meal away as Quench came in.

He talked regularly with this old man. Quench wore a custard-coloured jerkin and ragged purple corduroy trousers. His grey, grizzled, shoulder-length hair framed a pallid face. He hobbled about with the aid of two wrist-strapped metal crutches.

"I say, Osvaldo, things are shifting," Quench announced. Only Quench and Visandia called him Osvaldo.

Carotid, preoccupied, didn't answer at once.

"Cat got your tongue, eh?" Quench winked and smiled, revealing rotting, uneven teeth.

Quench's manner, though blunt, was unthreatening; he seemed simply an old man battle-scarred by life. Deeply-ingrained creases ran from beside his nose down past his lax mouth to the chin. His loose skin smelled strongly of ripe cheese. His hands were spotted and scarred, his fingers callused. He seemed to enjoy chattering away about city life.

"Ever heard of the Master?" he asked, seating himself without invitation beside Carotid.

Carotid hesitated. He assumed the old man meant the Master of the members of the Lamprey Lodge. He glanced around, making sure they were not overheard.

"It seems to be a secret," he responded, his voice low.

Quench smiled crookedly. "You need to know about the Evokari." He raised his eyebrows. "They know all about you."

Carotid frowned, puzzled.

"The Evokari are everywhere..." Quench leaned forward 'til Carotid could smell his breath. "Even in our dreams."

Carotid shook off the mystique. "I'm happy here." He avoided Quench's gaze, toying with his napkin. "This city has made me so."

Quench nodded, as if he understood precisely. They sat together quietly, gazing out into the courtyard where street hawkers' bustle and buskers' songs filled the air with noise, and the sun shone through the lattice of the cafe's garden wall making a fretwork of light on the dusty street.

Carotid depended now on his meetings with Quench. They often talked like this, slightly cryptically, yet apparently to their mutual satisfaction. Carotid had come to consider Quench, initially simply a local character, a friend. Quench rarely sat at table; he often preferred to stand. But he would take a cup of strong, dark coffee when Carotid offered it, and this helped draw them together.

Later, on finding the Lodge quite empty, Carotid wandered down a long dark corridor to the building's rear. At the open back door, he gazed out over the grass beneath the twilit overhanging mulberry boughs. Wind rustled the leaves, swirling little eddies of dust around gnarled tree roots. Cicadas still chirruped their insistent grating. The insects' high thrumming and scraping sounded constantly. These were the small insects, he knew, mere cousins to the giants which arrived but once in an age. Carotid considered the way a bare-branched tree rose ghostly against the orange-streaked sunset sky.

That night he prepared cold rabbit for supper, and Visandia brewed some piquant tea. Her smallest movement was surpassingly beautiful to him. After dinner, she sat in a high-backed chair to read, leaning the volume on her knees. He watched her drowse, her black-tinted lashes lowering over half-closed eyes.

As evening wore on, she found renewed energy and walked about, expanding on her hopes and dreams, her painting, her love of the city.

"There is so much I want for us!" Her white hands, emphasising her thoughts, seemed to float in front of her slim body, which was draped in a velvet purple cloak clasped at the throat with the sign of her House—a totemic gold insect with jewelled eyes.

Later that long evening, lying with Visandia in his arms, Carotid watched the undependable light from outside shifting on the ceiling. The weather turned, the cicadas fell silent, and cold rain beat hard against the glass. He imagined grey mist sweeping the marshes surrounding the city—the marshes, with their weedy thrusts of vegetation and their treacherous walks.

At length, he thought he heard voices—*was it chanting?*—from else-where in the Lodge, but before he could focus more intently on the sound, he drifted into sleep.

———※———

"I'm not happy with my painting," muttered Visandia. Her current piece was upon the easel, and she was dabbing the brush at it, her lips compressed with effort.

"Why not?" asked Carotid, pulling on his shoes. "It's wonderful." Her work always impressed him.

"The original hologram I copied from had elements which I've lost in the transfer." She frowned and glared at the canvas. Today she wore a beaded orange bracelet, and two ornate silver rings. She was painting a landscape, its subject one of the old whitewashed city walls, partly obscured by fruit-vines running to tangled bramble.

"I'll leave you to your work," he said. "See you later."

She waved goodbye without turning away from her painting.

Outside, he surveyed the scene before commencing one of his rambles. Overhead, the hot morning sky, pale amethyst, was peppered with insects and squawking, planing gulls. A trio of birds cackled raucously, wheeling down and fluffing up their feathers as they perched upon the gables.

After his walk, which took him the length of Egamini St, he went to drink at the cafe and chat with old Quench. As the afternoon drew on, a temperature drop betokened an impending electrical storm. An unseasonable chill crept out from the alleyways. The leaden air tasted like salt. Beremythos citizens shut up their shops for the day.

Soon it began to pour. The storm littered the avenues with leaves from the trees which ran from Salton Clough to the city's oceanward edge. Tired of awaiting a lull, Carotid pulled his collar tight and stepped onto the rain-slicked pavement.

The street was dark and a little fetid where rainwater swirled in dirty pools and crevices. Streetlamps hung like eerily glowing eggs at intervals along the avenues beneath the bleached sky. Wind gusted up Abrahadabra Street, a blustery chill draught that stung the eyes, making them water. Mist pawed at Carotid's shins like grey, soft hands. Folk bumped into him as he passed.

He found himself in the de L'Isle Quarter, where the wind whistled and keened down mean alleys. Though rain spilled from the sky in a steady torrent, he toiled on, unconcerned about getting drenched. Raindrops showered out of the flame-trees; a silvery light edged the clouds. The waxing moon hung there like a lustrous grinning face.

He reached home close to midnight. Visandia's landscape had progressed well, and she had gone to bed. Carotid undressed and bathed, and went to her bedside. Her face was a pale oval in the dim light. The night outside was still as a crouched hare.

"Osvaldo? You're safe," she murmured sleepily.

The night's strange feel decided him. He reached behind the bedside cabinet and carefully withdrew something precious.

"I've been making you a love token," he said. From behind his back, he produced for her a brightly-painted mask crafted from papier-mâché. It was shaped like a bee's head, complete with mandibles, proboscis, antennae and all. The crafting had taken him weeks. "I'd like you to…perhaps you could wear it when we make love," he said, a little shyly.

She drew a deep breath and propped up on one elbow, rubbing her eyes. She took the headdress uncertainly, turning it in her hands "Oh, Osvaldo, it's beautiful. But I don't know."

"Do it for me?" he urged. "It would give me pleasure…"

She smiled, placing the mask upon the bedstead's pommel like a promise. He lay down beside her, allowing weariness to take him.

Next morning when he awoke, Visandia was asleep on her side, the sheets pulled tight around her neck, one tress draped across her cheek. In the slanting morning light, she was paler than ever. He listened to her quiet, even breathing. She rolled away, her back to him, still in sleep's clutches. Something—like a pair of vestigial wings—was protruding from between her shoulder blades. For some reason, he was unsurprised.

Then, reaching out for the bee headdress and placing it gently over her head, he moved her body against his, kissing her between the shoulder blades, between those curious buds, gradually moving down the curve of her spine. She made a slight sound, only faintly aware of his lips' light touch on her skin.

Carotid turned her to face him. She sleepily opened her eyes, putting her hands flat against his chest as he drew her close and opened her smooth thighs with gentle movements of his hand. The headdress, with its black-and-yellow stripes, swayed as she moved her head dreamily from side to side. He was surprised how quickly the heat rose in her as she placed one hand in the small of his back, encouraging him, and he slipped inside her.

Afterwards, with the mask removed, they lay holding each other in the hot little room, listening to the lodging-house sign creaking in the wind outside.

"The High Council has spoken," said silver-haired Darius Chaeish in his usual reedy tone, leaning easily on his long-bladed sword. "We must obey."

Beyond the parapet apartment's window, the dying sun struggled futilely with encroaching dusk. Insects in from the marshes, viridescent and delicately-winged, hovered thrumming, or darted tremulously past Chaeish's head. An acrid tang, borne upon the winds blowing in from the outlands, polluted the air and lay bitterly on Darius's tongue.

Annihilation Jezek answered him. "We need to be careful, Chaeish." The Jezek was a huge, dark-locked warrior, his massively muscled frame clad in blackened chainmail. His canny eyes shone with absolute devotion to the Evokari and their cause, but he would take only well-calculated risks.

"The Council believes the time is right," Chaeish countered. "A year ago, the city was too dangerous to bear even talk of such a thing. Circumstances have changed out there since the sacred cicadas' return." He gestured outward, downward from the Lodge's parapet room. "We have our instructions. There are no two ways about it."

"Easy for you to say," muttered the Jezek. He paced, his own sword dangling from one strong hand, its tip swinging pendulum-like to the rhythm of his thoughts. "But what if it's a lie, or a trap designed for us?"

Darius was obdurate. "The Council doesn't work that way. Nor does the Master." His obedience to the Evokari was unquestioning, and he would not be swayed.

At this, the Jezek looked grim. He kicked his boot against the step of the cold hearth. "Let's go then—if we must."

---

Carotid had lost his fondness for dreaming, but the dreams still came. They transported him—sometimes back to a childhood clubhouse his father had built for him, sometimes to misty mornings back in Ghrynne trudging to his work. Sometimes they took him to weirder places: corridors with false turnings, halls which narrowed so extremely he was unable to follow them further; city streets he seemed to know, but where he lost his money and other belongings and wandered aimlessly, unable to intuit how to rectify the loss.

One night, as forked lightning shattered the night sky to fragments, he dreamed of some stranger. The unknown man, his body covered head to toe in black ashes, was parading along, waving aloft the upper part of a torso, complete with head, on a long pole. Sunlight boiled down on them; a gangrenous glare shone in Carotid's eyes, half-blinding him. Before the dream ended, it altered, gradually accumulating strangeness until a huge wave, black and threatening, arose beside him, and crashed down over his head. His clothes became soaking wet, so heavy he was afraid he would drown. He woke sweating, in panic.

Visandia turned her head on the pillow, brushed her fingers across his cheek. "What's the matter?" she asked, raising herself up to look him in the face. She laid her delicate fingers across her throat, half-concealing the swell of her creamy breasts.

It was an awkward question. He shook his head. "Just a dream."

She was quiet a moment. Then she murmured "You dream so often!" adding, "It's all right," as she stroked his hair with soothing fingers.

Carotid was sceptical of premonitions, but the dream seemed like one; its unsettling impression lingered throughout next day. Visandia had business in the city, seeing a merchant about selling some of her work. Carotid busied himself, meanwhile, rehearsing for his next performance at the Kaminski. Laughter and music from a smoky bar across the street reached his ears. Laying down his instrument, he got himself a glass of water and gazed out the window overlooking the Fusion Galleria as he drank.

That night, he went to bed alone. Visandia often returned late; he assumed she would come in after him. But in the small hours, when he half woke and reached out for her, she was not there.

He adjusted the fireworm and looked around the room. Something was wrong. His glance fell on the bed's pommel, where the bee headdress had rested since the night she accepted it. It was missing! *Could she have taken it?* But a hollow feeling in his gut warned him some harm had befallen her.

He slept no more that night, making ready for first light. He went early in search of her. After retracing familiar streets, he found his anxious way to the railway tracks by the river. The air smelled of burnt diesel, rotting vegetables, blue-metal throwing off heat in the sun. The riverbank itself was sweet with the scent of lemon-grass. Wind-buffeted bells in distant towers in the town tolled gently. The atmosphere was singing with heat and light, despite which a damp, salty mist clogged the air. His eyes studied a hawk which floated languorously on the air currents circulating above the coastal swamp. Flights of birds wheeled and performed wave manoeuvres in the warm thermals of the valley below Beremythos. Carotid could hear the fluttering of wings as more birds soared aloft. But these were mere distractions from his worry.

Suddenly feeling vulnerable, he glared anxiously around. Nothing seemed out of the ordinary. The horizon was a smooth curve distinguishable by the ocean's cobalt turquoise-blue; above the horizon line, the sky shaded from light blue to sky's pale azure. *Deep calls to deep*, he remembered—his grandfather's words. Gazing back towards the city, he saw its revetments and battlements rising in clear relief against the sky. Away from the city, the countryside gleamed vividly. Thick mottled clumps of oaks and beeches waved green-yellow leaves; the low ground was studded occasionally with primrose.

He made to return home, when a sudden rushing sound alerted him. They were on him from behind before he could react. A black bag was forced over his head, his arms were pulled roughly behind him and secured. His eyes watered from dismay and shock.

His assailants shoved him ahead of them. He cried out: "Where are you taking me? What's happening?" but the heavy hood muffled his voice, and no answer came. They talked amongst themselves. Their words were unclear, but he thought he heard one man, with a nasal, reedy voice, mention, "The Yellow Sword" and "The Evokari." The first of these names meant nothing to him, the second little more.

Though effectively blind save for smudges of light visible through the opaque black cloth, he sensed they were following the trail, dotted with dwarf oaks, elder, ivy and hawthorn, which led back via the Quarrion Gate to the Lodge of the Lamprey. Eventually, they ascended two flights of steps. They had arrived back at the Lodge.

*Visandia!* he thought. *What if she has returned?* But somehow, he doubted it.

They took him up to his room and tied him unceremoniously to a chair. An hour or two passed. He wanted her safe, but now he was glad she was not home. He heard the men moving around, whispering amongst themselves. Carotid made several attempts to query them, but sharp blows curtailed his attempts.

He concentrated on easing the grip of his bonds. In time, he managed to loosen them. With a sudden action, he thrust them aside, snatched the bag from his head and in moments, was through the door, downstairs and out the back, running for safety.

It was already early evening. As he scrabbled over the uneven rocky ground behind the Lodge, the wind blew hard, blustering through his hair, spraying stinging grit in his eyes. Snatching a glance back over his shoulder, he saw the lighted gallery of the Lodge silhouetted against the star-punctuated sky. He tried to be swift and silent, but seed-pods and leaves cracked under his shoes as he fled. Above the sounds, he could hear the pounding boots of his pursuers.

Within minutes, they caught him. They used no lights and he could recognise none of them.

"By the gods, Jezek! He nearly got away," said the reedy-toned voice.

This gave Carotid one of the men's names, but he didn't recognise it. He was all at sea. One of the men jostled him roughly back towards the Lodge with forceful pushes in the back.

The other man answered in full-throated tones. "But he didn't."

———————◇———————

E ventually, the men took Carotid, hooded once more in the eyeless black cloth sack, out into the moonless night. They wended their way along ancient lanes, pushing him stumblingly ahead of them. His nostrils caught the scent of untended, night-fragrant gardens. "Nearly there, Chaeish," said the full-throated voice. Now Carotid knew both men's names, but it did him no good; both were strangers. He sensed they were gradually ascending an incline.

A great scouring wind swept the serpentine back alleys. Carotid detected dry lightning trembling out over the marsh. The wind in the treetops sounded like surf roaring on some uncharted shore. Or was it, he wondered, only the sound of his rising anger pounding in his ears?

Finally, the men jerked him to a halt and snatched off the hood. Dazed and disoriented, Carotid found himself outside the city's Great Hall. Chaeish and the Jezek, his captors, were fearsome-looking and fully armed; he dared not try to break away again.

A broad paved square surrounded the massive building; it was lined with tottering, ancient houses with small-paned windows. The Great Hall, its bronze cupola streaked with rust, towered above a votive statue of a giant cicada the colour of the leaves floating across the square and lying in drifts on its stony-winged back. More leaves swirled, whipped like wild spirits, swirled across the square's ground.

Stars glimmered on the harbour, though the lower town itself was largely invisible here. Townspeople crowded outside the Great Hall. Their purpose was unguessable, though none seemed perturbed by his humiliation at the hands of these men. He thought he glimpsed the dancer, Ione Jonak, amongst them, but in the semi-dark he could not be sure.

The people gathered around him holding lanterns in his face. He was jostled by elbows preternaturally soft, pressed by stomachs and chests abnormally pulpy.

The faces surrounding him were curious, peering, and unkind. The lanterns they held up made eldritch, drunken constellations in the dark; he shielded his eyes with his hand from their dazzling brightness.

Chaeish and the Jezek appeared at his side and forced him ahead through a dim black doorway into the Great Hall's entryway. Carotid had never felt more intensely aware of his own skin, muscle, and bone. *Perhaps*, he thought stupidly, *it's something to do with being in danger.*

Beyond fluted columns rising at intervals, he glimpsed the high walls of the chamber's interior, which were pierced with lanceolate windows. The walls themselves were nacreous, shining with a continually shifting opalescent light. They were interspersed by rich hangings of gold, vermilion and purple. The floor, of great uneven flagstones, had long ago been painted arterial red, but so covered was it in thick dust—little puffs of which rose up at each step Carotid took—that its original colour was no longer discernible. The space seemed illuminated by a sort of subterranean starlight.

In the great chamber of Euchronium's High Council, Osvaldo Carotid was shoved bruisingly to his knees upon the rough stone. His breeches and jerkin were sweat-stained and dirty from his ordeal. At first it was eerily silent within the Great Hall, save for the sputter of tall flaming braziers which lit the central space.

Loud stridulations suddenly racketed through the space—the unmistakable sound of cicada song.

A figure loomed up nearby, and Carotid, who had been staring about wildly and murmuring to himself in undertones of low astonishment as he entered the place, recognised with bewilderment that the figure was the old man, Quench. Momentarily he smiled, glad to see his friend; but then his heart turned cold.

Quench no longer wore his customary shapeless custard-coloured jerkin. He had donned richly red robes, the hood thrown back, the fabric woven with gold thread and bearing upon the breast the sigil of the Evokari. At his side hung a sword in a yellowish scabbard, but it remained sheathed. Quench's long tousled hair was no longer grey but dark; his face smooth and unlined. He advanced upon Carotid with perfect facility, his crutches abandoned. Carotid felt he should be angry. Instead, he only felt mild irritation. The old man had played him for a fool!

In one bright, sizzling breath, Carotid guessed the truth. Not only was the old man now young, but Carotid recognised him as, in some sense, his grandfather. *How could this be?* By some nameless sorcery, his grandfather—perhaps others here—had unnaturally prolonged their lives.

Quench—or was it Lenten?—flashed him a conspiratorial, yet apologetic smile, opening his knotty palms as he approached. The weak mouth, so familiar to Osvaldo from his youth, when Lenten had regaled him with tales of faraway times and places, opened. "I'm sorry for this, boy, but it is…necessary."

Carotid, feeling dwarfed by the chamber's titanic vaulted masonry, laughed bitterly, and gasped: "Who are you? Are you—the Master?"

"I am only the leader," said Quench. "The Master you will meet later. For now, you have been brought before the Evokari."

"The Evokari!" repeated Carotid, his cheeks suffusing with bright blood.

A sound of indefinite scrabblings: then from the chamber's black depths, there emerged a swarm of dim, indistinct figures—subservient, hybrid things. They were the servitors of the Council. A noxiously pungent odour of decay accompanied their entry. Moments later, Carotid heard the sounds of people from the square trooping into the hall.

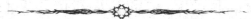

From his demeaning position, Carotid looked up and around. Shocked, he saw that a succession of alien beings had emerged from the darkness to surround him. As his vision adjusted he realised, with wonder and horror, that these bizarre visages belonged to the High Council's officers—the fabled Evokari. Each was assisted to enter the chamber by the dwarf-like, black-winged servitors who manoeuvred the tall, robe-draped figures into place via moving platforms. Each human body, peering down at Carotid, was encased in a preserved, vividly-painted carapace, each from a different species of sacred cicada.

Immediately before him was a Tiger Prince, its carapace painted black-and-orange, restoring its living appearance. Craning his neck to see around the circle of swaying, bobbing cicada heads, Carotid beheld next a Green Grocer, its exoskeleton an incredible emerald green; next to it, the great Yellow Monday with its black-and-orange head; a brown-bodied Chocolate Soldier; and further along, an extraordinary Blue Moon, whose shell he found particularly beautiful, despite his growing terror.

As he scrabbled around on his knees, taking in the whole circle, he saw leaning towards him the great swaying heads of the Masked Devil (a black masklike pattern between its eyes), the Cherrynose with its dark stripes encircling its thorax, legs and red-spotted proboscis, the Razor Grinder with its dull brownish-black body, and the Bagpipe, named for its hugely swollen belly. Some councillors wore male shells and some female, complete with ovipositors.

Completing the circle were the Floury Baker, its light floury markings striping a green body; the Golden Emperor with its incredible golden wings; the Sandgrinder with its distinctive white-banded black body; the Double Drummer with its orange-black body and loud amplified call; and the Brown Bunyip, with its long, slender lightly-banded brown body. Lastly, the Black Prince, its great matt-black shell glistening like an obsidian mirror.

Darius Chaeish and the Jezek, their weapons unsheathed, had retreated to one side, outside the circle.

Euchronium's sacred myths rose again in Carotid's mind. His grandfather's explanations—how Euchronium's peoples believed only the mature adult insects, or imagos, with their fully-formed wings, partook of the sacred power. The shells of even giant nymphs were never used. The gigantic insects would moult frequently during their short life-spans, but it was true: only the last of the shed exoskeletons were held suitable for the Evokari's sacred rites.

Quench seemed to read his thoughts. "In years like this, the Year of the Return," he told Carotid, "we send harvesting teams into the wastelands. They search out discarded exoskeletons attached to the sides of ruined cottages, or to tree-boles there. The harvested shells are brown, their original bright hues lost when the great sacred insects burst forth in their periodic excursus from under the earth. The people carefully unhook the enormous claws and carry the casings back to the city, to be lacquered and shellacked for use as colourful ritual costumes for the High Council." He gestured towards the High Councillors. Then, looking back at Carotid: "But you have been told all this. Now you behold them."

Carotid knew also that the exoskeletons were virtually weightless, but because their petrified bodies and limbs were brittle, immobile, the unhuman servitors were required. The servitors made it possible for the Evokari to enter the Chamber having donned their stiff carapaces. For matters of high state, the Councillors were placed facing the Circle's centre.

The Evokari's expressionless insect masks served to hide their intentions, their lacquered eyes blankly unreadable. Carotid felt the 'faces' of the figures surrounding him might as well be fashioned of wax. Though he knew they were at least partly human, Carotid could only think of these beings as creatures—the insects as which they dressed.

Suddenly the Chocolate Soldier spoke in a hoarse, percussive tone, "The Evokari know all."

The Black Prince responded in a resounding roar, "The Evokari see all."

The Razor Grinder continued the litany, its voice shrilly piercing, "The Evokari hear all."

"Knowing, seeing, hearing—all are one to the Evokari," intoned the Floury Baker.

The city people, who had formed an outer circle around the Evokari ring, responded in kind, their lanterns flickering only dimly now in the cavernous space. "Knowing, seeing, hearing—all are one to the Evokari," chorused the voices.

The formidable Cherrynose spoke in its rattle-like voice, "The Evokari are the guardians and emissaries of the Master."

A ratcheting, susurrating noise echoed around the chamber as the entire circle of Councillors lent their insectile voices to repeating this chant.

Swiftly, Quench drew the red hood of his robe over his head. He motioned to the servitors, making certain ritual hand gestures and intoning in some unfamiliar tongue in a deep, baritone voice which raised more strange childhood memories in Carotid's mind.

At this, a weird green flame sprang up in the chamber's centre. It was a sickly, chlorotic light rising in a belching column almost to the shadow-drowned ceiling, which was coated with a venomous verdigris from its continual upflow. Carotid struggled to his feet, swallowing. Alien music reached his ears. His mind filled with images of brooding hills and dusky darkness.

The Evokari began, under the Black Prince's direction, to drive Carotid towards a barred enclosure at the rear of the Great Hall's main chamber. The circle of people broke, as the councillors swarmed, forcing Carotid on; the cicada shells glared down on him with bulbous, empty eyes. The lurid shimmering of the greenish flame washing the walls suggested the insidious lapping of sunless waters. Chaeish and the Jezek came behind.

Inside the enclosure, where hordes of damnable servitors awaited, Carotid pulled up before rows of torture chairs like complex evil thrones. On ranks of shining tables, lay serried rows of elaborate cutting implements with wicked-looking curved and serrated blades.

Beside one of them, a woman curled foetally on the floor. He blanched. It was Visandia, her head lolling at an ungainly angle. The missing *papier-mâché* bee headdress, which must have played some part in her abduction, lay nearby. She still breathed shallowly, but her face was pallid; blood trickled from the corner of her mouth. The top half of her high-collared embroidered gown had been torn away, and something was wrong with the skin of her beautiful back.

As Carotid neared her, he realised the redness meant her flesh had been flayed raw. A sharp, dark pain flared up in his gut. "Visandia! No!" He surged across the floor towards her, but strong arms grasped and restrained him. So furious was he that they had to beat him to comply; the heaviest blow knocked him half-unconscious and he slumped. Several of the ungainly servitors removed his clothing and strapped him, naked, despite his screams, into one of the chairs. Immediately, they administered the drug.

Wide-eyed with fear, Carotid stared around the cavernous space, eyes flicking from one assailant to the next. "What is this?" he cried out. "I have been *invited* to this town. You have no right!" he shouted defiantly. He fought the panic, his heart racing, glancing wildly around at the lichen-mottled walls carven from solid rock. The place was a Stygian grotto, a hellish temple of unknown darkness.

"You are foolish, and shallow," said Quench. "You have read much but observed little. It is decreed you should serve the Master. For here, blood calls to blood, and deep calls to deep."

Carotid couldn't imagine what he meant. One of the servitors motioned him to stillness and placed a metallic thing like a grappling hook around his head to secure it. Carotid's eyes darted from side to side. A thin film of perspiration beaded his upper lip. Some gelatinous substance dripped from the device attached to his temples.

"Why are you doing this?" he rasped incredulously. Only silence answered him. "I'm no more than a bower-bird," he husked, amazed to hear the words amplified in a desperate, hollow voice. They disregarded his distress. He tried to heave himself out of the chair, but this time he was trapped more securely. A servitor struck him again on the temple; blood streamed from the wound, and his body went slack.

As the drug entered his bloodstream, his mind was filled with protean shapes.

Ⅎll feeling in his body receded, but his mind swam giddily with visions of a land of vast primeval plains where huge conifers, gingkos and cycads grew profusely. At first, he seemed suspended above a world of ancient pines and tree-ferns. His consciousness traversed floodplains and estuaries and beheld vast coastal forests.

As his drug-induced nightmare deepened, he seemed to walk unending mudflats, knowing himself to be in Gondwana, that ancient continent which preceded the formation of the Great Southern Land, in Euchronium's dimmest past.

His mind or spirit body seemed to roam through aeons of time, pausing here at the site of a vast asteroid-inflicted crater, and there at places where dinosaurs—vast stegosauruses and sauropods—stood drinking at the water's edge, or tearing trees from the ground with their massive claws and sharp teeth.

Now and again he glimpsed in the distance creatures which seemed gargantuan masses of protoplasm. His bodily form appeared to have solidified. He shivered, steeling himself for some awful moment when he might need to defend himself from these huge, unidentifiable puffed things. His teeth chattered wildly with cold and fear. Terrifyingly vast masses, like shapeless congeries of protoplasmic bubbles, with myriads of temporary eyes forming and un-forming as pustules of greenish light, the creatures moved sluggishly through nautilus-strewn landscapes. He stumbled away across opalised backbones and fossilised fins of reptilian sea-creatures, across red earth built up upon unbelievably ancient reefs.

Once, he stood on the shores of a secretive, immemorial inland sea filled with lungfish and turtles, and surrounded by lush rainforest. He lost all sense of time; he might have been here for millennia. Then, looking up, he saw the demon star Algol blazing in the heavens, and with that, he lost consciousness again.

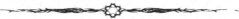

The next thing he knew, Carotid was returning to his physical body in the torture chamber. As he awoke, eyes crusted from his drugged sleep, his head pounding, he realised he had been unbound from the chair and was stretched out on the floor. Darius Chaeish and the Jezek were out of sight. But the ghoulish, tittering servitors formed a semicircle around the main chamber's blazing fiery column; the ghastly flame threw capering shadows against the gold, vermilion and purple hangings. Carotid felt something was locked up in his skull, scrabbling to get out. Dazed by his prehistoric journey, he stared helplessly at the servitors. They seemed lost in adoration of the sick, unhealthy flame, which radiated deathly corruption as it spouted volcanically from depths inconceivably far below.

Beyond the windows, false dawn lightened the sky. Burning away his terror, his resentment was rising, boiling up in him. He struggled up again. *Visandia—where had they taken her?*

Carotid's heart thumped angrily in his chest. Whatever he feared seeing, the reality of what he saw next was far worse.

At the torture chamber's furthest extremity was another enclosure, its space created by a series of massive metal bars running floor to ceiling, like a huge prison cell. Into the bars was set a grilled metal portcullis; chains to raise and lower it were entwined around supports on either side. Beyond the heavy vertical bars, a shadow moved in the darkness.

As the shape advanced towards the bars, flashes of a mucoid yellow half-light illuminated it at irregular intervals. What Carotid saw was neither a mantis nor a spider, yet somehow like both—not altogether a writhing mass of decomposing and pustulous tentacles, or a squamous-skinned amphibian, or a giant suppurating whip-scorpion, but some weirdly misshapen, monstrous hybrid of them all. Its multifaceted eyes imparted to it the look of implacable cruelty characteristic of most insects. It was a look Carotid had long believed humans consider motiveless since they were unable to comprehend the insectile mind.

The thing was definitely staring at him. Its jointed legs, which looked too thin to support its weight but were undoubtedly enormously strong, moved unevenly up and down. Clots of dried blood clung to them, and to its long and pointed palps. Algol's light shone from it and Carotid instinctively felt the creature existed equivocally, as though located in both deep stellar space and here on this plane. The light emanating from its own body, both alluring and alarming, glistened off splashes of red—like alien birthmarks, or the bright spots of colour one might see on a poisonous fungus, disfiguring its hideous skin.

Horribly fascinated, Carotid gave vent to an involuntary gasp. An overpowering stink of gore emanated from the enclosure. Choking, he tottered forward for a closer view, but the thing's incredible, impossible size stopped him in his tracks. "The Master!" he breathed.

It was distorted, fabulous, beyond logic. Ever-changing biolumin-escent threads flickered through its body, lighting the skin from within. Though repellently huge—Carotid sensed the visible portion was the merest hint of its actual bulk—it seemed somehow provisional, indefinite, as if at any moment it might lose its hold on existence. A pungent smell of electrical energy, like the charged aftermath of a lightning-flash, filled the air. Carotid wondered if the sacrifice of a life to this fitfully moving abomination was intended to make it stronger.

Carotid's hair stirred with horror, and a chill crept up his spine. The geometry of the place was all wrong. Everything in there was frangible, subject to strange physics irrelevant to the outside world. Carotid could hear the muffled clack of the creature's mandibles; its flagella flailed menacingly. The thing emanated an aura confusing to the senses. Carotid's head swam anew, and he witnessed a multiplicity of selves emerge and retreat sickeningly within his mind.

Even from this distance, he was sure he saw bones in the enclosure. Some were white, picked clean; others still carried gobbets of raw flesh. Against one wall lay the remains of a human ribcage. The enclosure's rough floor was stained and spattered with half-congealed blackish blood, out of which hanks of hair and scraps of blood-stiffened cloth stuck up here and there. *How many have died in there?* he wondered.

Carotid began to shake. Tears rolled uncontrollably down his face. "Is it imprisoned?" he managed to ask.

A dry chuckle came from the chamber's dim recesses. Quench, or Lenten, or whatever his grandfather's real name might be, emerged once more. His contemptuous scowl pinned Carotid to the spot. "The master cannot be imprisoned. It *chooses* to dwell here." He motioned again, and servitors laid hold of Carotid, one at each arm. Their stench was unbelievable, and Carotid averted his head in disgust. He tried to wrest himself free, but they were too strong.

"You will bow before it, as we do. You should be grateful for a few crumbs from the Master's table," said Quench. "We will allow the girl to live, and you will have immortality." His irises veiled themselves in blackness. Uneven light blotched his face. He pointed across the room. "*There*—there is where you belong now."

Carotid gazed towards the room in which the Master roiled and writhed, its innumerable eyes shining like baleful, burning orange suns. Transfixed with dread, Carotid laughed hysterically on a high, sustained note, which wavered and fell away. "Why should I believe you?" he demanded.

"The Astral Sacrifice must go willingly to the Master," declared Quench.

Carotid suddenly felt the fight go out of him; further resistance seemed pointless. His shaking subsided. Quietened by shock, he stopped tugging and struggling.

Beyond the chamber windows, the sky brightened with flare-lamps. They were being fired off by the crowd outside and sucked into the sky's ravenous maw. In the main chamber, the flame's leprous light still washed unnaturally over the walls; its flickering greenish glare hurt his eyes.

He stared down for a few moments at his shoes. A movement along his arms caught his eye: chromatic patterns of light, like those which pulsed in the Master's body, wormed up and down his forearms beneath the skin.

Carotid drew a long, ragged breath. Escape was impossible for him now. From the corner of his eye he saw Visandia brought into the light, supported and escorted to a place of safety by Ione Jonak. He knew he had no choice. He had been born for this—for her.

Two of the malformed servitors raised the heavy portcullis, whose chains rattled as it went up.

As he was prodded forward towards the space where the Master—
that great, amorphous, star-spawned being—squirmed and floundered,
Carotid lowered his head and in another moment, without so much as a
fleeting backward glance, he entered the enclosure and was swallowed
by the lightless entrance.

# WAITING FOR CTHULHU

## A Play in Which the Stars Come Right, Twice

Act I

*A country road. A star. Evening.*
*Whateley, sitting on a lone Mound, is trying to take off his boot.*
*He pulls at it with both hands, panting. He stops, exhausted, rests,*
*begins again. As before.*
*Enter Pickman.*

Whateley: (*giving up again*). Nothing to be done.

Pickman: I'm beginning to come around to that opinion.

Whateley: Why don't you help me?

Pickman: The most merciful thing in the world, I think, is the inability of the human something to correlate all its contents. Who said that?

*Silence.*

Pickman: Charming spot. Inspiring prospects. Let's go.

Whateley: We can't.

Pickman: Why not?

Whateley: We're waiting for Cthulhu.

Pickman: Ah! (Pause) You're sure it was here?

Whateley: What?

Pickman: That we were to wait.

Whateley: He said by the tree.

*They wait.*

Pickman: That passed the shadow out of time.

Whateley: It would have passed in any case.

Pickman: Yes, but not so rapidly. That was as rapid as the

decomposition of the old man in 'Cold Air.'

*Pause.*

Pickman: The stars, look at the stars.

Whateley. Were they not there yesterday?

Pickman: Yes, of course they were. Do you not remember? We nearly killed ourselves trying to make them come right. But we couldn't. Do you not remember?

Whateley: You dreamt it.

Pickman: Is it possible that you've forgotten already?

Whateley: That's the way I am. Either I forget immediately or I never forget.

*Pause.*

Whateley: We always find something, eh Pickers, to give the impression that we exist?

Pickman. Yes, yes, we're magicians. But let us persevere in what we have resolved, before we forget.

*Enter Upton and Angell. Upton drives Angell, who wears a Dagon tiara, by means of a rope passed around his neck. Angell carries a heavy bag, a folding stool, a picnic basket and a strange metallic object of undetermined interstellar origin.*

Whateley: Is that him?

Pickman: Who?

Whateley: (trying to remember the name) Er…

Pickman: Cthulhu.

Whateley: Yes.

Upton: I present myself. Upton.

Pickman (to Whateley): Not at all!

Upton: You took me for Cthulhu.

Pickman: Oh no, not for an instant, sir.

Upton: Who is Cthulhu?

Pickman: Oh—he's a kind of Old One. A friend of ours.

Whateley: Nothing of the kind. We hardly know him.

*Upton and Angell picnic on goods from Angell's basket—chicken, bread and a bottle of wine. Angell slavers, then kicks Whateley violently in the shins.*

Whateley: Oh, the swine! He's crippled me.

Upton: (ordering Angell to lecture): Speak, pig!

Angell: Given the existence as uttered forth in the *Necronomicon* of the Old Ones quaquaqua alas alas on the skull the skull the skull in R'lyeh abode of non-Euclidean geometry...so calm... unfinished...

*His tiara falls off.*
*Exit Upton and Angell, Angell on rope as before.*

Whateley: We can still part, if you think it would be better.

Pickman: It's too late now.

*Silence.*

Whateley: Yes, it's too late now.

*Silence.*

Pickman: Well, shall we go?

Whateley: Yes, let's go.

*They do not move.*

CURTAIN


Act II

*Next Day. Same Time. Same Place.*
*Pickman's boots front centre, heels together, toes splayed. Angell's Dagon tiara at same place. The tree has four or five tendril-like suckers.*
*Enter Whateley agitatedly. He halts and looks long at the tree, then suddenly moves feverishly around the stage. He halts before the boots, picks one up, sniffs it, manifests disgust, puts it back carefully. Comes and goes. Halts extreme right and gazes up at the sky as though scanning distant galaxies, shading his eyes with his hand. Comes and goes. Halts extreme left, as before. Comes and goes. Halts suddenly and begins to sing loudly:*

Cthulhu came from the Outer Spheres
Mankind to dominate
He lay in R'lyeh eternal
With nought to do but wait.

Then all the sailors came clambering
And found his watery tomb...

*He stops, broods, resumes.*

Then all the sailors came clambering
And found his watery tomb
And wrote upon R'lyeh's walls
For the eyes of those to come.

Cthulhu came from the Outer Spheres
Humankind to dominate
He lay in R'lyeh eternal
With nought to do but wait.

Pickman: We are happy.

Whateley: We are happy. *(Silence)*. What do we do now, now that we're happy?

Pickman: Wait for Cthulhu. (Whateley groans. *Silence*) Things haven't changed since yesterday.

Whateley: And if the stars don't come right?

Pickman: (after a moment's incomprehension): We'll see when the time comes.

Whateley: Everything oozes.

Pickman: Look at the tree.

Whateley: It's never the same ichor from one second to the next.

*Pause.*

Whateley: All the dead Old Ones.

Pickman: They make a noise like tentacles.

Whateley: Like suckers.

Pickman: Like tentacles.

*Silence.*

Whateley: They all speak together.

Pickman: Each one to itself.

*Silence.*

Whateley: Rather they susurrate.

Pickman: They gibber.

Whateley: They leer.

Pickman: They gibber.

*Silence.*

Whateley: What do they say?

Pickman: They gibber about their lives.

Whateley: To have lived is not enough for them.

Pickman: They have to gibber about it.

Whateley: To be dead is not enough for them.

Pickman: It is not sufficient.

*Silence.*

Whateley: They make a noise like Shoggoths.

Pickman: Like shantaks.

Whateley: Like Shoggoths.

Pickman: Like night-gaunts.

*Long silence.*

Whateley: Say something!

Pickman: *Cthulhu ftaghn*!

*Long silence.*

Whateley *(in anguish):* Say anything at all!

Pickman: What do we do now?

Whateley: Wait for Cthulhu?

Pickman: Ah!

*Enter boy right. He halts. Silence.*

Boy: Please, Mister. *(Pickman turns)*…Mr Albert?

Whateley: Off we go again. *(Pause).* Do you not recognise me?

Boy: No, sir.

Pickman: It wasn't you came yesterday?

Boy: No, sir.

Pickman: This is your first time.

Boy: Yes, sir.

*Silence.*

Pickman: You have a message from Cthulhu.

Boy: Yes, sir.

Pickman: He won't come this evening.

Boy: No, sir.

Pickman: But he'll come tomorrow.

Boy: Yes, sir.

Pickman: Without fail.

Boy: Yes, sir.

*Silence.*

Pickman: Has he tentacles, Cthulhu?

Boy: Yes, sir.

Pickman: Yellow or…(*he hesitates*)…or green?

Boy: I think they're mottled, sir.

*Silence.*
*Exit boy, right.*

Pickman: We'll hang ourselves tomorrow. (*Pause*). Unless Cthulhu comes.

Whateley: And if he comes?

Pickman: We'll be driven mad.

*Pause.*

Pickman: Well? Shall we go?

Whateley: Yes, let's go.

*They do not move.*


CURTAIN.

# THE HORROR IN THE MANUSCRIPT

## with Lindsay Walker

*Letter to Inspector William H. Morrison, Boston Police Department, from Hollis Chalmers, Solicitor, River St, Arkham:*

14 July, 1955

Dear Morrison,

**Y**ou may have heard that my old friend Arthur Danvers passed away about the middle of last month at the age of seventy-four. Although years my senior, he was on very good terms with me for the greater part of his adult life, and presumably for that reason appointed me, shortly before his death, the executor of his will. Now, knowing you to be busy at this time of year, I will come straight to the point: among Danvers' papers was a curious document which I have enclosed, since it has a bearing on a case with which you were involved here about twenty years ago, and because it may be of personal as well as of official interest.

Danvers left no instructions as to either its preservation or destruction, and his two sons have informed me that the disposal of the miscellanea is entirely in my hands, so I feel justified in forwarding it to you. It purports to be a record of the events leading up to the disappearance and suspected murder of John Symes. You will remember that attempts to question Danvers thoroughly about the matter either at that time, and on all subsequent occasions, proved fruitless. Doctors at St Mary's Hospital advised restraint, surmising that probing could have caused a recurrence of the breakdown that had resulted in his being there. The investigating officers, finding that even cautious questions on the subject made Danvers hysterical, reluctantly agreed. As there was no other person known to have been in contact with Symes just prior to his disappearance, the public assumed that he had followed the example of his house's previous tenant and departed for regions unknown. The police, after further attempts at questioning over the next two years, each time with the same lack of results, filed the case as 'unsolved.'

The document states that there was in fact another witness, a doctor from Arkham. With the idea of finding out whether or not he knew anything about the affair. I made inquiries but found that the only doctor dwelling in Salstonstall St at the time of Symes' disappearance died several years ago. As to the facts of the account, it seems evident to me that Danvers must have written it while still under an appreciable mental strain after his breakdown, for his writing towards the end is agitated and incoherent, and almost neurotic in its implications. The papers among which it was found were very old, and perhaps Danvers had forgotten about its existence, or else might have destroyed it himself. He certainly displayed no signs of mental unbalance in the last twenty years of his life, though he apparently lost interest in his extensive art collection. However, you must form your own opinion — I would be interested to know what you make of it.

Yours,
Hollis Chalmers

*The Manuscript of Arthur Danvers*

# I

John Symes had always been a close friend, although in later years I had seen very little of him. His studies, which I understood to be extremely taxing, were presumably the reason for his solitary existence. He had once been renowned as a Boston socialite, and had startled all his friends with his sudden departure to the old family home at quite a distance from the city. His popularity arose from his organisation of séances and Ouija sessions at his own home and at those of acquaintances; I was amazed, as he was so knowledgeable in the realms of the occult, that he would condescend to arrange such parlour games for the pleasure-seeking elite of Boston. Some thought his decampment from the city the result of a widely rumoured romance with the wife of a prominent citizen; but this explanation I found most unlikely. The affair was, in all probability, the result of a number of social calls and a barrage of idle gossip. He did leave, however, after receiving a small shipment of books from overseas and I assumed he had retired to study them and perhaps write his promised thesis on ancient myth and religion. Yet, I became deeply disturbed as his seclusion dragged from weeks into months and the public heard almost nothing of him. None of his friends had seen him for at least six or seven months, and his tersely worded telegram came as a pleasant but unexpected surprise. Without any explanation, he insisted that I join him immediately, and although my children had of late occupied my attention almost exclusively, in an effort to forget the saddening death of my wife, innate concern added to a certain curiosity impelled me to obey my friend's summons.

My drive through the cold New England evening recalled to me strongly our early years together, as we had often travelled through this region on our way to visit various mystics and antiquarians in the archaic, legend-haunted town of Arkham further inland. We had both been deeply interested in an intellectual way, though not greatly involved, in the occult. I had been interested mainly from the angle of amateur psychological analysis, maintaining that those who practised the occult were to some extent deluded. Symes, on the other hand, was convinced that something substantial lay behind many of the preternatural events of which reports continually appeared in newspapers nationwide. My enthusiasm for the esoteric had waned over the years, though I was still an avid collector of the strange and grotesque in the form of statuary and artwork. Symes' interest, I knew, far from deteriorating, had grown into a passion bordering on obsession. This bent for the fantastic had driven away all but two or three friends of long standing, myself amongst the latter, who refused to let it affect their respect and feeling for him.

I knew that I was now nearing his house, and as I turned off the main road, I felt the full impact of the depressing surroundings. The trees by the road were low and gnarled, and the streams that flowed sluggishly under the bridges I crossed from time to time were swollen with rain. As the darkness under the thick foliage deepened, I switched on the headlights of the car, but they were of little use, seeming unable to pierce the dark wall of trees or to reach far ahead into the blackness. Driving was hazardous and made more difficult by the manoeuvring necessary to avoid the bumps and potholes in the rough road, which wound on until it reached the base of the sloping hillside directly ahead. At that point, the trees opened out and I saw at some distance Symes' partly derelict mansion. Unsurprisingly, only one room had a light burning in it, for he had dwelled alone since his retreat to this backwoods region of the country.

The land on which the house stood had once belonged to an ancient

Indian tribe and for this reason the characteristically superstitious native farmers, few though they were, would not venture near the area. The house itself was an architectural nightmare, built as if under constantly changing plans. The original structure had been erected in the middle eighteenth century and had been added to by later generations of the Symes family, resulting in extensions of rambling wings, which jutted from the bulk in all directions, and attics that mushroomed atop the building, giving it the appearance of another storey. The effect of the ungainly creation was one of complete dominance over its surroundings; the only break with its antiquity of appearance was the power lines which ran from the house along the side of the hill in the direction of Arkham. Left untenanted since Symes' great-uncle, Banfield Symes, had left for overseas where it was presumed he died, the house was in only a moderately good state of repair as far as I could see; moreover, the grounds were unkempt and a sinuous, vine-like vegetation grew profusely around the base of the building.

I swung my car into the overgrown driveway and could see the weeds becoming thicker and taller as I drew near the side of the house. To my annoyance, I had to pull up twenty-five yards or so from the house to avoid possible damage to the car if I tried to force it any further through the obstructing weeds. I got out, leaving in the car what little luggage I had brought with me and made my way through the weeds until I reached the short stony path leading to the main entrance. The paint, I noticed, had almost completely flaked off the weatherboard walls, and as I reached the door, I saw what appeared to be a slightly phosphorescent glow emanating from the bare, dark boards around it. This occurred in irregularly spaced patches, and as I leaned towards the wall for closer inspection, a pungent odour assailed my senses. So strong was it that I was forced to lean heavily against the door in order to keep my balance.

The door was slightly ajar, however, and gave way, resulting in my stumbling into the hallway most unceremoniously. Recovering my faculties, I looked around for my host, whom I assumed would be in the hall by now, but I could see by the light issuing from the drawing room that it was empty save for myself. Confused, I went along the hall to the dining room. Perhaps, I thought, something had delayed Symes from laying out dinner. However, turning on the light, I again found the room unoccupied. Approaching the dark, mahogany table in the centre of the room, I discovered that it was set with a meal for one; by the plate lay a leaf torn from a notebook. Upon it was a message, scrawled in apparent haste and addressed to me:

*Arthur—Sincerest regrets. Shall be out all night. Treat the house as your own. Shall see you in the morning—John.*

This was not at all typical of Symes who, prior to his retirement to the country, had always catered to the needs of his guests in hospitable style, and I was somewhat irritated by his absence. He had called me down urgently, and it was due to my reasoning that such a summons must have been justified that I had consented to travel directly to Symes' house. It now appeared that my presence was unnecessary, at least for the next twelve hours or so; time which I could have spent finishing the cataloguing work on which I had been engaged at the time of Symes' message.

Not feeling particularly hungry, but out of politeness (undeserved as I felt it to be), I sat down to eat the dinner he had prepared. The food itself was rather tasteless, but as of old, the accompanying wine was excellent, and after fully savouring it, I retired to the library, which I had seen only briefly on the one occasion I had visited the house, just after Symes moved in. Again, I was overwhelmed as I entered by the size and extent of the library, of which Symes was so justifiably proud. The dark and sometimes cobwebbed shelves contained many hundreds of books, and some of the oldest occult manuscripts in America. My irritation at Symes' non-appearance slowly ebbed, as I perceived the opportunity for several hours of pleasant browsing through the vast collection.

After a period of studying some of the titles, I came to the most used section of the library, as evidenced by the conspicuous absence of dust on the cases and books. A small coffee-table had been drawn up in front of the shelves at this point, but the chair which could reasonably have been expected to be in close proximity to it was actually standing in quite a different position—at the other side of the room. Symes wished, perhaps, to divert attention from the fact that he studied often in this section.

I moved the table a foot or two in order to examine the books on the shelf before which it stood, and began to marvel anew at the array of priceless volumes presented there. Amongst them stood such ancient, forbidden tomes as the *Book Of Dzyan*, *Death And Resurrection* by Ibn Khanu, and von Junzt's *Unaussprechlichen Kulten*. These were quickly relegated to the back of my mind, as I took in the array of even more terrible books surrounding them. There was an incredibly rare copy of the Comte d'Erlette's *Cultes Des Goules*, *Res Occulta Viscerum Mundi* by Veneficus, volumes on mythology, mind transference and conjuration including *Dream Prophecies*, the sinister *Cthaat Aquadingen*, and another of particularly evil aspect, de Niye's *Secrets des Vides*. Of some of these

I had heard mention in my studies on the occult and knew them to be shunned and abhorred texts in many circles of occult practitioners. The pages of most had been studied at length, it seemed, since the books through which I proceeded to look fell open in various places.

Replacing a beautifully illustrated edition of Fraser's *The Golden Bough* and deciding to study de Niye's eldritch legacy to students of the arcane in greater detail, I took the volume down, laid it on the table and let it fall open where it would. Someone had underlined a passage on one of the pages at which it opened, and I began to read:

*Verily hath it been said yt They shall come again, and in this com'g shall make use of Their minions on Earth and in ye spaces surround'g it and in ye various times for ye open'g of ye gates between ye Spheres and for ye overcom'g of ye Elder Sign. And of these minions, none is of more import than yt race which now rules ye worlde, which is to say man, who came after ye great'r be'gs. Some of ye members of this race hav'g a certaine susceptibilitie to, and less often an affinitie with, Their thoughts, these men be'g of extreme raritie, are able to receive ye mind-impressions which mould their thoughts to ye will of Cthulhu, and thus has it been from ye time yt man was formed from ye clay of Earth, yt They influence him by means of dreams and vari'd mental projections of surpass'g strangeness which when ye Cycle is complet'd shall aid in Their liberation and freedom to possess ye Earth as of yore and make of it Their kingdom once more...*

This passage disturbed me. Much of it meant nothing to me, but some dim recollection of Symes' interest in telepathy indicated that he had a definite reason for underlining it. I turned farther into the book and found star-charts predicting the best times to perform certain unnamed conjurations. I shuddered as I began to understand the purpose of the book, but irresistibly drawn on, kept reading.

Someone had inserted a mimeographed page after the star-charts; it was a manuscript in the crabbed hand of a clergyman who signed himself Rev. Ward Phillips, and was an extract from a manuscript copy of *Thaumaturgical Prodigies in the New-English Canaan*, as denoted by the title at its head. Disregarding much of the elaborate and technical language, I detected the underlying meaning of its message and shuddered again. The aforementioned conjurations, sourced from *Res Occulta Viscerum Mundi*, were to be used not to call forth the daemons mentioned in the underlined passage, but to allow them to enter the mind of the conjurer. The daemons themselves were generally referred to as the 'Great Old Ones' or 'Ancient Ones', and upon turning several more pages, I came across a line drawing entitled 'Yogge-Sothothe'—one of the Old Ones I then presumed—a presumption I have since discovered to be correct.

The actual sketch was extremely vague, as if the artist himself had been unsure as to what he was drawing. (I thought of a phrase Symes had once pointed out to me in the Miskatonic University Library's copy of the abhorred *Necronomicon* by a certain mad poet—"By Their smell can men sometimes know Them near, but of Their semblance can no man know..."). The result was a singularly disgusting image of an amorphous being from whose upper parts extruded a set of repulsive tentacles, partially obscured by a kind of congeries of globes.

As I stared at the hideous representation of this abominable being, I received a momentary impression of a figure moving across the door-way. I turned to see part of a shadow, low down on the wall by the door, projected there by the light from the dining room opposite, pass from view as though the person casting it had continued up the hall. The suspicion that a thief had entered the house crossed my mind, but I quickly dismissed it. It would have been a highly unlikely occurrence considering the position of the house, which stood so far away from any town. The nearest of any substance was Arkham, about ten miles away.

I had just risen to investigate when the lights in the hall, dining room and library simultaneously went out. Cursing, I left *Secrets des Vides* on the table and made my way towards the door, where I fumbled for the switch. Locating it at last, I attempted to turn the light on, but there was no result. Relying on my scant previous knowledge of the house, I spent ten minutes locating the kitchen. I secured a box of matches and managed to find an old hurricane lamp under one of the sideboards. Dusting off the accumulated grime and lighting the smoky wick, which quickly settled down to giving off a steady glow, I carried the lamp before me up the hall. There was no sign of anyone along its length, so I began a tedious search of the entire house—no mean task in any circumstance, let alone under the conditions now prevailing. However, luck was with me, for dust covered many of the rooms in the disused parts of the building, and I realised that if anyone had entered them recently, their footprints would be plainly visible. This enabled me to search whole wings with some alacrity, and after a half hour, I found myself back near the dining room and library.

The intruder, if he was such, had thus far eluded me, and I was by now inclined to believe myself mistaken in thinking I had seen a shadow. Nevertheless, I determined to check the remaining rooms. The drawing room and the study yielded no results and while in the process of checking the dining room, I became aware of the sound of footsteps in the library. I crossed to the door of the dining room and looked out into the hall, only to see the front door slam.

Running down the hall, I wrenched the door open, looked out and held my light quickly aloft in an attempt to spot the position of the intruder; but the dark grounds were empty as far as the small pool of light allowed me to see, and there was nothing to be heard. I stood in that position for another minute or so, peering vainly into the night, but I discovered no further evidence of the intruder. I assumed that my reappearance had driven him off. I was puzzled by the fact that he had braved the house's reputation of standing on evil ground, but as he had caused no obvious damage, I forbore investigating further. Closing the door, I returned to the library to replace the book left on the table during my search of the house. If Symes did not wish me to look at the books, I would not give him any reason to suspect that I had done so.

The sight that met my eyes on entering the library threw me into a state of confusion—the coffee table was bare and *Secrets des Vides* gone! With increasing alarm, knowing the extreme rarity and value of the work, I scanned the shelves, but in vain; the intruder must have taken it with him.

I ran towards the front door again, hoping that I might catch the thief before he got completely away. Flinging open the door, I stumbled out to my car, gunned the motor into life, and swung off in a tearing arc down the rank drive and onto the road. The most obvious escape route was right, in the direction of Arkham, and I turned that way, but after a few minutes, having seen nothing, I stopped in helpless despair and drove back towards the house. Whatever the thief's identity, there was no chance of apprehending him tonight. Important as it might be, the matter would have to wait until morning, since the bridges between the house and Arkham were none too safe even in daylight, and Symes had no telephone, so communication with the police was impossible until then. I cursed Symes' lack of foresight in this regard, but calmed down on reaching the house, and told myself that it was not his fault. I dreaded facing him the next day to report that I had carelessly failed to prevent the theft of his book; but there was nothing to be done, so I resolved to get as good a night's sleep as I could.

My watch showed 10.45—only half an hour had elapsed since the footsteps in the library had attracted my attention. I brought my luggage inside, and after hanging up my coat, mounted the stairs to the bedroom I had used on my previous visit, once in bed falling into an uneasy but dreamless sleep.

## II

When I awoke in the morning, it was quite late, and as I rose and dressed, I recalled the events of the previous evening. The unpleasant but necessary duty of informing Symes of the loss of his book once more confronted me. On stepping out into the sunlit upstairs hall, my gaze was drawn to the portraits lining its walls, and which I knew had been recently restored to their original condition. They depicted various members of Symes' family, and as I moved closer to a rather grand study of his great-grandfather, I discovered that although the paintwork seemed to be clean and renewed, dust thickly coated the surface of the glass covering the canvas, as it had been neglected for some weeks. I soon found the whole of the hall to be in this untended condition and was again surprised, as I had been at the note the previous night; such an occurrence was quite out of keeping with Syme's character and sensibilities, who was usually so attentive to the care of his possessions. On the other hand, he had behaved rather differently in a number of ways since moving away from the city, and I put it down to enthusiasm for his new work, the nature of which was still unknown to me.

I descended the stairs and made my way to the dining room and there found a light breakfast set out on the table, again accompanied by a note, which read:

> Detained in study all morning. Deep regrets for any resulting
> inconvenience — John.

Most annoyed, I threw the note back on the table and sat down to eat. Occupational enthusiasm aside, this was no way to treat a guest, even such an old friend as I, and I determined to see Symes despite his message. The sooner I informed him about the theft of *Secrets des Vides*, the better, as far as I was concerned. It would probably drag him away from his work for a while, and we could drive into Arkham to report the matter to the police.

I went to the kitchen, hurriedly washed up the used breakfast utensils and then directed my steps towards the library. Going through to the study entrance, I smelled the same noxious odour, though not nearly so strongly as on my arrival at the house, lingering in the air around the walls. It reminded me greatly of the putrescent air of decay, yet conveyed in its presence something, an impression, of what I could only feel was *impurity*, as if its source were corrupt. I noticed from across the room that the study door bore traces of the phosphorescence, and continued purposefully across the room.

Knocking heavily on the blackened oak panelling of the door, I called Symes' name loudly. There was no reply. "John!" I called again, and still no answer came. I tried the door-handle and as I had half-suspected, found it locked; I began shaking it. "Are you all right?" I called out, a guilty feeling spreading suddenly across my mind.

Then, at last, I heard a voice from within. It was so unlike Symes that I had difficulty in recognising it as such and was shocked at the apparent poor state of his health. "Yes," he said, painfully slowly, in a voice that seemed to gurgle more than speak, "...yes, I am all right, but feeling ill. I will see you this afternoon, but please leave the door and do not approach the study until then."

My emotions were confused by this order. As I realised Symes' probable condition, I was ashamed that I had not done so earlier; and yet I was hardly to be blamed in view of his continual avoidance of me, concerning which I was considerably vexed. On reflection though, I realised that he could not be incapacitated or seriously ill, or he would have been unable to prepare my meals. It was now after one o'clock, and since I had practically only just broken my fast, I decided to forego lunch and take a stroll around the grounds.

I left the library and, pausing only to take my coat from the hallstand, went outside. Moving slowly about the house, I wondered at its immensity and general disproportion; it was vast and rambling, and seemed as I traversed its exterior, to go on indefinitely. Finally, reaching the rear of the house, I saw in the distance a structure, which appeared to be of stone, topping a barren hill a mile or two away. Observing a path heading in its general direction, and having nothing better to do, I decided to follow it, in the hope of reaching the monument, as the structure apparently was.

I had been travelling on the path for half an hour or so, and it had diverged very little from the desired direction when I noticed the cropped nature of the grass, and the plants growing on either side. It seemed as though someone using it regularly had recently cut the undergrowth in order to make it easier to pass. Yet the cutting was irregular, as if the work had been deliberately concealed. I puzzled over this for some time, wondering who could be using a path with any frequency in this remote area. Symes I dismissed, owing to his incapacity for such work due to his illness, which to judge by the sound of his voice had taken hold some time ago.

The air was growing cold, and gathering clouds foretold rain, but I pressed on. Ahead of me loomed the apparently ancient stone structure. It was not, after all, a monument, but a circle about thirty yards in diameter of huge, crumbling, moss-grown blocks of stone, in the centre of which lay a large rectangular slab. An aura of gloom hung over the place and the few, feeble rays of sunlight which managed to penetrate the covering of leaden clouds seemed somehow less bright in the precincts of this primordial fane-like ruin.

I could not help wondering who could have built it, but I had no answer to my mental question. The stones were obviously much more ancient than the white man's civilisation in America, and I doubted greatly that the early Indians could have erected monoliths of such proportions. In any case, I had the odd impression that they had been there since the beginning of Earth, and time; they seemed to radiate the knowledge of millennia, and the outré experience of aeons.

A thin drizzle had broken, but I wanted to examine the smooth, green-black centre-stone more closely. It looked disturbingly altar-like and the mouldering undergrowth surrounding its base gave it an added sinister aspect. As I reached it, something dripped down the side to the ground. I put out my hand to touch the top of the stone and it came away wet with fresh blood. I shivered with the cold, the coat whipping around my legs in the rising wind. Suddenly an unholy gibbering sounded in my ear, and I leaped back in fright. Black storm clouds were now on the horizon, and a rumble of thunder broke the silence. My mind jumped to the obvious solution for the disturbing noise, but it had sounded quite unlike thunder.

The black clouds in the west were rolling quickly across the sky and seemed to pile up as though preparing for an attack. I ran down the hill, clutching my coat tightly about the neck, but was only about halfway to the house when a gigantic clap of thunder broke the comparative soundlessness of the afternoon and an icy, scourging rain began its assault. I was by now out of breath and exhausted and realising that I was doomed to a soaking anyhow, slowed down and jogged the rest of the way to the house. Lightning scarred the sky in great bolts as the storm clouds whirled across it in wild turmoil and the wind screamed through the hills. I glanced back over my shoulder at the stone circle and saw it silhouetted above the horizon in gargantuan majesty, the seeming centre of a vast maelstrom of crashing fire and rain.

I finally reached the house and made my way to the front door, stepping inside and pulling the door to behind me.

It was quite a time yet before I would see Symes, if he was true to his statement of the morning, but the interior of the house was in almost total blackness except when illuminated by the occasional flash of lightning. I reached for the light switch and, snapping it down, realised that the fuse, which must have blown the previous evening, was still not functioning. I did not want to venture out into the storm again, so resigned myself to another evening lit by the hurricane lamp, thinking to repair the fuse the next morning. I hoped the darkness had not inconvenienced Symes, but thought that perhaps he was sleeping since he would surely have told me had he needed the light.

The raging elements were still battering the house's exterior as I proceeded to the kitchen, dried myself in front of the outdated wood-burning stove and tried to decide how to occupy the time until my meeting with Symes. The remembrance of that unearthly gibbering which I had seemed to hear on the hill came back to me, and I sought to find a reasonable explanation for it.

The thunder had not been the cause, and yet I had seen no one beside myself in the area, nor would have expected to. I was at a complete loss and I could do nothing but put it down to imagination—a fanciful delusion caused by the oppressive atmosphere and the mystery surrounding Symes' reasons for ordering me here. However, I could not bring myself to completely accept this explanation.

Walking down the hall to the dining room, I looked in, and seeing that once more a meal was set on the table, I went in. Once more, a note accompanied the meal, this time not even signed:

'*Do not concern yourself over the light—I can manage. I will see you at four in the study*'.

I seated myself, thinking that perhaps at last Symes might reveal the nature of his work. It would set my mind at rest concerning his state of health, which certainly appeared bad at the moment. I lingered over the food in order to fill up the time before the appointed hour of the meeting. It was now that I became aware that the storm had subsided to a mere drizzle of rain, and the absence of the sound of thunder and wind was a contrast to the past couple of hours that made me vaguely uneasy. The silence seemed stifling, and I experienced a reversal of my earlier wishes for the storm to abate.

My mind wandered back to what I had found in *Secrets des Vides*. Surely, I reasoned, this indicated that Symes was studying the 'Old Ones', though I had not the faintest notion of his object. A conviction was growing upon me that these apprehensions were more than idle fancy, although I knew that I had no firm grounds on which to base my mental conjecture.

My only reasons for thinking thus were the incidents which had occurred since my arrival, added to an impression, a kind of foreboding which I would normally have ignored, but which now seemed most significant. Surely if there were any truth at all in the legend of such detestable primeval beings as the Old Ones, and I had experienced too much of the bizarre during my youth to dismiss the possibility completely, Symes could be in danger of a kind almost too terrible to contemplate.

However, becoming aware of the fact that my present state of mind was hardly conducive to helping Symes or solving the mysteries persistently worrying me, I calmed myself and tried as well as I was able to put such musings out of my mind. My watch showed a few minutes to four o'clock, so I left the library, lantern in hand and proceeded to the door of the study, where I knocked lightly.

There was a pause, and just as I was about to knock again, there came the same gurgling travesty of Symes' voice, which bade me enter. I opened the door and stepped into the room, the lantern casting a dim half-circle of light in front of me. Yet again, the nauseous odour that had previously shaken my senses assailed me. The front part of the house seemed entirely pervaded by what was here almost a stench, as of rotting meat. My thoughts were cut off when a cry of protest arose from Symes, who must have been sitting in a chair behind the large desk in the centre of the study.

"Wait! Take the light away. You may leave it in the library."

Taken aback, I hesitated a moment, but obeyed the odd request, and took the lantern back to the library, leaving it on the coffee-table, which reminded me of the painful confession I had to make to Symes about his book. I re-entered the study and shut the door. Symes directed me to a chair by the window. The heavy curtains were drawn, but fortunately, a steady draught of air ran out from behind them. I could make out very few details of the room or its furnishings, or for that matter of Symes himself — all I could see was a hazy outline of his body in the armchair behind the desk.

"I have a reason for not wanting the light present at the moment, but I shall come to that in due course," spluttered Symes, the typically friendly tone of his voice all but lost in the guttural, semi-liquid croaking issuing from his throat. "First I must explain to you the purpose of my request that you visit me. No doubt you've been wondering."

I snorted an assent.

"Well," he began, "as you know, I have been seeing very little of the outside world for the past few months. I have been experimenting with what could be called a new type of meditation; it involves hypnotism."

"Ah." I began to understand. In our earlier years together, Symes and I had used hypnotism in our studies on occasion and had become proficient in its use and practice. "But how have you supported yourself without working for so long?"

A movement indicated that Symes waved his hand deprecatingly. "I'm alone here—the place was full of furniture. I sold most of it long ago." I was on the point of making some comment when he abruptly took up his narrative again. "I have employed a tape-recorder in my self-hypnosis experiments so far, but that method hasn't yielded the results I have been hoping for. Tape-recording is slow, and cannot, of course, capture physical reactions. I need closer examination in my trance state and your assistance would be invaluable."

"But surely—" I began. He cut me short.

"Please keep your questions until I've finished. You now, of course, understand my immediate reason for summoning you. I regret the inconvenience you must have suffered since last night, but an error of judgement on my part resulted in my thinking that your presence here was required at once. As it turned out, I was a day ahead of myself. You are the only person I can trust; it is a matter of great importance that you maintain complete secrecy. I'm sure my confidence in you is not misplaced."

My mind was bursting with questions to which I longed to give voice, when I noticed on Symes' desk—my eyes having become accustomed somewhat to the semi-darkness—a bulky shape that seemed somehow familiar. I leaned forward, peered intently through the gloom and discerned the 'stolen' copy of de *Secrets des Vides*, unmistakable in its garnet-studded binding! I was immediately plunged into confusion greater than before. Had Symes apprehended the intruder and not told me? Had the thief returned the book for some incomprehensible reason?

Symes must have realised the cause of my uncertain forward move. "Ah, yes," he said quickly, "I haven't explained about the book. A rather elaborate ruse, but a necessary one, I'm afraid. I wanted to explain the purpose of my experiments in my own way and at the right time, so I removed *Secrets des Vides*, from your reach."

"And made it appear stolen?"

"Yes."

"But I searched the house. How could I have missed seeing you?" I asked incredulously.

"I turned the light off at the fuse-box, making it an easy matter to avoid you in the dark. I heard you follow me down the hall, so I entered the dining room. You went straight past me and must have gone over the back part of the house. When you returned, you went to the drawing room; I crossed to the library and took the book. I heard you open the study door, and knew you must be looking there, and then you walked back to the dining room. I went through the study to the front door, opened it and swung it shut, moving back into the study before it closed. As I had hoped, you thought that someone had left through the front door and tried to follow."

I was speechless; such action as Symes had just described seemed insane. All my forebodings about his work came flooding back, but I controlled myself sufficiently to ask the question that perhaps would do most to enable me to judge the situation properly. "I can't say I understand your actions, but in any case, what are you doing that requires such measures to maintain secrecy?"

"I'm coming to that," Symes managed to articulate through the grotesque croakings to which he was also giving vent. "What I am going to explain to you may be very difficult for you to comprehend as a possibility, but I hope to convince you of its truth.

"It was nearly three years ago that I first came across references to the subject I am studying, while visiting Miskatonic University in Arkham. As you know, books on occult subjects form a major part of the library there. While engaged in compiling material for my paper *Religious Symbolism in the Art and Literature of the Peoples of the South Americas*, I found repeated allusions to a race of prehuman beings referred to variously as the 'Ancient Ones', the 'Outer Beings' and the 'Great Old Ones'. Some months later, I again encountered a reference to these god-creatures, as they apparently were. The passage also mentioned that Abdul Alhazred, the Arab scribe and poet, gave more detail in the *Necronomicon*.

"It was about this time that I was obliged to move to my present place of habitation owing to the tumult surrounding that imagined 'affair'. Since there was no major project on which I had to engage immediately, I decided to follow up the reference to Alhazred's *Necronomicon* and went into Arkham with a view to examining the book in the library at Miskatonic.

"Much to my surprise, on my requesting access to the volume, the librarian questioned me closely as to my professional status before he would even admit that the library possessed a copy. I knew from previous experience that the Miskatonic kept the *Necronomicon* under lock and key because of its rarity and its terrible reputation among searchers after the forbidden; but I had assumed that I would be remembered. It appeared that the librarian was taking no chances. I had to go through the same rigmarole as on the occasion I had previously examined a portion of the book—with you, as I recall. My answers to his queries apparently satisfied him, however, and directing me to a glassed-in reading-room, he told me to take a seat and to await his return. He departed, but was back in a few minutes bearing the huge, leather-bound tome, which he placed on the desk before me. Warning me that I had but an hour to study it, he left me alone, and I fell eagerly to reading, although I had some difficulty in translating several sections of the stilted Latin.

"The subject matter of the section to which I had been directed consisted of hideous rites and unearthly ceremonies for 'opening the Gates between the Spheres' and allowing certain of the Old Ones to appear on Earth. According to the passage, They had held sway in prehistoric times, before becoming involved in a cataclysmic battle for domination of the cosmos with another, more benevolent race, the Elder Gods, who defeated Them. The Elder Gods had imprisoned and banished the Old Ones to various parts of the galaxy. Great Cthulhu had been incarcerated in the sunken city of R'lyeh beneath the Pacific. Hastur (sometimes mentioned as He-Who-Must-Not-Be-Named) had been banished to dim Carcosa in the Hyades. Noxious Yog-Sothoth, the All-in-One and One-in-All, was sent to an unnamed or unnamable extremity of the universe; and the daemon-sultan Azathoth to the centre of Chaos, where he babbles mindlessly. But the progeny of the Old Ones on Earth, and those men whose minds They could reach and influence, forever wait for the stars to come right and the Cycle to be completed, and prepare the way for Them when They should come again."

Symes' laboured breathing had become increasingly fast and his speech practically unintelligible. As he broke off at this point of the account, his voice had taken on a wild note. I had recognised the story of the Old Ones from the books I had leafed through in Symes' library, and feared that my thoughts about his work were proving correct. Meanwhile, Symes had relaxed in his chair and after a few seconds took up where he had left off.

"I was fascinated and as I read, made feverish notes of what I considered to be important points. In several places, I encountered a couplet of strange portent and haunting ambiguity, which I have now gone some way towards comprehending:

> *'That is not dead which can eternal lie*
> *And with strange aeons even death may die.'*

Infuriatingly, Alhazred would go no farther in some parts of his work than to hint at the nightmarish things of which he apparently had some inner knowledge but which he thought safer not to discuss fully.

"I was unaware of the quickly passing time, and after what seemed no more than ten minutes, the librarian silently reappeared and informed me that my time was up. Regretfully handing back the book and gathering up my notes, I made my way out. I imagined as I was leaving that the librarian looked at me a little queerly, but my mind was awhirl with ideas and I took no notice, returning home immediately.

"I began to devote myself entirely to searching for information on myth-cycles similar to that of the Ancient Ones, and within a few days had found several among the material on the Mayas I had collected for my last paper. The Mayan priests had preached to their people that history and past events repeat themselves, an obvious link with the cycle of star-positions on which the Old Ones are dependent.

"An even greater parallel was the legend of the god who had come down to Earth with the purpose of instructing the people. He was described as being different from the Indian people in that he had white skin, long hair, a flowing beard, blue eyes, and was of remarkable height, a description which corresponded nearly exactly to that of 'Umr-at-Tawil, the embodiment on Earth of Yog-Sothoth as given by Alhazred. This god incurred the wrath of another, whom I identified with Nodens of the Elder Gods. He left, though promising to return. This represented his banishment by the Elder Gods.

"In succeeding weeks, I became increasingly convinced of something which it is likely even you will find hard to understand. I believe, indeed now know beyond dispute, that there do exist certain entities or powers, often worshipped as gods in the form of such beings as the Old Ones, which lurk just outside the consciousness of man, entering his mind when it is in an open state to communicate the most valuable of all things—knowledge."

I had followed these ramblings in silence up until this moment, but now could not help protesting loudly. "Surely you cannot believe such a thing! Your experimentation has caused your health to deteriorate; it would be wiser to abandon it altogether. It can lead to no good." I could see Symes move uncomfortably in his chair, and a familiar movement of his arm denoted his impatience and annoyance.

"Let me finish. I am still confident that you will want to assist me when I have explained fully."

I could think of nothing to say in reply, so I let him continue.

"Sleep, of course, leaves the mind in an open state. One night on retiring to bed excited by my discoveries, I could not at first sleep, but eventually lapsed into slumber. It was then," he said, leaning forward in his armchair, "that I had the first of a number of dreams through which the Old Ones, to use Their mythical name, have communicated with me. It was of extremely short duration, but left a lingering impression of reality after I woke, as sometimes happens.

"I seemed to be standing on wet, slimy ground among heaps of strange Cyclopean stones, the like of which I had never seen before. The sun's rays were beating down from a cloudless sky and almost blinded me. In places stood gigantic deiform statues of an exquisite primitive weirdness, hewn from green-black stone. My sight must have been affected by the shimmering haze which hovered around the huge, beslimed blocks of masonry, for it seemed to me that their surfaces shifted and changed almost imperceptibly in perspective. At times, I found it difficult to believe the evidence of my senses as to their form. There were sometimes cavities where one would expect corners or edges; and where corners did appear, their apexes curved off indefinitely in apparent defiance of the geometrical laws of linear space. Certain of the blocks were carved in relief or inscribed with unusual pictographic designs, and even the shapes and colours of these seemed subtly altered from the normal.

"I shielded my eyes from the glare and looked around. I thought for a second that I caught a glimpse of some hunched shape shambling across the top of a heap of ruins in the distance, but the light was so intense that I could not be sure my eyes were not playing me tricks. I decided not to make any move towards climbing over the heaps of stone since with that curious, unreasoning sureness that is a common feature of dreams, I had an absolute conviction that to do so would be dangerous; those deceptive stone surfaces could not be trusted.

"The dream ended abruptly and I awoke. I hardly gave it a second thought until experiencing the same dream the next night—or rather, the same dream up to the point where it had ended the night before, but then being extended. I had just decided not to climb over the stones and was moving around on the oozy ground of the clearing seeking some other means of exit, perhaps a gap in the enclosing rock, when I caught sight of an immense tower standing high above the chaos of rubble at a considerable distance from where I stood. Constructed of the same greenish-black stone as covered the ground around it, and garlanded for the most part with barnacles and dripping slime, it was of the same titan proportions as the rest of the masonry. High on the side of the wall facing me was inset a slab of grey stone, which bore a symbol, or design of some sort. Moving closer, I made it out to be a roughly-shaped five-pointed star enclosing a kind of broken diamond rather similar to an eye, and surrounded by tongues of flame.

"At this moment something began to obtrude itself into my mind. It was a voice, intense and with a powerful timbre; it was speaking in a language which sounded phonetic, but which I could not comprehend at first. Gradually, however, I began to understand snatches of the semi-articulated words and discordant combinations, though I had the feeling that it was I who was being adapted to the speech, and not it to me. Entranced, I stood staring at the sea-spawned tower.

"Ia! Azathoth!…whose laughter…not be. To Nyarlathotep, Father of the Million Favoured Ones, the Messenger…seeker after truth…the Gate and the Way in Yog-Sothoth…curves and angles of the known cosmos…to teach them to scream and laugh and show them the Key… allegiance and transformation…granted…wonder and glory…the Universe, the finite and the infinite…of the dream and the reality…"

"There followed a series of unintelligible phrases which I could not now render, then suddenly, almost before I had grasped the meaning of the speech, I felt dizzy, and my field of vision darkened, I fell to the ground—and felt it drop away from beneath me. With an icy shock, my awareness returned and I found myself hurtling at colossal speed between outer-spatial clusters of matter which were constantly spinning, dissolving and erupting towards, only to find myself, an instant later, an incalculable distance across the galaxy. I was rocked by explosions of incredible force and swallowed into multi-coloured sprays of galactic mist. Propelled into a slipstream vortex of spectral radiance, I was whirled beyond the circuit of the known planets; my mind and body were buffeted by new dimensions and I emerged from enveloping nebulae and swirling clouds of gaseous crystals, only to be blinded by macrocosmic panoramas of interstellar flashes. Utterly unable to orientate myself, I was swept along in the path of some gigantic force through the dark wells of angled space and beyond, to unmentionable horrors in the blackest depths of the cold, howling void. Senses were wakened in me that have lain dormant in man since the dawn of time. I began to discover that which I sought to know, and more besides…

"I awoke drenched with sweat, with the details of all I had experienced in my dream state already fast fading from my mind. But one thing remained clear. The names I had heard had been those of the Old Ones! I knew not what to think, but after another such dream in which I was once again subjected to the terrors and wonders of the Universe, I began to suspect that the dreams were more than coincidence. Certain common factors denoted the fact of conscious planning.

"On the morning after the third dream, I realised that I was speaking as I awoke, and that I was relating the visions of my dreams. I determined to set up a recorder to tape my next dream and put this plan into effect. The result was a recording mainly consisting of gibberish, but in which I definitely referred to my *contact* with the Old Ones. My experiences had seemed realistic because some part of me, perhaps my subconscious, had actually undergone them! You have no conception of the things I now know about the origin of what is known to us as the Earth, about the actual significance of what man in his ignorance calls 'colour'; revealed to me are things more horrible than were painted by Dore or Pickman."

Symes' voice began to exhibit again the same excitement as he had displayed when referring to his discovery of the legend of the Ancient Ones. I imagined that his eyes were glittering fiercely with the light of fanaticism. He broke into what must have been a quotation, his cracked voice trembling. "Great holes secretly are digged where Earth's pores ought to suffice, and things have learnt to walk that ought to crawl..." I tell you, Danvers, the corners of space hold more than most men could hope to see and remain sane! And yet, I need to know more— They have offered me..." He collapsed deeper into his chair, panting hoarsely. "But these things do not concern you directly," he continued. "Let me finish what I was saying.

"After a series of unclear tapes, I began to fear that the knowledge gained in my nightly experiences would be lost if I was unable to find some means of conveying it accurately, as the mind cannot be guided and questioned for clearer information in the sleeping state. The same thing naturally applies to hypnosis when there is no outside questioner. You must help me!"

For what must have been a full minute, I remained speechless, stunned by these pronouncements, which proclaimed in no uncertain terms the unbalanced state of my friend's mind, which must have been becoming increasingly more prevalent since his isolation began. It would do no good to point out straight away that the dreams were probably caused by Symes' over-devotion to the study of the Old Ones. The best thing would be to ease him out of his present excitability and get him calm enough to take a rest. That would do as a first step. I would pretend to go along with him. "Why have you never had these dreams before?" I inquired.

"I believe it is because of my living in this area, where the influence of the entities is particularly strong. I suspect that the Old Ones were actually worshipped by some of the members of the old local families."

"In New England!" My incredulity at this was obvious.

"Stranger things have been known to happen when the decadent families of the New England backwater towns are involved. I could name many unusual instances."

"But you're unwell. I suggest that your experiments be...postponed. What price besides that of your health must you pay if you continue them now?"

"The price to be paid is only that which would be expected of any servant by his Master—that he serve faithfully in all possible ways. In any case, it is far outweighed by the rewards, the knowledge to be gained, and becoming—but that you shall see for yourself. Go and bring the lamp; you must be prepared for certain—changes. Once you are back I will place myself under hypnosis and very soon afterwards I shall be contacted. I have made sure of that."

Something in the way Symes expressed that last sentence made me wonder what he meant, and then I realised with a shock. "You don't mean—the altar on the hill—the blood...?" I stammered.

"I have merely made a small but sufficient propitiation, coupled with readings from a certain book, as a token of my readiness to be contacted, and to ensure a receptive state of mind. The stone circle is a kind of focus of power; the altar-stone is actually a fragment of a building in lost R'lyeh," said Symes calmly. He continued, "When I start talking under hypnosis, it will mean that I am conveying the information I am being given, as has happened before. Turn on the tape-recorder and be ready to question me if I am unclear on any point, which is quite likely. Do not leave me in the hypnotic state for more than half an hour. For now, go and bring the lamp." He made a gesture which I took to be a signal to leave the room.

Saying nothing, I turned, opened the door and went through to the library. Symes' plans were lunacy, and I would not foster his madness by taking any part in them; but I dared not let myself think that his ravings were due in any way to the things he claimed to have seen. I kept my mind firmly on the line of his seclusion and preoccupation with unhealthy matters. He must be prevented from going any further, but I needed light—the strain of listening to that ghastly voice through the darkness had told on my nerves. Now, however, picking up the lamp which was still burning on the coffee-table, I brought my emotions under control and turned back to the study doorway prepared to withhold Symes, forcibly if necessary, from proceeding with his 'experiment'.

Stepping into the room, I could see clearly the front of the desk, and beginning to tell Symes that I would not assist him, I moved forward and placed the lamp upon it. I fell back in horror as I saw the thing to which I had just spoken.

It was Symes, although on his mouth and chin a beard-like growth of long flesh-coloured tentacles hung. His head was swollen and misshapen and his hands were revolting, pendulous shapes protruding from his dressing gown. I do not know whether I screamed the word aloud, but my only thought was for a doctor.

Running from the room, I dashed to the front door and out to the car, which was parked in the driveway. Without a thought, I was driving through the deathly-still twilight towards Arkham. The town was ten miles away and the roads were merely ruts, but I succeeded in arriving within twenty minutes, managing to avoid going through a bridge into the river by sheer good luck. I knew of only one doctor in the town and I raced the car towards his house in Salstonstall St and pulled up outside.

In reply to my banging on his door, a grey-haired old man in night attire answered the door. He has since told me that he could not understand most of my garbled outpourings, but extracted enough information to know where he was needed and to realise that something was terribly wrong. He told me to wait while he dressed and after a few minutes hurriedly re-emerged. He ran to his car, signalling that I was to go to mine, jumped in and sped off up the road. I followed as quickly as I was able and we arrived together in a little over the time of my outward journey.

The door was ajar, and as we hastened towards the study, I again noticed the noisome odour, which had assailed me previously. The doctor entered ahead of me and gave a grunt of alarm; I blundered in after him and a quick glance told me that Symes was no longer in the room. "Where to now?" said the doctor, turning to face me.

Something flashed across my mind. "The hill!" I yelled, and without waiting to see whether or not the doctor was following, I hurled myself back through the doorway and through the hall to the back of the house and once outside ran at full strength up the trail towards the stone circle on the hill. A vague suspicion was taking form in my mind, a suspicion so monstrous that I did not dare let it intrude wholly into my consciousness. In a short time the doctor, bearing the map I had left behind on the desk in my hurry, caught me up and we ran together. I suddenly noticed something that must have been in my line of vision all during my run from the house—a strange greenish glow was softly lighting up the top of the hill.

As we neared the stone circle, I ran ahead of the doctor and could see the light pulsing around the stone slab in the centre. Yet my attention was not drawn to it, for barely five yards away lay a shocking bloated object, which lumbered painfully towards the altar-stone. Its glaucous, leathery hide was covered with small tentacles and its shape bore no relation to anything living or dead. I screamed with horror and as I turned away saw the doctor hurl the lamp in the direction of the loathsome obscenity. The thing burst into flame and as it writhed, I could see sickening eruptions of ichorous fluid breaking out all over its upper surface. Then, as it slowly subsided into a bubbling gelatinous mass I perceived the final cataclysmic truth, which threatened to shatter my sanity.

I fell fainting to the ground, and recollect nothing more until waking in a state of hysteria in a ward of St Mary's Hospital in Arkham, whence I was released after a time, supposedly well again. Though the doctor who was with me saw the thing within the circle of stones, and living in an area where the unaccountable is commonplace, has kept his thoughts to himself, he has no knowledge of the actual reason for my uncontrollable shuddering whenever the affair is mentioned. He is unwitting that what he destroyed so felicitously for myself and the world on that hillside was an embodiment of pure evil. For what I beheld, before the final descent into dissolution in which my reason passed from me, on the ground near that which withered and boiled in the flames, were the scorched and tattered remains of the dressing-gown of John Symes.

*Letter from Inspector William H. Morrison, Boston Police Department, to Hollis Chalmers, Solicitor, River St, Arkham.*

20th July, 1955

Dear Hollis,

Your enclosure on the old Symes case is certainly most unusual, to say the very least. Had you not assured me of the fact that Danvers appeared mentally sound in the years between the case and his death, I should have said that whatever event had led to his breakdown and the writing of the document (probably the real truth about Symes' disappearance) had also left him permanently unbalanced.

I can only agree with you that it was written immediately after his breakdown while he was still in a disturbed state. It is hard to tell where the truth ends (for the account consists in part of undeniable fact) and where the fantasy begins. It is possible that Symes was involved in researching some outlandish cult, and that his disappearance could have been connected with it, but of course no credence can be given to Danvers' wild ramblings about the involvement of 'alien intelligences'. Although it casts no real light on the case I shall, after one more reading, file it with the police in Arkham for future reference. Personally, I feel inclined to destroy the manuscript as the useless ravings of a man gone temporarily mad; but perhaps at some time it will be of value in further investigation, however remote the possibility might seem. As far as I am concerned, though, the case remains and will continue to remain unsolved.

Yours faithfully,

William Morrison.

*Extract from THE BOSTON TIMES July 21, 1955*

### POLICEMAN'S FATAL ACCIDENT

A man was found badly injured and unconscious at his home in George Street this morning and later died on his way to hospital. He was Inspector William Morrison, unmarried, 43, of the Boston Police Department. Morrison was discovered at about 2.30 pm by two colleagues from the Department after he failed to appear for work. He was found lying on the floor of his study with his skull fractured, the injury eventually proving fatal. Doctor N. Arkwright, who examined the body, found that fragments of bone had pierced the brain and stated that some sharp, weighty, metal object had most likely made the wound.

Police believe that Inspector Morrison struck his head in falling, against the corner of his private safe, having fainted and toppled from the chair in which he was seated. Yesterday's overwhelming heat was the probable cause of his swoon, the doctor said, since there was no evidence of heart failure. The police have dismissed the possibility of murder, owing to the circumstances. There was no sign of forced entry and nothing appeared to have been stolen. The only objects on his desk were a letter from a solicitor, a sealed and unposted letter apparently written by Morrison in reply, and a document headed in Morrison's handwriting "Symes Case - Item 28." The latter was face down on the desk and bore on the back of the last page the phrase "4th June 1955" and the initials 'A.D.'

# THE ROOMER

I been through a bit of a lean period this last couple a years. Not much left of the old life, a few things chucked in a suitcase, whaddya need after all? Cuppa coffee in the mornen, bit a tucker through the day, enough piss a course, whatever ya can get, beer, wine, preferably somethen to eat at night as well but if not fuck it. Somewhere to kip is good, sometimes you can go without if yer on the sauce, but it catches up on ya so a few hours here and there's always gonna pay dividends. Yairs, oh yai-rs.

The roomen house was a fucken shithole but then whaddya want for thirty bucks a week? Most of the blokes stayen there were OK, truck drivers a lot of em. Some of em had a wife back in Wauchope† or wherever. Others, who knows what they ever did before, but now they were wearen old ill-fitten suits Vinnies would reject. Always seemed to have enough shrapnel to scrape up for the next beer, though. One or two of em'd buy me a drink sometimes and if I was cashed up I'd do the same, but mostly they'd keep to emselves. I did the same. If I wasn't up in me room lighten a candle and mutteren dark prayers, I'd be sitten in the downstairs bar most days, lighten up a smoke and nursen a beer, looken out at the traffic. Sometimes a girl'd go by, but in this part a town it was usually fucken old codgers shufflen and kids in pants so fucken baggy they looked lost in em, guys unloaden stuff from trucks into the shops—newspapers, cartons of softdrinks, all that shit.

Alexandria's a bit of a shithole as well, but it's all relative I reckon. I've slept in the fucken street a few times too many, even in between jobs sometimes when I was worken but haven yer own bed is fucken heaven. The missus woulden like it, the bed I got in this room, the mattress is kinda bulky and that, springs sticken up into yer arse if you go too far in one direction, but jeesus bloody christ I'll tell ya what it's

† A hinterland town near the Australian east coast.

a fucken paradise compared to some dumps I've been in. Ya can have a bit of a wash at this handbasin thing in the room if ya want one. The publican doesn't care if you fucken leave yer cigarettes and yer black candles burnen on the side table, the things burnt to fuck as it is, so what's another few scorch marks gonna do?

I'm usually skint a course, hangen out for the next dole payday, so most of the time it's a waiten game. Mondays I generally put a few bets on down at the TAB[†], sometimes the trifecta if I'm feelen really lucky, but I've never won a fucken thing. Except one time a horse I had twenny bucks on comes in at ten to one and I get two hundred bucks in the hand. I had it down, thought I'd figured out the ideal system. Two hundred bucks! I shouted the whole fucken roomen house ales that night, even old Johnno who's drunk nothen but VB the last fuck knows how many years, I talked him into a scotch! Kidded on I'd come into an inheritance. Only fucken thing, I went back to the TAB next day tryen to repeat the success, tried exactly the same system and was well and truly fucked. Didn't eat for the next three days, hung on like grim death for the end a week payment. Fucken typical. Occasionally its way up or its way down, but usually it's in the middle, that's the rut.

I call it a rut, but it's not so bad. You don't have to answer to anyone, there's no nice soft woman to get into bed next to, but you can fucken smoke and drink and stare out the fucken window all day long here, as long as you put yer thirty bucks down at the beginnen a the week. That kinda luxury on the soul is welcome I'll tell ya, no fucken domestic dramas, no tearful scenes bout this and that, no tryen to keep up fucken appearances. Jeesus christ, isn't it enough to wake up and walk around and try like fuck to figure out what's goen on without all that fucken baggage? I reckon that's why I only walked out with a suitcase when we split, I didn't even wanna take it, but I wanted to have me coat and me good boots with me, and the suitcase was fucken there, so I took that and me leather book that me dad gave me and left. The rest, she's got the lot, I don't give a fuck, it's not what it's about to me. I can fucken take it or leave it. So I left it.

Some days I play poker with Johnno and Alec. Alec's a fucken dirty old bastard, what I mean is his personal habits are not that clean, but as Johnno says it's not the fucken Ritz is it, so what's the diff? Johnno usually shuffles the cards in his big, cracked hands and keeps one eye on the teev. There's a big fucken teev on the pub wall near the bar. It's always blaren the latest race info and that, gives me a fucken headache. Johnno usually coughs a lot, that phlegmy smoker's cough like he's

† TAB – Australian betting shop (Totalisator Agency Board)

about to bring up a lung.

Sometimes I look at the teev but when playen cards I prefer to concentrate on the game. Anyway, I never bother to study the form anymore after that business with the two hundred bucks and the system I had. What's the point? Johnno, but, he can keep a poker face and take in the race odds at the same time. How the fuck do ya do it, mate, two things at once, I ask him. He just smiles that crooked smile a his and takes a long drag on his coffin nail.

Alec sits there in his threadbare t-shirt, coughen and splutteren, he must have chronic bronchitis or somethen worse, I don't wanna think too closely about that. Every now and again he'll fucken sneeze and drag out a big handkerchief that musta been white once but now its grey, never fucken washes this thing, just wipes the snot away with it and shoves it back in his pocket, all balled up. Jeesus, mate, I say, would it hurt ya to wash that flamen snotrag once in a while. Might be a good idea. He fucken ignores me every time.

Ah well, they're a good pair a blokes to play cards with. I know nothen more bout em, they know fuck all about me and that's the way we like it.

Me coats a great coat, it's a greatcoat, that's a joke ha ha! It's a real heavy fucker, good in winter, keeps the cold off ya like nuthen else, hangs all the way down to near the feet, and with me boots on I can fend off wind and weather like you wooden believe. Saved me from freezen to death a few times, that coat has, walken between towns in the freezen cold. Walkens good, I always like it, taken in a few cows and horses along the way, in the view a the countryside I mean, walken that gravel or the hardtop on the highways.

Occasionally if you're travellen you'll get a lift into the next town, and the blokes that drive the car always comment on me coat. That's a fine coat, they'll say by way a conversation, some suit on his way to an insurance conference or some fucken shit like that. I never answer, just smile me best knowen smile. Too right it's a fucken fine coat, it belonged to me dad when he was in the war and they're not getten it just for given me a lift, no way. I pull it tighter around me. One bloke picked me up one time tried to get me coat off me, claimed I owed him for the lift or some such shite. I had to do me magick on him as I got out the car. I pulled me big leather book out the greatcoat pocket and blasted him with the Koth spell. Wasn't much left of the bastard after that. Just a small black stain of ash on the front seat.

Now I come to the roomer, I keep the coat hangen up behind me door and I always lock me door so no fucker can get in unless I invite em.

We don't need to go down the local from here, cause this *is* our fucken local! We wanna drink we just yell out for Jane and she brings the beers over and she sticks em down on those little cardboard coasters that are always on the tables. Good sort, Jane. I don't like em, the coasters, cause they always stick to the bottom of the fucken glass, they're a general bloody nuisance.

As far as food, you can get a bit of a counter lunch. Jane does a fairly good bangers and mash. Or you can get pies and potater chips at the bar, that sorta shit. In the evenings I usually go out, there's a Turkish pizza place, it's a bit slow but the food is good when it finally gets there, those Turkish breads with sausage and egg and stuff on em. The bloke there, Tony, he's great and we usually have a good yack. He could talk the leg off an iron pot. Or sometimes I'll do baked beans or scrambled eggs on toast in the cooker up in me room. Then I might do an invocation or three before I cop some shuteye.

Christ almighty I thought to meself this one evening, there must be something going on man I mean it's so boring staying in all the time, do ya know what I'm sayen? There was some ginger-haired bastard I never seen before at the bar drinken, but no-one else was payen him any attention. I decided to go out to eat and then after mebbe to another pub. Mebbe I'd run into some other blokes I knew, old Charlie, that would be good, we could have a laugh and talk about politics or whatever the fuck. Topics peripheral to football, I still like to have a debate sometimes, I'm not so far gone as some of these fuckers who find it hard to get the ball rollen, I can talk till the bloody cows come home.

I'm of the opinion that you need a bit of hangen out with mates now and again. I mean what do you do when you're gaspen for a smoke? Ya can smoke on your own, but it's better to sit down with someone over a middy and chew the fat awhile.

Thinken bout smoken made me realise I was out of fags[†]. Me pecuniary situation was a bit light. I went across the road and stopped into the bottle-o. I says to the guy "The state of the exchequer's not real flash, pal, can you see us through till dole day?" He knew I was from the roomer across the road. He let me have some fags and a lighter, and a couple of packets of potater chips to stuff in me pocket. I might get hungry on the bus on the way to Charlie's.

I went outside and thought about setten off up the road. What I had in mind was to find somewhere to eat and get some good grub inside me, then to strike out for this other pub where I thought Charlie and

† Slang for cigarettes

some of the guys from the old days might be. He'd be in the saloon of his local, the Earlwood.

He had a room up on the top floor there now, all he had was a pair of jeans and an old PC to write his stories on. His sister had all his stuff in storage. Down in the saloon, I could imagine it, it would be the stale cigarette smoke, the kerchink of slot machines in the back room, the men's room stinken of piss, a few semi-attractive barmaids collecten the emptied glasses in big tiers in a bored sort of way. It would be good to see old Charlie, but.

It was hard lines that he'd had to move out of that other place. A half-decent rented place he'd had, sharen with a couple of other fellas. Friggen no-hopers. Then he'd started worken those long shifts and had no time to clean up. The other blokes were oxygen thieves—curdled milk in the fridge, no food in the cupboards, only leaven enough pizza crumbs around the lounge-room for mice to infest the sofa. Charlie couldn't handle it any longer. He was about to move out, when the word came from the estate agent that they were all evicted.

Charlie always appeared to be amused by that. It took them an inordinate amount of time to realise the state the place was in, Charlie said, with a wheezy laugh. Inordinate, that's the word he used. That was a strong point. Evict us eh? Well fuck you, said Charlie. Anyway, it was after that he'd moved most of his stuff up to Coffs[†] to be stored by his sister, and moved himself into the pub. I could have a laugh with old Charlie. Yairs, oh yai-rs.

I had the fag in me hand and was standen on the pavement waiten for the next bus. I snapped the lighter and made sure the flame came on, shelteren it in me cupped left hand from a slight breeze that was kicken up the hill.

The bus was not comen. I was smoken me fag and kind of pacen up and down a bit. People went by—blokes headen out to the pub mebbe, or comen back from the supermarket with a few plastic bags of groceries.

One thing I had learned, you had to make yer own way in the world. The bus was not comen, but that didn't mean it wouldn't come. There was no sense getten pissed about it. Sometimes buses were late. At least I had a bit of dough in me pocket. That horse at Randwick on Thursday had come in at 16 to 1. 16 to 1! I'd only had five bucks on it, that was all I had at the time, but those winnens were enough to buy me dinner every night this week and still have the bus fare to get to Charlie's and that. I was doen fine. Ya just had to push on and get things done, that's what ya had to do. Where the fuck was this bus?

† Coffs Harbour – a seaside town on the east coast of Australia

It was starten to get cold. The wind was whippen around the old ears, maken the tips start to feel chilled. I pulled me collar up a bit around the neck, tryen to keep warm. I was getten soft, I thought, mebbe I would have to start a few exercises, a few dumbbell lifts or somethen back at the roomer. I would have to start the exercises.

A bus came along but it was the wrong one. Another bloke got on, headen into the city probably. The bus pulled out and away and I rubbed me hands together, it was getten really bloody cold now. The coat kept the worst off, but the extremities man, that was the part ya had to worry about. Mebbe I could get meself a pair of gloves in a week or two when the weather started really turnen. I glanced at me watch, I'd been waiten nearly forty-five minutes. This was beginnen to get on me nerves.

Suddenly I didn't feel like goen to see Charlie after all. Not goen was too easy, I knew—a soft option. But fuck it, I could make up me own mind. Charlie wasn't expecten me anyway. I couldn't be fucked lumpen all the way out to Earlwood and then haven to get back on the bus later. I threw the cigarette butt down and stamped it out with me foot. A wisp of smoke curled up from the butt, and there was a small black stain of ash on the pavement.

I saw the bus I wanted comen up the hill. I was teeteren bout whether or not to go. I could get on the bus without thinken about it and then I would be on me way. Or I could just turn back. No point worryen about it. What difference did it make?

Fuck it, I thought to meself, I'll just go back to the roomer. It was kinda irritaten maken a plan and then changen it, but what the hell, there was always tomorrer. Charlie would still be there. Tonight was too fucken cold to go roamen around the place. And there was that new ritual I was wanten to try out from the book. I rubbed behind me right ear, it was sore there for some reason.

I turned around and headed back down the street to the roomen house. There was a lot of noise comen from the street, it was starten to grate on me—loud cars, and somewhere a circular saw grinden. Fuck sake, it was nearly nine p.m! Who'd be usen a circular saw this time a night? I shook me head.

I pulled another smoke from the pack as I walked back to the roomer. Only the next thing would be it would start rainen. It was looken ominous—big black clouds gatheren over the street. Nah, it was better to stay home tonight. I could go to the boozer tomorrer. Right now, I was tired. I hadn't realised how fucken tired I actually was.

I turned into the front hallway of the roomer. Lie down on the bed upstairs, that'd be the go, not even botheren to take the boots off. *Sleep.* I stood inside the doorway, me eyes were almost starten to close for fucks sake, I couldn't believe I felt so shagged out.

I get up to me room, unlock it, and throw me greatcoat on the bed next to the big black book. And lo and behold if some ginger-haired fuck doesn't spring out from just down the corridor, jump into me room right behind me, and snatch the fucken greatcoat off the bed. I have to hit the bastard. I don't enjoy hitten him, to be honest it makes me sick, but certain articles are not for the taken and me greatcoat is one of em.

He flakes out on the floorboards and drops me coat. It occurs to me I've got just what I need for that new ritual. I shut the door and lock it. Then I set me altar up by putten me breadboard across the washbasin and lighten up the black candles and maken the obeisances before the Sign of Koth that I keep wrapped up in a clean rag under the bed. Then I get me bread knife off the table out and lay it next to the black book on the bed.

But before I start in with the spell, and the cutten, I hang me coat up real careful behind the door.

# THE MUSIC OF ERICH ZANN

## A Screenplay

**TITLE 1**. AZATHOTH PRODUCTIONS PRESENT (Wash-out)

**TITLE 2**. (Burn down). THE MUSIC OF ERICH ZANN (cut to Title 3)

**TITLE 3**. A Horror Phantasy. (Wash-out then cut to Slide 1)

**SLIDE 1** Adapted for the Screen
By Leigh Blackmore
From H. P. Lovecraft's
Story of the same name (Cut to Slide 2)

**SLIDE 2**. Photography…K. Aldridge
Effects & Lighting…D. Threlfo
Audio…J. M. Blaxland (Cut to Slide 3)

**SLIDE 3**. CAST—
Erich Zann—J. M. Blaxland
Arthur Danvers—Leigh Blackmore
M. Blandot—D. Threlfo (Cut to Slide 4)

**SLIDE 4**. SOUNDTRACK—
Gloomy Sunday
Devil's Trill Sonata (Fade out)

**FADE IN** on CU of a handwriting, in what is obviously a journal. Already written are the words, under the of 18th August, 1765, 'I have almost given up hope of finding the Rue d'Auseil or the strange old man again.' The hand writes 'But perhaps it is for the best, although I am haunted by the vision of that dark street.' Camera scans page, giving plenty of time to read entry, and slowly fades out.

**FLASH-BACK**: Fade in 'Gloomy Sunday.' LS of Danvers walking slowly along a dark narrow street with overhanging roofs. Tighten to MCU of his face as he catches sight of a sign on one of the houses. Pan to CU of sign which reads 'Rooming House. Landlord—M. Blandot.' He walks towards it.

**CUT TO** inside the house (dilapidated as possible). M. Blandot is writing at a shabby desk. Cut to CS of Danvers knocking and entering. Blandot's POV. Danvers gestures and Blandot rises, and nods. Camera follows approximately 1 foot as they turn (2S) and go out by the door through which Danvers entered, closing the door behind them.

**CUT TO** Blandot opening a door in a different part of the house. Danvers pays him (2S) and enters. Track in and stop as Danvers unbuttons his shirt and sits on the bed. Viol music is heard from a distance, and Danvers stops and listens. It does not re-occur, so he continues preparing for bed.

**NEXT DAY**. 2.00pm as shown by MS of clock in background. Cut to Blandot's office. Danvers is gesticulating as though playing a viol, with an enquiring look on his face. Blandot points to the name 'Erich Zann' on the list of tenants on the wall, and picking up a hand-bill, headed New World Theatre, points out Zann's name amongst those of the orchestra at the bottom. Repeat Part 2 of Scene 4 with slight variations.

**CUT TO** Danvers knocking on the door of Zann's room, which is opened by Zann. BCU on Zann as Danvers introduces himself. They enter the small dingy room (2S) which Zann inhabits. MS as door closes behind them.

**CUT TO** inside of Zann's room. 2S as Danvers again gesticulates as though playing a viol, and Zann nods and opens his viol case. Pan to Zann as he plays a short air (MCU varying with CU of fingers playing). Pan back to Danvers, who thanks him and tries to whistle some of the music he heard the night before; whereupon Zann clamps a hand over Danvers' mouth and looks around furtively.

**CUT TO** Danvers' bedroom that night. He is reading, when he hears faintly one of Zann's weird melodies. He gets up.

**CUT TO** outside of Zann's door where Danvers is listening to the music coming from within. Suddenly, there is a cry from inside. Danvers knocks repeatedly and the door is finally opened by Zann (CU as he does so) terrified and shaking.

**CUT TO** inside the room as Danvers enters and helps Zann to a chair. S to Zann. He writes a note and hands it to Danvers (2S). It says, and the camera scans it CU, 'I implore you in the name of mercy, and for the sake of your curiosity, to wait where you are while I prepare a full account in German of the marvels and terrors which beset me.' 2S of

Danvers settling down to wait and Zann's pen flying across a sheet of paper.

**CUT TO** same scene but with Danvers almost asleep and a larger stack of papers beside Zann's elbow. A low musical note is heard from beyond the window. Zann immediately seizes his viol and starts playing wildly. ('Devils Trill Sonata' MIX other FX). S of Danvers' startled face. Zann's playing grows louder and wilder, but a single continuous note from beyond the window is audible above it. The shutters begin to rattle and then fly open. The window breaks and wind rushes in, scattering the manuscript sheets. CU of Zann's eyes, which are growing glassy; he is playing mechanically. Danvers tries to save sheets of manuscript but the wind bears them out of the window. He moves towards it and looks out (FX Danvers' POV). He turns to run but stops briefly to look at Erich Zann, whose eyes are bulging, face icy-cold, and who is still playing. He exits.

**LS OF** Danvers fleeing down the stairs and into the street. He melts into the shadows.

**FADE IN** to Danvers' journal. Hand has now written under what was there before: 'The discovery that Zann was dead but still playing was almost as terrible as that which came immediately before. But I am not wholly sorry for the loss in undreamable...' Here the hand is writing as the camera scans: '...abysses of the manuscript which alone could have explained the music of Erich Zann.'

**THE END**

# THE RETURN OF ZOTH—OMMOG

## (Found Among the Papers of the Late Jack Leyton, of Sydney)

*I*t was a star-spawned abomination, a monumental cosmic horror from a universe beyond imagining. The thing lumbered towards me, its great faceted eyes protruding, its membranous and semi-transparent squamous flesh quivering, slime dripping from its ravening maw. It was a god awakened from slumber, a being of hideously appalling size and terrifying vastness. It crashed across the temple's rock platforms, its cone-shaped body dwarfing the gigantic eel whose size had shocked me before this even more massive creature had appeared.

"Zatomaga! Zatomaga!" chanted the Pohnpeians, massed to witness the spectacle in their ritual temple.

The abominable creature slowed in its lumbering tracks and extended hideous appendages which sucked and chewed at the air, writhing blindly as they sought prey. The thing was a behemoth, positively Brobdingnagian. Extending one of its appendages to the nearest chained Pohnpeian, it ripped the head cleanly off the screaming man. Blood spurted ten feet through the air, splashing me on the chest. The remains of the man's body slumped to the ground. The gargantuan thing had four broad, flat, starfish-like arms with suckers, but it seemed to prefer to use its head-tentacles to clutch and grapple. It was a god, an incredible mutation, sheer muscle and killing power.

Zatomaga! Yes, and Zoth-Ommog—for despite the native name for the creature, I knew this was the Dweller in the Depths, the One referred to in the Ponape Scriptures. Dozens of feet above us, Zoth-Ommog brandished the man's head in its tentacle—a revolting trophy, dripping blood.

I backed against the temple's cold stone wall. The natives brandished their weapons, giving full vent to their fury. In hellish ecstasies of adoration they howled their god's name. "Zatomaga! Zatomaga! Zatomaga!" Their god, the one they had worshipped for generations, was making a rare, if shocking visitation. It was the time of the Red Haze, and Zoth-Ommog had come again!

My name is Jack Leyton. It is now ten years since the events of which I am about to write. I am not an overly imaginative man. At least I was not, until unexpected adventure befell me. Now, my dreams are shockingly haunted, and I intend to seek with my gun the peace which I can find in no other way.

I am without heirs or relations in this world. I leave this diary account of my adventures in Pohnpei for whoever may stumble across it, for I am almost maddened by glimpses of forbidden aeons, of shattering truths that flashed out at me from the abysms of ignorance in which I was sunk until that fated year of 1863.

"*Pwoahng Mwahu*," said my companion, Sturges. "That means good night." He lay down with his back to me.

Since escaping our captors, we had eaten our fill of bananas and breadfruit, and then later cooked yams on our campfire. We saw a large monitor lizard in the distance. Sturges told me they will eat chickens and occasionally a small piglet. I wondered if we might catch meat tomorrow if that monitor didn't sample us for breakfast. I don't remember falling asleep; I was so exhausted from our escape.

We had awoken to the sound of heavy bodies smashing through the jungle's perpetual green daylight. To our night-camp came the crunching of branches as they splintered, the splashing of naked feet in shallow water. Startled birds—sooty terns, brown noddies—screeched as they wheeled up and away from the column of men that bore down upon us.

I rolled over on my grassy bed, my eyes crusty with sleep, my spine knotted, and my legs racked with cramp. I scrabbled for my knife, my backpack, the few remaining possessions I had with me. Folding stiffly into a half-crouch, I turned my head to listen. I could still hear the thwack and stomp of men chopping their way through tangled knots of jungle growth. The ship's masters might send men from the *Lady Armitage*, which yet lay moored in the lagoon that separated Pohnpei from its surrounding reefs. It may have been natives. In any case, we didn't want to be caught.

I gestured to Sturges, pointing forward through the rain-drenched forest canopy and we plunged forward through the plumeria, bougainvillea, thick stands of pandanus. Before we had gone far, we quickly climbed one of the plentiful monkey-pod trees to elude our pursuers. Rain came again and the splashing muffled any noises we were making. Our pursuers lost us, passing on the muddy, overgrown trail beneath. We waited a long time in that tree, listening past the rain for any sound of danger.

It was only three months ago that I was enjoying the rum of Sydney town. In 1863 the colony's publican houses were the stalking ground of press gangs. I was a landlubber, too naïve for my own good, and I didn't expect to be whacked on the head, certainly not by naval troops.

I had finished work and passed along the Rocks' cobbled twilight streets. Everywhere muffinmen rang their bells, pigs'-trotter men plied their trade, pipeclay sellers and piemen cried out for people to buy their wares. I arrived at the Hero mighty thirsty after my day's work.

The Lord Nelson was built from sandstone brought up from the Argyle Cut, where I had been working. The Beehive was another pub built with stone from the Cut, but I didn't want to drink at places reminiscent of my workplace, so I usually drank at the Whalers Arms or the Hero of Waterloo. Tonight it was the Hero. The place had been an inn long before the famous 1815 battle, and was a favourite drinking spot for Garrison Troops, but its open log fires and well-stocked bar provided welcome relief from the ramshackle, rat-infested dwellings of the Rocks' mean streets.

I often drank there and had never run into any trouble before. I was generally careful not to enter Cockroach Lane or Frog Hollow, more dangerous slums of the colony, which were filled with unsavoury grog shops and shanties. I was not as down on my luck as some of the area's debauched and unhappy residents; at least I got paid a decent wage. I usually didn't venture to Gallows Hill, either, though many fellow convicts liked to go there with the large crowds to watch the hangings in the old jail near George Street North.

On this particular night, however, a sinister atmosphere seemed in the air as I downed my pint at the bar. Rum smugglers were said to use the place, but I had no idea that tunnels ran from the hotel's cellar down to the Harbour. I liked my rum as much as any man, so I hadn't been about to complain.

This week had been hard. After a couple of hours I was full as a boot. Just as I thought of heading home, two men clad in rough blue naval dress accosted me, suddenly gripping my arms from both sides. A stunning blow to the side of my head sent my vision black as I slumped to my knees.

Before I could recover, I was dropped through the trapdoor into the cellar. Kegs of beer rolled away from me as wrought-iron gates opened on rusting hinges. I was half-dragged, half-carried through a maze of stone cellars, smelling the sweat of my captors and the dankness of the underground tunnel that led from under the hotel to a house nearby.

I had no time to regain my senses or look about me, before the same two men took me from the house. They manhandled me down to the wharves, where many whaling ships were berthed, and unceremoniously bundled me aboard a foul-smelling clipper. They thrust me into the hold, rough quarters for a motley crew of other gang victims—some (I soon learned) as shocked as I was to find themselves there, aboard the *Lady Armitage*.

"Slogger Ball got ya, did he?" one of the sailors jeered.

"Who's he?" I asked groggily, fingering the tender spot on my head, where I could feel a patch of bloody, matted hair.

"Press ganger. Does the Darling Harbour beat. Hard to miss—wears a stovepipe hat and frock coat. The back rooms of his house have hidden trapdoors. Poor bastards like you get shoved into the dungeons there before they turf you out to crew this sorry ship."

I tried to think. "No, I was drinking at the Hero of Waterloo, down Lower Fort Street."

"Ah, matey, that place is just as notorious. Could have been the naval press gangs, then. They're licensed to roam the streets and seize any able-bodied man. Or maybe it was the larrikins from the Rocks Push that got ya. Well, make the best of it—you're bound on a voyage for Micronesia!"

*And you*, I thought, but said no more, for shock overcame me at this moment. Upon my recovery, it wasn't long before I concluded the crew of this ship constituted ruffians of every description. Many had been pressed into service from the gaols. Others had been taken from their places of employment, or (like me) simply kidnapped off the streets or out of the bars. Some had tried to bribe their way out of it, but still couldn't escape.

❖

Once at sea, I realised the conditions on board the full-rigged ship promised to be little worse than those I had endured in servitude. The masters reminded me of the brutal guards at the Argyle Cut, where I had been doing hard labour cutting sandstone with hammers and chisels, and witnessed the first horrific experiments with explosives. The place was becoming the underground home of thugs, petty gangsters and rats, and cases of plague had started to clean out the convict labourers.

Most of the crew endured rough treatment at the hands of the master, Henrik Janssen. Under Janssen, there was Karl Jacobs, the bo'sun; and

Dan Metcalfe, the second mate. The men all slept in bunks in the ill-fitted berth below decks.

I wondered at my change of fortune. One place was as good as another if I was a free man. Maybe I'd even be better off sailing all the way to Micronesia. The warm dark nights refreshed me, as did the ringing of bells at the various watches, the sky's blue during the day, the rolling of the waves. It was an illusory freedom, but I started to feel free at sea. The masters still treated us brutally, but at least I began to make acquaintances amongst the crew.

"We're bound for the Carolines," snapped one of the men when I asked our destination, but he didn't seemed to know. The master played his cards close to his chest.

But I began to think I could manage to make my escape if the ship made landfall. Meanwhile, we sailed north, towards the large archipelago of widely scattered islands in the western Pacific, northeast of New Guinea.

Over the course of a month the ship sailed north, up Australia's East Coast, north through the vast landless reaches of the Coral Sea. Heading further northwards, it reached the Solomon Sea. I thought we may make landfall in the Bougainvilles, but instead the ship pressed on, sailing past New Ireland and further north. After another month we crossed the Equator, past tiny Kapingamarangi Atoll, and kept going. In my dreams I imagined escaping when we made landfall, but each time we weighed anchor for supplies we were beaten below decks and hardly saw the earth, let alone the green forests of those islands in all that time.

Eventually, three months out of Sydney, we came into the region of the Eastern Carolines.

One night after second dog-watch I was scrubbing the deck around the after-deckhouse—one of my allotted tasks to earn my meagre provisions—and overhearing snatches of conversation between Jacobs and Metcalf, who leant over the rail smoking.

I learned one of the reasons for them heading for Micronesia. The sea around Truk and other islands in the region was full of sunken wrecks, they said. Some contained treasure, and more wrecks lay off the islands of Eten, Fefan and Uman. Some, the men said, were in lagoons, under only a few feet of water, shallow enough that it would be simple to salvage whatever treasures were still aboard.

"Those wrecks are going to make us rich," said one man to the other. "Just think of all that gold!" At one point they discussed heading for the mysterious and darkly-rumoured Sequeira Isles in the West Carolines, but after arguing they decided to head for Ponape, a place previously known as Ascension Island.

There was a place on the island called Nan Madol. Some legends, the men said, told that Nan Madol's canals had been formed by a giant dragon or lizard. Jacobs ventured that this may have derived from the New Guinean crocodile, a large species that often swam in the open sea, but Metcalf held the legend true, superstitiously believing that the giant lizard or eel still dwelled in a secret chamber in Nan Madol's largest temple.

I contrived to win the confidence of one of the crew. Ship's provisions were meagre; we lived on ship's biscuit, tins of corned beef, salt butter and tea. By saving some of my corned beef, I managed to get Eli Sturges to engage in conversation with me. Initially surly, he warmed to me after I offered him my extra corned beef, and I found he was simply being guarded.

Sturges was a tall, lean man who had worked up north with the Kanakas in the Queensland cane fields. He had been a blackbirder, one who specialised in stealing young Melanesians to put them to work in Australia's cane fields. He confessed as much.

"We used to lure 'em on board with promises of treasure—muskets, mattocks and axes, pipes and tobacco were treasure to them. Naïve, they were. Then we'd take 'em back to Australia and put 'em to work for our wealthy colonial betters. The owners found us white scum died if forced to labour in Queensland's tropical heat." A bitter laugh escaped him. "I earned good money to stand over the kanakas on horseback, with a stock-whip."

I shuddered. Sturges seemed proud of his former job, which amounted to no more than slavery. In fact, he was morally little different from the pressgangers. How galling he found his enslavement now! Despite my repugnance, I kept up our conversation, for I hoped in the stories he offered might lie something useful to aid my escape.

Sturges had also been in the Carolines before. Full of wild tales about Pohnpei, and what had happened to him there, he had travelled widely, and talked of idol-capped monoliths in other lonely places. He had seen more than he dare reveal, but he had witnessed strange rituals, and cryptic obeisance made before ancient altars.

As we stood together up near the forepeak one evening, he began to reflect upon some peculiar lore which preoccupied his thoughts.

"Ever heard of the *Ponape Scriptures*? It's a manuscript found in the Carolines by Captain Abner Ezekiel Hoag sometime around 1734. It was old even then." He eyed me narrowly to gauge my receptiveness to his statement. As I didn't react, he went on.

"The book's pages were made of palm leaves; it was bound in a now-extinct cycadean wood. It was lettered throughout in Naacal—the language of Mu."

"Mu?" The name sounded strangely on my ears.

Sturges looked around furtively. "Mu—Lemuria—can't tell you everything at once. I knew an army man from Ceylon. Churchward was his name. He got in with those priesthood cults—studied various megalithic civilisations, especially in the South Pacific Ocean—was entrusted with the secrets from certain stone tablets. He was full of tales of a great early civilisation, known as Mu or Lemuria. It vanished beneath the sea 25,000 years ago. Imagine that! Mu was an immense continent covering nearly half of the Pacific." He waved vaguely to the southwest. "Mu sank under a great volcanic eruption. Now fifty million square miles of water cover it over. Churchward said Mu's history dated back 200,000 years."

These were numbers and measures of time for which I had no reference. I couldn't help but shake my head. Sturges scowled.

"Well, Hoag wasn't making it all up. That's all I'm saying. He managed to translate the manuscript. But when he tried to have it published, religious leaders strongly objected to the book's references to Dagon and the publishers turned him down. I know some copies survived amongst secretive cults such as the Esoteric Order of Dagon."

I didn't know what he was talking about. "Esoteric Order of—Dagon?"

Sturges reached into his inside coat pocket. He drew out a volume bound in dark cloth, stained with salt and water-marked on its covers. "Here. You'll need it where we're going."

I couldn't imagine how he had kept the thing secret, but I followed his practice of keeping it hidden at all times. In my bunk below decks, and by the feeble light of a stolen stump of candle, I read it through that night; it was the testimony of a crazy man. It claimed that the original *Ponape Scriptures* was authored by Imash-Mo, high priest of a being known as Ghatanothoa, and his successors. This Ghatanothoa was from a race of beings known as the 'Old Ones.' The book claimed these Old Ones ruled the earth before there were any humans. They were gone now, inside the earth, and under the sea, but their dead bodies had told their secrets in dreams to the first humans, who formed a cult which had endured throughout the ages. The author raved that the *Ponape Scriptures* detailed the story of the legendary lost continent of Mu and of Zanthu, high priest of Ythogtha, another of the Old Ones.

Paging further through the volume's tattered pages, I read pencilled annotations which Sturges must have scribbled in the margins: *Churchward says temple built over network of cellars and crypts connected to a canal. Centre-room shaped like pyramid. Similar ruins (to Ponape) at Kosae, near village of Lele. Huge enclosures—cone-shaped hill surrounded by high walls. Natives say people here very powerful—travelled east and west in great vessels. Some believe legendary lost continent of Mu, or Lemuria, may lie off its waters. Nan Madol, ritual centre, built as mirror image of sunken city that, at time of construction, could still be seen lying beneath water's surface?*

I hid the volume away and fell into a restless sleep haunted by visions of distant wastes and dark places. Hoag's words seemed to appear before me in letters of black flame: *"Someday the Old Ones will call, when the stars are right, and the secret cult is always waiting to liberate him."*

My reading of Hoag's book, and Sturges' recent bizarre rantings, confused and bewildered me. But there was a weird credulity to the tales that almost convinced me despite myself.

*"What has risen may sink, and what has sunk may rise!"* said Sturges. "We have to try and stop what's happening on Ponape."

I fell to studying the volume's contents with ever-increasing fascination, keeping an eye on the captain's cabin to ensure my secret studies were not observed. I would be soundly flogged if the senior crew discovered me slacking off my on-deck duties.

Starboard lay Kosrae island. The sailors whispered anxiously of its ill-rumoured ruins, which stood on the smaller island of Lelu. Off to port we glimpsed the atoll Ngatik; but we would make landfall at Ponape.

The weather on our voyage had been mainly fine, but we weathered a small typhoon once we reached the Carolines. Fortunately the ship was undamaged.

Every now and again we saw other sea creatures—lionfish, sting-rays, and the occasional school of barracuda. We had heard of hammerhead sharks, which the natives called 'Baku,' but saw none.

Gradually we sailed closer to the islands, coming in through the coral atolls, with their sprinklings of coconut palms. Sturges pointed out the peak of Mount Totolom, easily seen from out at sea. Occasionally a cortege of sea turtles would cross the clipper's wake. Gorgonian fans of bright coral loomed up beneath us.

Another night, Metcalf and Jacobs talked of the strangeness of Ponape. "Did you ever hear tell of old Captain Obed Marsh?" asked Jacobs. "He learned of strange creatures he called the Deep Ones. Alien, half-fish and half-frog things, he said they were. And there was old Zadok Allen, from Innsmouth. I got him drunk one night—not that he needed much help! He loves that bootleg whisky!—and he told me about an island east of Otaheite. It has a lot o' stone ruins older'n anybody knew anything abaout, kind o' like on Ponape, in the Carolines, but with carvins' of faces that looked like the big statues on Easter Island."

Metcalf responded with rumours of bountiful gold and fish offered to people in certain South Seas areas, exchanged to humans for human sacrifices. He had heard that the swindling Australian ship Captain Charles 'Bloody' Hart, master of the British ship *Lambton*, had in the 1830's traded with the Deep Ones, who had given him fine pieces of a special tortoise shell in return for unnamable sacrifices—members of his crew. Sometimes, he whispered, the fish-frog things even mated with the humans, producing hideous hybrid entities. Their vast underwater cities lay beneath the sea, and the alien creatures lived in them for millennia. There were other whispers, about brooding reefs and black abysses, and an underwater city, Cyclopean and many-columned Y'ha-nthlei, which some thought lay beneath the harbour at Ponape's mysterious Nan Madol complex. Some said this was identical with a legend of a sunken city the Pohnpeians called Kahnihniweiso.

---

*Zoth-Ommog had returned! As I backed against the temple wall, I thought how foolish I was to have ventured here. Zoth-Ommog's cult had consumed the people on Ponape, and I been captured through my careless enthusiasm for adventure, and the lure of the mystery of Nan Madol's bizarre architecture.*

*Zoth-Ommog thrashed colossally before my eyes. Its head was tremendous, razor-fanged and reptilian, but covered in tentacles. Bending forward, it extended another prodigious tentacle writhing with mouths, each lined with viciously sharp fangs. The tentacle snaked towards the next man in line—it was Janssen, master of the Lady Armitage. Though he had done me no kindnesses, I didn't wish to see him die. But I could do nothing to prevent it. Janssen pulled out a flintlock musket he must have hidden on his person. Before he could fire, the tentacle lashed around, smashing him across the face. Half the skin was flayed off at the first blow. The musket clattered to the floor.*

*The tentacle returned, whipping gigantically around and opening fully in front of the terrified man's head. The teeth gleamed an instant in the red maw, then the mouth snapped shut, splitting Janssen's skullcase with an awful* crunch. Zoth-Ommog, stupendous in his alien ghastliness, undulated, shook Janssen's limp body furiously, then tossed it aside. The natives shouted, in a hoarse chorus of approval: "Zatomaga! Zatomaga!"

Zoth-Ommog roared its mountainous satisfaction. I now knew this to be Great Cthulhu's third son, imprisoned by the Elder Gods beneath the seabed near Pohnpei. I had read neither The R'lyeh Texts nor the fabled Zanthu Tablets, but enough had been whispered to me by my compatriot Sturges for me to know Zoth-Ommog was perhaps the most dreaded of the Great Old Ones.

The creature known as Zoth-Ommog slobbered and groped, a gelatinous immensity that promised nothing but fear and death. It roared again, and the temple walls shook. I knew I was about to die.

A beautiful young Pohnpeian woman with eyes like the dark moon was suddenly beside me. It was the girl I had seen earlier on the island, and who had not given away my presence. She was offering to help me escape! As she cut my bonds with a stone adze, she said one word: "Pwoakapwoak." As I looked into her dark eyes, I didn't have to speak the language to know that meant 'love.'

She gestured to a dark recess, an exit, in the temple wall nearby, and pulled at my wrist. I needed no urging to run with her, desperately seeking refuge from the monstrous horrors I had witnessed. A shout from manifold throats rose behind us as we made our escape.

This was not my first escape in recent times. As I ran hand-in-hand with the girl, my mind swam back to Sturges. Had he known what fate awaited him the night we escaped from the Lady Armitage?

---

Sturges and I had decided to escape as soon as the *Lady Armitage* entered the lagoon near Nan Madol. The night before, I grabbed a canvas bag and stowed in it what supplies I could. I have only vague memories of what we went through as we climbed overboard and took the dinghy towards the shore. Someone on board raised the alarm. They fired on us, shots ringing out over the open waters. We were sitting ducks in the dinghy.

"Dive!" I called out to Sturges. We were a long way from shore, but we dived into the sea in a rush of bubbles, and struck out hard. The water was not cold, but the distance was long. By the time we got near shore, I could tell Sturges was as exhausted as I was. Then there followed our scrambling out of the water, standing on an exposed rockshelf, shivering on the edge. Crabs crawled around my feet as I reached down to help the dripping Sturges from the pounding surf. The wind's stinging fingers struck ice into my veins. I remember little else. Memories of wide, cold ocean splashing up against the shores—pools of water topped with slippery algae scum, covered the rock—wind buffeting—then merciful unconsciousness as we dragged ourselves to the tree line and collapsed.

When we awoke, we found ourselves on the mountainous high island—Ponape. From our position on the coast, we could see that numerous volcanic peaks dominated the place. Some looked to be over 2,000 feet above sea level.

"The name Pohnpei means 'upon a stone altar'," said Sturges. "I don't understand why, but that's how it translates."

We looked around. Dense forests surrounded the lagoon, within which the Lady Armitage lay at anchor. The coastline consisted of seemingly endless fringing reefs, inlets and coves. The most spectacular outcropping was a place Sturges pointed out to me as Sokehs Rock. It was a sheer basalt cliff face nearby—the boldest natural landmark, rising 500 feet.

"You get mainly tidal flats and mangrove swamps on the coast," said Sturges. "The interior is more treacherous—it's filled with hidden brooks, snaking rivers, and secret and hidden valleys."

I agreed with him we didn't want to venture too far into the interior rainforest. The moss-covered trees and abundant rainfall there would make it difficult to reach and harder to get out of.

One morning we stole an outrigger canoe from the beach and hid it in the forest on the point at Metalanim Harbour. To my puzzled queries, Sturges would only reply: "Insurance."

"We have to watch out," he added. "They don't like the Westerners here. If the ship's crew doesn't get us, the locals will. The people here regard their home as sapw saraw—sacred land. In 1854, the whaler Delta brought smallpox. An outbreak of sores followed the fever. I saw the aftermath—there was a sickening odour as the sores broke and oozing pus spread. Hundreds of natives were affected, groaning and dying through the breadfruit groves. People were buried in shallow graves, some still living. It was a horrible time. Sometimes those buried alive returned to their families dressed in their burial clothes. Over half the island's population died, including many chiefs. The epidemic abated, but they blame the Westerners—if they catch us, we're dead meat."

"That was only nine years ago!" I exclaimed.

Seeing the look on my face, he added, with his bitter laugh: "Oh, it's quite safe now."

We climbed a hilly rise, and found it looked out over a local village.

Standing on a bare stone ledge, we could see huts made of mangrove wood, thatch, rope and bamboo, all painted in contrasting colours. Most backed onto pens of squealing pigs. Baskets spilling bananas and yams sat outside some of the thatched huts.

A couple of the natives sat making wood carvings—dolphins, sharks, turtles. Another dark-skinned fellow worked on an outrigger canoe model. I could see sitting on the ground next to him some models of manta rays which he carved from the nut of an ivory palm.

"Clever people. They use hand-twisted coconut sennit rope to tie the beams. Look at how the wood pillars are set on stones so as not to touch the ground."

"They seem really peaceful," I said. Boys wearing loincloths played with dogs which ran about, or lazed on the paths. Moss-covered stone walls straggled here and there. "But you don't trust them?" I asked him, as dark-furred fruit bats circled overhead, and screeched towards the treetops.

"Keep your head down," he said, flinching. "Not at all. They have their sinister and fanatical side. Let's hope we don't find out about it." He looked away into the distance. His eyes saw unbidden memories and his jaw set tight.

Women wearing hibiscus skirts were sitting bare-breasted in the streams doing laundry. Through the day's heat, young children ran laughing and naked. Men walked about in their traditional fibre clothing, occasionally spitting a squirt of chewed betel nut. Some of them were adorned with brightly coloured trochus-shell necklaces and beads.

Many of the men seemed heavily tattooed, mainly on the arms and legs, with complex and cross-hatched patterns. Some of the women were tattooing their men as we watched. The design that recurred most depicted a writhing creature with a tentacled head.

"And what about the tattoos?" I asked.

Sturges shrugged. "The *pelipel*? These people wear their histories on their bodies. Clan histories and great events in the island's life show up in them. They see the ability to endure pain as honourable. You know how they usually do it? They take 'em to an isolated hut. For up to a month, the person being tattooed withstands the ordeal of having elaborate patterns etched into their skin with an ink-dipped thorn. Sometimes they use sharpened animal bones. Colourful, aren't they?"

The women were also tattooed, largely around the thighs and buttocks, though Sturges told me they were often also tattooed around their genital regions. I grimaced.

"You think that's bad," he said. "Another male rite of passage is the *lekilek*—the castration of the left testicle." He laughed at my obvious discomfort.

Sturges pointed back to the forest, and we made our way back to our camp-cum-hiding place. Just as were making our way into the trees, I turned around, and saw a Pohnpeian woman, one of the most beautiful island girls I'd seen, staring after me with eyes like the dark moon.

A red orchid decorated her hair, and her brown skin glistened. For a moment I stood stock still, terrified to have been spotted. But she smiled shyly, and inclined her head in a way that signalled me to keep going. Perhaps she had seen something about me she liked. I continued into the cover of the trees, and saw her go back to work, weaving her net, saying nothing to those around her.

Sturges and I hid in the forests for two weeks. Bored with eating breadfruit and fresh mangoes, we surreptitiously made our way to the beach, carefully so as to avoid being observed. We caught fresh fish in the lagoon's shallow waters, a tasty variant to our normal diet.

Back at our camp, Sturges told me another Pohnpei story he considered important.

"Eight years ago," said Sturges, "in July 1855, an unusually dense, smoky haze surrounded the island, and the sun and the moon took on a red glow. The *sanworos* (priests) got upset. They thought it the work of Isohkelekel, displeased over the people's failure to perform *karismei*, the first offering of breadfruit season. They immediately made feasts to his principal priestess to propitiate the god. Soon afterward, the Red Haze disappeared. It was around that time I was taken captive. I nearly lost my life then. They get worked up on such occasions. Something's brewing again now." He looked worried and wouldn't say more. But that night I noticed that the night sky was tinged with red.

We were, I learned, in the Madolenihmw district where Nan Madol is found. I enjoyed watching the people from afar. They worked hard producing copra, and also cacao and taro. One day I could smell the Pohnpeians preparing *sakau*, a potent narcotic brew like *kava*. They had taken pepper plant roots and were pounding them upon huge basaltic sakau stones made from rounded river rocks. The men would then squeeze the roots through some inner bark of the tropical hibiscus, which contributed a viscous sap to the *sakau*.

An atmosphere of anticipation began to build amongst the people. Sturges recognised it as ominous preparations for a major ritual. The people held a canoe-building competition, feasting, singing, dancing and *sakau* drinking over a number of days. Gradually they worked themselves into a state of frenzy. We saw them drink the *sakau* from coconut shells, passing it around communally, usually at sunset, and always with the *nahnmwarki* (district chief) served first.

Meanwhile, I felt my obsession to see Nan Madol also growing.

Eventually, we crossed from the jungle to the tidal flats of hilly Temwen Island, where we beheld Nan Madol. Mysterious megalithic ruins of ancient walls…dykes…columns…Cyclopean stoneworks…all built of black basalt rock by pre-modern inhabitants. The Venice of the Pacific!

*T*he island girl and I fled that poison temple of madness through a secret exit known to her, running for our lives across the outer precincts. Why did it seem that the stones were oddly angled beneath our feet, the endless vistas of rock seeming phantasmally variable and prismatically distorted?

*The girl took me to the islet's edge. Behind us were a thousand angry Pohnpeians and a raging Old One, an aeons-old immensity that lumbered and floundered after us.*

*We had one advantage. It would take Zoth-Ommog some time to find a way out of the temple. The black-haired girl guided me skilfully through the twisting waterway; without her I wouldn't have had a chance. I rowed the canoe back through the canals.*

*She pressed into my hand a flintlock musket; it must have been the one Janssen had dropped. It would be no use against Zoth-Ommog's might, but perhaps it would help me somehow.*

*The moon shone fitfully down over the scene. Behind us, a thunderous crashing told us that Zoth-Ommog had broken out through the temple wall. I felt a pulsing of alien thought pressing on my mind, threatening to overtake it. The star-spawn was using its telepathic powers to try and sway me, but it was not close enough. It wouldn't take long to catch us, though.*

*Leaping off the canoe and back onto the fringing beach, we ran for the shelter of the coconut palms. The ground trembled beneath our feet. Looking back over one shoulder I saw It through the Haze—a cloudy impression of great wings, of writhing head tentacles, and a face only an Old One's mother could love.*

*The grotesque monstrosity came on after us, its outspread starfish arms clawing at the midnight sky. With a few strides it crossed from Ihded islet to the very shore where we had stood scant moments before. We scrambled forward through the jungle, over rocks and fallen trees. Our one hope lay in the dark, and in the Red Haze, which now lay low above the ground. From Zoth-Ommog's height, we puny humans would seem the merest insects.*

*Zoth-Ommog's misshapen head turned to sight us. Its stupendous legs crashed on the ground. Trees splintered and fell before It as It entered the forest in search of us. The girl cast terrified glances behind, but I tried to urge her forward.*

*Thank God that Sturges and I had stowed that spare outrigger canoe around on the point of Metalanim Harbour. If we could just reach it and get off the island!*

*I didn't think Zoth-Ommog could stray far from his lair, for I had seen the graven seals on the rocks around Nan Madol, and now I knew what they were. They were the ancient seals and signs of the Elder Ones, the immemorial gods who had imprisoned Zoth-Ommog here in the South Pacific. The return of the Red Haze had allowed the Old One to rise, but we still had a chance. We must get out to sea!*

*As we continued to stumble through the jungle, my thoughts returned again to Nan Douwas, to all that had led us here.*

---

Sturges and I descended from Temwen island. There they were: ninety-two islets made by human hands, across eighteen square kilometres, covered thickly with liana and mangrove. I could see that in places the fast-growing tropical trees, underbrush and vines were starting to destroy the ancient stonework.

We descended the rock footpath through scattered ruins to the reef towards the artificial islet complex. Nearest us was Nan Douwas, the largest structure on Nan Madol. Some of the corner-stones here might weigh fifty tons, I thought.

"This place was by built by the Saudeleurs," said Sturges. "They were a line of tyrannical stranger-kings from Katau Peidi in the west, who had won control of the land and imposed their will on Ponape's people. They dominated the area for five centuries. Pohnpeian oral traditions link these rulers to the Thunder God. His temple is a large, three-tiered platform on Pahnkadira Islet—that's it over there, where the Saudeleur lived. The Thunder God's son, the legendary Isokelekel, is said to have established a new political order presided over by a high chief called the *nahnmwarki*."

Naturally formed logs of intrusive basalt lay in long strips, piled skilfully atop each other to form walls in some cases up to twenty-five feet high. These immense megalithic prisms were often fifteen feet in length and must have weighed tons. I could see the gaps between stones were filled up with grit and coral rubble. Immense seawalls and breakwaters protected the island centre from the Pacific's unrelenting waves. The islets were connected by a network of waterways.

Sturges continued to lecture me. "Nan Madol was an elaborate residential and religious compound. This complex was been their royal residence. Their *nahs* or meeting houses were usually pole-and-thatch, but the temples were stone-built. Many of the residents were chiefs, but most were commoners. Nan Madol helped the cruel Saudeleur chiefs organise and control potential rivals. In the thirteenth century, after the Saudeleurs, the Nahnmwarki invaders led by Isokelekel were victorious. At its height, Nan Madol was a vast capital. It supported more than a thousand people –Ponape's ancient elite chiefs (the *Saus*) and their servants—on the islets alone," he said, gesturing around us.

I was stunned. This was a city built by people as sophisticated as the ancient Egyptians.

"I've studied this place intensively," said Sturges. I believed him. "Each islet had a specific purpose; for instance one was used for building canoes, another for processing coconuts. One was a residence for servants, another was a burial place of ancient tombs. The earliest buildings date from a thousand years ago. The major constructions here probably began around 1200 AD. There's been two thousand years' of continuous occupation here."

He shrugged. "Let's get cracking," he said. "We can approach by canoe from the open lagoon and then move along the central lagoon that leads through Madol Poew," said Sturges.

Numerous outrigger canoes were pulled up along the stony beach near the entrance to the canals. We commandeered one. The high tide enabled our small canoe to navigate the grid of twisting mangrove-choked waterways and shallow canals which wound through the complex. The place must have been vast in its day. Some of the stone walls towered as high as fifty feet above our heads.

Looking over the canoe's side, I glimpsed variegated coral through the crystal-clear waters. Passing jungle-covered islets on both sides, we caught glimpses of Nan Douwas' southwest corner through the lianas and trees.

With Sturges steering the canoe, we maneuvered and slowed, sliding up beside the west front's main entry landing. I gazed up in wonder at the magnificence of Nan Douwas' west façade—the stately podium, the noble entryway, and the steps ascending to interior courts, enclosures and tombs. Enclosing walls surrounded the huge crypts.

The site's dramatic impact was staggering. Thousands and thousands of columnar volcanic basal blocks, probably weighing thousands of tons each, formed the walls of different temples. The walls were built in basketwork fashion out of loose bricks, with no masonry.

"The basalt blocks were probably cut at Ponape's north coast," said Sturges, "and taken across to the east coast to build Nan Madol. They had placed these giant slabs with fill on top of submerged coral reefs to form raised platforms. These supported their elaborate ritual and ceremonial complexes. The stones were so big that there's widely varied speculation about how the local people could have transported them—an amazing engineering feat. Certainly, the stones did not originate locally. The blocks were somehow transported overland through impassable jungle."

"How did they do it?" I sat in the canoe staring awestruck.

"Well, there are the oral traditions," smiled Sturges. "The most popular legend tells that at Sokeh lived two brothers, Ol Sipha and Ol Sopha. Ol Sopha set himself up as Ponape's first supreme ruler. They decided to build a sacred place to the gods, demons and ghosts, and made offerings to the turtle god Nahnsapwe. Their first shrine at Sokehs Rock collapsed due to the waves' action. Eventually they founded Nan Douwas, with the people digging canals, tunnels and walls.

"Another legend claims the brothers had magical powers, and the basalt blocks were brought from nearby Sokeh and made to fly through the air, settling down in the right positions to form Nan Madol."

The prevailing northeasterly ocean breezes ruffled our hair as we continued gazing up at Nan Douwas.

"How do *you* think they did it?" I asked. "Did this black magic have anything to do with it?" I asked.

Sturges shook his head. "I don't reckon so. There's yet another—more credible—theory that the prisms were dislodged by large fires built at their bases," he said. "The stones were rapidly cooled and fractured by the seawater, then placed on rafts and floated within the fringing coral reefs to the building site."

"You can see that not all the stones reached their intended destinations," said Sturges. He gestured to the coastal lagoon's bottom, where I could see long blocks lying on coral and sand. Some appeared to have mysterious carvings, like signs or seals engraved on them. Clearly, moving and placing the basalt stones had been highly labour intensive, taking hundreds of years to accomplish. The sunken blocks suggested coral-encrusted formations in the deep, and I thought again of the book, with its suggestion that a vast sunken city underlay Nan Madol.

Sturges shrugged again. "They may also have used levers, maybe inclined coconut-palm planes. They would have made strong hibiscus fibre ropes. Moving megaliths was definitely within their capabilities. They're a smart people, even if I don't trust 'em."

"What's the area to the northeast?" I asked.

"That's Madol Powe," said Sturges. "It's the upper town, the ritual and mortuary sector. They built major tombs there—the biggest is a central stepped tomb—and that's where the *Saus* lived. Mortuary activities and burials also happened along the lagoon breakwater islets. Nan Madol is divided into two main areas separated by this central waterway. To the southwest is the lower town, known as Madol Pah. It used to be the administrative sector—the royal dwellings and ceremonial areas."

A cycle of whispered legends clustered around the practices of the ancient peoples who had built and worshipped at Nan Madol, averred Sturges. Some of the legends centred on Zoth-Ommog, a being of the Old Ones, who had been spawned near the double star Xoth. He was the eldritch progeny of Great Cthulhu and the female being known as Idh-yaa.

"So why is it called Nan Madol?"

Sturges needed no encouragement to display his knowledge. "'Nan' meant 'place', and 'Madol' was Ponapean for 'between places', so that Nan Madol meant 'space between' or 'the place between places'."

I could see that 'space between' could be a reference to the canals which intersected the islets. But that didn't seem to be a full explanation. What could that phrase possibly mean?

"Is that all?" I pressed him.

"Well, the Sadeleurs originally called it *Soun Nanleng,* which means 'Reef of Heaven'. But they renamed it when the Old Ones trickled down from the stars. I think it's a reference to the Old Ones' rulership of the city. I once read a copy of Abdul Alhazred's *Necronomicon.* There's a passage in that book I know by heart."

His gaze became distant as he recited. "*The Old Ones were, the Old Ones are, and the Old Ones shall be. Not in the spaces we know, but between them, They walk serene and primal, undimensioned and to us unseen…They walk unseen and foul in lonely places where the Words have been spoken and the Rites howled through at their Seasons. The wind gibbers with their voices, and the earth mutters with their consciousness …The ice desert of the South and the sunken isles of Ocean hold stones whereon their seal is engraven, but who hath seen the deep frozen city or the sealed tower long garlanded with seaweed and barnacles?… They wait patient and potent, for here shall They reign again…*" Sturges stared at me, challenging me to call him crazy.

"*Not in the spaces we know, but between them!*" I thought of the seals on the sunken rocks—"*...the sunken Isles of Ocean hold stones whereon their seal is engraven.*" Despite my reluctance to believe Sturges' more outlandish ramblings about the Old Ones, the evidence seemed to be piling up in their favour. We clambered out of the canoe and onto the islet.

We hadn't gone more than a few steps onto the rocky platform when, out of the shadows came a party of Pohnpeians, armed with slings and stone adzes. We were captured!

They took us, struggling and cursing, to the main Pah Kadira islet. The whole temple complex seemed ominously desolate under the moon's dim glow. Many of the stone platforms were littered with used shell tools, ornaments, pot shards and stone tools. We were unceremoniously thrust into a bamboo cage, and locked in. It was an uncomfortable night, and I dreaded what was to come.

Next day, the tribe assembled. From our bamboo prison we saw them bring forth a great turtle, which they anointed with coconut oil and hung with ornaments. They loaded the turtle into a boat and paddled down one of the canals. Despite our plight I was fascinated. The priest stared hard at the giant turtle, seeming to blink every time the turtle blinked. An integral part of the ritual, I guessed.

Then they brought the turtle back onto the main platform. The chief priest killed the turtle with a blow from a club, breaking its shell. The men cut it up, cooked it, and served it to the priests, with muttered prayers and ritual.

"It's a *kamatihp*, a feasting ceremony," said Sturges. The men seemed to forget about us. For the feast, they killed and ate a dog, and served giant quarter-ton yams. Native women arrived in canoes, and the Pohnpeians worked themselves into an orgiastic frenzy. They fell to having sex, openly fornicating and continuing the feasting and lascivious celebration.

That night we were transferred to Idehd, the Place of the Sacred Eel, where the Pohnpeians kept us captive in a bamboo cage for a fortnight while their bizarre ritual built to its climax.

In this place there were square wells within the courtyard full of sacred eels. The canals allowed sacred eels to enter from the sea.

In many of the pools, there was a great variety of eels, from multicoloured dragon morays to snake eels, and large *conger oceanicus*, some as long as three or four feet. These brutes would weigh upwards of a hundred pounds each and could take a man's fingers off. The natives usually fed them live food. Sometimes they threw in mackerel flapper, removing the backbone and tail and allowing the flanks and innards to flutter in the water.

Sturges told me the Pohnpeians also periodically brought green-backed turtles to Nan Madol, keeping them in an artificial basin on the islet of Paset. Then later the captured sea turtles were brought to Idehd, where they were killed, cooked and their entrails fed as a sacrifice to the eels.

The natives' wild ceremonies were now building to a crescendo. Next, the priests made an offering of cooked turtle innards to Nan Sanwohl. During this bizarre ancient ritual, the natives loudly chanted "Zatomaga! Zatomaga!" and "Nan Sanwhol!" The latter was the name of the Sacred Eel, also known as 'the Thing That Lies in Wait.' The priests, who lived on the islet of Usendau, came to Idehd for the ceremony. The chief *Sau* performed a ceremony of atonement for himself, for the other priests and for the people.

"The Saus take this very seriously," said Sturges.

After a fortnight of near starvation, we were taken into the vast precincts of the main temple, its stacked prismatic walls glittering darkly. A low monotonous chanting greeted us—voices raised in dark praise. Two tattooed Pohnpeian acolytes dragged us forward and bound us to a stump of upright rock with hibiscus-fibre ropes that chafed our wrists. I knew this must be the place Churchward wrote of as being mined by cellars and crypts connected to one of the canals. I inclined to believe Churchward's theories now, for the temple's inside was shaped like a vast pyramid.

In the temple's central precinct was a huge dark pool, surrounded on all sides by tattooed Pohnpeians bedecked in beads and other ornaments. It seemed that human sacrifice was to be the culmination of the ceremonies.

The Sau chief picked up a large, bound volume, and began to intone some incantation from its pages. I recognised it from its palm-leaf pages as a copy of the fabled *Ponape Scriptures*.

There now lay revealed such a horror as threatened to overwhelm us. What Stygian depths yawned beyond the frightful pool we shall never know, though I suspect that some accursed infinity of lightless pits led down towards the ocean's nethermost reaches. God knows what unhallowed elder worlds exist in those ghastly caverns of inner earth where Nyarlathotep, the mad faceless god, howls blindly in the darkness to the piping of amorphous idiot flute-players.

Next to the pool, on the square basalt cobble paving, tottered aeon-old mounds of broken turtle shells, where the Pohnpeians had cast the remains of the food that they fed to the Thing That Lies in Wait. The shells seemed mixed with more—unidentifiable—remains. From where I stood they looked suspiciously like human bones.

Beside us were chained several of the local women—like us, potential sacrifices. Beside them were chained the captain, the first mate and the bosun of the *Lady Armitage*. Evidently, they had been careless enough to make their presence known to the locals as they tried to track us and take us back to the ship.

Now they were in deep trouble. They cast around in panic, struggling against their bonds, or stared at their feet, awaiting their desperate fate.

The Pohnpeians tethered Sturges at one end of the line of native prisoners, and me at the other. I looked helplessly at the faces of Janssen, Jacobs and Metcalf. They seemed to sense that death was near, but they could hardly have anticipated its nature.

One of the Pohnpeians brought forth, with great ceremony, a turtle-shell bowl containing a pale blue transparent sea creature. I could see it had tens of long straggling tentacles and guessed it was a deadly sea wasp or box jellyfish, its tentacles armed with thousands of nematocysts or stinging cells. The man, careful to pick the thing up with an instrument resembling wooden tongs, threw it to a nearby turtle, which gobbled it down, apparently with no ill effects.

The chanting from the assembled Pohnpeians grew louder and more intense as the native with the bowl drew forth another jellyfish, its long tentacles dripping with brine, and walked the length of the line, stopping finally before Jacobs. Jacobs screamed as the man thrust the jellyfish at his face. The thing wrapped itself around his head.

I knew as the venom went into his face that the attack on his nerves and heart was immediate. Someone called his name, but I doubt he heard it; the pain must have been excruciating. I could see that the thing's tentacles were becoming sticky and adhering to his flesh, leaving his face bloody. In a few moments he went into toxic shock and, no longer able to breathe, contorted, fell to the ground, writhed for a few moments, and then lay still.

The natives picked up his body and threw it onto a raised basalt platform at the edge of the pool. I recognised this with a shudder as a *pei*, a stone altar of incredible antiquity—*perhaps the very stone altar that gave this island its name.*

There came a stirring in the black water at the pool's centre. A ripple of dirty foam formed a widening V as something began to emerge from the pool.

The eel was not simply gigantic. It was stupendous, titan, horrifyingly enormous. Most of its gargantuan bulk lay submerged in the pool's brackish water, but its vast head and upper body gave a clue to the ghastly enormity of the whole. We all stood horror-struck. It was a gigantic Viper Moray, its immensely strong curving jaw and rows of needle-sharp pointed teeth on view as its maw gaped ravenously. Further back in the jaw were huge flat-surfaced molars, each as big as one of the native's *sakau* pounding stones. Normal morays would use them for crushing shellfish. I shuddered to think what this one might use them for.

I threw a glance back at the line of native women prisoners. The *Sau*'s men were bringing forth more turtle-shell bowls, each containing a deadly box jellyfish, which they started placing over the faces of the helpless women. Each in turn writhed, screaming in agony as the poison took effect and then fell in their death throes.

I knew it was only moments until I met the same fate. I looked back at the pool, with its hideous oceanic denizen. The creature's disgusting body smelled half-rotten—greenish-brown, with leathery skin covered in hideous purple brown blotches. It was a creature that ought not to exist in this world. One could only speculate on its nameless origins. Had it come from the incredible oceanic deeps of the Mariana Trench? For thousands of years it must have lain here in the dark waters, being worshipped and fed by the Pohnpeians.

Suddenly, it reared up, snapping its massive head towards us. The few prisoners still alive reared back in panic as it slithered mountainously out of the pond towards where we were tethered. I knew the conger eels on the smaller islands could stay alive for long periods out of water. This anomalous horror of the nighted ocean depths could undoubtedly do the same. If the smaller eels could take off fingers or toes, this massive creature could undoubtedly bite our heads clean through or chew us in half.

The thing came onward, its slavering jaws exuding the foulest stench imaginable—some hellish concoction of crab, cuttlefish and squid, commingled with turtle—its normal food as supplied by the natives. The Pohnpeians waved their spears and chanted. The beast's thick, leathery skin was proof against any weapon. Of course, we had no defence. The high priest intoned a passage from the *Ponape Scriptures,* as the assembled Pohnpeians bowed in supplication before the creature.

Sturges was unable to dodge the thing, which lowered its great ugly head towards him. He screamed. Razor-sharp teeth sank deep into his flesh. The rope that bound him broke, but he was now lodged in the filthy thing's massive jaws. It tossed its head this way and that as it savaged him. Blood spurted from Sturges' neck and chest. His arms still flailed, but his chest had been pierced by the needle-like teeth, and the Thing Which Lies in Wait smashed Sturges' body upon the stone altar of the podium.

His skull cracked loudly as the body slammed into the rock. His attacker started rending him limb from limb, chewing the human flesh, bones and all, and within a few minutes, what remained of Sturges had been chewed and gouged into an unrecognisable state.

I closed my eyes. Through gaps in the temple walls, I could hear and see great crested terns and frigate birds wheeling overhead, crying like banshee children. More than that—I could see the sky had become a Red Haze. It was the time of Zoth-Ommog!

*Z*oth-Ommog *was catching us up. The closer It came to us, crashing destructively through the trees behind us, the more strongly I could feel the intensity of Its alien thought-forms. My head swam with visions of strange geometric cities, monstrous and maddening arcana of daemoniac palaeogean horror. As we came out on the sand and continued our desperate rush for the canoe, our last hope of safety, the girl fell beside me, clutching her head.*

*Surely she saw the same things I saw—incredible inclined planes and walkways, vast alien cities of abnormal and unimaginably non-anthropomorphic construction, beneath iridescent skies filled with triple crimson suns, and far-flung gaseous nebulae of unguessed-at cosmic alienage.*

*I pulled her to her feet. "We have to keep going!" I shouted at her. She couldn't speak my language, but maybe the sound of my voice would get through to her. "Snap out of it!"*

*She shook her head, trying to free herself of Zoth-Ommog's intrusive thought-forms.*

*We stumbled across the moon-lit beach, wisps of the Red Haze drifting around our heads. Just the other side of this distinctively shaped rock was where Sturges and I had hidden the canoe. I scrambled to a halt, clutching my companion in shock. The canoe was gone!*

*Zoth-Ommog appeared hugely above the trees. His enormous wings flapped thunderously against the still-present Red Haze. The Haze was blocking his senses somewhat, but his head-tentacles wavered in search of us.*

*I cast around for the canoe, hoping against hope. There it was! The very tip of a prow was jutting out from beneath a pile of fronds he had used as camouflage. Sturges must have covered it up with palm-fronds as I searched for fresh water.*

*The girl pulled me forward, for she too had spotted the canoe. We threw off the palm fronds and pushed the vessel the short distance down the beach to the water's edge, where we steered it through the shallows. Leaping in, we began to paddle it into deeper water.*

*Zoth-Ommog, silhouetted gigantically against the moon, advanced implacably onward. Trees fractured like matchwood as It stomped onto the beach, sending up an ear-splitting howl that echoed out for miles over the darkened waters.*

*We looked back as we continued to paddle our hardest. The outgoing tide was with us, and the outrigger, built by the natives for fast travel, cut swiftly through the waves, making good time. But would it be fast enough?*

*Zoth-Ommog was now at the water's edge. It waded in, sending up great plumes of spray, displacing tons of water as it ponderously crashed forward into the ocean. It continued striding colossally after us. I could not believe we would escape it. My heartbeat thumped in my ears. We couldn't stay ahead at this rate. The distance between the creature and us began to diminish by the moment. The girl screamed, her dark eyes flashing.*

*"Keep paddling!" I yelled.*

*Zoth-Ommog let out a howl of triumph as It lashed one of Its starfish arms into the ocean beside us, causing our tiny craft to rock uncontrollably.*

*We were prepared to be crushed, dismembered by the almighty Old One, when its roar changed timbre. A plaintive note of anger had crept in—then one of terror, as it lashed its head tentacles in frustration.*

*A stone column, barnacled and dripping with weed, was rising slowly from the ocean surface. As the girl righted our canoe, I peered down through the waves and from the seabed came another, then another, rising like dripping sentinels, forming a ring barrier between the gigantic monstrosity and our vessel. They were the seal-engraven columns of the underwater city, long set in place by the Elder Gods to protect humankind, setting a boundary which Zoth-Ommog could not cross.*

*The monster flailed helplessly as our canoe continued out to sea. Later we would head for Yap or another island whence we could return to civilisation. For now it was enough that we escaped.*

*The last we saw of Zoth-Ommog was Its mountainous form surrounded by the fading Red Haze, covering its hideous head with its tentacles as it averted its face from the aeons-old seals of the Elder Gods—and retreating back to land.*

My companion, whose name was Lipahnmei, remained my devoted friend through all that followed. She travelled with me, working for our passage back to Sydney, sharing in adventures comparatively mundane. Lipahnmei learned to speak English quickly, but sadly no children came to bless our marriage bed. Perhaps the trauma of that night had taken something of the life from both of us, for I always dreaded Zoth-Ommog's return.

We both remained troubled by the memories of the mighty Old One. One day I found my wife tattooing herself on the thigh with the seal of the Elder Gods, a final, desperate attempt to stave off the madness that seemed destined to overtake us.

She died last year, of natural causes. Now I lie alone at night without her strong arms to hold me in the dark.

Of late, a strange red haze has been reported drifting about some of the islands in the South Pacific. I do not care to keep living on a planet where alien monsters may yet be liberated, and rule again over a puny and defenceless humankind.

Here, on my desk, is the flintlock musket given to me by my wife, and with its aid I shall, tonight, bring an end to the horrors I have known and can no longer stand.

# AUTHOR'S AFTERWORD & STORY NOTES

*"There's an itch in my brain and I gotta scratch it..."*

– Todd Rundgren/*Utopia*

*Stories are like demons—like wild beasts that hunt you, haunt you, demanding to be told—but life interferes.*

Thirty-five years ago I had hopes of perhaps making a career as a writer. As this book appears, in my 64th year, it's clear I will never be prolific enough to do so. Nevertheless, writing is always going to remain a major preoccupation. In the last decade or more, I believe I have found a voice, and some level of competence that was not present earlier.

*You try to write stories. Relationships start and finish. Your discipline strengthens, wavers, strengthens again. You move house too often, you work a demanding job, you try and hold it all together so you can do the only thing you really care about in the whole fuckin' world—writing stories. Some people manage to write a lot of them, some only a few. So far, I'm in the latter category.*

Lack of lived experience is always a frustrating thing for a writer; but for me now, having been married and separated and found new relationships, having been a member of occult societies, having tasted some of the best and worst that life offers, I believe I have more to say and a more fluid way of saying it. While this collection is ninety percent horror—darkness has often preoccupied me—my recent work is trying to broaden the palette somewhat. This may be evident in several later tales gathered here.

Horror is my main theme; though I started out in my teens by imitating Moorcock and Lin Carter and the Hyperborean fantasies of Clark Ashton Smith, I have never desired to add further to the wealth of fantasy tales dealing with truculent elves and palace intrigues. The stories in this book took me more than forty years to write. I write painfully slowly, piecing tales together like jigsaw puzzles. Some stories here lingered long in my files, in stages of completion ranging from completely plotted but needing a polish, to bare unresolved situation sketches. For the latter, I have in some case finished and reworked the tales so that they are completely new stories. Naturally, due to the long lapse of time between conception and completion, such tales no longer resonate with my current beliefs about technique.

So why publish these earlier tales now? Perhaps the reader will find a certain pleasure in witnessing a stylistic progression from the start to the finish of this volume. As for me, I *need* to have a book of my stories on the shelf with my name on it. Call it ego, if you will. But after forty-plus years, it's time. I'd like to have *more* stories. I'd like to have a few *better* ones, even though I'm proud of some of these. But the time has come. If I wait any longer I'll go absolutely apeshit—screaming, bugfuck crazy. And, gentle reader, none of us want that, do we? So here's a few words about the stories and how they came to be.

Several shorts here date to the very outset of my writing, around age 16, though I first hit print with poetry, which I continue to publish to this day. I trust readers will forgive me for presenting these apprentice efforts. **'The Last Town'** (1975)—pure fantasy rather than horror, though with a grimly ironic touch—was penned while I attended high school in Newcastle NSW, inspired by the fables of Lord Dunsany in his *The Food of Death and Other Tales*. The black-and-white polarity represented here was instinctive with me, and still is; it is reflected in the magical name I took in 1990 (LVX/NOX—which means light and darkness—OK, "light" and "night" if you're a Latin literalist) and which I used for twenty years until changing it in 2010.

**'The Sacrifice'** (1975) was also written while I was at high school. It was inspired by a still photograph from Ingmar Bergman's *The Seventh Seal* and was written quickly under school examination conditions. I let my friend Danny Lovecraft publish this and a couple of other pieces of my juvenilia in his 1990s fanzine *Avatar*; they are printed here again simply because they're early children of which I'm fond, despite their brevity and naivety of approach.

The little screenplay **'The Music of Eric Zann,'** based on Lovecraft's evocative tale, was also penned in 1975 for our amateur film production company Azathoth Productions (which was me, Lindsay Walker and our fellow schoolmate J. Michael Blaxland). It was unproduced, though segments of our other production, a version of Clark Ashton Smith's 'The Double Shadow' were filmed on Super-8 and are still extant in my archives.

**'The Horror in the Manuscript,'** (1975), co-written with my friend Lindsay Walker, was also written in high school. We had just discovered and become infatuated with the writings of H.P. Lovecraft. The conception of the tale was Lindsay's, but the writing was done in more or less equal shares, my portion in a blue-covered exercise book with the crest of Newcastle Boys' High School on it. The tale was submitted overseas. Both Brian Lumley and Ramsey Campbell (then and now, well-known writers in Lovecraft's Cthulhu Mythos) looked at it—but after it was (kindly) rejected by Campbell for his anthology *New Tales of the Cthulhu Mythos* (damn! I could have been in an Arkham House hardcover at the age of 16!), it was never submitted elsewhere. I still treasure the long rejection letter which Ramsey Campbell sent us. He called the tale "one of the better unsolicited items I've seen for that book...a good deal more carefully written and, in particular, composed than most of the work than by unknown writers I've been sent. You seem to have understood well HPL's basic principles of careful buildup of atmosphere and detail. On the whole I didn't feel any elements were particularly jarring or inappropriate." He rejected it as being too familiar in its details—some Lovecraft, and Derleth's 'Return of Hastur' in particular (ironically, a tale neither of us had read at the time). He went on to write..."Now, I take it from your reference to 'pressure of schoolwork' that you are both as young as that implies. If so it's a very impressive and promising performance—promising enough for you singly or together, to develop your own style." That was exciting and immensely encouraging! And he suggested learning from the work of other writers in the field such as Blackwood, M.R. James, Leiber, Aickman and others; this was a lesson I took to heart. Even at this long interval, I am grateful to Ramsey Campbell for such sage advice. 'The Horror in the Manuscript' also has the small distinction of having an original paragraph contributed by Brian Lumley. I'm happy to present the tale in this volume, despite it being an artefact from a time long ago.

(I missed out a second time on being in an Arkham House hardcover in the mid-2000s, when Robert Weinberg and George A. Vanderburgh took over the editorial reigns at the famed publisher, and Mr Vanderburgh invited me to contribute to an anthology called *The Arkham Garland*. Now *there* was a project that revved my writing motor! But alas! The project was stillborn before I completed my submission; *The Arkham Garland* was never published).

I wrote other tales in the seventies that have still not seen the light of day and maybe never will. Some stories benefit from resting, accumulating detail over a long period. Others give up the ghost, with a whimper that recalls Eliot's end of the world, refusing to ever find a true shape of completion.

The science-fantasy '**The Guardian**' (1978) was written when I had moved to Sydney and was living in an old schoolhouse in Rozelle with friends. The tale was the basis for a musical project collaboration with guitarist and synth-player Greg Smith. The deadly worms were inspired by similar scenes from *Biggles Hits the Trail* by W.E. Johns, while the underground cavern and some of the prose style owes much to Rick Wakeman's concept album of Jules Verne's *Voyage to the Centre of the Earth*. One finds the word for a building spelled firstly as 'aedifice,' due to a naïve youthful fondness for archaism and obsolete spellings (see 'An Horror Fantasy' as the subtitle of the Zann screenplay), though later in the tale it appears (inconsistently) in its correct modern form as 'edifice.' And those worms are said to be 'featureless,' though in apparent contradiction they are also said to possess mouths. Such infelicities stand here uncorrected. Greg painted two scenes from the tale (now lost) and we wrote a suite of music for it on synthesisers (also non-extant). Greg's only contributions to the tale were to name one of the Servants 'Roland,' and a galaxy in the story 'Korgian,' based on the brand-names of two synthesisers on which we composed the music!

*Life interferes.* For most of the early eighties I was concentrating on my music, not on writing fiction. I was playing in my band Worm Technology, starting out on my 25-year career in the book trade. (The band tapered off around 1985, the bookselling not until twenty years after that). *But the stories are demons. They demand to be told. They itch at your brain, worming around in there, telling you — "one day you're going to write me down." You go to work, and scribble notes along the way. You come home and do the chores, and scribble some more. Gradually (very gradually in my case) things take shape, and the stories let you alone. Or that particular one does. Of course, another is always there ready to take its place. Scratch, scratch: "Write me down! Let me out of this dark place inside of you!" Scratch, scratch.*

'**By Their Fruits...**' (1985) (the title is a Biblical quotation—go look it up, OK?) is another story influenced more by Ramsey Campbell than by any other writer. Campbell remains one of my major literary heroes; I still appreciate his atmospheric writing and collect and read his work. The story was writing-as-self-therapy for a broken heart— the first of several doomed early romances. Unable to write a complete tale, I patched it together from drafts written years apart during the eighties. In this time, I was struggling to escape the influence of other writers, and to find my own voice. Submissions have never been my strong suit, and the tale has never found a home—until now.

'**The Infestation**' (1986) was written partly at my parents' place at

Thornleigh, shortly after I had abandoned my second early attempt at a degree, after attending Sydney University for two years. I also wrote it partly, memory tells me, at a house I shared at East Sydney with my friend Richard Trowsdale—the same neighbourhood that inspired me to write **'The Squats'** that year. While the former tale is perhaps a little strong on the disgust factor, it was greatly influenced in mood, again, by the stories of Ramsey Campbell. I hope it works as an attempt to narrate a tale from the monster's point of view; that, anyway, was its intention. Steven Paulsen read this full version on Rick Kennett's Melbourne radio programme 'Pilots of the Unknown,' though the actual prose has never seen print prior to this collection. Via the crew that was producing the later banned-in-three-states *Phantastique* comic, artist Gavin O'Keefe illustrated a graphic novel adaptation of it, from a script by me abbreviated from my tale. Now, here's the story as originally written.

*As I've said, life interferes.* Between 1987 and 1993, I was concentrating on editing and publishing, not on writing fiction. With Chris Sequeira and Bryce Stevens, attempting to foster the local Australian horror scene, I put out three big issues of *Terror Australis* magazine in those tumultuous years, springboarding to a book contract for an original anthology by the same title. We were having fun, and learned a hell of a lot on that particular strange excursion.

*Life continues to interfere. But the stories are still there, like wild animals demanding to be let out, caged beasts whose shape you can't fully see, until they emerge into the light. They paw and whine until you notice them, these stories like beasts, they muscle up to the bars of the cage, snapping their jaws. You can't ignore that forever.*

**'The Hourglass'** (1993) was written at Leichhardt, in those heady experimental years when I was exploring anarchism, magick and other ways of breaking out of various society-imposed psychological straitjackets. Included in my *Terror Australis: The Best of Australian Horror* anthology, it was a further attempt to exorcise ghosts from the same relationship as 'By Their Fruits...'—ghosts that were finally put to rest when I finished this tale. It's the first story I wrote where I felt my own voice was coming to the fore after nearly twenty years of arduously learning, through failed experiments, how to portray characters and how to plot, it felt so sweet to finally get down the vision that was in my head and have it hold together on the page. It was, at the least, a stage in the level of competence of my output. Rob's name is significant in view of his character, which I based largely on my school friend Lindsay Walker but with an evil twist. David is

269

transparently me, as Honey is my first love, Heather. My original title was 'Sand and Honey,' since the image of Honey dead, with the sand trickling out of her hand, was part of the tale's earliest conception. But to get there, I developed the symbol of the hourglass, relating it to the physical computer icon and David's iconographic worship of Honey. The computer icon was included because this was the first story I wrote entirely on a PC (new technology then!); the icon it displayed when saying 'wait' or saving work fascinated me. An hourglass tipped on its side looks like a lemniscate — the symbol for infinity; and the traditional figure of Death holds an Hourglass, as in the poem by Addison used as the story's epigraph. Although I mention the iconographic nature of the Pre-Raphaelite painters' works, I didn't discover until *after* I'd written the story that Evelyn de Morgan actually produced a painting titled 'The Hourglass' (1904-05) — see Jan March's *Pre-Raphaelite Women* (p. 132). The first sentence is a take on Nietzsche's warning not to gaze too deeply into the Abyss, lest it gaze into you. There are some direct tributes to R. H. Barlow's 'The Night Ocean' especially the phrase 'Foolish marionette' (whose use here becomes a pun on Honey/Heather's real first name, Marion). In Honey's death, too, a faint echo of the ending of Lovecraft's 'The Rats in the Walls' where de la Poer devours his friend. There are also semi-disguised quotations from a poem of Blake: "To see a World in a grain of Sand...Holding infinity in the palm of my hand..." The mask Rob wears is a combination of the Balinese turtle-shell mask that *Terror Australis* magazine co-editor Chris Sequeira had given me, and the ritual skull from the cover of Throbbing Gristle's *Force The Hand of Chance* album. There is another echo of the ending to Lovecraft's 'The Rats in the Walls' in "Now I'm in this barred cell at Goulburn" — as indeed the psychological ambiguity of the character is meant to be similar to de la Poer's, "They must know that I did not do it..." All too referential, too self-conscious? Certainly, but also a case of using what I knew.

*Life interferes.* I entered a major relationship in 1995 and was divorced in 2001. For half a decade I was concentrating more on being in a committed relationship, than on writing fiction (though I did tinker in that period with novels, novellas and short stories, such as one of my favourites, the still-unpublished 'Reading the Alien.' Some tales from that period still await completion). Following the divorce, I attempted to crank up my output and publication level, with at least some success. *Snap, growl! Okay, okay, I'm getting better at writing you down, give me a break!*

'**Dr Nadurnian's Golem**' (2001), written at Earlwood, grew from a dream I had in the mid-nineties about a man who screams about "colours behind the sky." I had this line in my notebooks, and the image haunted me for years before I managed to find a use for it. The tale slowly took shape in my head over a prolonged period after my divorce, and its blackness may have as much to do with the separation as with continually walking home at night, after work, through a dismal swamp bordering Ghiraween Park in the Sydney suburb of Bardwell Park. It wasn't until I had spent several years in a Sydney-based occult secret society that I was able to do this tale justice on the page. Other main influences on the tale include the work of occultist Kenneth Grant, and the weird fiction of Thomas Ligotti, before whose *oeuvre* I prostrate myself. The name 'Nadurnian' comes from a combination of 'Nada' (nothing) and 'Saturnian' (Saturn's influence is traditionally an ominous or maleficent one in occult studies). The atmosphere draws heavily on the work of Ligotti, but the relationship between Nadurnian and the narrator derives primarily from that between myself and Fr. Numa, my initiator and Lodge Master for several years in the Ordo Templi Orientis. It wasn't until I saw Samuel Beckett's *Endgame* (which I had read over twenty-five years earlier) on stage in the Sydney Festival of 2003 that I realised how the image of Hamm (immobile in his chair, wearing dark glasses, yet still commanding) had stayed in my mental vision and contributed to my image of Nadurnian in this story. As part of the drama unit of my Creative Writing degree, I workshopped a dramatic rendering of the story in 2008.

I talk about **'Uncharted'** (2002), also written at Earlwood, in the afterword specific to that story. For me, despite being more writing-as-self-therapy (and perhaps all writing is that?) this tale was a break-through; it wasn't just the sense of absolutely writing in my own voice, but being able to use my own experience and feelings about the world, whereas all my previous writing had been some form of pastiche. 'Uncharted' is, despite a detectable M. John Harrison influence (which mainly relates to technique) the most 'me' story I've yet written. Margi Curtis has pointed out that this tale's narrator, David, could well be the same David as the narrator of 'The Hourglass.'

I was lucky enough to have a couple of stories published around this period and started to feel that one day I could produce fiction of high enough quality to get published regularly.

**'Cemetery Rose'** (2003), again written at Earlwood, had its genesis in two things—one was a longstanding desire to write a tale set in Sydney's incredible Rookwood cemetery. I started out with a tale called '29 Necropolis Drive,' to which I had kept returning over the years, but my conception of the plot slowly mutated. The tale went through many drafts. Despite my horror colleagues Bryce Stevens and Rick Kennett having collaborated on their tale 'Rookwood,' also set there, my tale begged for a different approach. The impetus to write it properly finally arose when I read of 'the cemetery rose,' a particular breed of rose that does indeed grow in cemeteries. My rose, though, was different again. The tale was read on American radio (The Writing Show) as part of the Australian Horror Writers Association's Six Days of Hallowe'en in 2006, together with a recorded interview with me)—a rewarding experience.

*Life interferes, in ways both good and bad. In 2004, I met my wonderful new partners, the writer Margi Curtis and her husband Graham Wykes. I left my job in bookselling, moved to the Illawarra, and recovered from a serious dependence on painkilling medications.*

*But the stories don't go away. They bug you, night and day, welling up from inside you, coming from a place that people who don't write will never understand. They push and pull you, scratching at your psyche as though you are wearing a hair shirt on your brain (if that's not too mixed a metaphor). They turn you this way and that, never letting up until you write them down. All right!*

In 2006, I enrolled in a mature-age Creative Writing & Journalism degree at the University of Wollongong. Journalism bit the dust in 2007 as I found grappling with a double degree too demanding, but I finished my Honours Degree in Creative Writing in 2009.

**'Imago'** (2006), is about wanting to change your own life but having to confront limitations that run way too deep. **'Wave'** (2006) is similar, though it draws on a real experience I had shortly after moving to the Illawarra. (And here's where I express my inestimable gratitude to my stepson Rohan Curtis-Wykes; he'll remember why). **'Leaving Town'** and **'Dream Street'** were written the same year. These little tales all saw print in campus publications of the University of Wollongong such as *Tertangala* and *Tide*.

The title for **'Water Runs Uphill'** (2007) (which I mistakenly believed I'd invented and thought was brilliantly original), and the story's plot, came to me all at once, during a trip with Margi to Melbourne for the 68th World Science Fiction Convention (Aussiecon Four), held on 2-6 Sept 2010. We were walking outside the Crown Casino Complex on the south bank of the Yarra River. Something about the look of the river running, and the idea of a combination of water and film and time running backward, caught my imagination. Much later, after writing and submitting the tale to *Aurealis*, who published it, it dawned on me that many years previously, I had read the second autobiographical volume by Robert Aickman, one of my favourite writers of 'strange stories' (his term)—*The River Runs Uphill* (written 1967; published 1986). It was primarily about his years campaigning to save the inland British waterways from abandonment. That subject was unrelated to my theme, but perhaps this title stuck in my head subconsciously. Oddly enough, I also learned of a nonfiction book on dreamwork by Jeremy Taylor, titled *Where People Fly and Water Runs Uphill: Using Dreams to Tap the Wisdom of the Unconscious* (1983). But Ovid was there first, with his 'rivers run uphill' (which may have inspired Aickman— 'nothing new under the sun,' and all that). My story's publication in *Aurealis* fulfilled an ambition of mine to appear in Australia's longest-running SF and fantasy magazine.

**'The Roomer'** (2009) began as a mainstream story in the vein of Booker-Prize-winning Scottish writer of the working-class, James Kelman, whose work I much admire. It was (reputedly) published as such in an on-campus magazine called *The Stack* by students at the University of Wollongong Faculty of Creative Arts. I was never sent a copy and thus cannot verify the appearance. (If anyone has a copy I'd love to see it). I subsequently rewrote the tale (2023) as a Lovecraft Mythos piece and am happier with it this way. Making my narrator a rough and ready average Aussie bloke was my idea of doing something a bit fresh with a Mythos tale instead of featuring the usual Lovecraftian scholarly gentleman dabbler into the dark side.

*Life interferes.* The last story I wrote in the 2010s was **'Beneath the Carapace'** (2013). Osvaldo Carotid's grandfather has many character-istics of my own maternal grandfather, whom I loved dearly (but who was, I recently discovered, a reprobate prone to violence). The city of Euchronium in my story is patently (or is it?) a variant of M. John Harrison's Viriconium, a city which has gone by many other names through the ages including Uroconium. While Harrison's Viriconium is located in Britain and is (in the novel *A Storm of Wings*), prey to plagues of locusts, Euchronium seems to be located in the Great Southern Land, witness Carotid's visions near the tale's end, and is ruled by a clade of great cicada beings. Australian summers of my boyhood were always a time for the cicada hunt. I was fascinated by the variety of their colours and poetic names. Boys would bring them to school in plastic lunchboxes, proudly displaying their finds. The rarest was normally considered by schoolboys to be the Black Prince, although we know now that these are more common along riverbanks than in the bush. Then, there were the vacated cicada shells that one would find on gum-tree trunks after nymph-stage cicadas had moulted; it was a great game to carefully remove these and attach them onto one's cardigan or jumper, where the insectoid shell (exoskeleton) would cling, due to its hooky claws. The utterly alien nature of the insectoid mind has always exerted a powerful fascination on me, and cicadas in particular have continued to intrigue me. In the late 1980s, my friends and I had delighted in the Australian rock band Outline and their classic anthemic song 'The Cicada That Ate Five Dock,' (look it up on YouTube) to which we used to dance at the Sydney inner-city pub The Civic Hotel, with its memorable carpet, so sticky underfoot from spilled beer that one could hardly extract one's feet from it to walk forward a step at a time towards the stage. Though my story originally had a different title, I settled on its current one partly from an utterance made by television detective Hercule Poirot: "Peel back the carapace, and the evil, it is revealed." There is little point, either, in denying that Lovecraft's memorable story 'The Festival' also exerted a great influence on aspects of my tale.

In the decade 2011-2022, I ran my own editorial and manuscript appraisal business. I also spent that decade publishing poetry and essays, and five overlapping years writing an occult thriller novel, *The Eighth Trigram* (forthcoming). The most recent story here is 'The Morsels,' (2023) which seemed to flow out of me, after I finished my novel, like paint out of a tube of Thalo blue. I had always wanted to write a story about a painter, but the plot of this tale came to me all at once, and I had outlined it fully before writing it. I cop to the influence of MR James's 'The Doll's House' for the stealthy emergence of the figure in Tom's picture. Some potent influences are just too hard to shake, and though it must be over thirty years since I read James' tale, I never could get that concept out of my head. Perhaps I've exorcised it now.

So here we are. A lineup of stories selected from over forty years of scribbling on and off. It seems a paltry sum of tales to me. Why haven't I got more? I'm not the kind of writer to sit down and crank out a tale in a day. Maybe it will happen sometime, but not so far. I would never have made it, back in the old days of the pulps, when they used to grind out a story a week to make a living. That just isn't my process.

Of course, there are in my files, as Australian sf and fantasy writer Terry Dowling says, "turkeys that you'll *never* see." But in reading this collection, maybe you'll be interested in the arc between the voice of the schoolboy who wrote 'The Last Town' and that of the 60-something-year-old man who wrote such tales as 'The Roomer,' and 'The Morsels.' I've tried to keep out the ones that gobble, but you can decide for yourself whether any of these are turkeys. I do hope you'll enjoy at least *some* of what's here.

I'm lucky to be blessed now with a partner who also writes and appreciates the imperative to do so. I still publish reviews and essays and poetry, but short fiction, with its necessity to create an entire world each time, is somehow far more demanding. I think I'll still be learning this craft in twenty years' time, but I've *started* to be happy with what I can put on the page. Bit of a slow learner, me, but it's starting to work.

And there will be more demons—uhh - *stories,* folks, I promise. Even though *life interferes.*

*– Mangerton, Wollongong, March 2023*

# Publication History (Summary)

The following elements of this collection have been previously published:

An illustrated/abridged version of 'The Infestation' appeared in *Phantastique* (1987). The full text of the story appeared first online at www.sffworld.com (Nov 2005). The full text version appears in print here for the first time.

'The Last Town,' 'The Sacrifice,' and 'The Guardian' first appeared in *Avatar* No. 3 (June 1995). 'The Last Town' also appeared online at www.sffworld.com (Nov 2005) and in print in *Aurora Borealis* 37 (May 2015).

'The Horror in the Manuscript' (with Lindsay Walker) first appeared online at www.sffworld.com (Nov 2005). It appears in print here for the first time.

'The Hourglass' first appeared in Leigh Blackmore, ed. *Terror Australis: Best Australian Horror.* (Sydney: Coronet, 1993).

'Dr Nadurnian's Golem' first appeared in Cat Sparks, ed. *Agog!: Fantastic Fiction.* Wollongong: Agog! Press, 2002, and online at www.ligotti.net (Dec 2005).

'Uncharted' first appeared (somewhat abridged) in Cat Sparks, ed. *Agog!: Terrific Tales* (Wollongong, NSW: Agog! Press, 2003). The full text appears here for the first time. Afterword to this appearance © 2004 Leigh Blackmore.

"By Their Fruits…" first appeared online at www.sffworld.com (Nov 2005).

'Cemetery Rose' first appeared online at www.sffworld.com (Nov 2005). The story was podcast, accompanied by an author interview, at www.writingshow.com (Hallowe'en 2006). The story appeared in the e-book Rebecca Lang, ed. *Dark Spirits.* (Sydney: Strange Nation, 2018). It appears in print here for the first time.

'Imago' first appeared in *Tertangala* (Oct 2006)

'Wave' first appeared in *Micro* [1, No. 1] [May 2006]

'Water Runs Uphill' first appeared in *Aurealis* No 38/39 (Sept 2007).

'Dream Street' first appeared in *And Then I Woke Up!* (Oct 2007)

'The Return of Zoth-Ommog' first appeared (somewhat abridged) in Rob Hood & Robin Pen, eds. *Daikaiju 3: Giant Monsters vs the World*. Wollongong: Agog! Press (2007). Reprints of the same text have appeared in Henrik Harksen, ed. *Eldritch Horrors: Dark Tales*. Denmark: H. Harksen Productions, 2009 and in Robert M. Price, ed., *Secret Asia's Blackest Heart*. Sweden: Timaios Press, 2021. The full text appears here for the first time.

'Leaving Town'" first appeared in *TIDE* (Oct 2008)

'Waiting for Cthulhu' first appeared in *Nightgaunt 4* (2016) in both English and in French translation by Adam Joffrain.

**The following elements of this collection are original:**

'The Squats'
'The Morsels'
'Cemetery Rose'
'The Infestation'
'Beneath the Carapace'
'The Horror in the Manuscript' (with Lindsay Walker)
'The Roomer'
'The Music of Eric Zann'